W9-BXX-645

JOURNEY OF
THE PHARAOHS

ALSO BY CLIVE CUSSLER
AVAILABLE FROM RANDOM HOUSE LARGE PRINT

Final Option (with Boyd Morrison)
The Titanic Secret (with Jack Du Brul)
The Oracle (with Robin Burcell)
Sea of Greed (with Graham Brown)
Pirate (with Robin Burcell)

CLIVE CUSSLER
and Graham Brown

JOURNEY OF
THE PHARAOHS

A novel from
the NUMA® Files

RANDOM HOUSE
LARGE PRINT

This is a work of fiction. Names, characters, places, and incidents either are the product of the author's imagination or are used fictitiously, and any resemblance to actual persons, living or dead, businesses, companies, events, or locales is entirely coincidental.

Copyright © 2020 by Sandecker, RLLLP

All rights reserved.
Published in the United States of America by Random House Large Print in association with G. P. Putnam's Sons, an imprint of Penguin Random House LLC.

Penguin supports copyright. Copyright fuels creativity, encourages diverse voices, promotes free speech, and creates a vibrant culture. Thank you for buying an authorized edition of this book and for complying with copyright laws by not reproducing, scanning, or distributing any part of it in any form without permission. You are supporting writers and allowing Penguin to continue to publish books for every reader.

Cover design: Mike Heath

The Library of Congress has established a Cataloging-in-Publication record for this title.

ISBN: 978-0-593-17170-7

www.penguinrandomhouse.com/large-print-format-books

FIRST LARGE PRINT EDITION

Printed in the United States of America

10   9   8   7   6   5   4   3   2   1

This Large Print edition published in accord with the standards of the N.A.V.H.

CAST OF CHARACTERS

THE HISTORIC PAST

EGYPT, 1074 B.C.

KHEMET—Former member of the Medjay, a group whose role was to guard the Valley of the Kings.

QSN—Orphaned child who gives information to Khemet, his name means **Sparrow** and the **Bringer of Sorrow.**

HERIHOR—Military commander who rose to become Pharaoh of Upper Egypt and then vanished.

NEW YORK CITY, 1927

JAKE MELBOURNE—Pilot, barnstormer and World War I ace, competing for the Orteig Prize.

CARLO GRANZINI—Head of the Granzini crime family.

STEFANO CORDOVA—Melbourne's friend and mechanic, Granzini's nephew.

THE PRESENT DAY

NATIONAL UNDERWATER AND MARINE AGENCY (NUMA)

KURT AUSTIN—Director of Special Projects, salvage expert and world-class diver.

JOE ZAVALA—Kurt's closest friend, the mechanical genius responsible for constructing much of NUMA's exotic equipment.

RUDI GUNN—Assistant Director of NUMA, a graduate of the Naval Academy.

HIRAM YAEGER—NUMA's Director of Technology, designed and built Max, NUMA's supercomputer.

PAUL TROUT—Geologist with a Ph.D. in Ocean Sciences, married to Gamay.

GAMAY TROUT—Marine biologist, married to Paul, most outspoken member of the group.

SCOTLAND

VINCENNES—Mysterious passenger on the fishing trawler.

SLOCUM—Smugglers' contact, part of the Bloodstone Group.

UNITED KINGDOM SECURITY SERVICE, SECTION 5 (MI5)

OLIVER PEMBROKE-SMYTHE—Former member of the SAS, currently Director of Counter-Terrorism Operations for MI5.

MORGAN MANNING—MI5 special operative, investigating the Bloodstone Group.

HENRY CROSS—Professor of Antiquities at Cambridge University, assists MI5 in identifying smuggled artifacts.

THE BLOODSTONE GROUP

SOLOMON BARLOW—Former mercenary, now an arms dealer and head of the Bloodstone Group.

KAPPA—Weapons specialist and Barlow's second-in-command.

ROBSON—Former street thug from a tough section of London, now one of Barlow's lieutenants.

DALY—Associate of Robson's, blames Robson for his incarceration.

GUS—Associate of Robson's, Daly's half brother.

FINGERS—Member of Robson's old street gang.

SNIPE—Another member of Robson's street gang.

ADDITIONS TO THE BLOODSTONE GROUP

XANDRA AND FYDOR—Brother-and-sister pair of assassins, they operate jointly under the pseudonym the Toymaker.

OMAR KAI—Flamboyant mercenary who is hired by the Bloodstone Group after they reach the United States.

FRANCE

FRANCISCO DEMARS—Grandson of the man who discovered the **Writings of Qsn,** lives in a château in France.

CAST OF CHARACTERS

SPAIN

FATHER TORRES—Catholic priest, serving at San Sebastián de las Montañas in Villa Ducal de Lerma.

SOFIA—Young child who introduces Gamay and Paul to Father Torres.

THE UNITED STATES

JAMES SANDECKER—Former Director of NUMA, now Vice President of the United States.

MIRANDA ABIGAIL CURTIS—Senior archivist with the FBI.

MORRIS—Lead agent in Sandecker's security detail.

THE NAVAJO NATION

EDDIE TOH-YAH—Old friend of Kurt Austin's, part of the Navajo tribal administration.

EDDIE'S GRANDFATHER—Leader of the local Navajo Council, Keeper of the Flame.

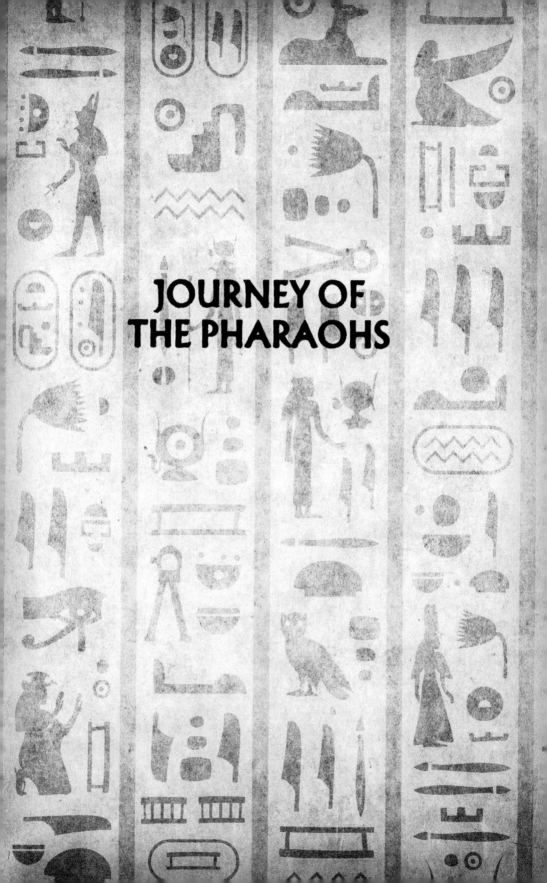

JOURNEY OF
THE PHARAOHS

PROLOGUE

Valley of the Kings, Egypt
1074 B.C., during the time of the 18th Dynasty

H eat shimmered in waves across the Valley
of the Kings as the merciless sun baked
the desert sands into clay.

High above the valley, at the edge of a cliff, a
bearded man named Khemet lay flat on his stomach, sweating beneath the noonday sun, looking
for any sign of movement. Sweat trickled down
the side of his face, a fly buzzed around his ear,
but nothing moved down below.

The valley was still—as the resting place of the
buried Pharaohs should be. The only movement
was a dust devil that rose from the southern end
and danced across the sand.

Khemet slid back from the rim. Several men
in linen robes crouched there. A boy stood next
to them. Khemet addressed the child. "What is
it you've brought us here to see?"

Villagers in Thebes called the boy Qsn, which

meant **Sparrow.** They used the term not because he was small for his age and tended to chirp as he spoke, but as an insult. To the people of Egypt, the sparrow was a nuisance, stealing food and spoiling fruit. The townspeople saw the orphaned boy in the same light.

Khemet knew differently. The child was a beggar, not a thief. In fact, he worked hard for the smallest of coins, watching everything with sharp eyes, gathering information. His size and age meant he was often invisible even in plain sight.

The boy crawled to the edge of the cliff, looked down into the valley and then tugged Khemet's arm. He extended a tiny finger, pointing. "Pharaoh's tomb has been opened. The stone has been thrown aside."

Squinting to see in the bright sun, Khemet looked past the magnificent three-story temple of Hatshepsut, with its long central stairway and rows of towering columns, and ignored the piles of rubble sealing the entrance of some lesser-known ancestors, finally focusing on a gap in the rock where smooth limestone blocks denoted the entrance to the tomb of Horemheb, one of the more recently buried Pharaohs.

His eyes weren't as sharp as the child's, but after shielding them from the sun he began to see into the shadows. The whitewashed slab that had been used to seal the tomb lay on the ground, broken in two where it had fallen. The path in front of the tomb was heavily rutted from the wheels of carts and trampled with the hooves of oxen.

"The boy is right," Khemet said. "The tomb has been violated."

"And just what does he want us to do about that?" one of the other men said.

The boy looked back, unafraid to address the adults. "You are the Medjay," he said in his high-pitched voice. "You are the servants of Rameses XI of Memphis. You guard the resting place of the Sons of Amun."

Khemet smiled. He had been a captain in the Medjay—a force of warriors appointed by the Pharaohs to guard the tombs of their ancestors—but his position had been swept away in the political upheaval that was dividing Egypt.

"Perhaps the Sparrow doesn't hear everything," one of the men said. "We're no longer needed by the Sons of Amun."

"But Rameses—"

"Rameses rules in Memphis and Alexandria," Khemet explained more patiently, "but this is Upper Egypt and Herihor has taken the title of Great House for himself."

The boy's face showed contempt. "Herihor is not only the High Priest, he is—"

"Here, he is a King," Khemet snapped. "There are those who would cut your tongue out for saying otherwise."

The boy shrank back.

Khemet allowed the lesson to sink in before adding, "Fortunately, we're not among them."

The men behind them laughed. The child looked relieved.

"Egypt is not what it was," one of his men said. "The weaker it gets, the more Pharaohs it needs. Soon there will be one in every region."

This brought more laughter from Khemet, though the boy looked stricken. He was still young enough to believe in concepts like duty and honor and, above all, the glory of kings descended from the gods. Those beliefs were not unlearned without great pain.

Khemet turned his attention back to the open tomb. "We should investigate and see what they've taken."

Leaving the cliffside, he led the group around and down a secret trail that took them to the valley below. These were hidden paths only the Medjay knew.

When they arrived, the light was brighter and more dazzling, as if they were walking the path to Heaven itself. Unlike the tawny cliffs around them, the valley floor was covered with pulverized limestone and white dust, chips and shavings from the great blocks that had been cut and worked and manhandled into place almost continuously for the past thousand years.

The reflected light caused Khemet to pull a

scarf across his eyes and he entered the tomb of Horemheb looking like a bandit.

Once inside, he removed the scarf and stood in the entry corridor. The cool air caressed his body while his eyes adjusted slowly to the darkness. As his pupils dilated, the splendor of the artisans' work appeared before him. Ceiling and walls, whitewashed and covered in hieroglyphics. Statues, carvings and other works of art. All lit up by the light coming in from the entrance of the tomb and from the torches mounted on the walls, which gave off an even purer light as they burned a smokeless blend of castor oil and natron.

Khemet took one of the torches and moved forward. His men followed close behind, the boy at his side.

Passing a second doorway, they entered the burial chamber reserved for lesser wives and servants.

Khemet stopped and pushed the boy back into a cleft in the wall. "Quiet, now," he said. "We're not alone." Reaching under his garment and pulling out a short sword, he waved the men to move up beside him. "Be ready."

Without a sound, Khemet stepped through the next doorway. He passed two statues of Anubis, the flickering torch in Khemet's hand casting shadows across the unmoving beasts on the far wall.

"Worthless guards," one of the men whispered

of the Anubis pair, "sitting idly by as robbers plunder the belongings meant to equip Pharaoh in the Afterlife."

The sound of a tool hitting stone could be heard up ahead. Moving into Pharaoh's burial chamber, Khemet found the source of the noise, a priest and a stonecutter carving a message into the far wall. Between them lay the stone sarcophagus of Horemheb. Its heavy lid had been thrown down and discarded. The golden coffin, death mask and mummified Pharaoh were gone.

The priest and the stonecutter noticed the flickering torch light. "It's high time you've returned," the priest said without looking back. "We have more items that need to be moved."

"You mean stolen," Khemet said.

Only now did the priest turn. "Who are you?" the priest demanded.

"I am Khemet, Captain of the Guard. And you are a thief."

The priest did not back down. "I am the hand of the Great House. Servant of Pharaoh Herihor. I do the Pharaoh's work. You men are trespassers and deserters."

And I will be a hero when I serve your head to Rameses, Khemet thought.

He stepped forward with his sword raised. "What have you done with the Pharaoh? Where are his gifts?"

"They have been relocated," the priest said, "to keep them safe from scavengers like you."

The priest's voice had turned snide and awfully bold for a scrawny man facing a soldier with his sword drawn. At the sound of movement, Khemet knew why.

An arrow flew down the corridor, piercing one of his companions from behind. The man fell with a grunt and nothing more.

A spear followed, catching another of the men as he turned.

Khemet pressed himself against the wall as a second arrow flew past. This one sailed into the burial chamber and hit the stonecutter in the stomach. He tumbled off the ledge and hit the floor, writhing in pain.

With the reflexes of a veteran warrior, Khemet dropped low and charged the archer in the hallway, upending him before he could nock another arrow. Thrusting his sword, Khemet pierced the man, yanking the blade back violently and pulling it free.

Seeing the last of his men speared, Khemet threw his sword, impaling the attacker. The man dropped to his knees and then fell sideways. Only the priest and Khemet remained, but the priest had used the fighting in the outer chamber to his advantage.

With Khemet engaged, the priest had drawn

a cobra-headed dagger from beneath his gaudy robes. He rushed forward, plunging it into Khemet's side.

Khemet twisted and slashed with a dagger of his own as he fell back. A hand closer and it would have been a fatal strike, but the priest had pulled out of range.

Falling to the ground, Khemet reached for the knife he'd been stabbed with. He could not remove it. The blade was deep, the wound burned strangely.

Fueled by anger, he stood, raising his weapon. The priest backed off farther but, curiously, did not flee.

"Face me," Khemet said, "and I will send you to the Afterlife you claim to adore."

He stepped forward trying to close the gap, but his feet were unsteady. He swayed to one side, placing a hand on the wall. Steadied, Khemet remained upright, but his head swam.

This was strange, he thought. He'd been wounded in battle a dozen times, and once he'd almost bled to death, but never had he felt like this. He reached for the dagger, pulled it from his side and noticed an empty niche cut into the center of the blade.

"The poison was meant for the stonecutter," the priest said. "To keep him quiet when his work was done. It will serve its purpose just as well in your blood."

Khemet threw the cobra-headed knife down. Steeling his resolve, he stepped forward again, but by now his eyes were playing tricks on him. The shadows around the tomb came alive. The Anubises and the crocodile moving and speaking.

The chamber began to spin. Khemet's own dagger fell to the ground, clanging against the stone floor as it hit. Fighting to remain upright and summoning the last remaining stores of his strength, Khemet pushed forward, lunging for the priest with his bare hands, grasping at the man's robe but catching nothing but air.

Khemet landed facedown on the stone and rolled over on his side. He heard music. Voices. But saw only the face of the treacherous priest. The man leaned over him, mouthed a curse, then straightened, raising a stone over his head, preparing to smash Khemet's skull.

Before he could strike, the priest's face tensed in agony as the tip of a blade burst out through his belly. The stone fell backward and the priest toppled over dead. And looked quite surprised to be so.

The boy appeared from behind the body.

"I'm sorry," he said, rushing to Khemet. "I shouldn't have told you. I am Qsn—the Bringer of Sorrow."

Khemet tried to focus on the child. As he did, a swirl of light and shadow grew behind Qsn, spreading like wings. In his delirium, Khemet saw the boy as a living bird, but not one so small and weak. "You are the falcon," Khemet told him. "You are Horus, the last protector of the Pharaohs . . ."

He reached out and laid his hand on the boy's shoulder. And then the world turned to blinding gold. And all he saw and knew vanished.

Qsn stood silent as Khemet's hand fell to the ground. The tomb was cold and silent and filled with death, but not the glory of the Pharaohs. He could think of nothing to do, no place to go, but he knew he would be killed if he stayed there.

Getting up, he rushed to the entrance and back out into the blazing sun. The ruts and hooves in the hard-packed ground led off to the south. A trail of thieves. He followed it almost without thinking.

By sunset, he'd caught up to a slow-moving caravan as its row of heavily laden carts neared the banks of the Nile. There, beyond a bend in the river, lay a natural harbor and more ships than Qsn had ever seen. Large ships, with long oars and masts built for heavy sails.

Some were tied up at the limestone dock, others waited their turn anchored in the quiet water, while still others were out in the channel, allowing the current to move them slowly downstream.

As the boy watched, treasures that belonged

to the dead were loaded on ship after ship. Goats and other animals were brought aboard as well. Foodstocks and amphoras of wine and sacks of dates and other fruits. In the midst of the commotion, the boy slipped aboard one of the ships, hid among the animals and soon fell asleep.

He woke to find himself part of a fleet under full sail heading south. They passed Memphis, the city of Rameses, in the dark of night. They sailed into the flooded Delta the next day. And then out into the sea.

By the time the boy was discovered and captured, the fleet had sailed from the mouth of the Nile and out beyond the edge of the known world.

Chapter 1

Roosevelt Field, New York
May 12, 1927

O n a pleasant afternoon that marked the middle of May, a small crowd gathered at an airfield on Long Island. A roped-off area was set aside for reporters, while farther back spectators from the general public jostled for position. Nearby, on a small platform, a brass band played.

A photographer snapped a picture of the crowd and the band. "You have to give Jake Melbourne credit," the photographer said. "He really knows how to put on a show."

Jake Melbourne was a World War I ace, a celebrity daredevil aviator and, as the photographer had noted, all-around showman. While other pilots wore brown leather jackets and drab wool pants for warmth, Jake wore a bright red leather jacket, adorned with epaulets. He wrapped his neck in a golden scarf and shod his feet in ostrich-skin boots. Over the years, he'd become famous, winning various flying contests and plenty of notoriety. Now he was going after the biggest ribbon in aviation, the Orteig Prize, twenty-five thousand dollars to the first pilot to fly nonstop from New York to Paris. Or vice versa. It meant hopping the Atlantic Ocean in one leap and many people thought it couldn't be done.

"What good is it if he gets himself killed?" one reporter asked.

"It makes for a good headline," a second reporter answered.

"Winning the prize would be a better one," another reporter said. "If anybody can do it, this guy can."

"You think Melbourne's going to make it?" the photographer asked. "You really think he's going to be the one? What about this Lindbergh guy?"

"Who?" the reporter said.

"The guy with the silver plane. He's parked over at Curtiss Field next door. Flew in last week from San Diego. Set a cross-country record on the way."

"Oh, you mean Slim," the reporter said with disdain. "Not a chance. His plane's only got one engine. Melbourne's got two and can carry more fuel."

"If you ask me, it can't be done," another reporter leaned in to say. "Four men have already been killed. Three other planes have crashed. And the French team in the **White Bird** are still missing. It's been a week. Wherever they are, they're not still flying."

The **White Bird** was the English translation of **L'Oiseau Blanc,** the name Charles Nungesser and François Coli had given their airplane. They'd left Paris on May 8th in spectacular style but hadn't been heard from since crossing the coast of Normandy. Searches for the plane and its crew were being carried out on both sides of the Atlantic even as Melbourne and other contestants prepared for their attempts.

"You wonder where Melbourne gets his money from?" the skeptical reporter continued. "Byrd has the Wanamakers, Fonck had Sikorsky."

"I heard Melbourne is funding the flight himself," the photographer said.

"And I heard he's flat broke and desperate for the prize money," the reporter replied. "Likes to gamble, you know."

The photographer considered that. "Well, it doesn't get much higher stakes than risking your life. Makes you wonder why anyone would even try it."

In a planning room, near the back of a hangar, Jake Melbourne and his financial backers were having a similar conversation.

Melbourne stood tall with his boots on, hair

slicked back and his red jacket hanging open. His meticulously trimmed mustache gave him a passing resemblance to Errol Flynn. He'd slept in very late in order to be rested for the long solo flight, but he looked tired and angry. "I'm not going," he insisted. "Not with that thing on board."

He was pointing to a compact steamer trunk, which, though it was small in size, was extremely heavy.

The men across from him seemed unimpressed by the outburst. There were three of them, very different from one another but with a family resemblance.

The older man in the center was thin and balding, with glasses and wearing a double-breasted mackinaw overcoat. Beside him was a bruiser who looked like he'd come straight from the bareknuckles boxing ring or jail. His nose was flat, one eye recently blackened, his ears chewed up like he'd taken a hundred punches to the head.

The third member of the trio was younger still, of more average height and build, and he considered himself Jake's friend. But that didn't count for much at the moment.

It was the older, bespectacled man who responded. "Listen to me, Jake. We're all here to help each other. Remember when the Irishmen wanted to break your hands for stiffing them on the three grand you owed? We paid them off for you. Not only did we do that, we bought out your other markers and helped you buy this plane. Now we need something from you."

"I was going to pay off those markers after I won the prize," Jake said, "that was the deal. You get half, plus we sell the plane. The rest I keep."

"That **was** the deal," the older man said. "We got a different one in mind now. In this deal, you get to keep the whole prize. You just have to deliver that trunk to a friend of ours on the Continent. He'll meet you in Paris after you land."

Melbourne shook his head. "If I put that thing on my plane, I'll have to off-load fifty gallons of fuel. One bad stretch of weather and I'll never make Paris. A little bit of a headwind and I might not even make the coast."

"You said going east instead of west puts the wind at your back," the older man insisted.

"I still need fuel."

"Maybe we could take out some other equipment," the youngest member of the trio said. "I've heard Lindbergh isn't using radio. I heard he doesn't want a parachute. Says the equipment is too heavy and unreliable." The young man turned to Jake. "You taught me how to dead reckon," he said. "You can use a compass and your watch."

"Lindbergh's crazy," Melbourne replied. "Once he takes off, he's gonna vanish just like the French. I need that equipment. And I need every gallon of fuel. Why don't you put the trunk on a steamship? Then I'll meet your friend in Paris and tell him what ship it's on."

The bruiser shook his head. "Hoover's boys are closing in fast and the docks are crawling with flatfoots looking for us. Besides, who can we trust?"

"Hoover?" Melbourne blurted out. "You're telling me the Bureau of Investigation is looking for this thing?"

The older man nodded. "We've had a misunderstanding with them," he admitted. "Why do you think we funded you in secret?"

Melbourne rubbed at his temple and ran a hand through his thick blond hair. Stepping forward, he grabbed the trunk, straining to lift it up, and then put it back down again. "Way too heavy," he said. Out of instinct, curiosity or just plain stupidity, he opened it to see what was inside. "What in the world?"

A boot slammed the top down so suddenly that Melbourne almost lost his fingers.

"I wish you hadn't done that, Jakey." It was the older man talking. His foot on the trunk, a revolver in his hand.

"You can't be serious," Melbourne said.

"Now what?" the bruiser said. "Those stones can tie us into everything. The guys we killed at the train station were carrying them. We get caught, it's the chair."

"I didn't see anything," Melbourne stammered. "Just a bunch of—"

Without finishing his statement, Melbourne threw a punch, knocking the revolver out of the old man's hand. As the weapon hit the hangar floor, Jake turned and sprinted for the door, but the bruiser tackled him around the waist, landing on him like a sack of cement.

Melbourne squirmed to get free and managed to slam an ostrich-skin boot into the man's already flattened nose. Blood spurted and the man grabbed his face, letting Melbourne go.

Jumping up, Melbourne froze in his tracks. The youngest man in the group had blocked his way and he now held a pistol as well.

"You have to fly it," the young man said. "Otherwise, we all go down. And that means you too."

Melbourne was past caring. He pulled open the top drawer on his desk, reaching for a derringer that lay there.

"Don't!" the younger man shouted.

It was too late for reason. Melbourne grabbed the pistol and spun. The fight ended with a pair of gunshots ringing out.

To the crowd outside, the shots were barely noticeable. Muffled by the walls of the hangar and masked by the playing of the brass band, no one could be sure if they came from bottles of champagne being opened, rimshots from the drummer or the backfiring of a nearby car or plane.

Any thoughts about the sounds were forgotten when the doors of the hangar opened and the crew pushed Melbourne's plane out into the sunlight.

The aircraft was beautiful. Painted bright red, with Melbourne's name on the tail and his personal emblem—a polished brass ram's head—on the side.

The plane was also a technological wonder, for its time. One of a kind, with an all-metal fuselage and a mid-mounted wing—design cues that foretold the future direction of aviation. It had twin engines, with in-line twelve-cylinder power plants that were water-cooled and had a capacity of 450 horses each. Its streamlined appearance and extra power gave it a top speed nearly twice what the average plane could fly. Its only weakness was that those engines consumed a lot of fuel. Melbourne's plan was to shut one engine down when he reached maximum cruising altitude, spend an hour slowly losing altitude, then fire the sleeping engine up and climb back into the sky. It was risky since twin-engine planes didn't fly particularly well on one engine, controlling them was difficult and restarting engines in flight had a spotty record of success. But Melbourne claimed to have practiced it and thought he could pull it off.

It was precisely this level of daredevil confidence that made the crowd love him. And when he came striding out behind the plane, in his red jacket, leather helmet, goggles and golden scarf, the crowd roared with delight. He bowed and waved and then climbed onto the wing of the plane.

From a spot behind the rope, the photographer raised his Ansco Memo box camera to take a picture. But just as he centered it on Jake, the reporter beside him pushed the camera down, the shutter snapped, and the photographer knew the photo would be blurred.

"What gives?" he said sharply.

"Never take a photo of a pilot before his flight," the reporter told him. "It's bad luck."

The photographer sighed. "Can I get the plane?"

"Wait until it's moving."

As the photographer waited, the band struck up a rendition of "Grand Old Flag" by George M. Cohan. The crowd sang along as Melbourne climbed into the cockpit. Within minutes, both engines had been fired up and the **Golden Ram** was heading toward the far end of the runway. There were no preflight checks, no delays, nothing that would cause the plane to spend more time on the ground burning fuel. It taxied out onto the runway, turned into the wind and began its takeoff roll.

The photographer took a photo and then lowered his camera.

With its twin engines thundering, the craft accelerated, but slowly. Halfway down the field, its tail wheel came up. Then, with only a quarter of the runway to go, it finally lifted off the ground, clawing its way into the air, fighting for every foot.

Everybody in the crowd held their breaths. Many of them had seen René Fonck's overloaded plane crash and burst into flames at the same spot the previous year. If they could, they would will the **Golden Ram** into the sky.

With the end of the runway nearing, the landing gear was jettisoned from the aircraft, the idea being that two hundred pounds of metal wasn't worth lugging all the way to Paris when one could land on the skid underneath the plane's belly.

Relieved of the landing gear, the plane climbed more easily, clearing telephone wires strung along the road at the end of the runway. Only now did the photographer snap his final shot. It caught the red plane turning east, heading for the coast, the sun glinting off its polished ram's head emblem. The Atlantic Ocean beckoned and, on the other side, Paris, fame and fortune.

The photographer developed his photographs the next morning. His pictures of the **Golden Ram** in flight would be used repeatedly over the next month, first in articles describing the great hope on the day of the flight, then during the unsuccessful search for the plane, which would go on for weeks after the **Golden Ram** vanished.

Despite the possibility of selling it for a large sum of money, the photographer would never publish the slightly blurred picture of Melbourne climbing onto the wing.

"Bad luck," the reporter had called it. And for the rest of his life the photographer would believe it had been just that.

Chapter 2

The North Atlantic, off the coast of Scotland
The present day

Gale-force winds howled across a hundred-foot trawler, whistling through the masts and booms that rose above the deck. Rain and spray blew in equal measure, lashing the windows of the bridge with blinding sheets, while the seas beyond the ship became a field of endless whitecapped swells rolling beneath the heavy gray sky.

A powerful Atlantic storm that had briefly been a hurricane had wandered north toward Newfoundland and then back across the pond toward Ireland. It was only the second such tempest to reach the British Isles in as many decades and it had come on faster than any of the predictions said it would.

Inside the trawler, three men occupied the bridge, one of them clinging to the ship's wheel, the other two holding tight to anything that helped them remain upright.

"Keep us square on," the captain shouted to the helmsman.

"I'm trying," he replied. "But the winds are shifting, Cap'n. We'll be getting blown over before long."

Both men spoke with a deep Scottish burr, a lifetime of northern heritage clear in their words. And despite their efforts, the trawler was struggling.

As it crested a long swell and dropped down the back side of the wave at an angle, the ship leaned hard to starboard and threatened to capsize. The helmsman had no choice but to turn downward and go with the wave.

Even then, it seemed like the ship might roll until the bow dug in to the bottom of the trough, the hull groaned loudly and the trawler's nose pitched up, shedding the seawater that had nearly swamped it.

Timing his steps to coincide with a brief moment of stability, the captain moved to the navigation computer. Holding on to the sides of the console for balance, he looked at the screen. The sweep of the radar beam showed an even heavier wall of rain to the north, but nothing beyond that. To the east, it picked up a small number of contacts and the rocky coast of the Isle of Skye.

As they neared the crest of the next swell,

spindrift blew back at them, raking the windows and sounding like hail. "It's no good," the captain said. "We'll never make it around the point. We need to find somewhere to shelter from the storm."

The third man on the bridge, whose name was Vincennes, took exception. Small in stature, thin-bodied, with a round, soft face, he looked anything but the demanding sort. Yet there was no mistaking the intensity in his unblinking eyes. "No diversions," he insisted, stepping closer to the captain and tapping a finger on the screen. "We go to Dunvegan."

Vincennes was neither an officer nor member of the crew, but he'd paid for the voyage and he intended to arrive at his chosen destination.

"Listen to me," the captain said. "The storm has passed far enough over that the wind is coming from the northeast. Right now, the Isle of Skye is between us and the worst of it. But the moment we pass Neist Point Lighthouse the waves will double in size and the wind will start ripping things off the boat. Things we need, like antennas, radar masts and life rafts. One bad wave and we'll lose a hatch or a window and then we'll start taking on water. Do you understand?"

Vincennes stared.

In case he hadn't gotten the point, the captain put it together for him. "We'll not be making Dunvegan tonight. The only thing for us to decide is if we spend the night sheltered in a bay or drowning out here."

The helmsman offered a solution. "If we put in to Loch Harport, we'll be safe from the storm. The loch is protected on three sides. And, from there, it's no more than twenty kilometers by road to Dunvegan."

By the time he'd finished making the suggestion, the boat had pitched forward once again, dropping into another trough between the waves. Everyone braced themselves for its bottom and the inevitable upward thrust that accompanied it.

This time the bow pierced the oncoming wave, submerging beneath it for just a moment. The crest of the wave flew back toward the bridge at a frightening speed. It slammed into the structure like a hammer, cracking one of the storm-proof windowpanes and staggering the boat.

The impact startled Vincennes. He flinched and ducked and then stood up slowly, looking surprised to be dry. "All right," he said, nodding to the captain. "Take shelter in the loch. But no radio calls. No one must know we're there."

The captain nodded to the helmsman, who'd already begun the turn.

Buffeted by the wind, the trawler swung ponderously to the northeast. It brought them on a course more directly into the waves. The awful twisting and rolling they'd been enduring for half the day was reduced.

Another hour brought them in sight of the loch's outer bay. The entrance was wide, but dotted with small rocky islands and submerged shoals.

"Watch the current," the captain urged. He could feel it pulling at the boat, slewing it around and drawing them off their intended course.

Waves were another issue. Out in the channel they were fairly regular and predictable, but as the boat neared the coast the wave pattern became more chaotic as the incoming swells bent around the rocky points and rebounded off the walls of the bluffs. One moment they would be getting pushed from behind, the next a wave would slam off the bow.

It didn't take long for them to find trouble. "We're out of the channel," the captain shouted while comparing their position to what was on the navigation terminal. "Hard to starboard."

"We're full over," the helmsman said.

Turning more, they were now fighting the wind as well. The combination was too much. The trawler was pushed farther out of the channel and dragged across a shoal.

The terrible sound of wrenching metal reverberated through the hull.

The helmsman tried to lessen the damage. He reduced the throttle at the first sound of impact, turned the rudder and waited for the leading edge of the next swell to roll in before returning to full power.

The arriving wave lifted them free, but the trawler was slow to pick up speed and they'd only just begun to make way when the bottom dropped out.

The second impact was more jarring than the first. The captain and Vincennes were thrown to the deck. The helmsman remained upright but slammed into the control panel. He cut the throttle once more as a bilge alarm went off.

"What's that?" Vincennes asked.

"Water coming in," the captain replied. "We've been holed."

"We're sinking?"

The captain ignored the question. "Full power," he ordered. "Go with the current until we're over the rocks, then make for the nearest shore. Our only hope is to run up on the beach."

The helmsman did as ordered, but the trawler was like a child's toy in the storm. Even with the throttle wide open, they were going nowhere. "Prop's not biting, Cap'n. Might've chewed itself up on the rocks."

"In which case, we're doomed," the captain replied.

Another wave hit from the side, swinging them around and shoving them even farther onto the shoal. They came to a jarring stop, caught hard on the rocks. The impact again threw the captain and Vincennes to the deck.

"Now what?" Vincennes demanded, attempting to stand.

The captain was up before him, looking out through the windows into a swath of sea lit up by the trawler's lights, where he saw the jagged tips of the rocky trap they were being held in. He knew the future. The waves would punish them as the rocks slowly tore his ship apart. "Now we die."

The trawler's approach had been noticed by the patrons of the McCloud Tavern, which sat up on a bluff sixty feet above a beach consisting entirely of smooth stones. They'd watched in fascination as the vessel approached the mouth of the loch with every light on board blazing.

A running argument divided the room, with one camp marveling at the bravery of the crew and the other marveling at the sheer stupidity of being out on the water in the first place.

"This gale has been comin' for three days," one man said.

"Aye," a woman replied. "But it's come on fast. And it's a wee bit worse than the dobbers on the TV said it would be."

"Ack," the man said, raising a mug. "You know you can't trust that lot. Even if you could, a man would have to be right doaty to be out in this weather to begin with."

The arguments went back and forth as quickly as the hot toddies and pints of ale. Hoping they made it, the bartender reserved a special bottle of scotch should they arrive in good health. But all the fun went out of the game when it became clear the trawler was in real trouble.

"They've run aground," one of the older men said as the ship's progress stopped. "I've nearly been caught on those rocks myself. Sharp as dragon's teeth, they are."

"There's been no calls," the bartender pointed out.

Like many small towns on the ocean, half the population here was fishermen. Marine radios were not in short supply. And during a storm everyone listened to the emergency channel.

The bartender picked up the phone to contact the Coast Guard.

"They'll never get a helicopter up here in time," the old man said. "And a rescue boat won't do. Not in this weather."

Despite the man's statement, the bartender stepped away to make the call. As he left the window, another man stepped forward, stopping at a spot between the other onlookers.

They looked at him sideways. He was tall, with a lanky build and silver hair. His face molded firmly but weathered by the elements. He wasn't a local, but he looked like a man of the sea.

The stranger took a brief look at the trawler through a pair of compact binoculars. "How far out are those rocks?"

"Just under a mile from here," the old man said.

The stranger raised the binoculars again, training them on a different location off to the side where a rugged spit of land stuck out into the bay. "And from the nearest point on that ridge of land?"

"A quarter mile," the old man guessed. "Maybe a bit more. Why?"

The stranger lowered the binoculars. He turned to the old man, looking at him with a pair of eyes that were deep blue in the gray light. "Because you're right. In this weather, a boat just won't do."

With that, the stranger turned and walked back through the pub. He met up with his friend near the bar and together they walked out through the front door.

The woman exchanged glances with the old man. "Who's that, then?"

The man shrugged. "Foreigners."

Chapter 3

Aboard the trawler, things had gone from dangerous to desperate. The boat had settled onto the rocks with a ten-degree list, water pouring in down below and the storm showed no sign of relenting.

The helmsman, feeling the sting of guilt and believing he'd failed the ship, turned to the captain. "I'm sorry, I should have swung wider."

"Nothing much you could do," the captain said. He got on the intercom, calling the chief engineer. "How bad off are we?"

"Three feet of water in the bilge. She's flooding fast. We need to abandon ship while we're still upright."

Vincennes heard this and shook his head vigorously. "No," he snapped, "we can't leave the boat. We have to get off these rocks."

"The rocks are all that's keeping us afloat," the

captain shot back. He pressed the INTERCOM button again. "Get the lads topside. We'll go out in the rafts."

With the order to evacuate given, Vincennes became livid. He pointed an accusing finger at the captain. "If this is some kind of a trick—"

Whatever else he might have said went unheard as a larger wave crashed against the ship, slamming the trawler broadside and rolling it farther over to starboard.

"You want to stay on board, you're welcome to it," the captain shouted. "My men and I are leaving."

Vincennes stared irately as men began coming up the stairs from down below. Unable to sway the captain, he waited for the last sailor to pass and then lurched in the other direction, making his way to the back of the wheelhouse and charging down the stairwell.

The helmsman made a move to follow, but the captain held him back. "He's my problem, lad. Get out on deck. Keep the men together. Launch the rafts as the waves crest, not before or after, or you won't stand a chance. Understood?"

The helmsman nodded, pulled on his life jacket and pushed out through the starboard door. As soon as he was in the open, the wind attempted to knock him down. He grabbed the railing and fought to stay upright on the tilted deck.

Things couldn't have been much worse. They

were over nearly twenty degrees now and leaning into the rocks. The port side of the ship was raised and acting like a bulwark against the onslaught of the storm, shielding the deck from being swept by every wave. But any boat that went into the water on that side would be slammed against the trawler's hull long before it could move away.

The starboard side of the deck looked more promising. The trawler was leaning that way and the edge of the deck was already awash. That should have made for an easier way off, but just beyond the rail lay a field of jagged rock spires.

The rocks vanished every time a wave crested through, only to reappear as it passed, emerging from the trough left behind like teeth in the jaw of some hungry beast. Still, he decided, a small chance was better than no chance at all.

He made his way down a ladder and then along the deck toward the midship's muster station. By the time he arrived, several of the men had begun inflating one of the boats.

The compressed-gas charges filled the raft quickly, but the wind and the rocking deck made it difficult to control.

"Secure the lines," the helmsman shouted.

Even as he shouted, the trawler shuddered with the impact of another wave. A blast of spray flew over them as green water a foot deep slid down from the elevated port side of the ship. It swept two men off their feet and took the raft into the sea.

Attached to the trawler by a sixty-foot lanyard, the raft was not yet lost.

The helmsman rushed forward. "Grab the line," he shouted, wrapping his hands tightly around the nylon cable. After two of the crewmen joined him, they pulled with all their strength, but they'd only managed to drag the raft a short distance before the next wave came surging through.

It swept over the ship and all around it, flooding in from both the bow and the stern. It caught the raft squarely, wrenching the line from men's stinging hands and flipping the raft as it carried it into the teeth of the rocks beyond.

One side of the inflatable boat was torn open upon impact. The orange craft lost its shape and was soon awash with seawater. The next wave finished it off, dragging it backward and wrapping its deflated fabric around one of the stone outcroppings.

The crewmen had seen the destruction up close. They all knew what it meant.

"We're trapped," one of the men shouted. "Even if we get another raft ready, we'll never survive that."

"This gale has a center to it, an eye," another of the men said. "If we wait it out, we might have a chance."

"The eye of the storm is hours away," a third crewman replied. "The ship will be scrap by then."

"Quiet," the helmsman shouted. He thought he'd heard the sound of an engine on the wind. He turned his eyes skyward, hoping to spot a Royal Navy helicopter. All he saw were churning gray clouds.

"There," one of the crewmen shouted. He was pointing toward the channel.

The helmsman turned, squinting against the wind and rain, and finally spotted a torpedo-shaped craft racing through the twilight. Whatever it was it pursued a curving path, disappearing behind the back of a large swell and then reappearing as the wave moved on.

"Are you lads seeing this?"

Murmurs of acknowledgment came his way.

"Whoever it is, he's got to be a bloody loon."

The bloody loon was a man on a high-speed watercraft similar in design to a Jet Ski but longer and wider, with an extended section aft of the seats, a bulbous nose and a noticeably broader stance.

The craft moved with great speed and agility and its pilot showed no fear, racing up one wave, coming down its back side and then heading directly toward the stricken trawler.

"He'll never make it past the rocks!"

The helmsman had to agree. But just as a bone-shattering impact appeared unavoidable, the next swell rolled through. The water rose, covering the rocky spires and lifting the oncoming machine above them.

Not only did the rider cross above the rocks, he raced straight onto the tilted deck of the trawler, ending his run in something like a controlled crash.

The crew rushed over, reaching the vehicle as the man climbed off and hooked an industrial-grade carabiner onto the second rung of a ladder near the trawler's superstructure.

"Are you all right?" the helmsman shouted.

He discovered a tall man in the wetsuit wearing a waterproof headset over a well-soaked mane of silver hair. The man's face hadn't seen a razor in a week, but under the thick stubble he appeared to be smiling.

"This is no place to moor a boat," the new arrival said.

The helmsman laughed, forgetting for a split second how dire their situation was. "Can't move it now. Any chance you can tow a raft behind that speeder of yours?"

The man shook his head. "Too much weight. We'd never get past the rocks before the next breaker comes through."

"Perhaps you can take a few of us at a time? As passengers?"

"I could, but that would take too long," the stranger said. "We're going to get you to safety the old-fashioned way."

As the helmsman watched, the man detached a cable from the tail section of his watercraft. Pulling it with a firm grip, it rose out of the water behind him, stretching out into the turbulent bay.

The stranger carried one end of the cable to the nearest boom, which the crew used to deploy the fishing nets. He climbed a set of rungs welded to the side and upon reaching a spot higher than any sane man should have climbed to in the storm he wrapped the cable around the boom in a figure eight, hooking it through one of the metal rungs and then onto itself.

With the cable secured, he pressed the microphone to his mouth and presumably spoke to someone on the other end of the line.

Somewhere in the distance, a winch started taking up slack. As it did, the cable rose out of the water. Only now did the helmsman realize what he had in mind. "A breeches buoy," he shouted.

"A what?" one of the crew asked.

"Think of it like a zip line," the helmsman said. "It'll carry us over the water and onto shore."

The stranger climbed down, shrugged the backpack off his shoulder and pulled out several harnesses, each of which was attached to a wheeled runner.

As he handed out the harnesses, the stranger explained what was about to happen. "The other end of the cable is attached to a trailer manned by a friend of mine down on the beach near the point. He has orders to keep the line taut and haul you in. How many on board?"

"Nine."

"Two trips," the stranger said. "Four people at a time. Then the last man goes with me."

The helmsman nodded and began directing his men to climb into the harnesses. The first four went up the boom and, one by one, hooked their new gear onto the steel cable and then to one another like a line of freight cars. With all four dangling out over the edge and the line sagging with the weight, the stranger spoke into his radio.

Instantaneously, a smaller secondary cable linked to the first harness pulled tight and the group began to move.

They went out across the water, dropping slightly and racing off into the distance. With the rain, the dim light and the blowing spray, it was hard to see them beyond the first hundred yards.

For the first time since they'd run aground, the helmsman felt a glimmer of hope. He looked back up at the stranger. "I'd like to say a proper thanks, but I don't know your name?"

"Austin," the man replied. "Kurt Austin."

Chapter 4

"Where did you come from?" the helmsman asked.

Kurt was the Director of Special Projects for an American government agency known as NUMA, the National Underwater and Marine Agency. Now was not the time to explain all that. "McCloud Tavern," he said. "We saw that you were in trouble. Crazy to be out fishing in weather like this."

"We weren't fishing," the helmsman said. "Just trying to get back to Dunvegan before the weather hit."

That sounded reasonable, except it meant sailing into the teeth of the storm. Heading south would have been far safer. Kurt filed the thought away and pressed the radio's TRANSMIT button connected to his headset. "What's the word?" he asked. "Has the first group reached you yet?"

———

A quarter mile away, close enough that an Olympic swimmer could cover the distance in four minutes, Joe Zavala stood on the back end of a trailer hitched to a powerful F-150 pickup truck. He was parked halfway up a deserted beach, watching as the winch on the trailer reeled in the cable.

Joe was Kurt's second-in-command at NUMA and his closest friend. He had a stocky build, short black hair and an easy smile that suggested things would be all right even when that appeared highly unlikely, considering the situation. This was one of those situations.

Despite being less than five hundred yards from the trawler, all Joe could see of the wreck was a shroud of light around the dim silhouette of the vessel. He strained for any sight of the men coming in on the line.

Finally, the cable began to bend, telling him there was weight on it, and four shapes emerged from the mist. They came sliding toward Joe, pulling their feet up as a wave tried to swipe them from the line, and crashed onto the beach in a four-man pileup.

Joe shut the winch down, hopped off the trailer and ran down to where they'd landed. He helped them out of their harnesses. "Get in the truck," he said, pointing to the crew cab of the Ford. "The heat's on. Make yourself comfortable, but don't play with the radio dial."

The men looked at him blankly, not getting the joke, and then stumbled toward the truck. As they opened the doors and climbed in, Joe pressed TALK on his own headset. "Congratulations, amigo. We've got four men on dry ground. Make that solid ground. Nothing's dry around here for miles."

"Roger that," Kurt said. "Get them out of those harnesses so I can pull the harnesses back and send over the next group."

Joe had already clipped the harnesses together and made sure they were secure on the cable. Heading back to the truck, he disconnected the brake on the winch, allowing the drum to spin freely and the cable to play out. "All clear," he said into the radio. "Use those biceps and pull to your heart's content."

Back on the ship, Kurt began hauling in the cable, pulling the harnesses back toward the foundering vessel. He worked quickly and without a rest. Finally, with his arms burning from the effort, the harnesses came into view. When they were close enough, he reached out and grabbed them.

"Next group," he shouted.

It took only a minute for the helmsman and

two other crew members to get situated in the harnesses and hooked onto the cable.

By Kurt's count, they were missing some men. "Am I confused or are we a couple of people short?" Kurt said to the helmsman.

"What?"

"These men are numbers five and six," Kurt shouted over the wind. "You make seven. But you told me there were nine on board. Where are the other two?"

The helmsman looked toward the wheelhouse. "The captain. He went down below to get our passenger."

"Passenger?"

"When we hit the rocks, he went below. The captain went down after him."

Kurt glanced toward the wheelhouse. With the lights on, it looked warm and inviting against the leaden storm, but it was no place to hide when the ship came apart. "Go with your men," he said. "I'll get your captain and this passenger."

The helmsman looked as if he was about to argue, but Kurt didn't give him a chance. He hooked the harness to the cable and pressed the radio's TALK switch to call Joe. "Next group ready to go. Reel them in."

The cable tightened and lifted the helmsman and his remaining crew off the gantry and out across the waves. As they rode toward safety, Kurt climbed down to the tilted deck and made his way toward the wheelhouse.

Just when he stepped inside the wheelhouse, the hull shifted with yet another wave, groaning in protest. If Kurt didn't find the captain and the passenger quickly, there would be no ship left to escape from.

Chapter 5

Austin stepped onto the bridge of the trawler and found it empty, then moved to the stairwell at the back of the pilothouse.

With the boat listing sharply to the side, the stairs resembled something from an amusement park attraction. "All ashore that's going ashore!" Kurt shouted.

His call brought no response and, with little choice, Kurt descended the diagonally slanted stairs. He found a short corridor with two doors on either side, the first on the right led to a radio room, the others to small cabins. All four proved to be empty.

At the end of the hallway another stairwell beckoned. Here, Kurt found a rope tied to the railing and trailing downward. The lights on the next level were out, so Kurt took a flashlight from a small pocket in the arm of his wetsuit and aimed it into the dark. Three feet of seawater was sloshing about at the bottom. But no sign of any person.

"Captain?" Kurt shouted.

Still no response.

Kurt followed the rope down and waded into the water. With the trawler rocking and the hull groaning with every passing wave, he wondered first about the captain and his passenger, then about his own sanity. "We're all out of our minds."

Panning around with the flashlight, he found another corridor and a second bank of accommodations. Six doors, three on either side. Pipes ran along the ceiling. And electrical conduits.

Aiming the flashlight down the length of the corridor, he spied a body floating at the far end. He rushed toward it, pushing a wave of buoyant debris ahead of him. Strangely enough, several life jackets, tied together in an awkward fashion, bobbed up and down nearby.

He turned the body over and lifted the man's head free of the muck. It was the captain. As his flashlight illuminated the face and head, Kurt noticed blood running from a nasty gash on the back of the man's skull. Bubbles by his nose and mouth suggested he might still be breathing.

Keeping the captain's head above water, Kurt pulled the floating mass of life vests toward him, untangled one from the others and strapped the captain in it.

"No . . ." the captain mumbled. "Let me go."

"Captain!" Kurt shouted.

The man's eyes opened a fraction. Kurt couldn't tell if they saw anything. "Can you hear me?"

A half nod, no words.

"Where's your passenger?"

The captain looked around in the dark. He seemed confused.

"Your passenger," Kurt repeated. "Is he down here?"

"He's dead," the captain blurted out.

"Dead?"

"Down below," he struggled to explain. "Drowned . . . the damned fool . . . I couldn't . . . get to him . . ."

Kurt nodded grimly. "Then we have no reason to stay. Can you stand?"

With Kurt's help, the captain got to his feet. The two of them waded through the muck to the stairs and climbed slowly back to the bridge.

"Who are you?" the captain asked.

"I'll explain in the pub," Kurt said. "Just stay with me and I'll get you out of here."

"What about my crew?"

"Already onshore."

That news lifted a burden from the captain's shoulders.

Kurt pushed the hatchway door open and helped the captain out onto the sloping deck. The wind whipped past and the rain came at them sideways. And footing proved treacherous. With the boat rocking every time a wave attempted to dislodge it from the rocks, before long the captain went down, taking Kurt along with him. In unnerving fashion, they slid toward the edge of the deck, stopping only as Kurt's feet hit against one of the cleats.

The captain took one look at the spires of rock ahead and shuddered. "Life jacket be damned. We'll never survive that. How did you get my crew off?"

"Breeches buoy," Kurt said. "But we're taking a more personal mode of transportation."

Kurt dragged the captain to the aqua sled, where it remained tethered to the ship's ladder. Each time a wave washed over the deck, the sled floated briefly, swung around to a new position and then settled again as the water drained away.

Kurt grabbed the handlebars and steadied it. "Climb on the back," he said. "Loop your fingers through those handholds. And whatever you do, don't let go."

As the captain got in position, Kurt climbed on the front. "Ready?"

"As I'll ever be."

Kurt fired the engine up, reached for the carabiner that held them to the ship and unlatched it. Another wave arrived, flooding the deck, lifting the aqua sled and banging it and them against the gantry.

Kurt shook off the impact and gunned the engine, pointing the nose away from the trawler. A rooster tail spraying out behind them, they rode straight off the deck and onto the bay. With the throttle pinned wide open, the aqua sled swiftly picked up speed, but, even as it did, the wave began dropping out from beneath them, creating a horrible, unsettling sensation just as they crossed the field of rocks.

Kurt leaned to starboard as an outcropping of mottled stone appeared in front of him. Avoiding that obstacle put them on a collision course with another algae-covered boulder. Kurt threw the weight of his body over the other way, split the gap and rushed out into the channel.

They were clear of the shoal and now out among the swells. To be safe, Kurt swung wide and headed for the shoreline below the tavern. Nearing the breakers, he timed his approach, slowing down and allowing the hill of water from behind to roll beneath him before speeding up once more.

By following the crest of the wave in and allowing it to crash and fan out, Kurt had given himself a watery carpet to ride up onto the stone-covered beach on. He took it all the way in, as far as he could go, stopping only when the aqua sled ground noisily to a halt on the shore.

Thrown forward by the sudden landing, Kurt pushed himself up off the handlebars. They'd come ashore at the tavern. A group of people already inside was rushing outside to help. They came down a crooked stairway that clung to the bluff and raced along the beach toward Kurt and the captain.

They arrived in joyous fashion, congratulating Kurt and helping the captain off the aqua sled. While a few of them helped him to the pub, several others helped Kurt lift the sled higher on the beach, where it wouldn't wash away.

The old man who'd stood beside him in the tavern handed him an open bottle of Talisker Whisky, proudly bottled nearby. "It'll warm your bones, lad."

Kurt had no doubt about that. He took a swig, handed the bottle back and walked with the small crowd back toward the cheerfully lit tavern.

Pressing the radio's TALK switch, he contacted Joe. "Did the second set of crewmen reach you safely?"

"They're in the back of the truck. Where are you?"

"I'm on the beach and heading up to the tavern for a drink," Kurt said. "Why don't you join me?"

"See you there," Joe replied.

Thankful that the rest of the crew was safe, Kurt allowed himself to relax. It was a truly euphoric moment, with one exception—the loss of the ship's passenger.

As he neared the warmth of the tavern, Kurt

wondered what would make a man run into the bowels of a sinking ship. It made little sense, considering the trawler was flooding and the danger was down below.

Something wasn't right. Kurt felt it. And even the whisky wasn't enough to drive that sensation away.

Chapter 6

Kurt met Joe outside the tavern as he pulled up in the F-150 they'd shipped over from America.

The trawler's crew piled out—some from inside the heated, dry cab, the rest from the open bed in back. Kurt hustled them into McCloud's, cutting off any more talk of thanks and appreciation.

"And would you believe none of them tipped me?" Joe said.

With the rescued sailors inside the tavern, Kurt jumped inside the truck and grabbed his duffel bag. Peeling off the wetsuit and getting into dry clothes felt terrific. The applause welcoming them when he and Joe entered the pub didn't feel bad either.

Before they could even say thanks, toasts were being made and food was being brought out from the kitchen. The sailors were treated to heaping plates of shepherd's pie, along with pots of hot tea and coffee. It wasn't long before townsfolk began to appear with other gifts. An older couple brought a basket filled with dry clothes. A younger man brought his son and daughter, explaining that the men who'd been rescued were fishermen like the children's uncle. A nurse, who everyone in McCloud's knew well, showed up and tended to the captain, putting antiseptic in the gash on the back of his head and getting ready to sew it up right there in the bar.

Trying to escape the fanfare as quickly as possible, Kurt and Joe settled into a booth in the corner of the pub. A fire crackled in a stone hearth nearby and the high walls gave them some privacy. A plate of food was delivered. Haggis and chips, which Americans call French fries.

Joe sampled the haggis. "So flavorful."

"You will literally eat anything," Kurt said.

"Food is fuel," Joe said. "And my tank is on empty."

Kurt traded whisky for coffee as a way of warming his bones. He took no milk or sugar. As long as it was piping hot, it was good by him. Taking a sip, he studied all the activity around them.

Everyone seemed happy and intent on celebrating. Everyone except for the captain. Then again, he'd just lost a ship and cracked his skull open trying to rescue a passenger who'd ultimately drowned. "You ever see a man run belowdecks on a sinking ship?"

Joe shrugged. "Some folks freeze up. I've seen people hide in closets instead of running out of a burning building. And last year we plucked those yachtsmen from the mast of their boat. Remember how they hung on until we forced them to let go?"

"True," Kurt said. "But in those cases, people were hiding from the danger, hoping desperately that it would stay away from them. The people in the building are hoping—irrationally, of course—that the closet door will keep the fire away. That if they don't see it, the fire won't get them. The sailors you're talking about climbed higher and higher. They'd have been smarter to get a raft off before the boat went under, but they were still trying to keep away from the danger. If the helmsman is telling the truth, this guy went down below and into the water after they hit the rocks."

"That is odd," Joe said.

"So is the captain's injury."

Joe glanced over at the man, who had his head down on a table while the nurse took out a suture kit. "We've all banged our heads on low-hanging pipes and hatchways," he pointed out. "If I ever go bald, you'll see a collection of scars on my noggin that go all the way back to my Navy days."

Kurt had a few of his own. "What part of your head?"

Joe ran his fingers through his hair, feeling for the scars. "Front and center mostly. One bad one, right on top."

Kurt nodded. "And yet our captain is getting the back side of his scalp stitched up."

"You think someone clubbed him?"

"Could be."

"Who?"

"Who else?" Kurt said. "The missing passenger."

Joe sat back, suddenly uninterested in the food. "Can't we just bask in the glory of this rescue like regular people? Does your suspicious mind have to work overtime?"

"Sorry," Kurt said. "When things don't add up, I look for reasons why."

"It's a bad habit," Joe said, shaking his head. "One I've tried to break you of for years."

Kurt shrugged and took a sip of the coffee. "I'm incorrigible. What can I say?"

Joe had finished the haggis and began stabbing the chips with his fork. Not satisfied with plain potatoes, he poured out a large glob of ketchup and began dunking the chips. "Since we're doing the paranoid thing," he said, "I'm wondering why that trawler was out in the storm in the first place. This cyclone has been all over the news for days. Plenty of time to head south or hole up somewhere."

Kurt nodded. "And yet they pressed on to Dunvegan."

"So, what's in Dunvegan?"

Before Kurt could respond, the fire shifted in the hearth, its flames tugged to the side by a draft that swept through the pub.

Kurt looked over to see the front door closing and three men standing in the entrance, shaking off the rain. They spoke with the hostess and made their way to the bar, taking seats at the far end.

Kurt studied them. They looked out of place. It was their clothing. They wore heavy wool sweaters, which were perfectly common to inhabitants of the area, but the ones these men had on looked fresh and new instead of well-worn and broken-in. And then there were the shoes.

"How are your boots?" Kurt asked Joe nonchalantly.

"Comfortable," Joe replied.

"Glad to hear it," Kurt said. "Are they clean and dry?"

"Not since we left London."

Kurt's were no better. He'd come to Scotland with two pairs of boots. By the end of the first week, both were covered with mud and perpetually damp. With fifteen days of rain out of the last twenty, it had proven impossible to keep footwear either clean or dry.

The shoes of every other patron in the tavern were in similar condition to Kurt's and Joe's and yet the new arrivals wore dress shoes with a half-decent shine and only the slightest hint of muddy residue around the edges of the soles. "I'd say they're not from around here."

"Neither are we," Joe pointed out.

"Yes, but we're local heroes now," Kurt said.

"True," Joe said. "What are you thinking?"

"You wondered why that trawler would be heading north to Dunvegan in the storm, I wondered why a passenger would run belowdecks on a ship that had been holed and was flooding. Both acts make little sense. Unless . . ."

Joe finished the sentence for him. ". . . Unless there was something valuable on that boat that had to be delivered to Dunvegan, something that had to arrive regardless of the weather."

Kurt nodded. As usual, he and Joe were reading from the same script.

"And if you were the customer waiting for this important delivery," Kurt asked, "and you heard the ship was diverting to another port nearby, what would you do?"

"I'd come to collect the package myself."

Kurt nodded once more, then sat back, keeping his attention focused on the men at the bar. So far, they'd done nothing but look at a menu.

"You realize it's none of our business," Joe said.

"What's not your business?" a voice asked.

Kurt turned to see a young woman who'd arrived beside their booth seemingly out of nowhere. Her hazel eyes sparkled with green and were accented by dark mascara, contrasted with ash-blond hair pulled back into a ponytail. She wore gray jeans and a cashmere sweater visible under an olive-colored raincoat. Her feet were shod in shiny black rain boots.

"The sinking ship," Kurt said. "It was none of our business, but we got involved anyway."

"So, you two are the gents of the hour," she said. Her accent was more suited to London than a small Scottish town. Her makeup and style were more city than country too. "Morgan Manning," she said, offering a hand. "Roving entry-level re-porter for UK News 1."

Kurt smiled and shook her hand. "Kurt Austin," he said. "This is Joe Zavala."

Joe shook her hand as well. "We're roving world travelers who can't seem to mind our own business."

"How can we help you?" Kurt asked.

She took a seat next to Joe and pulled a recorder from her coat pocket and placed it on the table. "You can change my luck," she said. "I've been sent up here on assignment. A crushingly poor assignment, to be honest with you. Get some foot-age of the storm, my boss said. Find some locals who want to ride it out—which appears to be all of them, mind you—and report on the dam-age to the coast, blah, blah, blah. All of it really boring stuff."

"I'd watch," Joe insisted.

"I wouldn't," she replied. "It's total tripe. We could film one storm and replay the footage every time another one comes in and no one would know the difference. But a trawler getting caught on the rocks, a couple of heroes risking life and limb to save the crew—now, that's a story."

Kurt went to cut the conversation off, but she was too quickly onto the next part of her pitch.

"Now," she said, "I've got some bloody great footage of the waves pummeling that boat, and even a shot of one of you riding out there, but I need something to tie it all together. To begin with, who are you and what are you doing here?"

Though he normally made a rule of avoiding reporters, Kurt found her hyperactive curiosity charming. He knew part of it was an act, but he'd seen worse.

She pressed a button on top of the recorder.

"We're American, as you can probably tell," Kurt said. "We work for NUMA—that's the National Underwater and Marine Agency—out of Washington."

"Yanks," she said. "I got that part already. Not the least from your accents as much as that monstrosity of a truck you're driving around in. And the ketchup . . . Do you really need to put that much ketchup on your chips?"

Joe looked down at his plate. It was swimming in the red sauce. "It's healthy. Lots of lycopene."

"Right," she replied. "But what are you doing on the Isle of Skye?"

Joe spoke up. "We're looking for the wreck of an ancient Viking ship believed to use copper plating as armor. It might not exist. But if it does, it would predate other metal-clad ships by several hundred years."

She seemed to find the idea suspect. "Is this really what the United States government spends its gobs of money on?"

Kurt jumped in. "No," he said. "We happen to be on vacation. Spending our own money. Which, unfortunately, doesn't add up to gobs."

"Not even half a gob," Joe insisted.

"And so far, we haven't found any sign of the ship."

Joe interrupted. "We have found copper artifacts with Nordic runes on them, but that was inland."

"So, no luck on your historical search," she said. "But you did turn out to be in just the right place at just the right time to risk your necks on that rescue mission."

Kurt sighed and took a sip of the coffee. "It happens more than you'd think."

"I, for one, found the risk well worth it," Joe said, trying to get Ms. Manning's attention back his way. "If you could have seen the look in those sailors' eyes as I reeled them in on the cable and helped them finally stand up on dry land—"

"You pulled them in?" she asked. "With your bare hands?"

Joe paused. "Well, the winch did most of the work, but I—"

"He had to press the button," Kurt said with a smile. "Injured his finger doing it. We might have to amputate."

"Very funny," Joe said.

The reporter turned back to Kurt. "So, you were the one who rode out to the boat. What did you find when you got on board?"

It was an odd question—oddly phrased, at least. "A crew of sailors needing rescue."

"Any cargo?"

"It's a fishing boat," Kurt said.

She laughed. "That's what I meant. Did you see any fish? Catch of the day, that sort of thing?"

"Didn't make it down to the hold," Kurt said. "And, as I understand it, they weren't fishing, just making for Dunvegan."

"Why stop here if they were heading for Dunvegan?"

Kurt shrugged. "I'd assume the storm forced them to put in here. But you'd be better off asking the captain or his crew."

She looked over her shoulder, then turned back to Kurt. "Great idea," she said. With the quick hands of a magician, she snatched the recorder up, switched it off and put it away.

With a smile that could melt butter, Morgan

Manning stood up and produced a business card. "I want to hear more of your story later. That's my mobile number at the bottom. If you think of anything else, give me a shout. I always answer on the first ring."

Kurt took the card and smiled politely as she walked away.

Joe looked upset. "Are we so flush with women that we're actively sending them away?"

"We do when they're distracting us," Kurt said. "Look around. Tell me what you see. Or, better yet, what you don't see?"

Joe scanned the room slowly. "The men with the polished shoes have vanished."

"So has the captain," Kurt added.

"That can't be a good thing," Joe said.

"Nope," Kurt said, finishing the coffee and standing. "It's not. You get to the truck and use the satellite phone to call for help. I'm going around the back. Be discreet. I have a feeling we're not the only ones on high alert at the moment."

Chapter 7

As Joe left the McCloud Tavern by the front door, Kurt made his way to an alcove next to the kitchen. Boxes of produce and pallets of beer lined one wall while the slope of the stairs ran above him on the other. At the far end stood a black-painted door with a four-paned glass window in the upper half. It was closing slowly.

Kurt reached it before it closed and kept it from latching.

He looked through the window. The view was blurred by the continuing rain and distortions in the hundred-year-old glass, but he could see the captain arguing with one of the new arrivals as they walked around the side of the building and stood under the shelter of the eave.

Kurt eased the door open, creating a small gap.

The cold air poured in and the words of the conversation came along for the ride.

The captain was pleading. "Listen to me, Slocum. There was nothing we could do. The storm came on too fast."

A pistol was produced. "Barlow doesn't like excuses, but perhaps he'll listen to you in person."

As the man spoke, a van pulled onto the pavers next to the tavern and stopped. The side door slid back, revealing the helmsman, bound with duct tape and gagged with a gray cloth.

"Leave my crew out of it," the captain said. "They have nothing to do with this."

Slocum shook his head. "Your incompetent crew are the only way to be sure you cooperate. It's just this one, at the moment, but we'll kill them all if you resist. Now, get in!"

The captain bowed his head and began trudging toward the van. The man with the gun turned to follow, staying far enough behind to prevent any attempt to disarm him.

Kurt used the moment to his advantage. He slipped through the door and sprinted across the patio. At a full run, he raced up onto a low wall and launched himself through the air.

One of Slocum's men saw him out of the corner of his eye. "Look out!"

Slocum turned, but Kurt's flying leap was already in progress. He came down on the gun-toting man before he could react, tackling him to the ground.

The impact sent Slocum tumbling backward. His hand smashed against the pavers and the pistol flew from his grasp.

Kurt went for the pistol, but the driver jumped from the van, raising a double-barreled shotgun.

Changing course, Kurt dove for the nearest cover, back behind the short wall.

The shotgun discharged and buckshot rattled off the old brown bricks. Kurt was unharmed. Expecting trouble from the second barrel, Kurt army-crawled to the far end of the wall and looked around the corner.

The captain had rushed to the van, where he'd pulled the helmsman free, only to be clubbed by the shotgun-wielding driver. The helmsman ended up on the ground as the captain was thrown into the van in his place.

By now Slocum had gotten up, hobbled over to retrieve his pistol and was limping toward the van. His men were reaching for the helmsman. "Leave him," Slocum shouted. "We have to go."

Kurt jumped up, ready for another run, but was forced back again as bullets tore into the damp ground in front of him. With little choice in the matter, he dove behind the wall once more.

Additional shots kept him pinned down. He had no idea where the incoming shells were being fired from, but sticking one's head up was a poor way to find out.

While Kurt stayed down, the van's engine revved loudly as the wet tires spun. The unmistakable sound of a vehicle backing up at high speed followed.

By the time Kurt risked a glance, the van had skidded to a stop, made a three-point turn and sped off on the road in front of the tavern. It fishtailed briefly, then straightened and raced off to the north.

With the area clear, Kurt ran to the helmsman lying on the ground. At almost the same time, Joe came around the corner. "What happened to being discreet?"

"I was never very good at that."

Kurt pulled the gag from the helmsman's mouth. It was soaked with bitter-smelling liquid. "Chloroform."

Kurt tossed the rag aside. The scent was pungent and he had no wish to smell it, let alone allow any of it into his system.

"He's out cold," Kurt said.

Unlike in the movies where two seconds of chloroform knocked a person out for hours, one usually had to breathe it in for an extended amount of time to pass out. "They must have had him for a while before they came to get the captain. How'd we miss that?"

"We were being distracted," Joe pointed out. "By a nosy reporter."

Kurt looked up. Morgan Manning should have been out there filming video and pouncing on what would be a highlight-reel scoop, but instead she was nowhere to be seen. "She's either the world's worst reporter or something else altogether."

By now the bartender and some of the patrons had come outside, including several of the rescued crewmen. Kurt waved them over to their mate. "Help him up and get him inside." He turned to the barkeep. "Get the police out here. You'll need an ambulance too. No telling how much of that anesthetic he's inhaled."

"I called the police already," the bartender said. "But the nearest barracks are in Dunvegan, and the road between here and there has been washed out."

Kurt stared through the rain. Dunvegan lay to the north, in the exact direction the van had driven. "If those men were trying to get back to Dunvegan, is there any other way for them to get there?"

"Only the Highlands path," the bartender said. "It's not much of a road, more of a winding track through a sheep pasture. It goes around the doon—the **big hill.** And Clagmore Castle is up there. And on the far side is East Brach."

"You can get back to Dunvegan that way?"

"It's rough country," the bartender said. "But if you were willing to go across it, then I suppose you could."

"Something tells me they're going to risk it," Joe said.

Kurt was already up and moving. "So are we."

Chapter 8

Kurt and Joe were belted into the front seats of the Ford F-150 as it charged diagonally across the big hill—or doon, as the bartender had called it. The footing was uneven, but the heavy-duty suspension and large tires handled it well. The higher they went, the less soggy things got.

"This hill is shaped like the back of a turtle," Joe said. "Aside from the ruts where the water's running, it's not bad driving."

"Just watch out for sheep," Kurt replied. "I've no interest in radiator-grilled lamb for dinner."

Joe laughed, but it was no joke. Scotland has millions of sheep, far more sheep than it has people. Out here in the Highlands, the ratio is perhaps a thousand-to-one.

"The rain is doing us one favor," Joe said. "The flocks are huddling under the trees."

Kurt gazed down the hill. Masses of what

looked like dirty clouds huddled around the base of the old-growth trees.

Beyond the flocks of sheep lay the Highlands road, a pair of tracks grooved into the earth by car and truck tires, with plenty of green growing between the grooves. Dark and muddy in color, the straight road stood out against the pale mossy hillside. Joe began to angle toward it.

"Hold off," Kurt said. "Keep to the high ground."

Joe stayed up on the top of the hill, running parallel to the road. Looking down toward it, he saw a pair of headlights cutting through the twilight. "You realize we're actually heading someone off at the pass. First time in history this has actually happened."

"Afraid not," Kurt said. "They're turning."

"Did they see us?"

"I don't think so," Kurt said. "They're heading toward the ruins of that castle the bartender mentioned."

Joe slowed down to a crawl. "I suppose you want to go down there and find out what they're stopping for?"

"That's why we came here."

Joe leaned on the wheel, looking over at Kurt. "You realize we don't have any weapons."

"We have surprise on our side."

Joe turned the wheel and began heading down the hill. "Last I checked, surprise doesn't fire any bullets. Or block them."

"I know that," he said. "But we have an investment to protect. We did a lot of work to save the captain in the first place, I'd rather not have all that go to waste."

Joe sighed. "Your logic is—"

"Impeccable?"

"I was going for the opposite," Joe said.

Joe brought them near enough to the trees that the clouds of huddled wool began to look like individual sheep. Stopping nearby, he shut the engine off. "We'll go on foot from here."

Kurt was already opening the door.

Joe got out of the truck, avoiding the huddled sheep and moving around back to where Kurt had dropped the tailgate.

Kurt had agreed with Joe's comment about having no weapons and figured they'd better improvise. He dug into the back of the truck and pulled out a pair of telescoping aluminum poles, which were normally used to attach cameras and sensors to a small ROV.

They were lightweight, sturdy and could extend to four feet in length, but they weren't exactly two-handed swords.

"Great," Joe said. "This will come in handy if I need to take a selfie."

Now armed, they moved across the road and down onto the grounds of the old castle, quickly reaching the outer wall. Slipping through a broken section, they closed in on the motionless van.

It had been parked near an archway that led into the castle. Once upon a time, there had been an iron gate, but it had long since rusted away.

"Looks empty," Joe whispered. "Maybe they switched vehicles. That's standard practice for a getaway."

Kurt crept up toward the van, confirmed it was unoccupied, then studied the ground. "I don't see any other tire tracks. But there's footprints leading into the castle. Maybe they have another vehicle parked on the far side. Let's see if we can catch them before they get there."

Kurt moved against the wall, leaned his head around the corner and looked into the castle for any sign of movement. Seeing none, they went inside.

On the other side of the castle, the men who'd abducted the captain brought him out into the courtyard. Kicking him in the back of the legs, they dropped him to his knees. One man held him down while Slocum stood over him with the pistol to his head execution-style.

No shot was fired. Another man appeared, coming out of the shadows of the castle. He had dark hair, a heavy brow and a large nose. He wore a turtleneck and black jeans.

"Are you Barlow?" the captain pleaded.

"You'll never meet Barlow," the man in the

turtleneck said. "I'm Robson. I'll decide your fate. Where is our merchandise?"

"It's on the boat," the captain said. "That's what I tried to tell these idiots. It's still there."

"And what about Vincennes?"

"He's out there with it," the captain said. "You can go see him, if you want to pay your respects."

Robson nodded a quick signal to one of his men. A kick came flying in and hit the captain in the face. He went down and tried to cover up.

"Pick him up," Robson said nonchalantly.

The two enforcers lifted the captain, trying to avoid the blood dripping from his nose and mouth.

"The next kick will be to a more vital part of your body," Robson said. "Do I make myself clear?"

The captain nodded. "I'm telling the truth," he said. "I tried to get it out, but Vincennes wouldn't help. He wouldn't come with me and he wouldn't leave it behind."

A hint of disappointment crossed Robson's face. "Not bloody likely," he said. "But we know there was another bidder. Did someone contact you? Did you kill Vincennes and divert to this little speck on the map to give us the slip?"

Robson spoke with a London accent—East End, maybe. He used fancy words, but his voice betrayed him. He was just another heavy.

"Why would I do that?"

"For money."

The captain looked up, his blackened eye and bleeding face defiant. "Running my ship aground doesn't sound very profitable, does it?"

This time Robson rushed forward and delivered a kick to the captain's midsection himself. "You could buy a fleet of fishing trawlers with what you've lost," he snapped, "with enough cash left over to purchase a small country."

The captain looked at Robson in shock. Only now did Robson believe his innocence.

"It's still on the ship," the captain said once more. "Just wait for the storm to pass and you'll be able to get it. All you need are a few good divers."

Robson looked at Slocum, who shook his head. "The hull is already breaking up. Even if it wasn't, this place will be overrun with investigators and police once the storm clears. We know that."

Before Robson could make a decision, another man appeared on the wall above. He'd been hiding among the old weathered stones watching the road with an infrared scope. "We have company. A couple of men on foot."

"Where did they come from?" Robson said.

"I couldn't tell you," the man replied. "The road has been clear."

Slocum reacted instantly, looking alarmed. "They might be the troublemakers from the tavern. They tried to stop us from taking him."

"Members of the crew?"

"No," Slocum said. "The bartender said they're from some American government agency."

Robson stared incredulously. He wondered if Slocum even thought about what he'd just said. "Men from some American agency tried to stop you from bringing the captain here and you just decided to tell me this now?"

"They're not involved," Slocum said.

"And how do you know that?"

"Because it has nothing to do with them," Slocum said. "And because Americans never tread lightly. If they were involved, they wouldn't send a couple of men who are good with their fists to deal with it. And those men certainly wouldn't announce who they were to the barkeep at some local tavern. It's a coincidence."

Robson shook his head. "Time for me to go."

"What about us?" Slocum asked.

"You stay here and figure out if these Americans are a bloody coincidence or something more." He turned to go, waving for the man on the wall to join him.

Slocum and his men held their positions. They hadn't been invited.

"What about him?" Slocum asked, pointing to the wounded captain.

Robson was already putting some distance between himself and the group, heading toward the opposite side of the courtyard. "Shoot him quickly. He doesn't need to suffer. He's an incompetent fool, not a traitor."

"And the men from the bar?"

"They're your problem," Robson insisted. "But I wouldn't let them live if I was you."

With that, Robson climbed through a gap in the far wall and disappeared.

Kurt and Joe were deep inside the ruined castle when they heard a shot. A single report that echoed down the corridor.

Judging by the echo, Kurt chose a direction. "This way."

Crossing a room knee-deep with muddy water, they came to a partition that had crumbled into a pile of rubble. Beyond it lay an open courtyard surrounded by ivy-covered walls.

Kurt moved to the edge of the room and crouched among the fallen stones. Out in the courtyard he saw the captain, lying on the grass, bleeding from a stomach wound. Two men stood over him, their backs to Kurt and Joe.

Kurt gripped the aluminum pole tightly. Every instinct in his body told him to rush out and attack while the men had their backs turned, but Kurt's mind worked with a cool efficiency. The more intense the moment, the colder it ran.

He pulled Joe down next to him. "There were three of them."

"We can't just leave him out there," Joe said. "He's going to bleed to death pretty quick."

"If they wanted him dead, he'd have a head wound," Kurt said. "They're using him as bait. We need to split up. You find the high ground. I'll run the gauntlet. When the third man shows his face, take him out. Preferably, before he gets a clean shot at me."

Joe nodded. "Give me thirty seconds."

As Joe backtracked, Kurt held his position and glanced at his orange-faced Doxa watch before returning his attention to the courtyard beyond.

The men outside remained focused on the captain, taunting him and kicking him from time to time, but neither of them turned Kurt's way.

As the second hand swept past the six o'clock mark, Kurt took a slow, deep breath, gripped the aluminum pole like a javelin and prepared to run.

Joe moved quickly, focusing more on speed and less on stealth. He found the opening in the ceiling he'd passed earlier, scaled the wall and pulled himself up to the next level. The seconds ticked past.

Sixteen . . . seventeen . . . eighteen . . .

On the second level, he discovered several ways to reach the outside world, but getting back to the courtyard was a little more difficult.

Twenty . . . twenty-one . . .

He climbed out through what had once been a window and found himself on the outer wall, exactly where he'd hoped to be.

Twenty-four . . . twenty-five . . . twenty-six . . .

Moving along the wall, Joe came within sight of the courtyard. He saw the two men and the captain down below. If there was a shooter set up to take Kurt out, the man would have to be on Joe's level. The best position was the ruined cupola of the tower to the right.

Twenty-eight . . . twenty-nine . . . thirty . . .

Should have said forty seconds, Joe mused to himself. Joe rushed toward the tower, running along the ancient stones with his arms held out for balance. He reached the cupola just as Kurt charged toward the two men in the courtyard.

At that moment a pair of hands holding a pistol in a two-handed grip appeared from inside the tower. Joe swung his aluminum weapon, bringing it down on the barrel, just as the gun discharged.

The shot hit behind Kurt, nipped at his heels. The men in the courtyard turned only to be clotheslined by Kurt throwing his body sideways and slamming into both of them at full speed.

Joe saw no more of the fight down below. He was fully engaged in a battle of his own. He'd knocked the pistol downward but hadn't jarred it free.

With hands that had to be stinging, the man wielding the pistol turned Joe's way to fire. This time Joe used the pole like a spear, jamming it into the man's forearm and pinning it and the weapon it held to the wall.

The gun discharged again, firing a shot into the stone wall. The recoil and ricochet shook the gun loose, but as the pistol fell the man spun free, pulled a knife and slashed at Joe's face.

Joe ducked, caught the man with his shoulder and rammed him into the wall. Expecting the knife in his back at any minute, Joe shoved the man to the side and out over the edge of the broken wall. He flailed as he fell, dropping ten feet, and landed on his back in the muddy grass.

He was banged-up but not dead or even out of action. And Joe realized he'd just created a three-on-one, with Kurt at a severe disadvantage.

He grabbed the pistol off the stone floor and found that the barrel had been damaged. Tossing the gun aside, he prepared to jump. As he stepped up on the wall, multiple shots rang out. They came so fast, Joe couldn't count them.

Below, he saw Kurt hit the deck. The three men he was fighting fell in rapid succession. None of them moved again.

Well aware of his exposure, and quite surprised to be alive and uninjured, Kurt crouched low and looked for the source of the gunfire. He found it on the upper wall as someone in an olive raincoat emerged from an archer's perch.

The figure pulled back the coat's hood, revealing a face with high Anglo-Saxon cheekbones, smoldering eye shadow—now slightly smudged by the rain—and a tightly wound ponytail of shimmering flaxen hair.

Kurt recognized her immediately. Morgan Manning.

Chapter 9

Kurt stood there in the pouring rain, surrounded by the fallen men, as Morgan Manning picked her way through the jumbled stones of the wall and made her way down to the courtyard.

Jumping onto the grass, she holstered the pistol beneath her raincoat and walked to where Kurt was standing by the captain. "Tell me he's still alive?"

"Sorry," Kurt said. "We were too late."

The captain was dead. By the look of it, he'd been dead before Kurt and Joe arrived. All the shouting and kicking was just for show. Part of a trap that had almost worked.

Morgan took a deep breath and shook her head. "Congratulations. You two have mucked up an operation that took months to arrange.

Now, instead of suspects to interrogate, I have four dead bodies."

"'Suspects to interrogate'?" Kurt said. "The news business must be rougher than I thought."

"That was obviously a cover story," she said, "made necessary when you got involved. I needed your names, voiceprints and facial profiles to run background checks."

"I don't recall you taking any photos," Kurt said.

"The voice recorder did it for me," she said. "It contains a hidden camera. Between the photos and the registration of your truck, I was able to confirm your NUMA backgrounds and rule you out as anything but overzealous bystanders who, unfortunately, chose not to stand by."

"Is that why you shot at me?" Kurt said.

She motioned toward the dead men. "I shot around you."

"Not here," Kurt said. "Back at the tavern. In the parking lot. It had to be you. Shots came from a high position. These men were at ground level and busy trying to get out of there."

She pursed her lips, pausing, before offering a reply. Finally, she nodded. "Very observant. For the record, I shot well ahead of you, into the mud. That way, you'd see the danger, pull back and take cover."

"And when I was behind the wall?"

"I had to keep you pinned down," she said.

"There was no danger. It's a small-caliber round. Not enough to punch through brick. It allowed these men to get away and me to follow them. So I could find out who they were meeting with and take them into custody. An act you've now prevented."

Having made his way back to ground level, Joe arrived in the courtyard just as Morgan finished speaking. "Ruining the best-laid plans of mice and men happens to be a specialty of ours." He took his jacket off and laid it over the captain. "Maybe we could have this discussion somewhere else. Like under what's left of the roof."

Kurt had gotten so used to the rain, he barely noticed it. With the wind dying down, it was almost peaceful out there. Still, it made no sense to linger in the open. The three of them moved to the shelter of Clagmore Castle, where the conversation resumed.

"Okay," Kurt said, "you know who we are. But who are you? More importantly, what organization are you with? And I don't want to hear that it's UK News 1."

"Security Service," she explained. "Section 5."

"MI5," Kurt replied. "And these men?"

"Part of an organization known as the Bloodstone Group."

"Never heard of it."

"You wouldn't have," she said. "But, trust me, they're very dangerous people."

Kurt didn't need to trust her on that, he'd seen

it. The bigger question remained—her presence in the mix. "And yet, you wanted to take them on by yourself?"

"Not necessarily," she said. "My team is standing by in Dunvegan. Our intel suggested a package would arrive there by sea yesterday. We've been watching everything and finding nothing. When I'd heard about the trawler mishap, I left the team behind and came up here on a hunch. Everything else happened so fast, there was no time to call for help. I wasn't even sure the boat was connected to the operation until Slocum and his men showed up."

It took guts to play a hunch and follow it through. Kurt had respect for someone who operated that way. "And what, exactly, were these men smuggling?"

"I'm not going to get into that," she replied. "You understand, of course."

"Of course," Kurt said. "I know all about the rules."

"Knows them," Joe pointed out, "but rarely follows them."

"I'm acquainted with that type of person," Morgan replied. The expression on her face suggested they might be cut from the same cloth.

"The thing is," Kurt said, "whatever these men were smuggling, it's still out there on the trawler."

Her gaze narrowed as Kurt spoke. "How can you be sure?"

"The captain and his passenger went below-decks to retrieve it," Kurt said. "They even made a raft out of life jackets to float whatever it was down the hall, which tells me it must be something heavy. What went wrong, I don't know. Probably an argument over what to do with it when they reached shore. Maybe someone didn't want to give it to these people and someone did. Bottom line—it's still down there. If it's perishable, like opium, you're probably okay just letting it go. But if it's something more substantial, it will still be in one piece. At least for now. We can help you retrieve it."

"I appreciate the offer," she said, "but I can't accept. I'll have a dive team up here as soon as the storm moves through. We'll go over every square inch of that boat. We'll find what they were bringing in."

"You won't," Kurt said. There was no malice in his voice, no spite, just the firmness of stating a simple fact.

Morgan's eyebrows rose as if she felt challenged by the statement.

Kurt explained. "After another twenty-four hours of raging winds and pounding surf, that trawler will be little more than scrap metal. Add in a renewed storm surge and multiple tide changes and you'll be lucky to find anything other than the engine and the anchor."

"I think you're overstating the danger," she

said. "The weather seems to be calming down already." She pointed to the sky, the overcast was lighter, the winds were tailing off, even the rain had slowed to a soft patter.

"This storm began life as a hurricane," Kurt said. "It might not have a true eye, but it has a calmer center than a normal weather front. That lull is reaching us now, but it's not going to last. We have calm winds for an hour or two and then the second half of the storm hits and you're shut down for the next day and a half. If you want to recover what these men were smuggling, you're going to have to do it now."

Morgan stared at Kurt for an extended moment. Her calm demeanor was momentarily replaced by a look of frustration. "You make a good point," she said, "I'll not deny it. But before I agree, I'd like to know why you're so interested. This won't be an easy dive and you've risked your life once already."

"Twice, actually," Joe said.

"Right," she said. "So why risk it a third time?"

Kurt grinned. To him it was as obvious as night and day. "I'm a sucker for a mystery," he said. "And so far I've been punched, shot at and thrown in the mud twice all because we tried to help someone. At this point, I'd really like to know why."

Chapter 10

The gusting wind had become a gentle breeze by the time Kurt, Joe and Morgan arrived at the beach. The sky above remained solid gray, and the spitting rain never quite cleared up, but conditions had improved. Studying the updated forecast on his cell phone, Kurt knew it was now or never. "This is as good as it's going to get. Let's be quick."

As Joe parked the truck, Kurt climbed out. With the reduced wind, the waves were no longer whitecapped, but they were still rolling in and crashing hard on the beach.

Morgan stopped and stared. She seemed taken aback. From down on the beach the waves looked even larger than they had from the road up above. "This is a little mad."

"This," Kurt echoed, "is a nice twelve-foot, left-hand break. Perfect surfing conditions."

Joe laughed and shook his head. "If you don't mind frigid water and being smashed against the rocks."

Having coaxed a nervous smile from Morgan, Joe raised a pair of binoculars to his eyes. "Lights are out," he said. "And she's almost completely submerged. Take a look."

Kurt took the binoculars from Joe and studied the wreck. Only the top of the wheelhouse and the booms used to deploy the fishing nets remained above the waterline. Every wave crashed over the boat and swamped it.

Lowering the binoculars, Kurt checked his watch. "Tide has nearly peaked," he said. "And the boat has settled a bit. Must be sitting flat on the bottom at this point. We need to get this done before the tide changes and drags it off the rocks."

"With the hull underwater, we won't be able to park on the deck this time," Joe said.

"No," Kurt agreed. "We'll need to be dropped off and picked up." He turned to Morgan. "This isn't going to be easy. How much diving have you done in rough weather?"

"Enough," she said. "I'm deepwater-certified and I spent three months training with the Royal Navy's Maritime Counter Terrorism Unit, subsurface and rescue. None of it in a swimming pool."

Kurt found her snarky tone charming. "Then it's best if you and I make the dive. Joe will be our chauffeur."

The plan was simple. Joe would pilot the aqua sled, drop Kurt and Morgan near the wheelhouse of the sunken trawler. While they went inside, Joe would move out into the channel and ride the waves, waiting patiently for them to signal him. As long as the waves remained steady and the wind held off, it would actually be safer for Joe to stay out in the swells than to come back to the beach, where he'd have to deal with the breakers on the way in and out.

With the helmet-mounted communication system, they would be able to talk through most of the dive, but each of them carried emergency equipment and flares in case the comm system failed.

After changing into wetsuits, Kurt and Morgan pulled on dive harnesses and tanks. While they'd brought a catalog of equipment on their expedition, they lacked something fairly simple—extra weights. As Joe readied the aqua sled, Kurt handed Morgan two mesh artifact bags used to collect things on the bottom of the sea.

"Fill these with stones and hook them on your belt. We'll be in rough water while getting in and out of the trawler. The safest way to deal with all that is to be heavily weighed down. Otherwise, we might be swept away."

Morgan filled both bags with smooth round stones and connected them to her dive harness. Between the gear and the extra weight clipped to their belts, it was difficult to walk onshore. But once they'd waded into the surf, she and Kurt fared better than Joe.

After almost losing the sled once, Joe hopped on board and goosed the throttle to keep the craft under control. Morgan climbed on behind him, Kurt climbed in third.

"Go!"

Joe twisted the throttle and moved them out into the surf. He cut power for a second, allowing them to drift back, as another wave loomed and then crashed. The white water swept toward them and Joe accelerated briskly, rushing out to meet the next wave before it had a chance to break over them. From there, it was a smooth ride, up and down the swells, out to the trawler.

With the trawler resting in a flatter position, Joe came in from the bow, which allowed him to avoid the submerged spires of rock. After some maneuvering to get past the booms, he pulled up beside the roof of the wheelhouse and held station by modulating the throttle.

"This is your stop," he called out.

Kurt was already off the sled, dropping into the murky water and sinking to the deck. He landed hard and grabbed for a handhold. One moment he was in ten feet of water with the throbbing aqua sled's engine and the cresting phosphorescent wave above him, the next moment he had to make sure he was off to the side so the sled, with Joe and Morgan on board, wouldn't club him on the head as it dropped behind the passing wave.

Now his head was briefly above water. He gave the thumbs-up and watched as Morgan slid one leg over the aft section of the craft. She dropped into the water as the crest of the next wave arrived. Sinking fast, but also being pulled away from the wheelhouse.

Kurt stretched out and grabbed her dive harness with one hand while he wrapped his other hand around the frame of the hatchway. For a moment it felt like he was being pulled apart, but the pressure relented and the water swirling past slowed.

Kicking with her fins, Morgan swam up next to him and grabbed onto the hatchway herself. "I thought the extra weight would do more than that," she said, her voice sounding flat through the comm system.

"Without them, we'd have been swept off the deck," Kurt insisted. "But we'd be smart to be extra-cautious."

She nodded.

"Follow me."

Kurt pulled himself inside the wheelhouse, which was filled to the ceiling with silty water.

Once inside, he flicked a switch on the lower part of his dive harness. It turned on a set of lights embedded in the gear. NUMA had learned long ago that the best way to light up the water without degrading a diver's vision was to position the lights away from the diver's mask. In this case, they were integrated into the harness itself.

And there was the added benefit of freeing the diver's hands.

"Switch on your lights," Kurt said, pointing to the right side of the harness.

Morgan found the button and pressed it. With both sets of yellow-green LEDs set on high, the wheelhouse went from a murky environment to one filled with definition and shadows. There was plenty of silt wafting around, but Kurt could see through it to the far wall. He quickly got his bearings. "Follow me."

Another swell rolled over the trawler. It rocked the vessel as it passed, creating a current inside, pushing Kurt and Morgan forward and then drawing them back. With the extra weights, it was only a mild distraction.

Kurt pressed forward. "Next stop on our walking tour—the stairs."

"Right behind you."

Kurt descended the stairway slowly, feeling like an astronaut on the moon. While the air tank and the harness restricted his mobility, the buoyancy acted like a low-gravity environment. Instead of walking down the stairs, he took a short hop and dropped easily onto the lower deck.

"Tell me more about this Bloodstone Group," he said.

"That's not part of our deal," Morgan said, landing behind him.

"I'm going to find out from my government anyway," Kurt said, "you might as well share the obvious stuff."

"Fine," she said. "They're arms dealers by trade. But they've been funding their activities with conflict diamonds and unethically sourced gems."

"Is that what they were bringing in here?"

"No," she said. "With the cooperation of Interpol and other government agencies, we've managed to cut into that trade. The big clearinghouses in Antwerp have assisted the effort by tightening controls and buying only from reputable sources."

"That's awfully nice of them."

"Partly," she said. "People cooperate more easily when things are in their best interest. They have no desire to see the market flooded with low-margin gems from desperate sellers."

"Good point."

"There are still loopholes," she added. "But the clamps have come down hard enough that Bloodstone has switched to another source of hard income."

"Which is?"

"Antiquities. Artifacts and relics from ancient cultures."

"Arms for antiquities," Kurt said. "I've heard that trade is growing again."

"What connection does NUMA have with antiquities?"

"We do a lot of archeological work. We've had to put extra security on at some of the more sensitive sites. Where does the Bloodstone Group source its relics?"

"Anywhere they can," she said. "They steal from museums, private collections and especially from active digs. Things that haven't been cataloged and recorded are more valuable because they can't be traced."

Kurt knew the rest. "They sell what they steal to wealthy buyers and use the cash to buy weapons."

"Exactly," Morgan said. "And then they trade the weapons to their old contacts fighting in the war-torn countries of the world."

By now they'd reached the second stairway. The rope he'd seen earlier was still tied to the rail.

"What's that for?" Morgan asked.

"Either to haul the cargo up or serve as a guide-line," Kurt said, double-checking the security of the line. "Considering the raft they tried to make out of life jackets, whatever they were carrying must have been pretty heavy."

Morgan turned so that the lights on her dive harness joined Kurt's in shining down the flight of stairs. Floating bits of sediment gleamed in the light like a field of stars. The trawler shifted gently as the waves continued to roll over it. Aside from the sounds of their regulators expelling gas and the creaks and groans of the hull, it was quiet. "Almost peaceful down here."

"Trust me," Kurt said. "It wasn't that way a few hours ago."

Kurt stepped off the top stair and propelled himself forward, then dropped down and landed on the lower deck.

His feet stirred up a small cloud of sediment as they hit the deck. It wafted around his legs as it thinned out. Kurt saw above him, trapped against the ceiling like helium balloons, the life jackets the captain had fastened together.

He moved forward as Morgan landed next to him.

"See anything of interest?" she asked.

"Not yet," Kurt said.

He moved past where he'd found the captain floating and arrived at a door that had been held ajar. A stainless steel crate lay wedged between the frame and the door. Kurt bent down to examine it. He found a heavy rubber seal where the lid met the body. It had a padlock attached for security.

"This must be it," he said, pushing the door back and grabbing a handle on the crate. With a solid heave, he pulled one end of the crate off the deck and then slid the crate forward. It was heavier than he'd expected.

Releasing the handle, he listened as the metal trunk hit the deck with a muted clunk.

"It's at least eighty pounds," Kurt said.

Morgan moved up and took a quick look at the lock on the crate. "We'll need a key or a pair of bolt cutters," she said and then slid past him and into the cabin beyond. "Let's see if it's part of a matching set."

Kurt joined her in the cabin. They found no additional crates, but as they turned to a far corner their lights fell across the body of a man sitting propped up against the bulkhead.

His arms were floating up as if asking for help while his hair wafted in the current and his lifeless eyes stared straight ahead. In the tinted light, his skin looked ghostly pale, almost green.

"Vincennes," Morgan said. "Our informant."

"The captain said he'd drowned," Kurt replied. "But this room had only three feet of water in it at that point."

Morgan was examining his neck. Bruising around the Adam's apple suggested he hadn't drowned. "His neck is broken. He was probably dead long before he had a chance to drown."

She ran her gloved hands through the pockets of Vincennes's jacket and then left him and drifted over to the far side of the room. There she found a computer bag and a cell phone. Dumping some of the rocks from one of her artifact bags, she slid the electronic equipment inside. "The boys at the lab will want to take a look at these."

Kurt looked through the rest of the room and found it empty. "Let's get that crate topside and call Joe to pick us up."

Back out in the corridor, they positioned themselves on either end of the trunk, grabbing the handles. "Ready," Kurt said. "Lift."

With the trunk in hand, they moved toward the stairway with Morgan walking forward and Kurt walking backward.

Chapter 11

Joe Zavala sat astride the padded seat of the aqua sled, riding the swells and holding station approximately two hundred yards from the submerged trawler. Out in the center of the channel, the waves rolled past with hypnotizing regularity.

Joe still had to deal with the occasional crossing wave or merger of two approaching swells, but for the most part he could time all his movements in advance, accelerating up the face of an oncoming wave, cutting the throttle near the top and then dropping smoothly down the other side.

It became easy, almost soothing.

That didn't really surprise Joe. He was at home aboard a machine like this. Unlike Kurt, who took some kind of masochistic pleasure from self-powered efforts like rowing on the Potomac or the even sketchier sailing where one depended entirely on the fickle wind, Joe preferred the horsepower of engines and machines. He'd begun rebuilding his first motor at the ripe old age of ten. He'd tuned and fixed cars all through high school and then had enrolled in engineering courses while in the Navy. Since then he'd designed and built boats, ROVs, submarines and even an airplane, which he'd yet to fly. He'd even created a self-powered diving suit that acted like a shell of artificial muscle, enabling a diver to swim twice as fast and several times as far.

In Joe's world, horsepower had been created for one reason—to replace human power—and his general rule of thumb was the more, the better. Even the aqua sled boasted a racing engine modified by Joe, a fact he gave thanks for every time he twisted the throttle.

He glanced down at the glowing display panel. Plenty of fuel, no warning lights, but a dwindling amount of time. The tide would soon be turning and that would cause rougher waters and a dangerous current trying to fight its way out of the loch.

At nearly the same time, the lull in the storm would end. Judging by the return of the white-caps, the wind was already picking up.

Joe eased down another wave, accelerated at the bottom and then put the spurs to his steed as the rising face of the next wave came on. Reaching its top, he eased back on the throttle again and glanced toward the trawler. He saw nothing to indicate that Kurt and Morgan had surfaced, but something else caught his eye, something in the distance moving just beneath the rolling clouds.

At first, he thought it was a bird—a wild albatross or some other seabird—that had ventured out during the lull in the storm, but the truth dawned quickly. The black spot in the gray sky was a bird, all right—a mechanical bird, a helicopter—and it was heading their way.

Joe thumbed the TALK switch and broadcast the information. "I hate to tell you two, but we're about to lose our exclusive claim on this salvage operation. We have a blacked-out helicopter inbound. Any chance it's from MI5 or the Royal Navy?"

Morgan replied first. "I haven't called anyone," she said. "I wouldn't count on it being friendly. Not if it's flying without running lights."

Kurt's voice came through next. "How soon will they be on our doorstep?"

Joe was dropping back down as the question came. When he looked over, the helicopter had closed a quarter of the distance. "No more than a minute. Are you two ready to get off that trawler?"

"We found what we're looking for," Kurt said. "Heading topside now. Meet us at the wheelhouse."

Joe didn't wait for the next swell to lift him up. He gave the throttle a nudge and sped off, curving to the right. This path took him to a position where he could approach the wreck with the waves coming straight at him. Like a plane taking off and landing into the wind, this angle gave him more control.

He timed the swells and eased forward, guiding the sled around the fishing booms that now stuck out of the water like dead trees. With a little side slip, he bumped up against the wheelhouse.

"Is that you knocking?" Kurt asked over the radio.

"Just wanted to let you know I'm here."

"Hang tight," Kurt said. "We're coming up the stairs."

Joe was pushed back, but as he came forward again he saw lights dancing around inside the boat. He heard heavy breathing and short grunts as Kurt and Morgan struggled with their discovery.

"Sounds like you're breathing heavy," Joe said. "You might want to spend more time in the gym once we get home."

"Very funny," Kurt said. "This little treasure chest is heavier than one might think."

Much as he wanted to help, all Joe could do was work the engine and stay in position.

He glanced back. The helicopter was over the beach when a pair of spotlights beneath its chin bubble came on. They were pointed straight down, lighting up the stony beach and then focusing on the white F-150.

The helicopter hovered there for a moment and then began to move again. Its circle of light crossed the beach, lighting up the foamy water in the shallows, and then picked up speed as it traveled out over the dark rolling swells.

Kurt emerged through the hatch as some of the water started draining away. He was walking backward, with the water swirling around his shoulders. Joe noticed he was holding his hands forward and down. Morgan was still inside the wheelhouse.

Kurt vanished as another wave rolled in. Joe goosed the throttle and moved forward so the aqua sled wouldn't be pushed back into the wheelhouse, then idled the sled in place.

Kurt reappeared just as the sound of the helicopter overcame the wind and the waves. It was turning sideways a hundred yards off. Its spotlights swung across the water and settled on the boat.

"Nice of them to give us some light to work with," Kurt said.

Joe shielded his eyes. He saw a figure in the doorway with his legs slung over the side and a long-barreled rifle in his arms. "Get down!"

Flashes from the barrel of that rifle reached them a microsecond before tracer fire began screaming overhead. Red streaks against the leaden sky, five potentially lethal shells.

Joe ducked and pulled away as shells tore into the wheelhouse. A second burst was short and to the right, tearing into the stern of the boat.

Kurt reappeared with Morgan beside him. Joe moved the aqua sled into position, but as they were about to lift the metal trunk aboard another burst of gunfire rained down, this one accompanied by a 40mm grenade.

The grenade exploded as it hit the water amidships. The shock wave pushed the aqua sled forward and knocked Kurt's and Morgan's legs from underneath them. They vanished beneath the water.

"Get out of here!" Kurt shouted over the comm system.

"Not without you two."

"You can't help us if you're dead. Go! That's an order!"

Joe twisted the throttle to full and the aqua sled shot forward. He raced out over the bow, heading out toward deeper water.

As soon as he looked back, he noticed a problem. The helicopter was following him.

Chapter 12

Racing out into the channel, Joe gave Kurt the good news. "If your plan was to palm these fellows off on me, it's working."

"Sorry," Kurt said. "But if you can keep them busy without getting shot, this could work to our advantage. We're working on a plan."

"Think fast," Joe said. He sped down the face of one wave and then up the next. As he emerged near the top, the helicopter appeared in his rear-view mirror. It was flying at a catty-cornered angle, crabbing along sideways so the sniper in the doorway could fire at him.

Out past the point, Joe had room to maneuver. He weaved to the right and swung in a wide circle, his path bringing him around to the nose of the helicopter. Even as it turned, Joe kept circling. And the gunman, with only the side door to shoot from, was always too far behind to get a bead on him.

Joe grinned at his own ingenuity. He wondered how many circles before the pilot and his sniper would start getting dizzy. "I can do this all day," he said out loud.

Just then, the helicopter stopped its rotation and spun back the other way. Joe noticed the change a second too late, ending up directly in the firing zone.

A wave of tracers tore into the sea in front of him and he turned instinctively. "Or not," he grunted, hanging on tight to the controls.

Suddenly the helicopter went dark and Joe lost track of it. He cut left and then right, trying to track the machine by the sound of its rotors. He assumed they had him on a night vision scope, which would give them a decided advantage, but there was little he could do about it.

He dropped down into another trough. When he came up to the crest, the helicopter was directly ahead of him. Spotlights came on, blinding him, and the sniper opened fire. One shell hit the windscreen, taking a section of plexiglass with it, another bullet blasted through the outside edge of the left-hand grip.

Joe pulled his arm back instinctively. His palm stung. His shoulder felt numb. Still rocketing forward, he raced directly under the hovering machine. If he'd had a spear, he could have thrown it inside and impaled the gunman.

One thing he could not do was continue to run and dodge.

Out in the clear, Joe tested his hand and found his grip strength okay. He grasped the shattered handlebar and turned once again. Good thing the throttle is on the right, he thought.

The helicopter turned to follow, but Joe had a new game plan. He was safe in the troughs because the crests of the rolling waves blocked him from the low-flying sniper's view. This time he stayed down, traveling in the trough of the wave as it rolled toward shore.

Having lost sight of him, the pilot made an obvious choice and climbed higher. The lights swept over Joe and then vanished.

To Joe's astonishment, the pilot had given up the chase. There could only be one reason for that.

He radioed Kurt. "Sorry, amigo, decoy season is over. They must have realized I'm not carrying any loot. They're heading your way."

"You did what you could," Kurt replied. "Get out of there. We'll take it from here."

"Tell me you're in the water and swimming."

"Not exactly."

As Kurt replied, Joe noticed the helicopter climbing, then lowering its nose and setting itself in a firing position.

Before Joe could utter a warning, it unleashed a furious barrage of missiles from pods connected to the stubby wings just below the cockpit. Five, ten, twenty—the projectiles kept coming. They tore into the partially submerged trawler in an unrelenting bombardment, blasting it apart. The deck was shattered, the wheelhouse obliterated. Orange explosions of fire erupted fore and aft. In the middle of it all the fishing booms toppled like trees cut down in the forest.

By the time the onslaught finished, the helicopter was shrouded in a cloud of smoke. As the smoke cleared, the helicopter's spotlights focused on the smoldering wreckage. They probed here and there and then suddenly went dark.

Lights off, the helicopter turned and rode with the wind, quickly vanishing in the deepening gloom.

Chapter 13

"Kurt, do you read?" Joe called out over the radio. "Give me a sign, amigo. I know you're out there somewhere."

Traveling slowly, his eyes scanning in front and to the sides, Joe circled the smoldering area of submerged wreckage in search of Kurt and Morgan.

"The helicopter is gone," he said, holding down the TALK switch. "I repeat, the helicopter is gone. I'm not picking up any transmission from your end. If you can hear me, send up a flare and I'll come over and pick you up."

Joe listened intently, but there was no response, not even a garbled or static-filled attempt.

He would ride the waves for another twenty minutes, crisscrossing the area, with the aqua sled's subsurface lights on, hoping to spot Kurt or alert him to his presence. He continued transmitting messages and getting nothing in return.

Finally, with the storm worsening again, and the low-fuel light on the sled blinking, he set a course for shore.

Arriving onshore, he climbed off the sled and ran to the trailer where the spare fuel was kept. Carrying a two-gallon container down to the sled, he opened its cap and poured the high-octane fuel in the sled's tank.

Running back to the truck, he opened the door, grabbed the key from under the mat and started the engine. With darkness nearly absolute now, he'd need to shed some light on the surf. He turned on the headlights and the auxiliary lights mounted on a bar on the roof of the cab. They lit up the beach and the white water thrown up by the crashing waves, but the sea beyond remained pitch-black.

Knowing that the tide had turned and would now be dragging Kurt and Morgan out to sea, Joe didn't waste a second. He grabbed another packet of flares, shoved them in a pocket and pushed the sled back into the surf.

He was just about to charge out when he spotted something coming out of the water a hundred yards down the beach.

Not one something but two somethings. Divers in gear, with pinpoint lights on their harnesses. As the undertow drew back, he could see that they were carrying something between them. From the way they stumbled, it looked heavy and bulky.

Joe turned the sled and sped toward them, every light on the machine blazing. He saw a wave knock them down as they came forward, but they dug their feet into the sand and held on to the object they were carrying.

Joe arrived as the water swirled away from them once more.

Too tired to speak or even gesture, Kurt and Morgan heaved the metal trunk up and dropped it on the back of the sled. As soon as it was secure, they grabbed onto the sides of the sled.

"Hold on!" Joe shouted.

He eased the sled forward and then sped up to avoid the next wave, which was rushing in behind them. They made it halfway up the beach before Kurt and Morgan let go.

Twenty yards beyond, the aqua sled beached itself, sliding to a stop once more. Joe jumped off and ran to Kurt and Morgan.

He found Kurt sitting on some loose stones, looking exhausted. He disconnected his oxygen line and pulled off his helmet, which he tossed away. Morgan was struggling to do the same.

"I looked for you," Joe said. "I had all the underwater lights on. Didn't you see me?"

"We did," Kurt said. "But we couldn't get to the surface with that crate in our hands—it weighs a ton—and we didn't feel like leaving it on the bottom to disappear."

Joe could hardly believe what he was hearing.

"You walked all the way back to the beach carrying it by hand?"

Kurt nodded. "Once we went overboard, we really didn't have much choice."

"It was a brilliant idea," Morgan added, holding up a hand and getting a weary high five from Kurt. "Truth be told, we were fine until we got closer to shore. Then all at once the tide changed and every step was a fight. If it wasn't for the extra weights we put on—and this bloody anvil of a trunk—we'd have been pulled back out to sea."

"Thanks for turning on the lights," Kurt said. "They helped us keep our bearings."

Joe grinned. "Every once in a while, we get something right."

"I'll bet it's more often than that," Morgan replied. She looked over at the aqua sled, eyeing the crate. "Now, let's open this thing and see what's inside."

Chapter 14

They carried the stainless steel trunk to the pickup truck and set it down in front of the lights. As Kurt stored their tanks and the rest of the gear, Morgan produced an extensive array of locksmith's tools from her bag.

"You came prepared," Kurt said.

"I **was** in the Scouts," she replied. "And smugglers are known to be fond of locks."

"That must have been an interesting Merit Badge," Joe said, grinning.

Morgan allowed a faint smile to cross her face and then went to work on the crate. She picked the lock with surprising ease, put the tools away and flipped the lid open.

The contents were far less exotic than any of them expected. In the center, supported by purpose-crafted foam, lay a stone object. Four-sided and narrowing to a point, it looked like a miniature pyramid. But the bottom edge was chipped where it had broken off of a larger piece.

"It's the tip of an obelisk," Morgan said.

Hieroglyphics were visible on each side. Kurt noticed a chiseled oval frame with markings inside it. "That looks like a cartouche. Possibly a royal name."

Morgan looked up at him. "You know your ancient Egyptian symbols. I'm impressed."

"Only enough of them to get into trouble," he replied. "I couldn't tell you what it says."

"Neither can I," Morgan said. She sounded disappointed.

Placing the pyramid-shaped stone aside, she pulled other items from the metal trunk. Slotted into the foam on either side of the obelisk were fragments of a stone tablet. They were wide and flat and perhaps an inch thick. A quick exam revealed more hieroglyphics and faded artwork.

Pulling the fragments out, Kurt and Morgan held two of them together. They connected like pieces of a jigsaw puzzle.

"Two halves of a whole," Joe said.

"Not quite halves," Morgan said. "Parts are still missing. And judging by the writing, I'd say a substantial part below the bottom edge."

A full search revealed more fragments, eleven in all. Some were thin, others thicker. "Parts of the tablet," Morgan suggested.

"More like several different tablets," Kurt said.

Joe shook his head. "After all we've been through, I was expecting nothing less than the golden mask of King Tut's brother. Or at least a second cousin once removed."

"This makes no sense," Morgan added. "If my informant is telling the truth, Bloodstone paid nearly half a million pounds for this. But you could find items like these at any underground antiquities market for a few thousand."

Kurt noticed something held in a mesh pocket on the inside lid of the crate. He pulled it free and found an object wrapped in waterproof plastic bags.

Opening the bags, Kurt risked a look inside. Faint writing in faded pen was visible, but the papers were dry and brittle. "Handwritten," he said, turning further pages and finding entries describing equipment and costs. "Logbook or journal."

"That's not from the Eighteenth Dynasty," Joe kidded.

"Definitely not." Kurt laughed. He leafed through the book and then handed it to Morgan. "Not sure how this connects with these other items, but it must have some value."

She closed the log, wrapped it up in the protective bags it had come in, then slid them back into the mesh flap in the top half of the trunk.

"Could there be more relics out on the trawler?" Joe asked.

"If there were, they're gone now," Kurt said.

"We looked," Morgan added. "Not everywhere, admittedly, but even if there were other crates hidden somewhere, it was this crate the captain and Vincennes chose to move first. Considering the situation, I have to believe they started with the most valuable items."

The three of them fell silent for the moment, gazing at the objects as if some answer might jump out at them. Before anyone offered another thought, Morgan tilted her head upward and began scanning the dark sky.

Kurt followed her gaze. He saw nothing but soon picked up the sound of rotor blades.

"Hope that's not our friends coming back for round two," Kurt said.

"Bigger bird, by the sound of it," Joe said. "Military or Coast Guard."

Kurt glanced at Morgan. "Friends of yours?"

"Possibly," she said. "Let's pack this up and be ready to move just in case."

With Joe holding the trunk open, Kurt and Morgan placed the stone items back inside where they'd found them. Each layer of fragmented stone was encased in foam and the tip of the obelisk rested in its niche on top. As he slid the obelisk into place, Kurt noticed a symbol that looked odd to him. He'd been speaking the truth when he told Morgan he only knew enough about Egyptian hieroglyphics to get himself into trouble, but the fact was they had a certain look to them and as Kurt stared at the marks he was convinced they weren't Egyptian.

The first visible signs of the approaching helicopter were red and green navigation lights on its side and a red beacon flashing under its belly. It came toward them from the south, rumbled across the mouth of the loch and then passed overhead.

Kurt recognized it as a Royal Navy Sea King. It touched down on a flat section higher up on the beach. As the side door opened, the exterior lights came on. A civilian wearing a life jacket stepped out of the craft and marched toward them, escorted by an armed enlisted man in a Royal Navy uniform.

As they grew closer, Kurt noticed something in the civilian's hand. At first, he thought it was a cane, but then he realized it was a swagger stick, a relic of British Army tradition.

"Be careful, now," they heard him say to the enlisted man. "Treacherous footing here."

Morgan stood to meet the new arrivals, stiffening her bearing and straightening her hair. "Colonel," she said in greeting, though she didn't salute.

With details of the man's face illuminated by the pickup truck's headlights, Kurt saw he was about fifty, with gray hair, cut close on the sides, and a thin mustache on his lip.

"Ms. Manning," the Colonel said. "You've stirred up quite a hornet's nest with this latest operation. I understand heavy gunfire and a barrage of missiles have been unleashed on this tiny hamlet."

Morgan didn't shy away. "I warned you about the Bloodstone Group. I told you they'd become desperate and aggressive. This is the proof. They wanted what Vincennes was smuggling and they wanted it badly."

"Yes," the Colonel agreed. "Badly enough to start a war, apparently. The question is, why?"

Morgan shrugged and shook her head. "I couldn't tell you. After seeing what they smuggled in, I'm more baffled than ever."

Kurt and Joe were just bystanders at the moment, watching the action from the sidelines. It was an arrangement that had never suited Kurt. "Information," he said bluntly.

Morgan and the Colonel turned his way.

"That's what they're after," he said. "The items in the crate aren't worth much, in and of themselves, so their value has to be what's written down on them."

With the Colonel's steely gaze focused on him, Kurt offered a hand. "Kurt Austin," he said. "And this is Joe Zavala. We're partially to blame for some of the chaos out here tonight. But you can rest assured we didn't fire the first shot."

The Colonel shook Kurt's hand with a grip of steel. "I'm aware of who you are," he said. "I must admit, you look about as I expected."

"How's that?" Kurt asked.

"I'll explain later," the Colonel said. "For now, let me say I'm glad to make your acquaintance in person—though it's a bloody awful night to do it on. Foulest weather I've seen in years."

"I'm afraid it's going to get worse before it gets better," Kurt said.

The Colonel raised an eyebrow. "You could say that about most things," he replied. "But at least you won't have to walk to London."

"London?"

"Yes," the Colonel said. "You're all coming with me."

The Colonel turned back toward the Sea King and began to march in its direction. Kurt looked at Joe, then over at Morgan. Nothing in her demeanor suggested this was a joke.

"Come along," the Colonel added, looking back and pointing his swagger stick at the stainless steel trunk at their feet. "And, by all means, don't forget the treasure."

Chapter 15

Grinstead Pumping Station, on the outskirts
of London

Solomon Barlow stood in the shadows inside
an abandoned pumping station just north of
London. Around him lay massive pipes and
heavy machinery, all of it covered in layers of dirt
and grime. Not one light of any kind illuminated
the industrial space, but the moon could be seen
through skylights above and it gave off enough of
a glow for Barlow to see his surroundings.

To the right and the left were circular turbines
the size of small houses. Behind him stood one
wall of the building. Fifty feet tall and made of
brick that had been stacked and mortared in
the 1930s, it had survived Nazi bombs through the
Battle of Britain—what the Londoners called the
Blitz—only to be covered by graffiti in the '60s
and '70s.

Barlow felt at home in this dark, abandoned
place, but he was not alone. Several of his men

stood scattered about the floor of the old station. One pair milled lazily near the back door, while another man leaned against the wall foolishly smoking a cigarette. A fourth man stood near the front, gazing out through a dirty window. His job was to watch the road leading up to the entrance. Barlow noticed him perking up as a point of oncoming light caught his eye.

Barlow stiffened. "What is it?"

The lookout studied the approaching light for a moment and then shook his head and relaxed. "Just a car turning around on the motorway."

Barlow sat down, unbuttoning his overcoat and easing himself onto a folding metal chair. It was an inauspicious throne for a man who'd once been labeled Prince of the Arms Trade.

He'd seen far worse, of course. Two decades fighting as a mercenary in political hot spots around the world told him it could always be worse. He'd lain in ditches running with raw sewage to escape machete-wielding rioters in Liberia, he'd suffered second-degree burns after getting trapped in a bombing in Sri Lanka. He'd nearly froze to death in the hold of a commercial airliner when a rival had attempted to "ship" him to a place where he would face justice.

It was a lifestyle that left him looking older than his mid-forties. His face was worn and scarred in places. He moved like an old boxer who'd fought one too many rounds. The substantial gut he'd grown since he started wearing suits and paying others to do his dirty work added to the appearance of decline, but he could still take a punch. And, more importantly, still deliver one.

"Something may have gone wrong," one of his men said.

"Of course something went wrong," Barlow snapped, standing. "Robson's three hours late. That doesn't happen if everything is running according to plan."

The men tensed at the outburst. None of them wanted to see Barlow's legendary temper.

"What do we do?" the man asked.

"We wait," Barlow said. "There's nothing else to do."

Barlow sat back down. He didn't show it, but he remained pleased that a hint of anger could put his men on high alert. As if to reward him, the phone buzzed in his pocket.

Reaching into his overcoat, Barlow pulled it out, pressed two buttons and waited while technology did its thing. Two programs in the phone had been activated. The first scrambled the location signal, preventing anyone from figuring out where he was. The second encrypted everything that was being said, which would prevent anyone from tapping the signal and listening in.

"This is Robson," an electronically altered voice said. The encryption system also modified all voices so that if anyone did manage to tap the line, a voiceprint identification could not be performed.

"Where the hell are you?" Barlow asked. "You were supposed to be here with the package hours ago."

"It couldn't be helped."

"The storm," Barlow said. "Is that your excuse?"

"We have bigger problems than the wind and rain," Robson replied. "They took the boat into another harbor and got hung up on the rocks. Vincennes called us and I sent Slocum down. But before we could do anything, a pair of outsiders got involved."

"Outsiders are of little concern to me," Barlow said. "What about the package?"

"It's gone."

"Gone? Where?"

"Destroyed."

Barlow stood up. He felt a great urge to smash something—anything, really—but he held back. Men in suits did not smash things, they spoke calmly and coldly, instilling fear through their very act of control. "You'd better explain yourself."

"The outsiders you so easily dismiss killed Slocum and his men and then went back to the trawler and attempted to recover the crate. I had no choice but to destroy it."

"The package?"

"The entire trawler. I thought it best to keep them from recovering it."

Barlow felt a tension headache crawling up his spine to his head. He reached back and massaged the nape of his neck. "You really should refrain from thinking," he said. "Reasoning is not your strong suit."

"It was either that or let them have it. I chose to deny them the opportunity to study it."

"And by doing so, you've denied us the opportunity to study it as well. Considering that only we know what the hieroglyphics are referring to, that makes this a net loss for our side."

As Robson went silent, Barlow thought about ways to punish his foolish subordinate. Means of torture and images of violence flashed through his mind. Before he'd chosen any of them, his attention was diverted by the sound of an incoming message reaching his phone. He pulled the phone away from his ear and studied the screen.

The message came from a numbered contact. It read simply

PACKAGE TO LONDON. MI5 IN POSSESSION.

"Thank the gods," Barlow muttered.

"What did you say?"

Barlow returned his attention to the phone call. "I said you've just been saved by your own incompetence. The artifacts must have been off the trawler when you destroyed it."

"Not possible," Robson insisted. "I know for a

fact that the divers were still on board. We heard their radio transmissions."

"Perhaps you missed them."

"Not likely. I assure you."

"Well, something happened," Barlow said. "Because MI5 has the crate. It's coming here to London after all. Only instead of you bringing it to me, these outsiders must be delivering it to Thames House."

After a brief silence, Robson volunteered, "Do you want me to go after it?"

Despite the temptation, Barlow knew blasting their way into MI5 headquarters would not be helpful. "Not yet. Just get yourself back down to London. Since we've lost Slocum and his crew, you'll have to pick up some local help. Can you do that on short notice?"

"I can bring in a few of my old mates. They're not soldiers, but they'll do in a pinch."

Robson had grown up on the streets of London. It would come in handy at this moment. "That'll work," Barlow said. "Round them up and get ready. When the moment comes, I'll need you to retrieve the package without destroying it."

"And just how am I supposed to do that?" Robson asked. "Since I'm not supposed to reason things out for myself."

"MI5 is still in the dark," Barlow explained. "They know we've been sourcing Egyptian treasures, but they don't know why. When they see the contents of the crate, they'll be even more confused. They'll attempt to decipher the information on the stones, but there are no experts in Egyptian writing on their staff, which means they'll have to seek outside help. Based on my knowledge of their previous work, I know who they'll choose."

"The Punter," Robson said.

"Precisely," Barlow replied. "When they go to him, you and your men will already be there waiting to collect."

Chapter 16

En route to London

Kurt sat in the back of the Royal Navy Sea King helicopter, enduring turbulence that felt like corporal punishment. Constant shaking was interrupted only by sudden updrafts that slammed everyone back in their seats or sudden downdrafts that felt like free fall. Near the edge of the storm, the air became so filled with lightning strikes that the inside of the cabin was illuminated like a strobe.

Silence reigned for most of the journey as all held on tight. But after one last round of buffeting, the helicopter got out in front of the weather and the ride settled down. Calmer air was welcome, as was the web of orange lights stretching out below.

"We're over the outskirts of London," the pilot announced over the intercom. "We'll be landing shortly."

The Sea King flew across London on a course

that took them directly toward the center of the city. They descended along the way, slowing to a hover over a dark, snaking void in the pattern of lights. Kurt recognized it—the River Thames.

An illuminated landing pad at the edge of the river came into view. The helicopter slowed and eventually hovered over the concrete before touching down.

Climbing from the helicopter, Kurt saw Big Ben in the distance, beyond which stood the famous London Eye.

"This way," the Colonel said, leading them to a stairwell that took them down to the Thames.

A patrol boat pulled up and they were ushered aboard. It took them across the river to a building known as Thames House, the official headquarters of MI5.

Inside the building, Kurt and Joe were separated from Morgan and escorted to a conference room. They remained there, uninterrupted, until an older woman brought them tea and biscuits.

"The Scots gave us whisky," Joe said.

"You're in England now," the woman responded politely. "We're a bit more civilized here."

She left without another word. With little to do but wait, Kurt poured himself a cup of tea. He stirred in some milk and picked up one of the rectangular biscuits. Having gone hours without much to eat, he was famished. "When in London . . ." he said to Joe.

He dipped the biscuit in the tea and waited for a brief moment before pulling it out. To his surprise, there was nothing left of the dipped end, as if it had dissolved in a pool of acid. After eating the part that hadn't disintegrated, he made a second attempt, retrieving the next biscuit more rapidly—and just in time to watch it crumble and fall back into the cup. He was on his third try when the door opened.

Morgan and the Colonel walked in together. She took a seat as he moved to the head of the table. "Sorry for the delay," he announced. "I trust you're being treated adequately."

Kurt cut to the chase. "That depends. Are we being held on suspicion of some wrongdoing or is this protective custody?"

"Neither," the Colonel said. "But it seemed best to bring everyone back here before explaining the situation. Let me begin by introducing myself properly. Oliver Pembroke-Smythe, formerly of the Special Air Service and the Royal Dragoons, now Director of Counter-Terrorism Operations for Section 5."

"Morgan addressed you as Colonel."

"Old habits die hard," Pembroke-Smythe said. "I'm retired. After twenty-six years in the Army, it's hard to say my name without including reference to my former grade. Also, I prefer to be called Colonel by those who work for me. It instills the right mix of confidence and fear."

Kurt laughed. "I know an Admiral who feels the same way. You were going to explain how you knew us?"

"It's simple, really. I'm well acquainted with NUMA. Not from your government website or dossiers, but from working with a rather extraordinary chap named Pitt years ago in the Sahara."

"You worked with Dirk Pitt?" Joe asked.

"**Worked** is not quite accurate, I suppose. We fought together, stormed a hellhole of a gold mine called Tebezza to rescue some prisoners and then spent what I was certain would be our last days on earth hiding in the remnants of an old Foreign Legion outpost. From behind those walls we fought off at least a thousand soldiers loyal to a mad dictator named Kazim. In the end, we managed to undo one of the most sordid regimes in recent history."

"That sounds like one of Dirk's adventures," Joe said.

Kurt nodded. He'd heard stories about the Sahara expedition, but most of it was classified above his level. All he knew for certain was that it had something to do with toxic waste poisoning the sea.

"Dirk Pitt is the Director of NUMA these days," Kurt said. "But I have to assume you already know that."

"Of course," Pembroke-Smythe said. "Spoke to him earlier this evening. First time in years.

Congratulated him on his promotion and his new family. And then asked for a favor."

Kurt shot a look in Joe's direction. "Here it comes."

Joe nodded. "What have we been traded for this time?"

"Nothing," Pembroke-Smythe said. "I merely explained the situation and asked Dirk if he thought you'd be interested in helping our investigation. Upon hearing the details, he suggested that, short of locking you up in the Tower of London, I wouldn't be able to keep you out of it."

Joe sat back. "Dirk knows us too well."

Kurt smiled. "I'd still like to hear those details," he said. "What, exactly, would we be signing up for?"

Morgan spoke up next. "Something right up your alley," she said. "A treasure hunt."

"That does land in our wheelhouse," Kurt admitted.

Pembroke-Smythe offered more. "As Morgan has already told you, the Bloodstone Group funds their dealings by selling stolen antiquities. We know they've been shadowing various archeological expeditions, bribing workers and guards— or threatening them—and siphoning off objects worth selling. They've also resorted to outright theft, having staged large-scale robberies at various museums and universities over the last two years. Based on information from one of Morgan's informants, we believe they're looking for a lost ship or fleet of Egyptian trading vessels."

Kurt leaned forward. "You have my attention."

"Mine too," Joe said.

Pembroke-Smythe continued. "We thought the delivery in Dunvegan might have been the fruit of their labors, but it seems to be just a step along the way. Your suggestion—that they want the information on the stones and not the stones themselves—is all we have to go on. But it's an intriguing idea."

"What about the journal?" Kurt asked.

"We were just looking it over," Morgan said. "It's not a journal, it's a logbook from an old aircraft. The final entry carries a date of December 1927. Because the ink has faded and the pages have turned brittle, most of the entries are unreadable. However, the last pages read like a diary, including notes that suggest the man who carried it had crashed in a remote area. He indicates taking a few items and attempting to hike out to civilization. It was a difficult task, considering he had an injured leg and nothing but dry scrubland and a rocky riverbed to hike through."

"Dry scrubland," Joe said. "Doesn't sound like England."

"Any mention of Egypt or artifacts?" Kurt asked.

Morgan shook her head.

They were clearly lacking information. It was

even possible the logbook/journal had nothing to do with the other artifacts, but there was no way to say for sure.

"What about your informant?" Kurt asked. "Any chance you can use him to get to the bottom of this?"

Pembroke-Smythe answered this way. "We think it's wise not to reach out to him at this moment."

"Why is that?"

Morgan explained. "My informant has an agenda of his own," she said. "He's a competitor of the Bloodstone Group, not in the arms business but in the world of stolen artifacts. We call him the Collector. He's known to spend large amounts on the black market. But as far as we can tell, very little of what he buys ever comes up for sale again."

"What's his connection to the Bloodstone Group?" Kurt asked.

"How does he know what they're up to?" Joe added.

"The association is a little murky," Morgan admitted. "We think he may have been a client of Bloodstone's at some point. Our best guess is, they had a falling-out, possibly a disagreement over price. Perhaps the Collector decided it's better to steal what he's after rather than pay Bloodstone for it. At any rate, where the Bloodstone Group wants to dig up these treasures to sell them, the

Collector seems more interested in keeping them for himself. And we've been using that desire in our efforts to stop them."

"The enemy of my enemy is my friend," Joe noted.

"Exactly," Pembroke-Smythe chimed in. "Whoever he—or she—is, this Collector has been spot-on in predicting what Bloodstone will do, though he must not have total insight because he labeled this delivery 'the big one.'"

"Relying on criminal sources for information tends to be a game of diminishing returns," Kurt said. "We used to do the same thing in the CIA. We found the informants would miss out on the most crucial details just when you really needed them."

"A scenario we're encountering now," Pembroke-Smythe said. "All of which leads to an important decision. Either we sit and wait or we take action. Since action is almost always preferable to sitting and waiting, we've chosen to move forward."

"Meaning what?" Kurt asked.

"We intend to cut the Bloodstone Group off at the knees by finding out what they're after and securing it before they do. That's where you two come in . . . if you're interested . . ."

"Take out their source of income and they wither on the vine," Kurt said.

Pembroke-Smythe nodded and then added a final touch to the sales pitch. "MI5 is simply not equipped for something like this. We stop smugglers, prevent terrorist attacks, arrest people. We don't search for lost treasure. And while we could go bring in university types and the like, putting civilians in the same arena as the Bloodstone Group would be considered bad form."

"Clearly," Kurt said.

"You two, on the other hand," Pembroke-Smythe said, "have proven yourselves willing and able to step into the breach. Based on that, and Dirk's insistence that there's no one he'd rather send into a fight, I'd gladly make an exception and welcome you aboard."

Kurt took a sip of the tea while considering the invitation. Tipping the cup back, he noticed a cake-like sludge at the bottom of the cup and wondered if a spoon might be in order. He glanced over to Joe. "We did come here to find an ancient ship. If we can't find a Viking one, maybe we can find an Egyptian vessel instead."

Joe nodded. "It would make our return to D.C. a triumphant one."

Kurt turned back to their hosts. "We're in. Where do we start?"

Both Morgan and the Colonel grinned. "By taking the items in that crate to someone who can decipher the hieroglyphics. That ought to shed some light on what Bloodstone is really after."

Chapter 17

The East End, London

The streets of London were never truly deserted. Countless pubs, coffeehouses and restaurants drew crowds late into the evening. And after the last of the night owls went home, a small army of delivery trucks, street sweepers and road crews appeared. They scoured the city, preparing it for the next morning's rush.

Still, the farther one got from the heart of London, the quieter things became. In the East End—beyond the gentrified sections—walking around the streets in the wee hours of the morning meant one was either hopelessly lost or criminally inclined.

Wearing a black leather jacket, black jeans and Army boots, Robson was more the latter. He walked the dangerous streets without a hint of concern on his face. And why should he worry? He was coming home.

He passed corners where he'd sold drugs, a dead-end alley where he and a few mates had fought another gang. He'd been knifed in the leg that night, but before he went down he'd broken one man's arm and smashed two of the interlopers in the face with punches assisted by brass knuckles.

The infection from the wound had been horrendous, but going to the hospital would have landed him in prison, so he'd waited out the pain with a bottle of scotch and some black market antibiotics.

Laughing morosely at the memory, Robson pushed on, heading for the docks. A few miles down the road, a brand-new section of the port loaded and unloaded ships twenty-four hours a day. He could see the lights from here. But the wharves nearby were abandoned. They lay silent and rotting, watched over by a pair of rusted cranes that hadn't moved in a decade. Every few years someone would promise money to refurbish the area and bring it back to life, but the money never came. And it never would.

Ignoring the blight, Robson passed along a graffiti-covered wall. He arrived near the dock and found he was alone. Disappointing.

Putting his fingers to his lips, he whistled loudly. "Come on, you lot!" he shouted. "Stop wasting my time."

The whistle and shouts prompted movement. Two men came out from behind the base of the old crane, two others emerged from the shadows of a blacked-out building with broken windows. One of them moved forward. "That really you, Inky?"

"I told you, it's Robson now."

"Oh really?" There was mockery in that response.

The men assembled before Robson. First in line was a long-haired man they called Fingers because he'd been pretty good with a guitar until someone broke his hand. Beside him was a short fellow with blocky shoulders who everybody called Snipe, though he hated the nickname. The third and fourth men were half brothers, Daly and Gus, a muscle-bound pair who'd been groomed as boxers by their scheming dad—a man who turned out to be the father of neither. As he looked at them, Robson was struck by how funny it was he couldn't remember any of their real names.

"The prodigal son returns," Gus said. Gus was a bruiser, a rugby player with a build to match, an amateur MMA fighter in his wildest dreams and in real life a part-time enforcer for a local heavy.

"Prodigal nothing," Robson said. "After tonight I'll never set foot in this slag heap again."

"Too good for this place?" Daly said, pushing between the others and pointing an accusing finger in Robson's face. "You royalty now or some fink?"

"Compared to you, I am."

Robson had expected a better reception but was prepared for the worst. Bad neighborhoods were the same all over—those people who got out were held up more as traitors than success stories. Daly had another reason to hate Robson, though it was all in his mind.

With Daly fuming already, Robson stood calmly with his hands in his pockets. He'd made sure to position himself so that the lone streetlight was behind him. It gave off just enough illumination to show him that Daly's eyes were bloodshot, raw and wild. That meant he'd been drinking for sure. Hard liquor, probably, cheap vodka being his go-to painkiller.

After drinking enough, Daly was always spoiling for a fight. And he was brutal when he got his hands on someone. He'd even busted up Gus a few times. Some said the only reason Gus was still alive was the fact that he and Daly shared a mother.

For now, Robson held silent, waiting for Daly's train of thought to wreck itself and start over. The inaction seemed to calm his old friend—for now.

Snipe asked the next question. "What's this really all about?"

"I have a job for you," Robson said.

"We heard that before. What's it pay?"

"Enough to get you lot out of here. Assuming you have any ambition at all."

Daly didn't seem to like that idea. Unknown to

Robson, he'd become more important in the local gang during Robson's absence. Daly's ego was wrapped up in it. He was something of a big fish here. He would never leave for a larger pond. And as far as he was concerned, neither would any of his boys. "We know how you got out of here," Daly spat. "Set us up. Snitched us raw on the last job, you did. Put me and Gus in the pound for three years."

"The fence gave you up," Robson said, "not me. I told you not to nick any of the jewels, just the cash, but you didn't listen. I told you to fence them in some other city, but you still didn't listen. That stupidity cost you."

Daly pulled out a butterfly knife, opening it in a flashing metallic blur. "It's going to cost you more than it cost me." He stepped forward, expecting Robson to back off.

Robson held his ground, eyeing Daly. "Careful, mate. Another step and I'll feed you that knife."

Daly lunged without warning, his free hand grabbing Robson's lapel while the hand holding the knife surged forward and upward. It was a quick move. And once he'd grabbed the jacket, there was no way for Robson to pull out of range.

Only he didn't need to.

With practiced calm, Robson pulled the trigger on the snub-nosed pistol in his jacket pocket. It blasted a hole in the leather of Daly's jacket and a bigger hole in his gut. The impact staggered the attacking man.

Robson fired again and Daly stumbled back, losing his grip on the jacket and dropping his weapon at the same time. The knife hit the ground with a soft clink, Daly landed with a heavy grunt. He rolled over, made a halfhearted effort to crawl away and then collapsed.

Stepping back and pulling the pistol from his pocket, Robson looked around. "Anyone else?"

He stared at Gus, but Gus had no real love for his half brother. Jealousy was their primary bond.

"Bloody hell," Fingers said. He'd dropped down to see if Daly was breathing. "You killed him."

"The bullet killed him," Robson said, "along with his own stupidity. Now, do you lot want to hear about the job or not?"

"The coppers will be down here before long," Snipe said. "You know they will."

Robson doubted that. A pair of muffled gunshots out near the docks in the middle of the night wouldn't be heard by anyone with any inclination to call it in.

"Dump him in the river," Robson said. "And then make your choice. You can stay here and waste away, pulling little jobs, selling smack and dodging the cops, or you can come with me. I've got a job that'll make you rich. And if you do it right, there's more to follow. But you decide now 'cause I won't ask again."

Fingers, Snipe and Gus remained frozen even as Robson began to walk away. Too much on their plates all at once, Robson thought. Too much at one time.

After a pause of indecision, they came to their senses. Snipe and Gus picked up Daly, dragged him to the edge of the dock, as Fingers looked nervously in every direction.

Robson heard the splash but kept on walking, heading for the nearest tube. He reached the stairs and went down without looking back.

Fifty yards behind him, the members of his former street gang followed, crossing the street against the light, which was flashing ominously red, and then pausing near the steps of the underground station.

They exchanged shocked glances, but no one said a word. The sound of a train pulling in rebalanced the scales. It was now or never. A collective decision was reached. They rushed down the stairwell, desperate not to miss the train.

Chapter 18

Cambridge University, near King's College Chapel

Kurt, Joe and Morgan arrived in the town of Cambridge at noon the next day. By then, the last remnants of the storm had passed and warm sunshine had settled over southern England. It was calm and idyllic, with birds chirping and butterflies fluttering about.

In terms of weather, it felt as if they'd traveled to another continent. In terms of scenery, it felt as if they'd traveled to another time. The Cambridge campus unfolded like an illustration from a storybook. Its Gothic buildings, complete with towering spires and stone archways, stretched toward the sky. Between them lay sprawling manicured lawns, crisscrossed by stone pathways and dotted with well-tended gardens. Through it all ran the waters of the River Cam, trickling no louder than a whisper.

As they passed the famous chapel of King's

College, Kurt gave voice to an odd thought. "I wouldn't be shocked if we ran into William Shakespeare."

Joe was thinking of a different writer. "Or Harry Potter."

Morgan had been to Cambridge a couple dozen times over the past three years. But even she couldn't deny that there was something magical about the place, especially in the warm light of late summer. "If you two are done gawking at the scenery, we have business to attend to."

Morgan carried a brown leather briefcase with her. Inside were high-resolution photos of the items they'd found in the metal crate—one of the flat stone fragments, for making a physical comparison. The rest of the artifacts had been left behind, locked up for safekeeping.

Kurt continued to gawk but also focused on her. "Tell me about this expert we're going to meet."

"Professor Cross," she said. "He's something of an old curmudgeon, much like you'd expect. He talks to himself a lot, but he's very sharp. He's an expert in ancient cultures of the Mediterranean and the dynastic authority on Egypt. He spent years abroad—mostly in Egypt, from what I'm told, but also in Libya, Ethiopia and the Sudan. His main interest is preserving and protecting history. He went over to Libya and Iraq during the wars in hopes of protecting the museums that were being looted and destroyed by the terrorists."

"Sounds like a man of conviction," Kurt said.

"He is," she insisted. "And well-traveled. If you give him the chance, he'll explain in excruciating detail just how many expeditions he's been on, and how many national museums he's partnered with."

As she spoke, Morgan rolled her eyes the way one does when talking about an exasperating parent or child who was also much loved.

"How long has MI5 been working with him?"

"Almost three years," she said. "Ever since the investigation into the stolen antiquities ramped up. Be careful what you say to him."

"Why is that?"

"He's got a photographic memory," she said. "He can even translate hieroglyphics without resorting to reference books or guides."

"Nice skill to have," Joe said, "considering the business he's in."

"What time are we supposed to meet him?" Kurt asked.

"Noonish," she said, taking them across one of the great lawns and down toward the river, which ran through the heart of the university.

Kurt glanced at his watch. "It's ten past noonish now. And we seem to be getting farther from the buildings."

"I know," Morgan replied. "We won't find the professor in his office on a day like this. He'd rather be out on the water."

Kurt smiled. "I like him already."

They approached the river and a bridge made of stone that looked as if it was right out of Camelot. Down below, the Cam trickled by a long wooden boat that was resting alongside a stone jetty.

A bespectacled man, wearing brown pants, a mustard-colored corduroy jacket and a flat cap made of tweed, was standing on the back end of the boat. Morgan waved to get his attention. "Afternoon, Professor. Sorry to bother you on a day like this but we have something we'd like you to look over."

"So I'm told," the professor said. "Please, come on down."

The trio made its way down a flight of steps and out onto the jetty, where introductions were made. The professor gave Morgan a hug before shaking Kurt's and Joe's hands. He agreed to look at the latest discovery provided they did it as far from the confines of his small office as possible.

"You'll get no argument from us," Kurt said.

They climbed into the boat, taking a seat on the bench in the center, while the professor used a long pole to push them away from the dock. With another shove they began gliding forward.

The flat-bottomed boat was known as a punt, the person in charge of pushing the boat known as the Punter. The professor initially seemed more than happy to do the job, but once they'd passed under the bridge he looked for a replacement.

"Punting is the best way I know to relax," the professor said. "It engages the body and the mind. But if I'm going to be reading and working, someone else will have to take over up here."

"Manual labor," Joe said quickly. "That sounds like a job for Kurt."

Kurt didn't mind. He stood up and reached for the pole.

"Come back here," the professor said. "Stand on the Cambridge end. Don't want to be confused with those miscreants from Oxford who do their work from the middle of the boat."

"Perish the thought," Kurt said in his best British accent. It drew a smile from the professor and a shameful shake of the head from Joe. Morgan couldn't help but laugh.

Standing up on the raised deck at the back end of the punt, Kurt tested the depth of the water. The pole went in eight feet before hitting bottom. By pushing down and back, while keeping his feet planted firmly on the deck, he got the boat moving again.

"Very nice form," the professor said. "If you need a summer job, don't hesitate to call."

Kurt laughed, pulling the pole out of the water and bringing it forward for the next thrust. As he worked, the professor sat down across from Morgan and Joe.

Morgan lifted the briefcase up and put it between them on the bench. She dialed in the combination and then opened it. Reaching in, she pulled out the dossier filled with pictures.

"As usual," she said, "everything we show you is an official government secret. Discussing this with others will result in severe penalties, up to and including you being thrown in the dungeon."

It was a formality they'd obviously been through several times.

"I've been in several dungeons," Professor Cross said. "Fascinating places."

"As long as you're just visiting," Joe said.

"Quite right," the professor replied. "Quite right."

He opened the dossier, read through the notes and turned to the photographs. "Interesting," he said more than once. "Intriguing." Finally, after studying the rest of the photos, he looked directly at Morgan. "I assume these have something to do with the thieves you've been chasing."

Morgan explained how the artifacts had come into their possession, even going so far as to mention having to shoot the smugglers. "Without anyone left alive to interview, we have no way of determining why they wanted these items so badly. What do you make of the inscriptions?"

The professor went back to studying the photos, making notes and even holding a few of the pictures up to the light like a doctor might study an X-ray. Next, he examined the flat stone with the writing on it. After looking over the markings, including the cartouche that Kurt had noticed, he spent what seemed like an inordinate amount of time feeling the texture of the stone and hefting its weight, even closing his eyes at one point as if to heighten his other senses. "Yes," he said. "Very interesting indeed."

Satisfied, he handed the stone back to Morgan and looked over the photos again. On the back of one he scribbled and scratched, crossing out a few things and then jotting down something new just below. "It has to be . . ." he muttered.

"Has to be what?" Morgan asked.

"I'm sorry," the professor said, "you're right. These relics are unique. They point to something very valuable. A treasure both vast and glorious."

"This is a treasure map?" Joe asked.

"Not a map," the professor replied. "More like part of a story. The hieroglyphics on each piece draw a word picture. Something like saying, **Over the hills and through the wood, / To Grandmother's house we go.** It's not a map but it gives you some idea of how to get there. In this case, if I might paraphrase, it reads **Down the Nile and out to sea, / With the Pharaoh's treasure we go.**"

"That's more like it," Joe said, perking up. "Which Pharaoh are we talking about?"

The professor grinned and adjusted his glasses. "Ever heard of a character named Herihor?"

Joe stared blankly and shook his head.

The professor looked at Kurt, who shrugged. "I'm afraid our expertise begins with Rameses and ends with King Tut."

"Nothing to be ashamed of," the professor replied. "Few people outside the halls of academia would recognize the name. But it's an important one nonetheless. Herihor was a man who changed the course of Egyptian history. Twice."

Kurt found it hard to believe such a man was unknown. "How so?"

"By uniting the kingdom during a time of war and then dividing it again."

Blank looks suggested that was not enough information.

"Can you be a little more specific?" Morgan asked.

The professor nodded, adjusted his tweed cap and began to explain. "Perhaps it would be helpful if I start at the beginning. You see, Herihor is a unique member of royalty since he began life as a commoner. Some say he wasn't even Egyptian, suggesting he came across the desert from Libya. And while that's probably not true, it gives you some idea how much of an outsider he was. At any rate, he first enters the historical record as a General for Rameses."

"**The** Rameses?" Joe asked.

"Not the character from the Bible," the professor said, "a later descendent. The eleventh Pharaoh to use that name."

JOURNEY OF THE PHARAOHS   151

"Like Henry here in England."

"Exactly," the professor said. "As one of Rameses's Generals, Herihor won several battles, culminating with a rebellion that he crushed in Ethiopia that had threatened to destroy the dynasty. For this heroic act, he was rewarded with Pharaoh's sister as a bride and, by this marriage, lay claim to royalty. At the same time, and of equal importance, Herihor was given the most exalted position in the religious order of the day—High Priest of Amun."

"Sounds like he had a good year," Joe said.

"A banner year," the professor said. "Titled and now married into Pharaoh's line, Herihor began his new life in Thebes—far from where Rameses ruled. Over a course of several years, he grew wealthy, and power-hungry, and sometime around 1080 B.C. he declared himself Pharaoh of Upper Egypt, splitting the civilization into Upper and Lower Kingdoms."

"Causing a civil war?" Kurt asked.

"No," the professor said. "It seems there was no conflict. Threats and posturing, of course—all the rumblings of war, that sort of thing—but no actual battles. Perhaps an agreement was struck or perhaps it was a cold war that never got hot. At any rate, six years after declaring himself Pharaoh, Herihor abruptly and completely disappeared."

Kurt, Joe and Morgan were looking at Cross with rapt attention, but the professor said no more.

"What happened to him?" Kurt asked. "Did Rameses kill him?"

"Doubtful," the professor said. "The truth is, we don't know. He vanished from the pages of history. Egypt was reunited and continued for the rest of the classical period as a single kingdom. As for Herihor, he was never heard from again. No record of his death has survived to modern times and no tomb bearing his name has ever been found."

Morgan asked, "Weren't the Egyptians known for trying to wipe out evidence of their ancestors and others they didn't like?"

"It was a common enough practice," the professor admitted. "Thutmose III tried to erase all memory of Hatshepsut, the only female Pharaoh and quite likely his mother. Rameses the Great allegedly did the same to his adopted son, Moses, if you believe the biblical account. But Herihor's name survived in many places, leading historians to believe he wasn't erased from history by some other ruler so much as he disappeared from it by choice."

"Why would a Pharaoh choose to disappear?" Kurt asked. "I thought they spent most of their reigns trying to build monuments so that they wouldn't be forgotten."

"An important question," the professor said. "We don't have an answer. But because he chose to do this himself, we must assume it was not on a whim. And the most likely reason that makes sense is that he was attempting to vanish to avoid his tomb being violated by grave robbers. They were the scourge of the time. Their acts were not only distasteful, but for a Pharaoh who wanted to enter the Afterlife with chariots and servants and gold and jewels, they were a great fear."

"So Herihor escaped them by hiding his death as well as his tomb," Morgan said. "Is that what you're telling us?"

The professor paused. "Most of us believe his grave is out there somewhere. More importantly, that it's never been touched by robbers."

"Bloodstone Group's interest in these stones suddenly makes more sense," Morgan said. "A tomb that hasn't been looted, like Tutankhamen's, would yield treasures worth hundreds of millions of pounds or more."

"Yes," the professor said. "But the discovery of Herihor's tomb would be many times more spectacular than the trinkets found with Tutankhamen. In fact, should it be found undisturbed, Herihor's treasure would rival anything found in history. It would almost certainly contain more artifacts—gold, jewels, statuary and furniture—than everything currently held in all the world's museums combined."

Joe and Morgan stared at the professor like mesmerized children. They were stunned by the estimate.

Kurt found himself surprised to hear what sounded like wild exaggeration coming from such a renowned source. The professors he'd known in his life tended to understate everything. "I'm not sure I follow," he said. "Why would a Pharaoh who only ruled half a kingdom for a short period of time be in possession of such an unrivaled treasure?"

The professor looked at Kurt with a glint in his eye and Kurt knew he'd been set up. Taking his spectacles off, Professor Cross explained. "Because long before he declared himself Pharaoh, Herihor was given that title in the priesthood that I told you about. As High Priest of Amun, he had unlimited access to every temple and burial chamber in the Valley of the Kings—a thousand years' worth of collected riches at his fingertips just sitting there for the taking. And make no mistake, he took it. He took all of it. Lock, stock and golden barrel."

"He looted the valley?" Morgan asked.

The professor nodded. "Everything that wasn't nailed down and many things that were. The collected riches of a civilization that spanned a millennium before he was even born."

"Just how much loot are we really talking about?" Morgan asked.

The professor shrugged. "Difficult to say. Maybe a hundred times what was found with Tutankhamen. Maybe five hundred times as much. You could expect at least forty golden coffins bearing the Pharaohs, along with all they'd have taken with them. Burial masks made of gold and lapis. Animal figurines carved from ivory and jade. Statues with sapphires and rubies for their eyes. Alabaster canopic jars. Weapons and other important items gilded in silver and gold. Not to mention the cache of papyrus texts and writings inscribed on tablets and walls that would give us a complete history of their rule."

The professor paused for a breath and then looked at Kurt and Joe. "I can only compare it to some future adventurer stumbling upon your National Archives and Fort Knox at the same time."

"That would be quite a find," Kurt said, pushing the boat forward with a smooth, easy stroke. "As will this."

"What would all this be worth," Morgan asked, continuing to probe. "In monetary value?"

"Oh, you couldn't hope to put a price on it," the professor said.

"The Bloodstone Group will."

"Right," the professor said. He paused and then threw out a number. "Billions," he said. "Tens of billions—if you could sell it all."

Morgan's mood darkened. "Even a small portion of that wealth could give them enough cash to fund a war."

Kurt had no doubt about that, but he didn't

want to jump to conclusions. "Just because Herihor had access to the Valley of the Kings doesn't make him a thief. How do we know he's the culprit?"

"Because he told us," the professor said, fixing the glasses back on his nose. "There are carvings in the walls of several tombs—KV57 and KV9, if I'm not mistaken—which tell us that Herihor, executing his sworn duty as the High Priest, had moved the contents of the tombs to a safer location. A process they euphemistically called restoration. Beyond that, we have the **Writings of Qsn.**"

"The writings of who?" Joe asked.

"Qsn," the professor said. "Qsn is the Sparrow. Stealer of the Harvest. The texts are attributed to someone using that acronym. A strange choice, considering Egyptian beliefs. At any rate, the writings themselves tell us a rather mysterious and controversial story in which Herihor is described as becoming a religious fanatic and creating a cult of his own followers who helped him collect his ancestors' buried riches.

"Interestingly enough, the hieroglyphics were written on broken stone pieces of facia originally designed to be affixed to a temple building"— he picked up the fragment of flat stone they'd brought with them—"very much like this."

"That is interesting," Morgan said. "Where were they found?"

"I'm afraid that's part of the controversy," the

professor said. "No one knows for sure. They first turned up in the private collection of a Frenchman named DeMars sometime in the late twenties, I believe. They disappeared during the war and haven't been seen since."

"Late twenties," Kurt said, seizing on the date. He glanced at Morgan, who nodded.

"Does the time frame mean something?" the professor asked.

Kurt wasn't about to answer, but Morgan did. "Along with the stones, we've recovered the log-book of an aircraft that crashed in 1927. We're still searching for a connection between the two. But if these stones have an odd provenance, then it's likely they were stolen and shipped. Perhaps the log is connected. It might help us find out where they came from in the first place."

"What else can you tell us about DeMars?" Kurt asked.

"He was like many wealthy men at that time, interested in adventure, history and making a name for himself as part of the New Enlightenment. He proposed an odd theory suggesting Europe—and France, in particular—had been colonized by the Egyptians a thousand years before the Romans named it Gaul. His interest and enthusiasm were admirable, his methods and lack of scruples less so. As you can imagine, part of the controversy surrounding the **Writings of Qsn** came directly from his unwillingness to explain where the stone pieces were found and how he gained possession of them."

"Could they be a hoax?"

"I think it unlikely," the professor said, "but perhaps only DeMars knew the truth."

With the sense that they were making progress in their quest, Kurt eased the punt under the next bridge. He ducked to keep his head from striking the underside of the structure. Gazing straight ahead, he saw the prow of the boat emerging back into the sunlight. As it did, a figure dropped onto it from above.

Short, stocky and wearing a wool cap, the man faced the passengers. He had his legs set wide for balance and a pistol in his hand aimed directly at the stunned occupants.

Chapter 19

The sudden appearance of a man with a gun surprised everyone.

While Morgan dove on the professor, covering him up the way a Secret Service agent would protect a high-ranking government official, Joe spun around, coming face-to-face with the business end of the gun.

Only Kurt had an advantage and that was his reach.

As the man landed on the boat, Kurt swung the punting pole out of the water and snapped it sideways across the boat. The tip of the pole, barely missing Joe's head, caught the gunman's outstretched hand.

Bones cracked, the pistol flew into the river and the man doubled over, cradling his wrist. Stunned and oblivious, he never saw Joe launching himself from his seated position.

With a powerful surge, Joe slammed a shoulder into the attacker, sending him backward and tumbling off the boat. He hit the water with a great splash and came up only after the punt had passed over the top of him.

They had been free of boarders for only an instant when two additional men jumped from the bridge. A thin man with long hair landed awkwardly in the middle of the boat, nearly capsizing it, while a bigger, bulkier attacker came down on Kurt's back.

Morgan raised her service weapon to fire, but in the close quarters scuffle, the second assailant grabbed her wrist and forced the weapon downward.

As they fought, the gun discharged once into the bottom of the punt, blasting a hole in the wood and letting in water. The taller man bent her arm back, twisting her hand until she could no longer hold on to the gun. It dropped, hit the edge of the boat and went overboard.

Using the leverage of his position, the man continued to twist her arm, forcing her off balance. She responded by driving a knee into his groin. As he doubled over in agony, she pulled him forward and tossed him into the river.

Kurt saw part of the brawl from a position flat against the tiller. The man who'd jumped him was a heavyset, muscle-bound type. He outweighed Kurt by a good fifty pounds and all of it was brawn. The man landing on him had pancaked Kurt to the deck and kept him there.

Somehow, Kurt was still holding the punting pole in his right hand. He brought it backward and upward over the top of his body and, at the apex, twisted his hand and snapped it down. It thumped against the man's skull, split the skin, drawing blood, and knocked him cold.

Kurt rolled to one side, shouldering the brute sideways and into the Cam.

The instant he was free, Kurt jumped up and shoved the pole in the water and pushed the boat forward with all his might.

He was on his second push when Joe shouted a warning. "Get down."

Kurt dropped and covered up. A man had appeared on the riverbank with a pump-action shotgun in his hands. He aimed, then hesitated.

Kurt kept his head down and pushed the boat forward again. He had no idea why the man hadn't fired, but he wasn't going to look a gift horse in the mouth—at least not until they were out of range.

"They're getting in a boat," Morgan said.

"Faster," Joe said. "This is the slowest getaway since the Stone Age."

The professor chimed in. "Hate to admit it. But if we're going to be racing, the Oxford way is preferred."

"Oxford way?"

"Down here. Press your feet against the seat back."

Realizing it would give him more purchase, Kurt made his way to the center of the punt. With each move of the pole he twisted his body as far as he could, pressing forward with his legs, shoving the boat along.

From his effort, and the new position, they picked up more speed, but it wasn't going to help. The pursuers had piled into a small boat with an outboard motor that was rushing toward them, its nose pointed high.

"Motorboats aren't allowed on the River Cam," the professor said, outraged.

"Hate to tell you, but that's not our biggest issue at the moment," Kurt said. "There's no way to keep ahead of them and we're severely out-gunned." He turned to Morgan. "How many shots left?"

"Plenty. But the gun is at the bottom of the river."

"And we're taking on water." It was the shore or nothing. Kurt turned the boat and angled for the right bank of the Cam, opposite where the shotgun-wielding man had been.

Unfortunately, the punt was ponderous and slow and now filling with water and it changed direction with all the agility of a tanker.

A shotgun blast ringing out overhead told him the race was over.

"Give us the briefcase," the gunman shouted from the bow of the approaching boat.

Kurt gripped the pole, ready for one last fight, but calmer heads prevailed.

"Give them what they want," the professor insisted. "Quickly."

Morgan looked pained, but with little choice she shoved the loose items into the briefcase, latched it and held it up. "Don't shoot."

"Throw it to us," the gunman demanded.

Morgan leaned back and then flung the case like a Frisbee. It spun flatly, soaring over the men in the boat and splashing into the water on the far side. Sealed, it was buoyant and bobbed to the surface, before starting to sink.

The motorboat turned instantly toward it, with the men on board dropping their weapons and grasping at the foundering case.

As they attempted to retrieve it, Kurt shoved the punt in the other direction and with three quick pushes reached the shore, stopping as the bow hit the mud. "Everyone off," he ordered.

Morgan and Joe helped the professor up onto the grassy riverbank as Kurt held the tiller steady. Without looking back, they rushed across the green lawn and headed for cover.

They needn't have bothered. Their attackers had collected the sinking briefcase and were heading downriver as fast as they could go, the grinding sound of the outboard at maximum power disturbing the peace and quiet as they went.

"They're letting us be," the professor said.

"They have what they came for," Kurt pointed out. "Now they have to get away before the law catches up with them."

"At least we're alive," the professor said. "But, with apologies to Sherlock Holmes, the game is afoot."

"Regrettably, they'll soon know everything we know," Morgan said.

"Not everything," Kurt said. "They don't have the logbook. Something tells me that lost plane is the key."

Chapter 20

NUMA headquarters, Washington, D.C.

Rudi Gunn had been in his office at NUMA headquarters for an hour when the sun rose over Washington, D.C. An early riser who liked using the quiet of the morning to get the day off to a good start, Rudi was the number two man at NUMA and the de facto handler of the day-to-day operational work. He was often called the XO, the executive officer, of NUMA, as compared to Dirk Pitt's status as captain.

As a former naval officer who'd graduated first in his class from Annapolis, Rudi didn't mind the analogy at all. He was well suited to the position. It required attention to detail, doing things by the book and running a watertight ship.

After reading a message from Kurt Austin, and a communiqué from the head of a foreign government agency, Rudi got the distinct impression that his ship might be going off course or perhaps taking on water.

The communiqué that made up the second half of his reading had come in on official channels from MI5 headquarters in London. It mentioned two incidents that took place over the past forty-eight hours and casually noted the involvement of Kurt Austin and Joe Zavala.

Rudi scanned the after-action report quickly, slowing down as he arrived at the personal thoughts of the MI5 Station Chief.

. . . possible involvement of major world arms dealers known by the moniker Bloodstone Group. Both Austin and Zavala acquitted themselves admirably and I extend my thanks for their continued assistance . . .

"Bad news?" a voice asked.

Rudi looked up to see Hiram Yaeger standing in the doorway.

Hiram wore blue jeans and a pullover sweater with a large red **S** stamped over the outline of an evergreen tree. He was the Director of NUMA's Technology and Information Systems Unit. Unlike Rudi, who always wore a pressed shirt, patterned tie and tailored jacket, Hiram seemed to possess clothing that ran the gamut from casual to extra-casual only. Such were the perks of running the IT department.

Rudi studied his longtime friend. The sweater caught his eye. "I must have fallen into an alternate universe," he announced. "When I went to sleep last night, Kurt and Joe worked for us, not British Intelligence, and you were a graduate of MIT, not Stanford."

"You're not dreaming," Hiram said. "Dirk loaned Kurt and Joe to the Brits before he took off for Japan."

"And your sweater?"

"My youngest daughter chose Stanford last week."

Rudi sat back. "Over MIT? You must be heartbroken."

"She's a misguided youth in full rebellion," Hiram said. "I blame it on the weather. We visited Boston in January and it was a balmy four degrees. The next week in California it was in the mid-seventies."

Rudi grinned. "And yet her choice is still more surprising than hearing that Kurt and Joe have been lend-leased to MI5 on a handshake. They were supposed to be on vacation."

Hiram came in but remained standing. "Vacation is just another way for them to find trouble. You could put those two on a desert island in the middle of nowhere and they'd still get into something."

"Isn't that the truth."

"I assume they need our help or we wouldn't even be hearing from them."

Rudi picked up the printed message from Kurt and scanned it once more. "They want us to look for a plane that crashed in December of 1927. They've narrowed it down to the 'drier parts of Europe'—France, Spain or Portugal, perhaps. In Kurt's words, that should make it easy."

"He's king of the optimists," Hiram said. "Then again, we've given him too many reasons to be confident in the past. Send me the details and I'll have Max search through the records."

Max was Hiram's artificially intelligent system, a one-of-a-kind supercomputer that he had built and modified over the years to the point that it had taken on a personality all its own.

"There won't be many government records that far back," Rudi said.

"I know," Hiram replied. "But old newspaper articles are often helpful in cases like this. Airplanes were few and far between in 1927. When one went missing or came falling out of the sky, that usually made the news."

Rudi knew he could count on Hiram. He handed the message over. "While you're at it, Kurt would also like to know about some ancient Egyptian texts, a missing Pharaoh and whatever information you can pull up on an MI5 agent named Morgan Manning."

"Starting with her phone number, no doubt."

"I'm sure he already has that," Rudi said. "It seems they're partnering on this investigation."

Hiram pulled off the wire-rimmed glasses he wore, cleaned them with the hem of his sweater and then slid them back on before studying the message. "Tell him I'll do what I can."

He turned to leave.

"And one more thing," Rudi said. "While you're helping Kurt, get me everything you can on this Bloodstone Group. I'd like to know exactly what Kurt is dealing with."

Chapter 21

Eurotunnel Folkstone Terminal, England

The Renault utility van eased along a concrete ramp in a slow-moving line of cars. Ahead of it, the other vehicles inched forward bumper-to-bumper, stopping at a security officer who studied their tickets before clearing them through. From there, the cars moved through a second set of gates and drove across a platform, lining up again, before disappearing into the side of a cavernous, rail-borne car transporter.

Robson looked at the hulking train, it stretched forward nearly twenty railcars before he saw what looked like the aerodynamic engine at the front.

"Never been in the Chunnel," Snipe said quietly. "Always thought people drove through it. Didn't know you had to ride a bloomin' train."

"No one drives through the Chunnel on his

own," Robson said. "Can you imagine if there was a crash or someone ran out of fuel?"

Snipe nodded.

"How's your hand?"

"Something's broke," Snipe said, holding out a swollen bandaged fist. "But I can still use the other one."

Robson looked over. "Keep it out of sight," he said, "in case it's been made part of our description."

As Snipe stuffed both his hands in the pockets of his windbreaker, Robson moved up until he was stopped by the uniformed officer. A graphic on the officer's jacket showed the high-speed train in profile underscored by the identifier TRAFFIC OPERATIONS CONTROL.

"Registration, insurance, travel papers," the officer requested.

Robson motioned to Snipe, who paused and then used his uninjured hand to retrieve the papers from the glove box. Robson took them and handed them through the window.

The officer studied the documents and then put his hand on the microphone clipped to his collar. Pressing the TALK switch, he called the information in and then waited for a response from his central command.

The reply did not come quickly. As the silence began to drag, Robson glanced around, looking for avenues of escape. Walls of concrete stood to the right and left, while going forward only led deeper into the rail yard. He glanced in the mirror and saw nothing but a line of cars going all the way back to the outer gate. There would be no getting through there either.

He forced himself to relax while allowing his hand to slide down the side of his seat, stopping only when his fingers touched the pistol taped there.

"Just as I thought," the officer said, handing back the papers. "You're the mechanics." He pointed ahead. "Down there. Next car."

The officer waved for another uniformed man to open the temporary gate and then directed Robson on through. Leaning in the car before allowing Robson to drive off, he issued a warning. "Remember. Once you get off the train in France, you'll be driving on the other side of the road."

Robson felt his pounding heart start to slow. He nodded, eased his foot onto the gas and moved the van forward.

Snipe whistled. "That was dodgy."

In the back of the van, Gus was recuperating from getting his scalp split open by the American with the pole. He wore a hat to cover it. Fingers had shaved off his long hair and now sported a punk rocker's Mohawk. They weren't a pretty crew, but it had got the job done.

With a careful twist of the wheel, Robson pulled

into the vehicle transporter, leaving the daylight for its well-lit, oversize interior. It didn't take long to realize it was a private car. A custom Maserati Quattroporte was parked in front of them. Just beyond that sat a Rolls-Royce Phantom.

With the engine off and the gearshift in park, Robson and his crew waited. Soon enough, the door to the transporter was lowered and sealed and shortly thereafter the train began to move.

The initial acceleration was so smooth that Robson barely noticed it. From there, speed was added methodically and quickly. They were soon traveling at over a hundred miles an hour, and heading for one hundred and fifty, and yet the rail system was so precise that even traveling at full speed resulted in only the slightest sensation of movement.

"When's Mr. Big coming?" Snipe asked.

"He's not coming," Robson said. "He's already here."

"Good. Then it's time we got paid."

"We get paid when the job's done," Robson said.

"I thought the job was done."

"Not yet," Robson said. "Not by a long shot."

Up ahead, a man got out of the Maserati. Robson recognized him as one of Barlow's personal guards. He waved him over.

"Stay here," Robson said. He grabbed the briefcase, got out and walked toward the Maserati.

After being relieved of his phone and both frisked and wanded for bugs, he was directed ahead to the Rolls.

The Phantom's rear door opened. "Get in," Solomon Barlow said.

Sliding inside, Robson sat. He handed the briefcase to Barlow, who opened it immediately.

While Barlow went through the contents of the case, Robson allowed his nerves to get the best of him. "I thought we were about to get nicked back there," he said.

"I told you I had it handled," Barlow replied without looking up.

"The mechanics?"

"If anyone asks, you're accompanying my cars to a show in Toulouse."

"Is that where we're going?"

"Farther on," Barlow said. "Down to the border with Spain." He looked up. "Is this everything?"

"That's all they had."

"Pity they didn't bring the actual objects with them, but the photos are enough for now. Wise of you to scan them and send them ahead. It allowed us to get a jump on things."

"Will it lead us to the treasure?"

"Not directly," Barlow said. "Regrettably, the important parts—the bits telling us where the treasure might be hidden—are still unaccounted for."

"Is that why we're heading to Spain?"

"We're not heading to Spain," Barlow replied. "We're heading to the border **with** Spain. Pay attention."

Robson didn't like Barlow's word games. "The question doesn't change. Why are we going there?"

"Because a French nobleman by the name of DeMars lives there. His family owned the original fragments containing the known **Writings of Qsn.** They might have information we could use. Specifically, some idea of where the rest of the tablet could be. They may even be in possession of other items that could help us in our search. Unfortunately, DeMars is an uncompromising fellow who doesn't like to share. We're going to provide him with proper motivation to change that habit."

Robson suppressed a laugh. Solomon Barlow and his long-winded speeches. He could've saved them both time and energy by saying they were going to torture DeMars. "Fine," Robson said. "First off, my men need food, rest and a down payment for their services."

"They'll get paid when I have what I want," Barlow replied.

"They won't be working on a promise."

Barlow turned cold. "They will find that to be an untenable negotiating position."

"How so?"

"Because you're no longer on point here,"

Barlow said. "After you nearly screwed the entire operation in Cambridge, I've decided to make a change. I'm putting Kappa in charge. His men will handle the rest of the operation. You and that rabble of yours are only there to provide backup."

"That rabble got back what your men in Scotland lost," Robson said, feeling oddly defensive about his old mates. "Mark my word, you're going to need their help before this is over. Especially if you're trusting things to Kappa. He wouldn't know a lie from a hole in the ground."

Solomon Barlow did not like being questioned, but he felt the odds had turned against them with the Americans and MI5 now teamed up together. He would put Robson and his street thugs away at some later date. For now, he knew they might come in handy.

"Fine," Barlow said. "Kappa stays on, but I'll let you handle the interrogation of DeMars. In the meantime, I'll see that you get some cash to pass around to your men. But I'm warning you. If you undermine this operation to make Kappa look bad, or if your men screw up in any form, it'll be your head that rolls. Understand?"

Robson nodded, pleased with the agreement. "So, how do you want me to treat this DeMars when we find him?"

Barlow glared at Robson as if he'd said something foolish. "How do you think I want you to treat him?" Barlow snapped. "We have a banker willing to part with a hundred million euros for every golden sarcophagus proven to hold a mummified Pharaoh, plus a dozen other collectors promising millions should we find anything at all. Get DeMars talking. I really don't care what he looks like afterward."

Chapter 22

Savoy Hotel, London

"No joy in Mudville," Kurt said. "The Mighty Hiram has completely struck out."

Kurt, Joe and Morgan were using a suite at the Savoy as a temporary headquarters while attempting to divine the final landing spot of whatever aircraft it was that had carried the **Writings of Qsn.**

Kurt sat at the desk near the front of the luxurious accommodations, studying his computer. Morgan sat in the adjoining room on the bed, looking at messages on her own laptop, while Joe was lying across the sofa, facing the fireplace, examining the pages of the logbook, hoping to find any information that would help them pin down the make and model of the missing plane or the pilot who'd flown it.

After hearing Kurt's announcement, Morgan looked up from her screen, bewildered. "Mudville?"

"Baseball reference," Kurt said. "From an old poem. The hero strikes out despite being supremely sure of himself."

"Something that never happens in real life," Joe said with a smirk.

Morgan's look remained blank. "Where, exactly, is Mudville?"

"It's not a real place," Kurt said.

"Then why bring it up?"

"You're missing the point," Kurt said. "What I'm trying to tell you is, after an exhaustive search our computer and records experts have found nothing to indicate the crash of any aircraft in any of the areas we've suggested they look during December of 1927. How's that for clarity?"

"Much better," Morgan said, smiling. "But a crash may not have been recorded if the area was rural."

"Perhaps not," Kurt agreed. "But a missing plane would be noted by the company flying it or by the operator of an aerodrome waiting for the plane to return. And if not by them, then at least by relatives of the missing pilot. Hiram and his crew have found nothing of the sort. They've even searched obituaries listing pilots. But they've . . . struck out."

"Ah," she said. "Now I understand. It's like getting bowled. Or ending up as batsmen with a sticky wicket."

Kurt stared blankly. "I'd say yes, but I honestly have no idea what you're talking about."

Joe burst out laughing. He needed to. Despite hours of trying to glean anything from the pages Morgan had stolen, he'd learned nothing new. He'd been over them a dozen times. He'd used a magnifying glass and then a special light that helped reveal faded ink. He'd even felt for indentations caused by something else being written over them.

Aside from the cryptic words, written by the injured and possibly feverish pilot, the notations were simple and irrelevant. Spark plug timings were noted, along with fluid levels and other mechanic's entries. The descriptions on the second and third pages referred to overhauls, misfiring cylinders and oil changes. They had nothing to do with the lost ancient writings.

Kurt looked his way. "What about you, Joe? Getting bowled or having a sticky wicket?"

"Neither," Joe said. "It was definitely a crash. Which makes me think Hiram is searching in the wrong place."

"He's covered all of Europe," Kurt said. "Where else can he look?"

Joe sighed. He had no idea. There was nothing to suggest where, just a description of an arid part of Europe with a high bluff and a river down below.

Ready to take a break, Joe sat up and allowed his mind to wander. He found his eyes resting on a small desk calendar. They'd done so much running around in the last week, he wasn't sure what day it was.

Studying the date, a realization came to him suddenly. He went back through the notes and the logbook entries. Once he realized what he was looking for, it became obvious. And he wondered how he'd missed it in the first place.

"Maybe we're looking in the right area," he said, "but the wrong time."

Kurt raised an eyebrow. "You're suggesting . . . time travel?"

Joe shook his head. "August 1st, 2019," he said. "How would you abbreviate that?"

"Eight-one-nineteen," Kurt replied.

Joe grinned, pleased with himself. "Morgan?"

She looked up from her computer. "Sorry, I wasn't listening."

"How would you abbreviate August 1st, 2019?"

"One-eight-nineteen, of course. Why?"

"Day, then month, then year," Joe confirmed. "European-style."

Morgan nodded.

"Has it always been that way in Europe?"

"As far as I know," she said. "I have a card from Granddad to my mum dated that way. Why do you ask?"

"Because you said the crash was on December 5th, 1927," Joe said. "We gave that date to Hiram to use in his computer records search. But if the plane— or the pilot—were American, then the notation five-twelve-twenty-seven would be May 12th as the crash date, not December 5th."

"What makes you think it's an American pilot?" Kurt asked.

"Because it's an American plane," Joe said. "And in those days that would almost certainly mean an American flyboy or -girl—er, -woman."

"You've figured out what kind of plane we're looking for?" Kurt asked.

"Not exactly," Joe said. "But I know what side of the Atlantic it was manufactured on."

Wanting to show them what he'd discovered, Joe brought the papers over to the desk. Morgan joined them. "Look at this," he began. "It's an entry regarding the maintenance on the engine. It includes a note about adding nine quarts of oil. Quarts, not liters or milliliters."

"It might have been a British plane," Morgan suggested. "In those days we used the imperial system too. The UK only changed to metric in the sixties. And if you ask my dad, that was a big mistake."

"Okay," Joe said, "but the oil is described as MHE 150 Aero-Oil. **MHE** is an abbreviation for **Mohawk Eastern.** Back in the twenties, Mohawk Eastern made oils for boats, cars and planes. They began production around the turn of the century and went out of business during the Depression. I have a vintage sign of theirs in my garage."

"You're sure that's the same company."

Joe nodded. "Absolutely. The thing is, Mohawk was a regional company. They never operated beyond the northeastern United States. In fact, you'd be hard pressed to find any sales outside of New York, New England and Pennsylvania. They never went west of Ohio. And they certainly weren't exporters. So if the mechanic is adding Mohawk Eastern Aero-Oil, then it had to be an American outfit flying the missing plane. That means the logbook would use American dates, not European. And that means the last flight took place on May 12th, not December 5th."

Morgan asked the obvious question. "What would an American plane be doing in Europe in 1927? Transatlantic flights hadn't even begun then."

Joe shrugged. "Maybe they were operating with a traveling air show or a barnstorming team. They might have been part of a cross-country race. Who knows? Back in the early days of aviation, pilots made money where they could. Wealthy big shots often held competitions or even invited performers to their cities, sponsoring air shows and other events. I've read about performers taking their planes over to Europe by steamship to work the summers on the Continent before heading back to the States in the fall. That would fit perfectly with the May date."

"You've convinced me," Kurt said. "I'll tell Hiram to run a new search using May as the focal point."

"Tell him to look for aircraft and pilots that were known to have operated on both continents. There can't be too many of those in the twenties."

As Kurt nodded and began to type the message, Joe stacked the pages and handed them back to Morgan, looking proud of the day's work.

"Thanks," she said absently while walking back to her computer.

"Something wrong?" Joe asked.

She folded the screen flat before responding.

"Professor Cross has completed his study of the hieroglyphics. He found nothing to indicate where the treasure was taken, only that the fleet passed Memphis and entered the Mediterranean. His suggestion is, look into the family who owned the **Writings of Qsn.** The DeMarses. Their descendants live in southern France."

"My calendar is open," Joe said, "no matter what dating system you use."

Kurt finished his message to Hiram and joined the conversation. "It's worth a try. And at the moment, as you said, we have nothing better to do."

Chapter 23

Southern France

After a quick flight down from London, Kurt, Joe and Morgan picked up a rented Peugeot in Toulouse and drove out to the DeMars estate. As they went west, the number of homes and businesses thinned out, giving way to sprawling farms and open country.

After they had been driving for an hour, Kurt's phone rang. He glanced at the screen. "It's Hiram."

"You mean, the Mighty Casey," Morgan said.

"Exactly," Kurt said with a smile. "One and the same."

He answered the call.

"I have something for you," Hiram said. "But not what you might have been expecting."

"Mind if I put you on speaker?" Kurt asked. "Only the three of us in the car."

"Be my guest," Hiram said. "Quite frankly, it

wouldn't matter if the bad guys were riding in the backseat."

Kurt switched to speaker and put the phone down. "You're on, Hiram. Give us the bad news."

Hiram cut directly to the chase. "I ran a search based on the new information. But as you might guess from my tone, we've come up empty once more."

"How empty?" Joe asked.

"Are there different degrees?" Morgan asked.

"Sometimes," Kurt admitted. "What do you say, Hiram? Did you find anything we can use?"

"You be the judge," Hiram said. "We found twenty-four documented plane crashes in Europe in the month of May 1927. I say 'documented' because many of the German and French records were destroyed during World War Two, while Iberian records suffered a similar fate during the Spanish Civil War."

"Twenty-four is a significant number of crashes," Morgan noted.

"Planes weren't very reliable back then," Joe noted.

"Correct," Hiram said. "We found some pilots crashing twice in the same month and living to tell about it. Obviously, we ruled those incidents out. We also ruled out incidents where the wrecks occurred in or near a populated area. Finally, we narrowed it down by focusing on American pilots or American-made aircraft. That gave us three possibilities."

"Sounds less empty than I was expecting," Kurt said.

"One plane burned to cinders, another went into a lake and the third was a minor accident on a grass runway where the plane was repaired within a week and sent up again. How does that information make you feel?"

"Empty," Kurt admitted. "What about American pilots in Europe who didn't crash in 1927?"

"Well, there's Lindbergh," Hiram joked. "But not too many others."

Kurt laughed. "Keep searching. There has to be some trace out there. Maybe you can dig up the records of Mohawk East and see who they sold oil to."

"I wouldn't even call that grasping at straws," Hiram said. "But I'll give it a shot."

"Call us if you find anything."

"Enjoy the wine country," Hiram replied. "My jealousy meter is hitting level nine right about now. Yaeger out."

"Does this Hiram friend of yours ever find anything in his searches?" Morgan asked politely.

"He literally never fails," Joe said.

"Hence, the Mighty Casey reference."

"But Casey did strike out," she said, sounding perplexed.

Kurt shook his head in resignation. "I'm just going to let you read the poem."

They were in the wine country now—vineyards had replaced the farms—and were closing in on their destination. After riding for several miles along winding roads, they came upon the Château DeMars perched atop a gently sloping hill.

"Now, that's what I call a château," Joe said.

The imposing Renaissance-style building rose four stories at its center and included turrets on its four corners. A garden maze of hedgerows could be seen from the road, while a vineyard covered the left flank of the hill and a pasture dotted with grazing horses occupied the right. A twelve-foot brick wall surrounded the property.

"Nice digs," Kurt said. "I'd hate to pay the electric bill."

"Something tells me they can afford it," Morgan said.

Kurt didn't doubt that. A half mile on he found the entry gate, complete with a guardhouse and security cameras. The gate itself was made of twin horizontal poles, welded together and filled with cement—a setup sturdier than it looked. The driveway was equipped with a line of raised metal spikes designed to blow out an intruder's tires if the gate failed to do its job.

"Someone doesn't like visitors," Kurt said.

"Actually, the château is used to host visitors

all the time," Morgan said. "It's trespassers they're worried about."

"Which category do we fall into?"

"Let's find out."

They pulled up to the gate and Morgan spoke to the guard in fluent French. She offered their credentials, smiled and quickly persuaded him to call Monsieur DeMars and request an audience.

He stepped into the guard shack and picked up a white phone. After a brief conversation, punctuated by a few nods and a glance at each passport, the guard hung up, came outside and returned their papers. "You may park in the breezeway between the carriage house and the main residence. Someone will meet you there."

"Merci," Morgan said, taking their credentials back.

Kurt put the car back in gear as the gate's poles went up. They passed beneath it and over the now retracted spikes. "Next time I get a speeding ticket I want you to handle it."

She looked his way, smiling again. "Are you saying you don't obey the traffic laws of your country?"

"Let's just say I wouldn't mind having a few autobahns in America."

Despite Kurt's penchant for speed, he found himself keeping the Peugeot in check. The driveway was a bumpy cobblestone road that looped around the property, past the vineyard and up to the house. They arrived at the crest of the hill and passed a stable large enough for twenty horses before nearing the majestic residence.

Pulling into the breezeway, Kurt parked directly across from a tall, slim man with wispy blond hair. The man wore a zip-up black sweater, riding pants and boots. He nodded politely as Kurt opened the door. "**Bonjour.** Welcome to the Maison D'être, our Home Away from Home."

Kurt recognized Francisco DeMars from photos they'd downloaded. He was the grandson of the man who'd found the **Writings of Qsn.** "At a home as splendid as this, one often meets a butler or a footman first."

"Most of my employees have gone back to their own homes," DeMars said. "And I prefer to greet my guests. Especially when they are—how do you say?—unscheduled arrivals. Do any of you speak French?"

Kurt stepped out of the way and Morgan came forward. They spoke briefly in French before DeMars reverted to English.

"I'm honored that both of your governments are interested in the work my grandfather did. It has been a long time since his efforts were given the proper attention. I will help you anyway I can. Please, come inside. Perhaps you'd like something to eat as well. It must have been a long journey."

He led them into the château and down a long

hallway replete with tapestries, paintings and other works of art. They passed a formal dining room, one of its long walls covered by a mural depicting scenes from the French Revolution. Finally, they entered a smaller parlor.

After suggesting they sit, DeMars called a servant, who arrived with a tray of puff pastries flavored with Gruyère cheese, baguettes of freshly baked bread and a wheel of soft Brie. Another servant brought a bottle of red wine and a bottle of Évian.

Kurt spread some of the Brie on a slice of the warm bread and took a bite. The entire creation melted on his tongue. "Heaven."

Joe was enjoying one of the pastries. "You'll have to try one of these next."

DeMars nodded. "Try one of each," he insisted. "As the saying goes, a meal without cheese is like a day without sun. Now, how can I help you?"

Morgan deferred to Kurt for the moment. "We're looking for information about a set of ancient Egyptian texts known as the **Writings of Qsn.** Your grandfather coined the term, I believe, after he found several stones with inscriptions on them."

"Yes," DeMars said. "That's correct. But they were lost to us during the war. The Germans took them and they were never returned to us. They seemed to have vanished. Why do you ask?"

"They may have reappeared," Morgan said.

DeMars's eyes grew wide. "I should be most interested to see them."

"Perhaps that's possible at some future point, but for now they're in safekeeping."

"Why?"

Morgan explained the threat that the Bloodstone Group presented and the hope that cutting off the supply of antiquities flowing to them would reduce the spread of illicit arms to the rest of the world.

DeMars took the news very soberly. "A worthy effort. How can I assist?"

Kurt went straight for it. "By telling us where your grandfather found the stones. Those details don't seem to be part of the historical record."

DeMars took a deep breath and sighed. "Because they have been kept secret."

"Why?"

"My grandfather's work was controversial. He believed the Egyptians had colonized Europe, settling the coasts of France and Spain, a thousand years before the Romans. He spent half his life searching for the proof, especially for a mythical fleet he believed foundered in French waters and for a pyramid he claimed had been constructed in the coastal area of Spain."

DeMars took a sip of wine, then continued. "To some extent, wild theories were common for the time period. I'm sure you know of the Nazi suggestion that Europeans, at least the Teutonic people, had all descended from that famous Aryan master race. A race that never existed. They spent years, and trunkloads of Reichsmarks, searching the Himalayas for their mythical origins. My grandfather spent years and half the family fortune looking for his mythical pyramid, never to find it. Today our family finds that parallel uncomfortable."

"Your grandfather's theory may have been outlandish, but that didn't make him a Nazi," Kurt noted.

"Far from it," DeMars pointed out. "The Nazi Party hated my grandfather's theory, particularly because it suggested North African origins for much of European culture and its population. When France fell to Germany in 1940, my grandfather was harassed and imprisoned. Much of what he'd found over the years was taken, including the **Writings of Qsn.** We assumed they'd destroyed the fragments. My mother, at least, hoped they had."

Kurt listened to DeMars speak, hearing a sense of sadness in the man's voice and a bit of shame. Unknown to DeMars, or even Morgan, NUMA had a surprising amount of inside knowledge regarding the Egyptians, some of which had only recently come to light. The truth is, Egyptian seafaring was more advanced than most mainstream scholars believe. They'd traveled farther and wider than anyone thought. One branch of Egyptian royalty had even wound up in Ireland. The possibility that others could have spread around Europe was not as far-fetched as DeMars imagined.

Kurt would share that data with DeMars at some point, but first he needed answers. "I appreciate the information," he said, "and I promise you we're not trying to interrogate you. But if you know where your grandfather found the stones, we'd appreciate knowing."

"They were found in Spain," DeMars replied. "But no one in my family ever believed that's where they originated."

Kurt said nothing. He could see where this was going.

"You see," DeMars continued, "our grandfather was so desperate to prove his theory, there were rumors that he'd begun seeding the ground with the type of things he hoped to find. All I can say is, it was a different time."

Kurt understood DeMars's sense of embarrassment. "Any chance the fragments were delivered to him by aircraft?"

"It's possible," DeMars said. "I suppose you might find the answer in my grandfather's journals. Though I warn you, he was a voluminous writer."

"We'd be grateful for the chance to look," Morgan said.

DeMars stood. "I'll show you the journals, but there are conditions. The contents and his opinions cannot be made public. And none of the journals are to leave this house."

"You have our word," Morgan said.

"In that case, follow me."

Chapter 24

JOURNEY OF THE PHARAOHS

DeMars led them out into the hallway and down toward the western rotunda. The circular space occupied the turret on one corner of the château. A statue depicting Joan of Arc astride her horse dominated the ground floor. It was rendered in extremely lifelike detail and gilded in gold leaf. As was customary, the Maid of Orléan held the reins in one hand and a staff bearing the French standard in the other. The banner had been crafted so expertly, it seemed to be fluttering in an invisible breeze.

"Beautiful," Morgan said, admiring the statue.

"She's our hero," DeMars said.

He led them up to the fourth floor and into the study. Shelves filled with material spanned the room. Reference books in one section, leather-bound journals in the next.

DeMars strode across the room to the wall of

journals and climbed a small stepladder. "These are my grandfather's expedition journals. If you're seeking information on the discovery, it will be in here."

Kurt eased up next to their host. He counted a dozen volumes covering 1927, ten for 1928, and eleven more for 1929. "You weren't kidding about your grandfather's notetaking."

"He was meticulous," DeMars said. "That will be helpful, no?"

"Helpful," Kurt agreed, "and time-consuming."

Kurt ran his finger across the spines, starting with those devoted to 1927, skipping January through April and stopping on the volume marked May. Opening it, Kurt saw the next problem. The writing was in flowing cursive longhand. It was also entirely in French. "We may need your assistance."

"Of course," DeMars said. He took the journal, sat at a desk and turned on a green-shaded reading light.

"I can read French too," Morgan said.

Kurt pulled a second journal off the shelf and handed it to her. She sat across from DeMars.

"I feel as helpful as a bump on a log," Joe said.

Kurt felt the same way. "We could search for terms," he suggested, turning to DeMars.

"My grandfather originally called the hieroglyphics fragments the red stones," DeMars said. **"Les pierres rouges."**

"And we're searching for a downed aircraft," Kurt added.

"Avion," Morgan replied. **"L'avion."**

Both Kurt and Joe took journals and got to work. Had the library been digitized, Hiram's computers could have searched through every word in a matter of seconds. By Kurt's estimation, the four of them couldn't do it in less than a full weekend. With nothing to do but get started, Kurt sat down and opened his book.

Darkness fell rapidly in the hill country of western France. As the sun disappeared behind the mountains bordering Spain, the air turned cool and the sky faded to a dusky gray.

With the slightest hint of orange light still glowing on the horizon, the security guard at the front gate settled in for what he expected would be a quiet evening. He said good-bye to the staff as they left and lowered the heavy gate.

Unlike earlier centuries, none of the staff lived at the château, they had homes and families of their own to go to. Aside from the security team and a butler, only the DeMars family remained overnight. And with most of the family away for the summer, the mansion was almost empty.

The guard laughed at the idea. The residence had fifteen bedrooms, almost as many bathrooms, two kitchens, three dining rooms and plenty of other spaces. Most of the time, it was all but vacant. Better for him, he thought. Many of the châteaux around France had been turned into tourist destinations and hotels. That meant endless foot traffic, screaming children and issues with theft. The DeMars château hosted only occasional weddings and corporate parties. If it ever became a tourist trap, the guard intended to put in for early retirement.

Sitting back and dividing his attention between the road outside, the ever-changing security feed from the cameras around the property and the music playing softly on his radio, the guard felt the peace of the evening settle on him. That feeling didn't change much even as a pair of headlights came down the road, slowing as they neared the driveway. He saw a turn signal light up, flashing amber in the dark, and found himself mildly annoyed as a delivery van pulled into the drive and stopped at the gate.

Grabbing his clipboard, the guard walked out to the van. "Catering and deliveries are not supposed to arrive after six. I hope you have a good reason for coming so late."

The window went down and the man in the vehicle looked over at him. There was something undeniably cruel about his face. "No delivery," he said in badly accented French. "Pickup."

Looking into the van, the guard noticed that the steering wheel was on the far side. That made it an English vehicle. The accent was English too. He wondered if this had something to do with the group that had arrived earlier. The woman had been English.

"Pickup?" he said, glancing at the clipboard and looking for anything that might be scheduled to go out. "What vendor?"

"Glock," the man said.

The guard froze at the sight of the Austrian-made pistol. He noticed that a silencer had been screwed into the barrel. That could mean only one thing.

He threw the clipboard and dodged to the side, but he was not nearly fast enough. Three muted shots were fired. Two hit him in the chest, the other in his right bicep.

He landed on the ground, stunned, bleeding and gasping for breath. He looked back to see a passenger climbing out of the van, but instead of finishing him off the man rushed into the shack and pressed the button to open the gate.

As the poles swung upward, a second van sped up to it, this one a larger, twelve-passenger model. It slowed, waiting for the gate to reach its zenith and the spikes in the pavement to retract. When the gate locked into position and the spikes disappeared, the van raced in.

Mortally wounded and bleeding out, the guard still processed what he was seeing. This was an assault. A planned attack. He had to call in a warning. He reached for the microphone attached to his collar and squeezed the TALK switch. "Code—"

A fourth bullet finished him off before he could say any more.

Robson stood over the fallen guard, waiting for an alarm to sound or a return call to come through on the guard's radio.

"If anyone heard that call, we'll be walking into trouble," Snipe insisted.

"Kappa and his men will find it first," Robson said. "But I wouldn't worry. It doesn't sound like anyone was listening. Get him out of sight and get back in the van. We don't want Kappa to have all the fun."

Gus and Fingers worked together, picking the guard up by his arms and feet and hauling him back into the shack. They laid him on the ground out of sight and closed the door. Meanwhile, Snipe had picked up the fallen clipboard. "Look at this."

Robson took it. It listed visitors and deliveries. He saw the names Manning, Austin and Zavala. Affiliations, UK and USG.

"The MI5 agent and the two Americans are here," he told the others. "Looks like we'll get to kill three birds with one stone."

Chapter 25

Château DeMars, fourth-floor study

An hour of reading had gone by in the blink of an eye. To his surprise, Kurt found scanning for terms amid words in a foreign language surprisingly hard. It was easy for his mind to wander as his eyes glossed over and stopped really seeing what they were looking for.

"This is like scanning the sea from a helicopter, looking for an orange life raft amid the endless blue," he said.

"That would be easier," Joe said.

Either way, it had the same effect—strain behind the eyeballs and the need for frequent breaks.

"Yes," DeMars said, standing up as he spoke. "Yes."

"Tell me you're not just agreeing with us enthusiastically," Kurt said.

"I've found something," DeMars said. "I think this is what you're hoping for. Come look."

Kurt gladly put down the journal he was reading and moved over to the table DeMars had occupied.

The journals covering May, June and July of 1927 sat beside him, stacked up neatly, effectively ruled out. Open in front of DeMars was the journal for August 1927.

With the others gathered around him, DeMars adjusted his glasses and began to read aloud.

Two days' mule's ride from Navia we finally arrived in San Sebastián. Here we are shown the items that the trader spoke of. Small golden castings, one in the shape of a crocodile, the other in the shape of an Anubis. They must be Egyptian. Proof that members of the dynasty were on the Continent.

He looked up with a grin and read on.

In addition to the golden items, these men have shown me flat sections of a reddish stone. The surface is covered with hieroglyphics. They have also a small, pyramid-shaped stone that appears as if it has been broken off the top of a marker or perhaps a small obelisk.

Turning the page, he found a rough drawing with some dimensions listed beside it.

"That's a good match for what we saw in the case," Joe said.

Kurt and Morgan nodded. DeMars continued.

I asked repeatedly where they dug the items up, but the old men shrug and do not answer. Perhaps they do not understand. I rephrase the

**words and ask how they came into possession
of the items. They indicate they were among
the belongings of a dead man who was found
by the river a full day's walk to the north.**

**I asked who this man was and where he
hailed from, but I receive only the same indis-
tinct shrugs. He was not one of us, I am told.
It is difficult to know what this means. I am in
Basque Country and they do not acknowledge
the government in Madrid. There is also the new
divide among those who count Spain as their
home. Communists and Nationalists are forcing
people to choose sides. All of this is making my
task of finding the truth more difficult.**

Kurt cross-referenced the dates with his knowledge of history. "Shadows of the Spanish Civil War."

"Indeed," DeMars said, then went back
to reading.

**Avoiding talk of the government, I ask how
the man died and what happened to his body.
They say he died from infection and loss of
blood. Some of the men buried him and they
brought his rucksack here. No one has come
for him . . .**

The next page described the items in more detail and the prices paid for them, but that was the
last entry for Spain. When the journal resumed,
it was five weeks later and the elder DeMars was
visiting a friend in Paris.

"He doesn't mention a plane," Joe said. "But the dead man's injuries match what was written in the logbook. I'd say it's a lock."

DeMars was smiling.

"You look happier than us," Kurt noted.

"Proud," DeMars said. "Many have considered my grandfather's work trivial or even fraudulent, me among them. This proves that the items didn't originate in Spain. But it also proves his discovery was serendipity, not deception."

Kurt put a hand on DeMars's shoulder. "And when we find what the **Writings of Qsn** are pointing us toward, he will be the biggest reason for a discovery of epic proportions. Now we just have to figure out where he was. Where, exactly, is San Sebastián?"

Kurt pulled out his phone, used to using the power of the internet for searches such as this. At the same time, DeMars put the journal aside and went to retrieve a large atlas from the shelf.

He carried it to the desk and placed it down with a soft thud. Leafing through the pages, he came to a section depicting northern Spain, just across the border from France.

"This is Basque Country," he said.

Taking out a magnifying glass, he scanned the page, searching the names of the towns and rivers. "Here," he said. "This is Navia. This is where they began. From there, two days by mule upriver would take them somewhere between twenty and perhaps forty miles at the most. That would bring them to . . ."

He checked the scale of the map and then placed a ruler alongside the river. At the twenty-mile mark, there was nothing, but nearer the top of the page, close to the forty-mile limit, was a small dot with two inked notes next to it.

DeMars got the chills. They were his grandfather's shorthand notes. They included dates in August of 1927. "This is it," he said, circling the town for the others to see.

Morgan and Joe came over to look. Kurt continued to wait on his phone to cooperate.

"It says Villa Ducal de Lerma," Joe pointed out.

"But the church is there," DeMars said. "San Sebastián de las Montañas—Saint Sebastian of the Mountains. That was my grandfather's way of saying where he was, by telling us which church he visited."

While Joe and Morgan looked over DeMars's shoulder, Kurt was about to give up on his phone. The mapping application had started and then frozen. It now indicated LOST DATA CONNECTION. The reception icon at the top of the phone, which had listed the name of a French Telecom company and had held steady at four bars during their conversation with Hiram, now indicated NO SERVICE.

"I'm not getting a signal," he said. "But earlier I had four bars."

"That's odd," DeMars said, pulling out his own phone. "We usually have excellent service. Though mine appears to be down too."

Seconds later the lights went out. First in the house, then outside along the grounds, one section after another, until the hillside was dark.

"Blackout?" DeMars asked.

Kurt's frame tensed. "Blackouts happen all at once," he said, "not a section at a time. Someone's tripped the breakers. Do you have a landline?"

DeMars pointed to a shelf on the far wall. On it sat an avocado green desktop phone, circa 1980. "Joe," Kurt said.

Joe grabbed the phone and held it to his ear. "Dial tone," he said, nodding. "It's working."

"Dial 55 for the security," DeMars said.

Joe pressed the 5 button twice, but the line went dead before the call could go through. Joe tapped the cradle a couple of times, but he got nothing. He looked across the room at Kurt and shook his head.

"What's happening?" DeMars asked.

"My money is on a home invasion," Kurt said, reaching into his jacket and pulling out a compact .45 pistol, confirming a shell was in the chamber, clicking off the safety with his thumb and moving toward the door.

"What about my security force?" DeMars asked.

"Something tells me they're already sitting this one out."

Chapter 26

Château DeMars, ground floor

Robson had caught up with Kappa and his mercenaries in the foyer on the bottom floor. Unlike Robson's men, who were from the street, Kappa's were straight-up mercenaries. They'd done plenty of dirty work in war-torn countries as part of Bloodstone Group's full-service menu. Never war-fighting on the front lines—they were too valuable to be cannon fodder in some Third World civil war—they abducted dignitaries, staged political assassinations, set off bombs and conducted what passed for crowd control in countries where peaceful protest was often met with bloody assault.

Including himself, Kappa had eight men at his disposal. He'd also brought a plethora of equipment—stun grenades, smoke grenades, body armor, night vision goggles, police scanners and even a high-powered transmitter that acted as a SERVICE DENIED jammer by overloading cell phone towers with a massive signal.

"Think you brought enough junk with you?" Robson asked, watching the crew set up.

"You don't understand the modern battlefield," Kappa said. "It's all about overwhelming your enemy. Makes them give up and run much sooner than in a fair fight."

The transmitter sat on the floor in the foyer. It looked like a garbage can with four antennas sticking out of it.

"Don't get too close," Kappa warned. "Not if you want to have kids someday."

Robson laughed but stepped back nonetheless. At that same moment, two of Kappa's men brought out the butler. They forced him to his knees in front of Kappa, who pulled out a knife.

"We're looking for the man of the house," Kappa said. "Have you seen him?"

"Upstairs," the butler said nervously. "In the study."

"Which floor?"

The man didn't answer.

"Perhaps you didn't hear me," Kappa said. "Let me clean out your ears for you." As one of the men cupped a hand over the butler's mouth, Kappa brought the knife down, slicing into the top of the man's ear. He began pressing downward and the blood flowed.

The butler squirmed and grunted, but Kappa's men held him in place.

"I'll ask again. If you don't answer politely, I'll turn you into the spitting image of Van Gogh. Which floor are they on? And in which room?"

"**Quatrième,**" he said. "Fourth floor. In the old study."

Kappa pulled the knife away. "Bind him up."

As the butler was pulled away and tied up, blood flowed profusely down the side of his face. "If you're wrong," Kappa said, "I'll come back and help you with your vision."

He turned to his men. "Cut the power and split up. There are two stairwells. Let's move like we have purpose."

Kappa's men divided up into two groups without delay. Kappa led one group down the hall toward Joan of Arc while the other group went in the opposite direction to the eastern tower and the second flight of stairs.

Robson and his men were left behind as the breakers were tripped and the château went dark.

With power off, the fans and air-conditioning unit shut down and the fourth floor turned stagnant and quiet. Kurt crept out of the study and over to the edge of the stairs. Windows and a skylight at the top of the rotunda were letting in just enough outside light for him to see.

Down below, he saw Joan of Arc on her horse, along with several men who were wearing night vision goggles and carrying short-barreled machine guns.

While one of the men remained on the ground floor to secure the stairs, the other three moved onto the steps quickly and quietly, traveling up them with military precision.

Kurt ducked back into the study. "Trouble coming up the stairs."

A second after he arrived, Joe returned from down the hall. "We have armed goons in the other stairwell as well."

DeMars was breathing rapidly. "Can't you shoot them?"

"They've got body armor and machine guns," Kurt said. "A shoot-out won't go in our favor. Is there another way down?"

"No."

"What about up?"

"Yes," DeMars said. "The roof is open."

"It's a start," Kurt said. "Grab the journal."

As DeMars picked up his grandfather's journal, Kurt holstered his pistol and grabbed an armful of books.

"Go," Kurt whispered to the others. "Stick to the wall."

"What are you going to do?" Morgan asked.

"Make a nuisance of myself while trying not to get shot. Now, move."

He didn't have to say it twice. Morgan, Joe and DeMars climbed the steps. They raced upward, hugging the wall and keeping low so as not to be seen by the invaders, who were now making their way past the second floor and climbing.

As Joe led the group, Kurt opened the books and bent the spines back to keep them that way. Upon hearing the click of the door up above, he heaved the books over the railing, tossing them up and over.

They dropped toward the ground, separating as they fell, pages fluttering.

The men on the stairs had been climbing in silence with their eyes on the landings and the railing, looking for signs of movement. They caught sight of the books a heartbeat too late and were taken by surprise. One man hit the deck, unsure if they were being attacked. A second jerked his weapon in the direction of the flying books and opened fire, spraying a dozen shells across the rotunda.

The gunfire punched holes in the wall across from him as the books slammed against the marble floor. The echoes from both actions covered the sound of the door to the roof opening and shutting.

Silence returned as the men regrouped. Kurt noticed red dots from laser pointers dancing along the walls. He lay flat on the ground until all the targeting beams had moved to the far side of the room and then leaned out just far enough to look down. This time the silence was shattered by the report from Kurt's .45. His first shot went straight down, hitting the man at the bottom of the rotunda in the shoulder.

The body armor was weak there and the .45 caliber slug hit hard enough to crack his collarbone and drop him to the floor. He fell with a grunt of pain, which was drowned out as his colleagues opened fire.

The response was tactical. Short bursts hit each of the landings and the other sections of the empty stairwell. Kurt rolled back into the hall just as a spray of shells tore into the space he'd been occupying.

As the silence returned again, Kurt heard muffled radio sounds as the men spoke into headset-mounted mics and replies came through the tiny speakers attached behind their ears.

He couldn't tell what was being said, but standard military procedure would be to call in the second group and get at Kurt from his flank.

Kurt decided to interrupt that plan.

He fired two shots down the hall toward the east end of the rotunda and then held the gun over the railing and fired back three more shots down and around sporadically.

Hoping he'd forced the men into cover, Kurt left his position and rushed up the stairs, firing twice more as he went.

The men below spotted him. They unleashed a hail of gunfire aimed in his direction. The bullets tore into the wall above, then trailed him as he ran up in a circle. For now, the marble steps prevented them from shooting through the floor. But he couldn't keep them at bay for long.

Reaching the top landing, Kurt had achieved a small advantage. He was directly above the assailants with two full circuits of the curving stairs between himself and them. From here, he could shoot the second they appeared.

They must have realized this because they chose a wiser approach, shooting a stun grenade in his direction. It landed across from him and half a circuit down, but too close for comfort. Kurt barreled through the door and onto the roof, diving flat, just before the flashbang explosion went off.

The blast was mostly contained in the stairwell, though it blew the door halfway off its hinges.

Kurt found himself on a flat roof with spires in several places and gables jutting out over the front side of the house. Joe, Morgan and DeMars were near the back edge, releasing the anchors on a small scaffold that could be lowered over the side.

It didn't look like a fast way down. But it was better than the stairs.

The sound of pounding footsteps racing up the stairway proved that. Kurt rolled to the side and got up, pressing himself against the thin wall of the turret's crown. A boot kicked the door open and a burst of gunfire poured through.

Kurt knew what would come next, another concussion grenade, tossed to prevent someone from hiding just the way Kurt was.

Kurt counted down quickly, imagining the man pulling out another grenade from his harness, grasping it solidly, pulling its pin and then getting ready to kick the door open again. Three . . . two . . . one . . . At that exact moment, Kurt launched himself forward. His timing was impeccable.

The mercenary kicked the door open and swung his arm underhand, hoping to toss the grenade softly. To the man's utter shock, the door he'd just kicked open snapped back on him, batting the grenade back in his face.

Had he been a little faster, he could have caught it, but the best he could do was knock it down. It exploded at his feet, blinding him and sending him stumbling backward. He hit the railing and tumbled over it. His drop ended abruptly as he was impaled on Joan of Arc's triumphal banner staff.

The two surviving attackers opened fire en masse.

There would be no trickery now, this was a full-on broadside assault. All Kurt could do was run as countless bullets ricocheted off the dilapidated steel door, tore through the walls of the turret and cracked and splintered the windows in the skylight.

From the mercenaries' point of view, what had looked like an impressive use of force turned into a slow-motion catastrophe as cracks spread in all directions, causing the entire canopy to give way. Large chunks and small angular pieces of glass, accompanied by a thousand shards and splinters, rained down like knives.

They had no choice but to cover up and hope the body armor would absorb any jagged, deadly trajectories.

The glittery storm ended quickly. After waiting for one last dagger-shaped shard to fall and explode on the tile down below, Kappa got up and began to move once again.

By then, Kurt had run across the open expanse of the roof and dropped over the side onto the slowly descending platform there.

Chapter 27

Joe and Morgan were letting out the ropes on the platform as Kurt landed in between them.

"Nice of you to join us," Joe said.

"I thought you didn't want to engage in a shoot-out," DeMars said.

"Apparently, they didn't get the memo," Kurt replied. "Is this as fast as this thing goes?"

"We had to manually release the cables," Morgan said, "since the power is out."

They continued down past the fourth-floor windows and down toward the third floor. Without warning, the cable on Joe's side jammed.

"Problem," Joe said.

The descent stopped instantly, but the jarring left the platform swaying from side to side. Kurt and DeMars grasped the wall of the château and used the handholds to steady the rig while Joe tried to release his line.

"No good," Joe said. He tied off the cable. Morgan did the same on her side, leaving the platform slightly tilted.

"We need to jump," Morgan said, gauging the distance.

"It's a ten-meter drop," DeMars said. "Thirty feet."

"We can't stay here," Morgan said.

"The ground looks soft," Joe added.

"Not soft enough," Kurt said. He was looking around for another option. He found it off to the side. "Joe, can you reach that window?"

Joe saw what Kurt had in mind. On his side was a recessed window. A six-inch ledge fronted it with shutters pinned back in the open position.

Moving to the edge of the platform, Joe climbed up on the rail and stretched out a leg. "I'm a little short."

"Hang on," Kurt said.

The platform was hanging by its two cables. By pushing against the wall, Kurt got it moving from side to side. It swung right, then left, then back to the right again. As it neared the window, Joe leapt nimbly onto the narrow ledge. He immediately wedged his hands against the window's frame to keep himself steady.

"Nice landing," Kurt said. "Can you open it?"

The window was latched, but the mechanism was old and flimsy. It had been installed decades ago, and a third-floor window on the back of the house surrounded by walls and security cameras didn't warrant much attention. With a firm shove from Joe, the latch gave way and the lower sash slid upward.

Joe pushed it to its stops and climbed into the darkened room. Turning around, he held the platform and reached out to the others. "Let's get a move on," he said, offering his hand.

Morgan went first and then DeMars. After swinging the scaffolding one last time, Kurt leapt to the windowsill and climbed inside.

As Kurt moved into the room, Joe slid the window shut.

"Now what?" DeMars asked. "Do we hide?"

Kurt looked around. The room was vast and dark. In the moonlight, he could tell they'd entered a bedroom suite. It had a canopied four-poster bed off to one side, a complete living area with love seat and chairs on the other. To Kurt's right stood a full bathroom with an old clawfoot tub sitting on black and white tile. It would have been a nice place to stay had the circumstances been different, but it offered little in the way of shelter or a place to hide.

"We've bought some time," Kurt said, "but that's all. It's not going to take them long to search the roof. When they don't find us up there, they'll start looking over the side. And once they see that platform, it'll lead them right here. We have to keep moving."

Nearest to the exit, Morgan had unholstered her pistol and put an ear to the door. "I don't hear anything outside. They're probably up top looking for us. We could head for the stairs now."

Kurt considered that a last resort. "These aren't the Keystone Kops we're dealing with. They're in communication with each other, using night vision gear and military tactics. They left people guarding the stairs. Accounting for us trying to get down and out."

"What about the east stairwell?" DeMars asked.

"We have no reason to believe that's not guarded as well. As soon as they see us, we'll be swarmed. We need another option."

Morgan turned to DeMars. "Did you grow up in this house?"

"Yes," DeMars said, trying to steady a pair of trembling hands. "I was born here."

"Did you play hide-and-seek as a child?" she asked.

"Of course," he said. "We played many games as children. Why are you asking that now?"

"When I was a child," she said, "we visited my aunt, who lived in a big country house out in Somerset. Our greatest joy was using the dumb-waiter as an elevator, until we grew too big. Even then, we could still use the laundry chute as a slide. I'm hoping you did similar things here."

Despite his trembling hands, DeMars genuinely smiled. "Yes," he said. "Of course we did."

Chapter 28

Robson and his men had been left behind as the shooting began. Considering the firepower and coordination of Kappa's team, he gave their adversaries only a puncher's chance of surviving. Still, he recognized the signs of overconfidence in Kappa's approach and he wondered if that would be Kappa's demise.

When the shooting began and the grenades went off, it sounded more chaotic than controlled. But when one of Kappa's mercenaries fell from the top floor and wound up impaled on Joan of Arc's staff, he took a twisted kind of delight in the failure. The puncher had landed the first blow.

"He's underestimated them."

"Bloody hell," Gus said as the barrage went full auto and a wave of glass fell into the rotunda.

"This is going badly," Robson told his group.

"Then why are you grinning?" Snipe asked.

"What's bad for Kappa is good for us. If enough of his blokes get killed, if he fails, we get back in the driver's seat. And that ups our piece of the take."

"What do you want us to do?" Fingers asked.

"You and Gus, get back to the van. Keep your eyes sharp for any sign of trouble and be ready to get out of here. Snipe, you're with me. Let's see what we can find in this bloody mess."

Robson and Snipe moved cautiously toward the rotunda. They passed the dead mercenary and came to a halt beside Kappa's other operative who'd been shot from up above. Despite a shoulder injury, the man maintained his position. He put a hand out to stop Robson and Snipe from passing.

"My orders are to guard the stairs."

"Your numbers are dwindling," Robson said, pointing to the dead man. "Kappa might need our help up there."

More shooting erupted as Kappa and his partner forced their way out onto the roof. "Go," the injured man said with a wave.

Taking the stairs, Robson moved quickly. Without all the body armor and equipment, he and Snipe were lighter and nimbler. Arriving at the fourth floor, they paused.

Footsteps pounding on the roof told him Kappa and his men were clearing sections of the roof. It was a big job, dangerous and time-consuming.

"Shouldn't we be helping them?" Snipe asked.

"We were ordered to stay out of the way, re-member?" Robson said. "Besides, the one-eared butler said DeMars and his guests had come up here. We might as well see what they were looking at."

They took the fourth-floor landing and entered the study. Milling about, Robson absentmind-edly pulled a few books off the shelf and glanced through them. He tossed them aside and moved to the desk, where the stack of journals remained. "They must have been reading these."

He gave them to Snipe and moved on. "Bring them with us."

"This is a waste of time. Let's just help them find DeMars and get out of here. Even I know you can't shoot up a big house and set off grenades without bringing the police down on your head. We need to go."

Robson ignored Snipe for the moment, but he was absolutely right. This operation had taken too long already. He glanced around, looking for anything else of importance. His eyes fell on a large atlas that had been laid down on another table and opened.

A magnifying glass rested on the page. Robson picked it up and peered through it, feeling like a silly Sherlock Holmes. And yet it revealed some-thing to him, something he soon realized was important. "I don't think we're going to need DeMars after all."

He studied the notes and the dates on the page. It was a narrow river valley in Spain. A town had been circled. The name rewritten in ink beside it. It had to be.

Robson ripped the page out of the atlas, closed the book and turned back to Snipe. "Time to go."

Up on the roof, Kappa and his men had cleared the spires and turrets and worked their way to the center, meeting in the middle. "We've covered every inch of the place," one of the men said. "They're not here."

"They didn't grow wings and fly away," Kappa insisted. "Keep looking."

"Over here," another of the men shouted.

Kappa jogged to the edge of the roof and looked down. A painter's scaffolding hung next to the wall. "What floor is that?"

"I'd say third," the man who found it estimated. "Back side of the house. Dead center."

"From both sides," Kappa said. "I want no mistakes this time."

The groups divided once more and backtracked to the individual turrets. Rushing down the stairs to the third floor, they slowed as they entered the hallway, moving quietly along the carpeted corridor.

Kappa pointed to a pair of doors aligned roughly with the center of the house. Readying his weapon, he silently counted down with his fingers. When he curled his index finger into his fist, two of his men kicked the doors open simultaneously.

Concussion grenades were tossed inside, with the mercenaries turning away and closing their eyes as the flashes went off. In the aftermath of the explosions, they rushed in, quickly covering every section of the room.

"No sign of them," the team leader reported.

Kappa's blood began to boil.

"We're way off schedule," one of his men said. "Five minutes over and counting. Every minute we stay makes it less likely for a safe departure."

"You think I don't know that?" Kappa snapped. "We cannot return to Barlow and tell him we've failed.

"Spread out and check every room," he said. "Stay on the radios. Any sign of them, call out. The sooner you find them, the sooner we leave."

Chapter 29

Kurt heard the commotion from inside a dark, vertical tunnel. He was suspended with his arms and legs spread outward in an X formation, each palm pressed firmly against a smooth wall, each booted foot wedged tight in an effort to defy gravity.

Below him, Joe was holding fast in similar fashion. Farther down, Morgan and DeMars had already reached the bottom of the tunnel, where a large hopper of unfolded laundry caught them.

The sound of Kappa shouting at his men carried through the wall and into the chute. He was yelling at his men, ordering them about. The stress in his voice was obvious. It brought a smile to Kurt's face. "We're getting to them."

"As long as they don't get to us," Joe whispered back.

Kurt doubted they'd be found. The door to

the laundry chute was hidden behind a panel that looked exactly like the rest of the wall, the wainscoting and wallpaper matching identically. Even DeMars had found the opening difficult to locate.

Outside, the argument ended and the mercenaries fanned out. Kurt heard the angry soldiers starting to lose their discipline. Their boots pounded the floorboards as they went from room to room. Furniture was noisily shoved aside and flipped over, belongings smashed. They'd given up any pretense of stealth and were now acting like a marauding army.

The noise only made it easier to escape. "Slide down," Kurt said.

Joe began to move, sliding a bit, stopping and then picking up speed over the last several feet until he dropped into the pile of sheets and overstuffed down comforters.

Kurt came down in a more controlled fashion, landing beside Joe.

Down in the basement, it was pitch-black. Kurt pulled out his phone, allowing the glow from the screen to illuminate the laundry room. "Excellent idea," he said. "Brilliant, in your English vernacular."

"Earlier, I saw the maid carrying a bundle of sheets," Morgan said. "She went down the hall with them and came back with nothing in her arms. I assumed she wasn't tossing them out a window. My biggest worry was whether we'd fit."

"Mine as well," DeMars said. "I was nine years old the last time I slid down this chute. Never thought I'd be repeating my escapades as an adult."

"I'm just glad there was laundry in the hopper," Joe said, looking comfortable amid the pile. "What's next? Underground tunnel to the forest?"

Kurt climbed from the basket and looked at DeMars. "I don't suppose you have one."

DeMars shook his head. "Sorry, nothing like that."

"What do you propose we do?" Morgan asked.

"They're still looking for us upstairs," Kurt said. "But they'll work their way down eventually. Before they get here, we should surprise them. Rising up like phantoms in their midst."

"The ground floor is the last place they'd expect us," Joe said.

"And that's exactly where we'll be."

Chapter 30

Under the light of Kurt's phone, DeMars drew a rough map of the basement. "You can take the servants' stairs from the pantry to the kitchen and then move through the scullery to the servants' hall, which connects directly to the east rotunda."

"Won't they see us?" Kurt asked.

"No," DeMars said confidently. "The servants' hall is back of the house. It runs behind the main wall."

"That's handy," Morgan said.

DeMars nodded. "When this home was built, the lords and ladies of the day wanted the servants to keep out of sight. Halls like this were common. They allowed cleanup and food service to happen without the two classes bumping into each other as they moved about. When you get to the formal dining room, you'll exit through a hidden door. It's designed to look like part of the wall, just like the opening to the laundry chute. From in there you'll be almost directly across from the stairs. You should have no problem taking them by surprise."

"Okay," Kurt said. "Joe and I will go. You and Morgan stay here and—"

"Not a chance," Morgan said.

Kurt wasn't having it. "If they get the jump on us, you're the last line of defense for DeMars. Besides, if things go sideways, Joe and I might need you to rescue us."

"Again," she added.

"What?"

"Rescue you again."

"Right," Kurt said. "Thanks for reminding me."

"Fine," she said. "I'll stay here. But I can't promise you for how long."

Kurt and Joe moved to the door, sliding it open and ducking out into the hall. With no lights, they had to feel their way along the wall. The stairs were where DeMars had promised and they climbed them to the kitchen.

Emerging into the open room, Kurt was surprised how easily he could make out the confines. By now their eyes had become so used to the dark that the filtered moonlight coming through the windows was enough to navigate by.

"Must be all those carrots I've been eating," Joe said.

They passed through the large kitchen and found the servants' hall. Even after hearing DeMars's description, Kurt was surprised at how narrow the winding passage really was. "How did they carry trays of food through here?"

"Carefully," Joe replied.

Kurt grinned and continued until they found the door. He eased it just wide enough to look out.

He'd been expecting Joan of Arc, but they were on the opposite side of the house. Here, a bust of Napoléon took center stage. The General, depicted in his classic bicorne hat, was staring directly at them from a marble pedestal in the center of the rotunda. The man assigned to guard the stairs crouched beside it, but he was looking upward.

Kurt saw DeMars's butler sitting against the wall nearby. His hands and feet were bound, his mouth gagged. And his face, neck and white shirt soaked with blood.

"Is he alive?" Joe whispered.

The butler's head had lolled over to one side. "Can't tell," Kurt said. "That's a lot of blood. Even if he is alive, he won't last much longer without medical attention."

Switching his attention to the mercenary, Kurt focused like a wolf in the forest targeting a kill. The man had a hand pressed to his ear. He was listening to the radio traffic as his teammates cleared the rooms above. His eyes worked in precise fashion. Scanning the stairs, then checking the hall, then glancing at the doorway to his right and then back to the stairs. A Heckler & Koch SP5K machine pistol rested in his hands ready to use. The weapon fired 9mm ammo and normally operated on semi-automatic mode, but after what Kurt had experienced upstairs he assumed this and the other weapons had all been modified to fire on full automatic.

One shot would have to do.

Kurt pressed his foot against the base of the door. With his hands free, he leveled the .45, holding it with a two-handed grip, exhaled calmly and pulled the trigger. The shot hit Kappa's mercenary in the face, shattering the night vision goggles and killing the man instantly. He slumped without uttering a sound.

"One down," Kurt said.

If Kurt had been in possession of a silencer, no one would have noticed. But the report echoed. No one came. In the shadow of that delayed reaction, Kurt and Joe rushed forward. Kurt went to the mercenary and took his gear while Joe ran to the injured butler and dragged him back to the servants' hall.

Kurt ducked in behind him and closed the door. Hidden once again, Joe checked the injured man for signs of life.

"He's hanging on," Joe said. "Looks like they cut off his ear. With his hands bound, he couldn't even stanch the bleeding."

"We need to chase them out of here and call for help," Kurt said.

As Joe wrapped the wound, Kurt picked through the mercenary's equipment. He'd needed to fire the lethal shot but now regretted destroying the night vision goggles.

Clipping the mercenary's radio to his belt and putting the headset over his ears, Kurt listened in on the chatter. He heard orders from Kappa and each member of the team checking in. They were waiting for the dead man to respond. When he didn't answer, they knew where the shot had been fired.

"They're coming," Kurt said. "Let's be ready."

He cracked the door a centimeter and put one eye to the gap. Someone was racing down the stairs. His approach slowed when the man saw his associate sprawled out and the butler gone. He stopped half a flight up and got on the radio.

"Gunther's dead. The butler is missing."

Kurt watched the man as he looked around in confusion. There was a jerky panic to his motions. Fear was creeping in as the hunter realized he'd become the hunted.

Another man joined him and then a third came running along the ground floor. They gathered beside Napoléon's bust, one on each side of the General.

Kurt yanked one of the concussion grenades he'd taken off the dead mercenary. He pulled the pin, waited a second and then flung it out toward them. It hit the floor, skipped and exploded directly in front of the three men.

The concussion grenade did its job, blasting the men backward and knocking them into states of delirium if not complete unconsciousness.

With the men on the ground, Kurt and Joe rushed forward, securing the men's weapons and ripping off their goggles. As the mercenaries regained their senses, one man went for a safety pistol hidden in his pant leg.

Joe spotted him. "Look out!"

Kurt turned and kicked the gun away, but another man went for a knife. Joe blasted the man's hand at point-blank range. A scream ended the rebellion, but the shooting was just getting started.

Without warning, gunfire rained down from above. Kurt and Joe dove out of the way. The mercenaries left behind took several hits. One was shot as he tried to crawl out of the way.

"They're shooting their own," Joe said.

"Dead men tell no tales," Kurt replied.

When the gunfire ended, all three men at the bottom of the stairs lay dead.

More gunfire upstairs ended with the sound of shattering glass.

Over the radio Kurt heard someone shouting, "Jump!" and then, "Get to the van!"

"They're making a run for it," Kurt said.

He pushed out into the main hall and took off

running for the foyer. At the main entrance, he rushed outside onto the driveway.

Kurt was too late. The smaller van was already speeding down the driveway while the larger van had just peeled out from the side of the château and was gathering speed.

There was no chance to follow. And, in truth, it was best just to let them go. After clearing the ground floor and linking up with Morgan and DeMars, they flipped the breakers, got the lights back on and discovered the jamming transmitter, which was immediately switched off.

With the cell phone signal restored, DeMars called the Sûreté and the Gendarmerie Nationale. An air ambulance arrived and took his injured valet to a hospital in Toulouse. But the men on his security team had all been killed.

"These men are savages," DeMars said.

"They come from a savage world," Kurt said. "Arms merchants selling death."

"Which is exactly what we're trying to stop," Morgan added.

DeMars seemed almost overcome. He fought to regain his composure and then presented his grandfather's journal to Kurt. "I've written the name of the town inside. Good luck with your search."

Chapter 31

Villa Ducal de Lerma, Spain, population 532

Paul and Gamay Trout arrived in Villa Ducal de Lerma after a long flight from Washington to Madrid and a three-hour car ride through the mountainous region of central Spain. The last hour took them on rutted dirt roads through an area of the country where the population had been dwindling since the '50s when everyone left the hill country and moved to the metropolitan areas.

The open land was both beautiful and desolate, with rolling hills and long-abandoned farmhouses and tumbled-down stone walls waiting quietly for someone to return and bring them back to life. After miles of such forlorn scenery, arriving in Lerma felt like returning to civilization from the great unknown.

"Look," Paul said. "A shining metropolis."

Ahead of them lay a collection of standing stone

walls, cobblestone streets and quaint wooden buildings with stucco-covered walls.

"Not sure I'm ready for the crowds," Gamay replied with a wink.

Paul and Gamay had been together since grad school, dating while attending classes and getting married shortly after graduation. They'd joined NUMA on the same day, being hired together, though Gamay always insisted she had seniority as her employee ID number was one lower than Paul's.

Since then, they'd traveled the world on various expeditions and adventures, making up a one-two punch of scientific knowledge, with Gamay's background in marine biology complementing Paul's expertise in ocean sciences and geology.

Equally at home in the field and the lab, they traveled well together, even when those travels took them to places with difficult working conditions.

Stepping out of the car into the cool, dry air of Villa Ducal de Lerma, Gamay sensed this trip would be less difficult than most. She stretched, shook out her dark red hair, which had been tucked under a cap, and took a deep breath. "The air is so clean."

Paul unfolded himself from the passenger seat. He was six foot eight. Traveling in what passed for a large SUV in Spain was a tight fit for him. He looked around. "I think I can see the whole town from here."

"It's that high vantage point of yours."

"Unfortunately, I don't see a tourist office."

Gamay laughed. "We're probably the first tourists to come here in years," she said. "Any word from Kurt and Joe?"

Paul checked his phone. "The last message says they're still dealing with law enforcement officials in France and won't be here until this afternoon."

"That's what they get for shooting up a luxurious home in the wine country," Gamay said. "Let's see how much we can get done before they arrive."

Locking the car and walking down a quiet dirt road, they saw only a few locals, all of whom kept to themselves. Admiring the beauty of the hills and the architecture of the old buildings, Gamay felt like she was on vacation. "We lucked out on this assignment," she said. "Remember when we were in Alaska two summers ago? And the mosquitoes reached levels of biblical proportions?"

"How could I forget?" Paul said. "I was down two liters of O positive by the time we got home. Not sure which was worse, that trip or six weeks in Antarctica in the middle of winter, all because Kurt and Rudi wanted us to study that subsurface lake. I'm still wondering what we did wrong to make them send us there."

Gamay smiled at the memory. It had been oddly romantic for her. "The two of us in an ice cave for six weeks. I enjoyed that one."

Paul laughed. "You know you have a strong marriage when you can survive for six weeks without a shower."

Gamay couldn't help but laugh. Perhaps she'd blocked that part out. "Maybe this is our reward for those other trips. I mean, when have we ever been given an expense account for buying shoes and dining at fine restaurants?"

"I don't recall anything about shoes in our instructions."

"We were told to blend in," she said. "That means shopping for shoes, along with eating tapas, drinking sangria and dancing lots."

Paul just beamed. His wife's effervescent personality was irrepressible. They knew it was a serious assignment and they'd been well briefed about the Bloodstone Group and the danger it presented. They didn't expect to find any members of the group in Lerma, but they'd been instructed to be cautious.

And, as Paul knew, none of that would interfere with Gamay Trout enjoying herself.

A small library in the center of town was their first stop. A town newspaper had been printed there for fifty years—little more than a leaflet—which, of course, didn't go back far enough to account for a plane crash in 1927.

Their second stop was a town courthouse, which was also the post office, the mayor's office—he wasn't there—and the archive of various town records. Most of what they found related to land transfers, political appointments and old legal decrees. They found nothing suggesting anyone knew about a plane crash, the **Writings of Qsn** or the short and fateful visit of Francisco DeMars's grandfather.

"We're striking out," Paul said. "And I'm famished. Time for tapas. Lots of them."

"This is why I married you," Gamay said.

They found a small café, but arrived just after noon.

The old woman who ran the place was happy to serve them. And though she didn't speak English, she listened politely as Gamay attempted to converse in Spanish, using what she remembered from high school mixed with the translation program on her cell phone. Eventually, the woman just nodded and walked away.

Gamay looked at Paul. "What do you think?"

"Either you ordered lunch or you told them you'd like to buy the place in an all-cash offer."

"Don't think our expense account is going to cover that," Gamay replied.

As she looked back at her phone, studying the translation once more, a smaller figure walked up to the table carrying two large glasses of sangria. She was a tiny thing who Gamay estimated could be no more than ten.

"Hello," the little girl said in well-practiced English. "My name is Sofia. My aunt says you're Americans. She told me Americans aren't allowed to learn other languages."

"That's not quite true," Gamay said. "But—"

"It's okay," Sofia said. "I'm learning English and American so I can work in Madrid when I grow up and then we can travel to the Big Apple."

"New York?"

"Yes, I want to go there too."

Paul had to laugh. "We should really enroll in a language class or two."

"The minute we get home," Gamay said.

She gave Sofia their names and requested two plates of croquetas de jamón—ham croquettes—and patatas bravas, a dish translated as **fierce potatoes,** a name taken from the tabasco sauce covering the fried slices.

As Sofia took their requests to the kitchen, Gamay tasted the sangria. The local fruit was especially ripe by the end of the summer. It gave the beverage a perfect sweetness. "Delicious," she said. "Now I know why they serve this in such large glasses. I still might finish this before our food arrives."

Paul took a drink and nodded in agreement.

With their taste buds invigorated and their thirst partially quenched, they planned out their next steps. "We're batting zero so far. We need to raise our game. How do we find a plane that went down a century ago if there's no record of where it went down?"

"Even Hiram can't find it with the satellites," Paul said. "We'd be better off looking for something that would be marked. Like the grave of the pilot."

"How's that going to help us?"

"Kurt said the pilot was buried near where the old men found him. Hopefully, he hadn't walked too far from where the plane went down."

"And he did have a broken leg," Gamay agreed. "So if we find the grave, it will put us in the general vicinity of the plane. I think that sangria has already sharpened up your mind."

"Not sure about that," Paul said, "but I'm willing to test the theory."

"The question is, how do we find the grave?" Gamay asked. "It was 1927. There's not likely to be anyone around here who was part of the burial crew."

"No," Paul said. "But Spain is a very religious country. Back in the twenties it was even more devout. Every small town had a priest and a church, even if it had precious little else. We saw a nice church on the outskirts of town when we drove in. DeMars even mentioned it in his notes. San Sebastián de las Montañas."

"How will going there help?"

"A dying man in a Catholic region most

certainly received last rites before he passed away," Paul said. "Once word filtered back that a man was dying farther up the river, a priest would have rushed out to administer the sacrament. Record of that, along with some commemoration of the gravesite, might well be kept in the church's records. They usually recorded births, marriages and deaths."

"The big three," she said. "Great idea. Let's visit the church as soon as we're done eating."

Chapter 32

San Sebastián de las Montañas, Villa Ducal
de Lerma, Spain

Paul and Gamay arrived at the church accompanied by Sofia and the woman who ran the café. They found it to be an architectural gem. Despite its age, it was well cared for. It had a classic Spanish façade, with a majestic bell tower up high and an arched doorway directly beneath. The walls had been built from local stone, cut and shaped by artisans brought in from Madrid in the seventeenth century. Their fine work had weathered and aged, leaving it gently discolored in places, but it remained sturdy, with the blocks fitting together snugly.

A courtyard in front of the church was shaded by a large almond tree and graced by a trickling fountain filled with water that sparkled in the midafternoon sun. To one side of the building lay a garden with lush trees and vibrant flowering plants. A man in overalls was tending a beautiful red bougainvillea that climbed an arched trellis.

Entering the church, Sofia and her aunt touched their fingers to a bowl of holy water and blessed themselves. They proceeded to the front, where they genuflected and offered silent prayers.

Paul and Gamay stood quietly in the back, turning as the man in the overalls came in from the garden.

Sofia saw him first. "Father Torres," she said, running back.

He crouched down and picked her up and gave her a hug and then spoke briefly to her aunt in Spanish.

As he put Sofia down, she introduced Paul and Gamay.

"These are my friends from America," Sofia said.

"Glad to be counted as friends," Gamay said, giving the priest their names.

Fortunately for them, Father Torres spoke excellent English. "It is always good to have visitors," he said. "Welcome to San Sebastián de las Montañas."

"Thank you," Paul said.

"Since we're in a church," Gamay added, "I want to make it clear for the record that we've only just met Sofia and her aunt. We don't want to proceed under false pretenses."

Father Torres laughed. "You have nothing to worry about," he said. "In truth, Sofia has never met someone who was not a friend."

Gamay laughed. "Good to know. It's a beautiful church."

"Not to mention a beautiful garden," Paul added.

"I am only responsible for the upkeep of the church," Father Torres said. "But at the risk of sinning, the garden is something I take great pride in. I find working with the soil most satisfying. If we can coax something to life from the earth, we are doing our best to imitate our Holy Father . . . Now, what may I do for you?"

Paul looked to Gamay. She was far better with words than he.

"We're looking for the records of someone who may have been buried in the area."

"We keep meticulous records," the priest said. "Thankfully, we have performed few burials in my time."

"Well," Gamay said, "this one wouldn't be a recent. We're looking for information on a man who died in 1927."

"That is a long time ago," Father Torres said, "but the records go back centuries. What was his name?"

"We don't know," Gamay said.

"How about the date of his passing?"

"We're not sure of that either," she said. "It would have been sometime during May of 1927."

Father Torres nodded. "There were more people living here in those days than there are now. The silver mine was still open. That said, there couldn't have been too many burials in a single month. Let's take a look and see what turns up."

"The thing is," Gamay added, "he was a pilot. His plane crashed nearby. And he wasn't buried here in town. He was buried somewhere upriver."

Father Torres nodded thoughtfully. "Very interesting," he said. "May I ask what you seek in regard to this man?"

Gamay hesitated. "Honestly, we're not looking for the man himself. It's his airplane we'd like to find. We believe there may be something of great historical interest in the wreckage."

"Ah," Father Torres said. "And when you say great historical interest, you really mean great monetary value."

Gamay blushed. "I wasn't trying to mislead you, I just . . ."

Paul had to look away or he'd have burst out laughing. Never had he seen Gamay so mortified. Meanwhile, Father Torres gazed at her with a stern face. He was young, no older than Gamay, but he pulled it off quite well. Still, there was something in the look that suggested it was too practiced, too over-the-top, to be serious.

A smile broke the façade. "Forgive me," he said. "I listen to many confessions. The story always starts with the mildest version of what happened. And so I've gotten used to the code words people use and the ways in which we all try to skirt the truth. It's become a game of mine to let the people know that I know what they're trying so hard not to say."

"It **is** of great historical interest," Gamay insisted. "And while it could be worth an enormous amount of money, that's not why we're looking for it."

"Tell the truth," Paul added. "Confession is good for the soul."

He tried to put his arm around Gamay, but she shrugged him off. "If you don't watch out, I'm going to have something more serious to confess soon."

This time Paul couldn't help but laugh. Gamay was at her most beautiful during the rare times when she was flustered.

Father Torres laughed as well. "Please, come this way. I'll show you what I showed the others."

Gamay took a step to follow and then froze as the word hit her. "Others?"

"Yes," the priest said. "Two men from an English university came here this morning. They asked the very same questions. They also did not admit to seeking anything of monetary value. But they had a feverish gleam in their eyes."

Paul and Gamay exchanged concerned glances. Father Torres noticed. "You seem worried."

"I don't think you have anything to fear here in the village," Gamay suggested. "But it's safe to say those men weren't from any university."

Chapter 33

Villa Ducal de Lerma, Spain

Kurt, Joe and Morgan reached Lerma by midafternoon and quickly found their way to the church. They discovered Paul and Gamay waiting with five saddled horses.

After introducing Morgan, Kurt pointed at the horses. "Have you two become caballeros in your free time?"

"Around here they're called **yegüerizos,**" Gamay corrected. "And, yes, since horses are the only way to get to the crash site."

"You know where it is?" Morgan said excitedly.

"We've got a pretty good idea," Paul said.

"How'd you find it?" Joe asked.

Gamay explained the discovery. "While you three were entertaining the French National Police, we spent our time learning from the local historians. Turns out the church records noted the burial of an unknown pilot whose plane crashed in the riverbed. The wreck is still out there. Some of the older citizens of the town recall seeing it, though it's mostly buried in the sand now."

Kurt glanced off to the north and the rising terrain. "How far?"

"About fifteen miles from here," Gamay said. "It's in a side canyon near an area called Falcon Point."

"We're told it's a rough hike," Paul added. "Not one you'd want to make on foot."

"What about ATVs?" Joe asked, eyeing the horses suspiciously.

Paul shook his head. "I already checked. This horsepower is the only form of all-terrain transport that will get us through. However," he added, "saddle sores won't be our only worry. According to Father Torres, a pair of men arrived here this morning asking him the exact same questions we did."

Kurt cocked his head to the side. "Did I hear you right?"

Paul nodded.

"Who were these men?" Morgan asked.

"They only gave Father Torres first names," Gamay said. "They claimed to be from Oxford, but Father Torres thought they looked more like military men. They had buzz cuts and bodies that looked like they spent plenty of time in the gym."

"Barlow's men," Morgan suggested. "Might even be the same crew that hit us in France."

Kurt agreed with that assessment. They certainly sounded more like the intruders from the château than the scruffy-looking hoods who'd attacked them at Cambridge.

Joe spoke next. "What I don't get is, how do they know about this place at all? We just found out about it last night."

"They must have found something in the château," Kurt replied. He turned back to Gamay. "How much of a lead do they have?"

"Four or five hours," she replied. "We don't know exactly when they left, but a rancher who lives at the edge of town came by this morning to warn everyone about the men who took several horses and a mule from his property. The description of the men matches up."

"He's lucky to be alive," Morgan said. "Barlow's people don't leave a lot of witnesses around."

Kurt summed things up. "Five hours is a long lead," he said, "but they still have to find the plane, excavate it, recover what they're looking for and then come back down the riverbed. If we hurry, we can surprise them."

With no time to waste, they mounted up and rode off, traveling into the winding bed of the river as it ran north from Lerma. For two hours they moved without a break. The first part of the journey was easy as the horses walked alongside the river, but halfway to Falcon Point the ground began to rise. The horses took the grade easily, managing to carry their riders up rocky slopes that no wheeled vehicle could possibly scale.

Beyond the steep sections they came to flatter ground once again. Here and there, the trickling waters of the stream became trapped behind natural dams in the landscape. As the water backed up, it formed a series of ponds and lakes, each of them surrounded by tall green grasses. The lakes were still, their surfaces reflecting the sky in mirror-like fashion, each of them a Spanish-style oasis.

An hour beyond the last lake, they finally came to a section of river with vertical cliffs on either side and a towering rock that had split off from the rest of the canyon. Beyond it lay a branch in the riverbed.

"This is Falcon Point," Paul said. He was navigating from a map they'd been given, double-checking their progress on a handheld GPS display. "Father Torres said the crash site is near here, in that side canyon."

A hundred yards ahead of them, a gap on the left led away from the river. It cut into the higher terrain and was surrounded by cliffs.

"Looks like a great place for an ambush," Joe said. He looked awkward on his horse.

"We know they're ahead of us," Kurt pointed out, "but they don't know we're coming. All the same, let's keep out of sight."

"Who would land a plane back there?" Gamay asked.

"Only someone who didn't have much choice," Kurt replied. "How far back to the crash site?"

"No more than a mile," Paul said.

Kurt looked at Joe and Morgan. Things were about to get interesting. He pointed to a shaded area fifty yards back. "Paul," he said. "You and Gamay tie the horses up over there and stand by. Joe, Morgan and I will go on foot. Watch the horses and be alert to any trouble."

If Kurt expected a protest, he didn't get one. "I don't mind staying behind," Gamay said. "But what, exactly, are you going to do?"

"Clearly, you haven't seen enough Westerns," Kurt said. "We're going to sneak up on them, pull our guns and tell them to reach for the sky."

Chapter 34

"There they are," Kurt said, looking through a pair of compact binoculars.

Kurt, Joe and Morgan had hiked past Falcon Point and into the side canyon. They'd kept to the shadows until they reached a boulder field, where the canyon's wall on one side had collapsed sometime in the last century. Kurt imagined it calving from the rock behind it like an iceberg from a glacier, shattering into a thousand pieces as it crashed to the ground.

The mammoth chunks now sat jumbled and piled on one another. Using this terrain as cover, they crept within a hundred yards of the wreck site before halting.

They lay there, flat atop a truck-sized boulder, peering over the edge, studying the men who'd already found the plane and begun excavating it.

"I count four of them," Kurt said. He saw

shovels and plastic water bottles strewn about. He saw rifles propped against a rock. Most importantly, he saw that the old aircraft was almost completely unearthed. "They've made good use of their time."

A deep trench had been dug alongside the fuselage, while another, like a sand trap on a golf course, had been dug underneath the tail. Smaller depressions had been excavated beneath each wing, exposing the engines and the stubs of the propellers, which had broken off in the crash.

He handed the binoculars to Morgan. "Definitely Barlow's people," she said. "I recognize the man in the middle. He's a mercenary named Kappa."

"What about the others?"

"No one stands out," she said. "But they're all cut from the same cloth."

She handed the binoculars to Joe, who noticed a serious lack of energy in the group. "Too bad they're not working at the moment," he said. "It would be a lot easier to sneak up on them if they were still digging with their backs to us."

"Maybe they're taking a break," Kurt said.

Joe watched as one man tilted a bottle up high, attempting to get every last drop of water from it, before tossing it aside. A second man was stretched out on the ground in the shade. The third man stood beside Kappa, who had a radio in his hands.

At their feet was a red nylon duffel bag with two straps for handles.

"Not break time," Joe said, "quitting time. Take a look at the bag. Ten will get you twenty that it's filled with the stone fragments we came here to find."

Kurt took the binoculars back and trained them on the duffel. He watched as the biggest member of the crew heaved it from the ground and over his shoulder and carried it to higher terrain. The bag's straps tensed with the load and after hauling it about twenty yards the big man laid it down and rubbed his shoulder.

Looking around, Kurt spotted the horses and the mule. They were tied up to a twisted canyon oak about forty feet downslope from where the men stood. The horses were chewing on the oak's leaves. The mule stood by like a statue.

"We could ambush them when they ride out," Morgan suggested.

Kurt focused on the man whom Morgan had called Kappa. He was shielding his eyes from the sun as he gazed into the distance. "They're not riding out," Kurt said, "they're flying. And, by the look of it, they're expecting to make a departure any minute now."

Morgan looked at the setup. The duffel bag had been dragged to roughly the center of the narrow canyon. The walls on either side were no more than fifty feet away. Their sheer cliffs rose two hundred feet, widening slightly near the top. She turned to Joe. "Would you fly a helicopter into this?"

"Nope," Joe said. "But they could always drop a bucket," he added, suggesting the only sane method of airlifting something out of the narrow gorge.

Kurt tilted his head and listened, picking up the unmistakable sound of an approaching helicopter. It was hollow and distant at first, the sound waves echoing off the walls in a ghostly manner, but it grew stronger with each passing second.

"Sounds like their ride is here," Joe said. "We need to hurry if we're going to delay their departure."

Chapter 35

Aircraft wreck site, Falcon Point

Kappa listened as the helicopter approached. He was tired, covered in sweat from excavating the plane, and sore from head to toe. When he called the extraction team, he let it show. "It's about time," he said, holding down the TALK switch on his radio. "We've been out here all day. We're tired of waiting."

"We've had some trouble finding you. The directions were very poor."

Kappa recognized Robson's voice as it came through the small speaker. Not a word of the apology sounded remotely sincere.

"We'll be overhead in a moment. Get your men ready."

"We're ready now," Kappa snapped.

Despite the fact that Robson had discovered the link to the aircraft and the wreck's location near San Sebastián, it was Kappa who'd been given the job of traveling here and digging the ancient plane out of the ground.

A booby prize, if ever Kappa had heard of one.

Still, it would all be worth it if he could personally hand the hieroglyphics-covered stones to Barlow.

Kappa pulled the radio away from his face and whistled to his men. "Let's go."

The others were tired and sore as well, but the arrival of the extraction team gave them some energy. They jumped to their feet and gathered around Kappa, gazing upward, waiting for the helicopter to appear.

When it finally showed up, it moved cautiously into position, adjusting its heading for the breeze and then holding station almost directly above them.

"Finally," one of the men said.

"We're not out of the woods yet," Kappa said. He raised the walkie-talkie. "You're in position. Lower the stretcher."

The side door of the helicopter slid open and locked. Kappa saw Robson swinging a rescue basket into place. The basket, in fact, was a thin, rectangular stretcher. It dropped toward them on a metal cable. Despite a secondary guideline to prevent the stretcher from spinning, it rocked back and forth in the downwash from the helicopter, twisting as it descended.

"It's going to be a bumpy ride up," someone said.

Kappa knew it would take at least two trips to haul himself and the stone-filled duffel bag and then the rest of his men up to the helicopter. Probably three. He was eager to get started. He pressed the TALK switch on the radio. "You're a little off to the west side. Straighten up and keep it coming."

The response couldn't have been more surprising. Robson's voice sounded panicked. "Kappa, you have targets approaching. Three intruders, forty meters from your position."

Kappa's first thought was that Robson was playing a juvenile trick on him, trying to get him to flinch, but then one of his men spotted movement and opened fire. Return fire came thundering back and Kappa dove for cover just as all hell broke loose.

Chapter 36

Kurt, Joe and Morgan had made it halfway to the wreck site before being spotted from the helicopter. Keeping his eyes on Kappa as they approached, Kurt noticed the sudden tension in his face as the radio warning came in. He knew instantly.

"Get down," he shouted.

Joe and Morgan heard the warning and scattered, finding safety just as Kappa's men began peppering the canyon with automatic weapons fire.

"I knew the peace and quiet was too good to last," Joe shouted, firing back.

Kurt surveyed the battlefield. With the chopper hovering overhead and the rescue basket nearing the ground, Kappa and his men had dropped into protected positions and were firing downhill at them. Kurt chose to look on the bright side. "The good news is, they can't load up without taking their eyes off us."

Morgan saw it the other way. "The bad news is, we can't move anywhere until they do just that."

"I've got worse news for the both of you," Joe said. "There are four of them. They can divide and conquer, with two of them pinning us down and two of them loading the stones into the basket."

"Pessimists," Kurt said. "I'm working with pessimists."

Kurt moved from one covered spot to another in order to get a better view of the terrain. He saw Kappa reaching for the swaying stretcher while his men poured on the fire.

From the tiny explosions of dirt kicked up by the flying bullets, Kurt could tell that Joe and Morgan had been targeted. Taking advantage of that, he moved into a firing position, sighted the most lethally armed of Kappa's men and pulled the trigger on his .45 caliber Colt 1911.

The man jerked to the side as Kurt's shot hit home. He fell, losing his grip on his rifle as he hit the ground.

Kurt ducked back behind a pile of rocks as the gunfire swung in his direction. Several near misses whistled past, others skipped off the granite around them.

Needing a new position, Kurt dropped flat to

the ground and army-crawled to where Joe and Morgan had taken cover. They were near the center of the gorge with their backs to a fallen tree that stretched across the dry riverbed. Its bark was long gone, its trunk bleached white from the sun, but it was thick enough and solid enough to keep the bullets away.

Morgan glanced at the helicopter. "We'll be in real trouble if someone starts shooting from the door of that thing. It's not a great angle, but I'd be happier if that helicopter was out of the fight."

Joe shook his head. "If we bring that thing down in this small of a space, we'll end up doused with burning jet fuel and riddled with shrapnel."

"Forget about the helicopter," Kurt said. "If they had a sniper, he'd be firing at us already. Considering they're planning to fly four men and several hundred pounds of rock out of here, they wouldn't come in with extra men on board. Two pilots and one crewman—tops. That means they have their hands full working the basket and keeping the chopper in place. Our best bet is to take out Kappa and the rest of the ground crew. If we do that, the pilot of that bird will turn tail and run."

Morgan pulled a small disk from her pocket.

"Top secret spy gadget?" Joe asked hopefully.

"Not exactly." With a flip of her thumb,

Morgan opened the disk, revealing a reservoir of makeup in the bottom section and a circular mirror in the top.

"This is no time for a touch-up," Kurt joked.

"A woman has to look her best," Morgan said, "and see her best."

She held the compact up, using the mirror like a periscope, studying their foes without exposing herself to gunfire. "They're still up on the flat area. Kappa's in the middle. He's got one guy on either side of him. Looks like he's going for the duffel bag."

Before she could confirm that, a well-aimed shot took the compact out of her grasp. She shook her hand and rubbed her fingers. "That cost fifty pounds at Marks & Spencer."

"We need to move," Kurt said.

"Considering one of them just shot a three-inch disk out of my hand, I vote against a frontal assault," Morgan said.

"I second that," Joe said.

Kurt's vote made it unanimous, but he had another plan. "You ever get hit with a ricocheting bullet?"

"Yes," Joe said. "Hurts bad enough. But it's not going to put anyone out of action."

"Turns you around, though." The gleam in Kurt's eye was unmistakable. He pointed to the canyon walls. They were flat, smooth granite, with no more than a foot of debris piled in a slope at the bottom.

"That it does," Joe agreed.

"Are you two trying to hit these men with bank shots?" Morgan asked.

Kurt nodded. "And when we do, they'll think we've flanked them. They'll adjust their aim to either side, leaving you open to fire right down the middle."

Morgan marveled at how casually Kurt threw out the idea. "Tell me you have another idea."

"We could let them get away."

She laughed at that. "Frontal assault it is. Just say when."

Knowing the helicopter was directly above the men, Kurt gauged their position by its shadow. Easing back from the fallen tree and sliding over to get the proper angle, he raised his Colt and took aim.

At the other end of the tree, Joe was easing into his own firing position. A nod from him told Kurt he was ready.

Leaning out to the side, Kurt opened fire, watching sparks light up the canyon wall as the shells caromed off it and toward the men beneath the helicopter.

He could hear Joe's 9mm being discharged in the opposite direction. When a barrage of return fire lit into either side of the canyon, well wide of

Kurt's current position, he knew they'd pulled it off. "Now!"

Morgan popped up, steadying her arms on the fallen tree and sighting Kappa's men. In cold repose, she pulled the trigger rapidly. Three quick shots felled the mercenary on Kappa's left, four more discharged the man on Kappa's right. They went down—and stayed down—but by the time she zeroed in on Kappa, he'd jumped onto the rescue basket and was lying flat behind the duffel bag, using it as a shield.

She fired at him anyway, but the stone-filled bag acted like a wall of armor. The bullets pinged off it.

"They've loaded the stones on the stretcher," she called out. "Kappa's riding up with it."

Not only were Kappa and the duffel riding up, the helicopter was moving. It had quit its hovering position and was accelerating down the throat of the canyon and out toward the main branch of the river.

Kurt saw this getaway attempt unfolding. Helpless to stop the helicopter, he did the only thing he could do, rational or otherwise. He holstered his gun, took off running and leapt toward the stretcher as it passed by.

He caught the edge of it with both hands, hanging on as it swung wildly.

The impact was so unexpected, it threw Kappa

off balance. He almost rolled off the side of the gurney. Grasping for a handhold to prevent his falling, he dropped his pistol. It hit the duffel, tumbled over Kurt's side and slid past.

For a brief moment, Kurt wished he was an octopus. Extra hands would have helped him to climb up and catch Kappa's gun as it fell. Or at least retrieve his own pistol. Instead, all he could do was hold on with his legs swinging beneath him as Kappa's pistol dropped to the ground.

The rescue basket stabilized as the helicopter moved down the narrow gap and out into the wider area of the riverbed. But it swung around like a carnival ride when the chopper swerved south and began to pick up speed.

As the helicopter straightened out, Kurt pulled himself up and threw one hand forward, reaching for the corner of the duffel bag. His plan was to pull it free and toss it down, then jump to safety when the helicopter inevitably slowed and turned back, searching for its lost payload. He tugged on the duffel, but it wouldn't budge. Kappa had secured it to the stretcher with three nylon straps, each pulled taut and locked in place with a metal tension buckle.

Still dangling from the basket—and painfully aware of the speed picking up—Kurt reached for the first buckle, dug his fingers under its lip and lifted. It came loose. But before he could slide the strap free, Kappa crawled up over the top of the treasure-filled bag and swung at Kurt.

The punch was an awkward lunging hook. Kurt dropped backward to avoid the blow, but that left him hanging beneath the basket once again.

Executing another textbook pull-up, he reached for the bag a second time. This time Kappa lunged toward him with a knife in his hand.

Kurt pulled his arm back, but the blade caught him anyway, slicing through his field jacket and into flesh. The pain was searing. But the bigger problem was, pulling his arm back so quickly had left him hanging from the basket by only one hand. Between the force of the helicopter and force of the wind, he wouldn't remain there long.

Instead of grabbing the stretcher again with his free hand, Kurt reached into his jacket and found the Colt in his shoulder holster. He pulled the trusty weapon free, aiming it upward, as Kappa lunged toward the hand gripping the frame of the stretcher with his knife.

Firing a single shot, Kurt hit Kappa in the shoulder.

The force of the bullet spun Kappa around and threw him off balance. He reached for the second-ary guideline as he fell backward, but it was just beyond his grasp. With a strange look on his face, Kappa tumbled off the stretcher and vanished.

Kurt didn't bother to watch him hit the ground.

He shoved the Colt back in its holster and grabbed the edge of the basket. With both hands, his grip was now firm, but by no means unbreakable. His left arm ached from holding on so long. His right arm bled through the gash in his jacket.

With maximum effort, he pulled himself up and rolled onto the rescue basket. Secure and stable, Kurt took a second to savor the victory before wondering what on earth he was going to do now.

Chapter 37

As the helicopter cruised down the canyon, Robson crouched in the back. He had one hand on the winch control and the other firmly gripping a handhold. He gazed through the cargo door at the fiasco going on down below.

The gurney dangled sixty feet beneath them, swinging wildly from side to side like a five-hundred-pound pendulum. With each swing, the cable strained and the fulcrum of the winch it was connected to groaned, the momentum so great that it was causing the helicopter to yaw and roll.

Trying to raise the basket proved impossible. "What's wrong with this thing?" he shouted, flipping the switch back and forth.

"Too much weight," the pilot shouted back. "When that guy jumped on board, it overloaded the winch. Something must have burned out."

Robson looked down once again just in time

to see Kappa tumble off the stretcher. Much as he disliked Kappa, Robson knew it was not good news. He gave up on the winch and pulled out his pistol. "Hold us steady."

"I'm trying," the pilot shouted.

Despite the pilot's effort, the chopper continued to slew around as if pulled by some invisible force. Straining to keep his balance, Robson aimed down with one hand while holding on with the other. The gurney swung beneath them, disappearing from view. He timed its return and fired the second it reappeared.

Austin did the same.

Lead bullets punched through the thin aluminum floor of the helicopter. One of them nicked the toe of Robson's boot. Another ricocheted to one side. A third went all the way through and punched a hole in the roof above him.

Robson dove toward the cockpit. While he assumed correctly that Kurt had no desire to bring the helicopter down, he sensed Austin wouldn't hesitate to do so if he felt it was his only option.

"Now what?" the pilot asked.

"Shake him off."

"What about the cargo?"

"The bag is strapped down and Austin isn't," Robson explained. "Shake him off."

"If he thinks he's going to die, he'll shoot us down before he goes."

"Not if he's low enough to jump," Robson said.

The pilot said nothing more. He poured on more power and aimed for the center of the ever-widening river valley. The helicopter descended, accelerating as it went. It was soon traveling at an altitude of less than a hundred feet, with the gurney beneath them only thirty feet above the ground.

Risking a glance, Robson saw Kurt bracing himself. "Turn," Robson ordered.

The pilot began a turn and then straightened up. Robson looked down and saw that Kurt was still in the basket.

"Harder," Robson ordered. "Circles. He can't hang on forever."

Kurt had wedged himself into the rescue basket. He had one hand on its frame and the other holding his Colt. His feet were jammed into the corners of the stretcher. He knew what the pilot was trying to do. But aside from shooting at the pilot's seat and trying to kill him or putting a few bullets into the engine or fuel tank, there was little Kurt could do to stop it.

He held tight as the helicopter sharply banked into a turn. The basket swung wide and then swung back. When that maneuver didn't shake Kurt, the pilot transitioned to a circular pattern. This had two advantages, neither one in Kurt's favor.

First, by flying in circles the swaying that threatened to pull the helicopter off course was eliminated. Once it began moving in a circle, it felt like nothing more than a merry-go-round, the stretcher acting as a counterweight. The ride was surprisingly smooth, the sensation of speed shockingly apparent.

The second issue—and the more disastrous one from Kurt's point of view—was that the circular pattern created an ever-increasing level of centrifugal force, one that would soon fling him off the gurney. Not only was there a limit to human strength countering such a force, the circling was also causing the blood to drain from Kurt's head, arms and hands. Even if he held on, he would eventually black out, like a fighter pilot pulling too many g's. At that point, he'd go over the edge like a rag doll, never even see the end coming.

With the strain building rapidly, Kurt needed to do something and do it fast.

Tightening his grip on the Colt, he aimed upward, thinking he might hit the cable or damage the helicopter enough that they would have to land, but as he extended his arm the gun grew heavier, wavered back and forth, soon feeling like a seventy-pound weight.

As he fought to stabilize his aim, the pilot tightened the turn further. Kurt's arm fell to the side and the g-force ripped the gun from his hand.

Kurt brought his hand back down and grabbed the frame of the stretcher.

The helicopter continued to circle, the turns getting ever tighter. Kurt began to feel dizzy. His heart was pounding, his arms shaking, his mind turning foggy.

With his vision fading, Kurt reached for the duffel bag. Feeling across its thick canvas, he found the first strap. He pulled it free from its buckle and then grabbed for the second strap.

Finding it, he tried to lift the lip of its buckle, but the thing wouldn't budge. Either it was stuck or his arm had grown too weak. He shifted his weight and lifted harder. This second effort moved it, but Kurt was close to losing consciousness by now. Everything was turning gray and beginning to go dark.

Kurt gripped his legs together and tightened his abs, trying to force the blood back into his head. His vision briefly returned to normal. He watched the ground flying past. It was no more than twenty feet below him. Sand and rocks rushed by, then trees and greenery, then finally dark water glistening in the early evening sun as they sped over one of the small lakes.

The pattern repeated itself as the circles tightened even more. Sand, rock, trees and greenery, water—everything passing in one giant, dizzying blur.

With his vision and strength partially restored, Kurt pulled up on the second buckle again. This time it unlatched.

The strap flailed in the wind and the duffel bag slid a few inches. But with its entire weight now straining against the single third strap, the tension grew tighter.

Kurt pulled hard but found it wouldn't budge.

The pilot banked the helicopter into a yet tighter turn.

Kurt primed himself for one last effort. He grabbed for the buckle and pulled. His hand slipped free. With the g-forces so high, he was unable to catch himself. His feet broke loose and his body came halfway out of the basket. His free hand found the duffel's fluttering strap and gripped it. It kept him from being ejected, but he was now holding on by his hands only, his legs were over the side of the stretcher and there was simply no way to overcome the centrifugal force and pull them back in.

His arms burned as he held on. Down below, the rocks now flew past. Now the sand. Now the trees. They were flying in one last circle and Kurt knew what came next.

He let go, flew through the air and plunged feetfirst into the center of the small lake.

Chapter 38

Kurt hit the lake at high speed. He plunged through the surface, spreading his arms wide, slowing his descent into the water as much as possible. He still hit the muddy bottom with enough force to embed his boots in its sediment.

Shockingly calm for someone who'd just been thrown from a moving helicopter, Kurt looked up. The murky water cut down on the light and, without a mask or goggles, the view was blurred, but the surface shimmered no more than twenty feet above him.

He saw no movement, no bubble trails announcing the presence of bullets fired into the water to finish him off. He saw only ripples from his own entry and the color of the evening sky in a circle beyond.

Reaching down, he dug the mud away from

his boots, kicked free and swam for the surface. He emerged cautiously and savored exhaling and taking a breath of air.

Looking around, he spotted the helicopter disappearing to the south. Rather than come back to make sure he was dead, they'd chosen to hightail it out of the valley. Kurt wasn't surprised. Doubling back was just asking for trouble. Their best bet was to reel in the duffel bag or land somewhere safe and haul it aboard by hand. Either way, the helicopter was gone—along with the **Writings of Qsn.**

At least Kurt still had his life.

He swam to shore, crawled out and found a rock to sit on. He was wringing out his socks when Gamay and Paul came along on their horses, trailing a spare along with them.

Both were obviously relieved to see him. Gamay made the first joke to lighten the mood. "An odd time to take a bath," she said, "but I hear the waters around here are healing."

"Lifesaving," Kurt replied.

Gamay led the extra horse over to him. "You told us to watch for anything dangerous. You never mentioned midair acrobatics with you hanging from a helicopter."

"I probably should have skipped that part," he admitted. "It was all for nothing anyway." Draping his socks over his shoulder, Kurt slipped his bare feet into his boots, pulled them tight and then climbed onto the saddle. He was dog tired, had a pounding headache and was not at all interested in hiking back to Falcon Point. "Thanks for having enough faith to bring me my horse. How did Joe and Morgan fare? Are they all right?"

This time Paul answered. "They secured the wreck site and radioed us about your stunt. We saw someone fall off a mile back. We were very glad to find out it wasn't you. Then we saw you fall and feared the worst."

"Let it be known that I jumped," Kurt said. "Just glad I didn't belly flop."

"So what do we do now?" Gamay asked.

"Ride back to Falcon Point and search that plane from nose to tail."

"Why?" Gamay asked. "Surely they took everything of value."

Kurt stretched and twisted around in the saddle, reveling in the glorious feeling of his back cracking and his spine realigning itself. "We'll never know until we check. They could easily have missed something. If they did, it'll probably be something small and hidden. But sometimes the smallest clue can make the biggest difference."

Chapter 39

With everyone gathered back at the site of the downed aircraft, Joe explained what he and Morgan had already learned. "All-metal construction," Joe said. "Twin engines."

"It's in good condition?"

"Part of it is," Joe said. "It's a tale of two parts, really. Everything that's been buried over the years is well preserved. Everything that's been exposed up top has been badly weathered."

The others looked on, following Joe's hand as he pointed things out. The line of demarcation on the plane was remarkably clear.

"It's not going to search itself," Kurt said. "Let's get to it."

Gamay nodded and moved toward the front of the plane. "We'll check the bow," she said, including Paul in her statement. "I mean, the nose. It doesn't look like they spent much time excavating that area."

"I'll take a look inside," Kurt volunteered.

"I'll join you," Morgan said.

"That leaves the rest for me," Joe said.

As the group spread out, Joe dropped down beside the fuselage to an area behind the wing. A section of the metal had been cut open and torn away.

He aimed his flashlight into the opening. The lower section was filled with sediment, though much of it had been dug out. He saw handprints and telltale scoops where someone's fingers had clawed through the soil. "Couldn't get a shovel in here, so they must have dug by hand."

"Can you tell if they found anything?" Kurt asked.

Joe studied the compartment. "Doesn't look like there was any cargo back here, just fuel pumps, rotted hoses and a large metal container that must have been the gas tank." He rapped his fingers on it. The tank reverberated like a muffled steel drum. It was half filled with sediment too.

"Pretty big tank for such a small plane," Joe said. "Whoever flew this wanted maximum range."

Kurt listened to Joe, but his mind was on his own effort. After climbing up onto the fuselage, he and Morgan gazed down into the cockpit. On its exterior, they spotted metal tracks indented in the sides.

"These rails look like they were part of a sliding canopy," Morgan suggested.

Kurt nodded, pointing to a spar jutting out in front of the cockpit. "It would have connected here to this stub of metal where a windscreen would have been fixed in place."

They found no remnants of the canopy or screen. The loss had left the cockpit open to the elements for years and it had filled completely with sand until Kappa's men shoveled it out.

Looking again inside, Kurt saw what remained of the instrument panel and pilot's seat, which was nothing more than some wooden framing, rusted springs and shreds of leather. The control stick had been broken off at the base and was missing. A layer of sediment covered the floor, far deeper in the corners than in the middle. Shovels had gouged the wooden boards beneath the seat, even breaking through it in places.

"Didn't exactly dig carefully," Kurt said.

"Something tells me they weren't interested in preservation," Morgan replied.

Climbing over the edge of the fuselage, Kurt dropped down into the cockpit. He sat almost as the pilot would have, facing the instrument panel. It was largely intact, though most of the glass in the gauges was broken and the insides filled with sand.

Touching the panel, he found it was also made

of wood. On the right-hand side he found a series of vertical scratches that had been crossed
through. They reminded him of the marks prisoners made on the walls of their cells to count off
the days and weeks in captivity.

"There's something behind the seat," Morgan said.

Kurt twisted around in the confined space and
spotted a small steamer trunk. Rectangular and
constructed of wood and leather, it had metal riv-
ets at the corners. Its thicker hide had survived the
years in better condition than the leather of the
pilot's seat.

Reaching around the remnants of the seat, Kurt
found that the trunk had already been pulled forward as far as possible. It was now wedged between
the base of the seat and the tubular framework of
the fuselage.

It was impossible to imagine that Barlow's men
had missed it, but Kurt pushed the lid up and
looked into it anyway.

"What do you see?" Morgan asked.

"It's empty," Kurt said. "Except for a layer of
mud at the bottom."

He reached down and dug through the residue, feeling for anything Kappa and his people
might have missed. He searched for pockets or
false compartments, then felt along the bottom
of the trunk and in all the corners, turning the

contents over with his fingers. The only thing he recovered were two chunks of stone, the largest one no bigger than a matchbox.

Scraping the residue off, he exposed its brick red color.

"Red stones," Morgan said, looking on. "Just like the **Writings of Qsn.**"

Kurt handed her one of the pieces and stuffed the other in his pocket. They would search every nook and cranny in the cockpit and even pull out the instrument panel and look behind it without finding anything else of interest.

Having exhausted every possible hiding spot he could think of and coming up empty, Kurt climbed out of the plane. "Anyone else having any luck?"

"Nothing up front," Paul called out.

"Nothing in the tail either," Joe said.

"I was hoping they'd have been less thorough."

"Maybe the plane itself can tell us something," Morgan suggested. She turned to Joe. "You seem to be the aviation expert of the group. What do you make of this relic?"

Joe stepped away from the plane and moved back a few feet. "From the maintenance logbook, we know it was built in '26 or '27. The fact that it's all-metal construction tells us something too. Very rare for that era."

"Must be aluminum or it would have rusted," Kurt said.

"Good point," Joe replied. "And the twin engines and large fuel tank mean it was designed for high speed and long range. Normally, that would suggest it was a mail carrier or a small passenger plane, but I haven't seen any room for cargo and there's only one seat."

"That's not all that's missing," Paul added. "This thing doesn't have any wheels."

Paul and Gamay had searched the front of the plane without finding any cargo, but they'd followed up by excavating farther beneath the aircraft.

"No landing gear?" Morgan asked.

"Just a skid under the belly," Paul said.

Kurt and Morgan hopped down and joined Joe. Together, the three of them moved to the front of the plane and crouched down to examine its structure.

Joe ducked under the nose and ran his hand along a ski-like rail. He followed it back to a spot on the fuselage where a rectangular indentation had filled with sediment. Using his fingers to dig out the debris, he found a solid metal pin and a hook linked to a braided metal wire.

"It looks like an attachment point for external equipment or munitions," Morgan suggested. "Could this be a warplane?"

Joe didn't think so. He moved farther back and came to another set of hooks that were positioned just aft of the cockpit. "It might not have wheels now, but it did when it took off. The landing gear would have connected here and up front. These hooks allowed the pilot to eject it after getting up in the air."

"Why would any pilot want to eject their landing gear?" Gamay asked.

"Because wheels and struts are heavy," Joe said. "They're also not very aerodynamic. They create large amounts of drag, which slows you down and burns up fuel in the process."

"They also help you land without crashing," Gamay pointed out.

"Actually," Joe said, "the pilot seems to have landed fairly safely. There's no sign of impact, no folds in the sheet metal, no compression in the nose or twisting of the wings. From what I can see, there's very little damage to the plane at all, even to the underside. I'd say the skid helped him put it down in the sand. A set of wheels would have sunk in and caused him to tumble end over end."

"Then how'd he wind up with a broken leg?" Kurt asked.

"Maybe he tripped and fell trying to walk out of here with a bag full of rocks," Joe said.

As Kurt and the others took that in, Joe stepped back from the aircraft. It dawned on him that this was more than a standard vintage aircraft. It was built for a specific task. "Maybe this was a racing plane," he said more to himself than the others.

"The pilot may have been trying to set an aviation speed record or . . ."

His voice trailed off. He looked the plane over with a new perspective, studying it from the nose to what was left of the tail. He calculated the length and wingspan, then went over the other details in his head. "Two engines," he said. "All-metal airframe. American pilot. Big, heavy fuel tank, for a plane this size, but a very small cockpit and throwaway landing gear."

He looked to the others as the truth dawned on him. "This plane was on a one-way trip," he said. "With some damage upon landing considered an acceptable outcome."

"What kind of trip?"

Joe didn't respond. He was lost in his own thoughts once again. His gaze came back to the front half of the plane, where he saw a circular mark the size of a small dinner plate. It stuck out slightly from the aircraft's aluminum skin and its coloring and corrosion were different than the rest and blackened.

He stepped forward and began scraping at the corroded surface. "Why didn't I see this before?"

"See what before?" Paul asked.

"This marker."

Gamay reached out and grabbed Joe by the arm. "Time for you to let us in on the secret," she said sternly. "What do you know and how do you know it?"

"I know what plane this is," Joe said.

"You mean what kind of plane, don't you?"

"No," Joe said. "I know exactly what plane this is because it's the only one of its kind ever built."

Using a knife, he pried chunks of corrosion from the disk. He then poured water from a canteen over it and, using his shirtsleeve, scoured it vigorously with a circular, polishing motion. Years of grime flaked off. And though the color didn't change from its tarnished black, details began to emerge.

The long nose of an animal appeared, first the nostrils and then the line of its mouth. Next came a sloped forehead and a single large eye. After more rubbing, Joe found what he was looking for—the curved shape of a ram's horn depicted in profile. The whole image a stylized Art Deco design.

"The **Golden Ram**," Joe said, looking up.

"The golden who?" Gamay asked.

"The **Golden Ram**," Joe repeated. "This is Jake Melbourne's plane. It vanished after he left New York on an attempt to cross the Atlantic in May of 1927. He was trying to win the Orteig Prize. The one Charles Lindbergh won a week later."

Gamay shrugged. "Never heard of him."

"People only remember the winners," Joe said. "No one remembers those who come in second or don't come in at all. Dozens of others tried to win the prize. At least six men died in the effort. Others vanished and were never heard from again.

A French plane known as **L'Oiseau Blanc** disappeared trying to make the journey from Paris to New York. They were trying to win the prize flying to the west. Melbourne's plane disappeared a week later, heading east."

Kurt turned back to the plane, looking upon it with a newfound reverence. "Are you sure about this?"

"Positive," Joe said.

Paul cocked his head to the side. "You said this plane disappeared a week before Lindbergh's flight. Since it obviously made it to Europe, does that mean Melbourne deserved the prize instead of Lucky Lindy?"

"Technically, no," Joe said. "You had to make it to Paris to win the prize and—"

"Still," Kurt said, interrupting, "it would make Melbourne the first person to cross the Atlantic without stopping. That would make him a hero in his own right."

"You would think that," Joe said cautiously. "But not really."

"Why not?"

Joe looked around sheepishly. "Because Jake Melbourne's body was found in a Brooklyn icehouse weeks after his plane took off. He'd had a gunshot wound to the chest and had been dead for a while. No one knows how long since the ice kept him, well, on ice."

Everyone's eyes grew wide.

Paul asked the obvious. "If he was killed in New York, then how'd the plane get here?"

"Someone else flew it," Joe said.

"The big question is, who?" Kurt asked.

Joe shrugged. "How should I know?"

Morgan joined the conversation next. "Let me get this straight," she said. "You're telling me this man Melbourne was killed and then some other pilot—unknown to history—took his plane and disappeared, trying to fly it across the Atlantic, only to crash here in Spain, die anonymously and vanish from history?"

"That's the only explanation that makes any sense," Joe said.

"Talk about rotten luck," Paul said.

"And you're sure this is his plane?" Morgan said, repeating Kurt's earlier question. "Not another one of the same kind?"

"There weren't any others of the same kind," Joe said. "Melbourne's plane was designed and built specifically for the contest. The ram's head embellishment proves it—that was Jake's moniker, his persona. They called him the Golden Ram. He butted heads with everyone but always looked good doing it. Trust me, this is Melbourne's plane even if Melbourne didn't fly it."

"Well, that's a very strange tale indeed," Morgan said.

"Stranger still," Kurt pointed out, "whoever this pilot was, he had the **Writings of Qsn** with him. Which means those tablets made it all the way to the New World before coming back here to Europe."

Morgan took the next step. "If we can figure out what happened to Melbourne and who replaced him, it might lead us to whoever really discovered the **Writings of Qsn** and where."

The members of the group looked at one another soberly, each of them calculating the odds in their own way. "It's a long shot," Kurt said. "But at this point, it's our only chance of beating the Bloodstone Group to the treasure."

Chapter 40

MV **Tunisian Wind**, forty miles north of the Spanish coast

Solomon Barlow stood on the bridge wing of an aging forty-thousand-ton bulk carrier that was partially filled with grain. The **Tunisian Wind** was registered in Panama, owned by an Albanian corporation that existed only on paper and used by the Bloodstone Group to ferry arms around the world.

Upon purchasing the Handymax-sized vessel, Barlow had considered changing the name to something like **Trojan Gift,** but he figured that was too on the nose, considering how he and his people used the ship.

The vessel itself chartered out to carry grain, filling its hold in various countries and delivering its product on time and intact, in a perfectly legal manner. It was crewed by professional seamen and passed all safety inspections.

What the world's authorities hadn't put

together was that the ship rarely made a delivery in the full amount of its cargo. Even when the holds were filled to the top, it routinely dropped off only half the total tonnage it was capable of hauling while down beneath all the remaining loose grain lay weapons wrapped in layers of protective plastic.

The **Tunisian Wind** had delivered mobile missile systems, tanks and helicopters from the former Soviet republics. Thousands of assault rifles, armor-piercing rockets and antipersonnel grenades had traveled in the bottom of the hold, along with enough plastic explosives to level a small city.

It had sailed this way for years. In all that time, the most anyone had ever done was open the hatch and test the grain for boll weevils.

Currently in between runs, the ship was anchored and awaiting an important arrival. Barlow checked his watch and scanned the horizon repeatedly, his patience fading. Finally, he spotted a helicopter approaching. "That has to be Kappa," he said. "Signal them with the lights."

The ship's master, who had also been with Barlow for years, did as ordered without question. He wasn't blind to the vessel's purpose and knew they were maintaining radio silence for a reason. He aimed the high-powered lamp in the direction of the approaching helicopter and began opening and closing the shutter, sending a message that directed it to land on the forward hatch.

A moment went by before the landing light beneath the helicopter flashed in response.

"They confirm," the captain said.

"Good," Barlow replied. "Weigh anchor. I want to be under way the moment they touch down."

As the captain made preparations to get under way, Barlow pulled on a jacket and left the bridge. It was quite a hike down the stairs to the main deck and then along to the bow. By the time Barlow reached the reinforced forward hatch, the chopper's wheels were touching down.

Barlow waited as several of the ship's crewmen secured the craft. While they worked, the side door slid open. Barlow was puzzled to see Robson standing there alone.

"Where's Kappa?"

"He's dead," Robson announced bluntly.

"And the others?"

"They died before he did."

Barlow's eyes froze in a look of anger. "Explain this to me."

Robson jumped down from the helicopter. "I didn't kill him, in case that's what you think. He got ambushed by the two operatives from NUMA and the woman from MI5."

"What about his team?"

"They lost a firefight where they had the high

ground," Robson explained. "In their defense," he added, "they got bounced at a bad time."

Barlow didn't bother with sentiment, but he was quick with figures and he was now down ten men thanks to Austin, Zavala and Agent Manning. "You seem to have emerged unscathed," he said. "I hope that means you've brought home what they dug up."

Robson reached back into the helicopter, grabbed the straps of the duffel bag and heaved it onto the ship's deck. "Unlike Kappa, I deliver what I've promised. Between that and the fact that there isn't anyone else left, I'd say it's time you put me back on point."

Barlow ignored the request for the moment. He dropped down on one knee and unzipped the bag. It was filled with flat, tile-like sections of stone—dozens of them, maybe a hundred—all broken up like pieces of a jigsaw puzzle.

"They were like that when we found them," Robson said.

Barlow pulled a palm-sized fragment from the lot, then looked over several more. There were hieroglyphics on every piece. All he had to do was put them back together.

He placed the stones back into the duffel and zipped it shut. "You've done well. The number one position is yours. Don't screw it up like Kappa did."

Because the Bloodstone Group operated like a pirate corporation, with the men earning their pay in percentages and shares, the simple promotion might add up to millions for Robson.

After giving Robson a moment to enjoy the news, Barlow gave a new order. "Take this to my cabin. We need to put it together and figure out its secrets."

Chapter 41

Villa Ducal de Lerma, Spain

Arriving back in Lerma meant a parting of the ways. After saying good-bye to Father Torres, young Sofia and her aunt, the NUMA team headed toward a small airfield forty minutes away. There, they found two jet aircraft waiting. One bound for London, the other for Washington.

Kurt climbed into the NUMA Gulfstream and spoke briefly to the pilot before coming back down the stairs. He waited until Joe, Paul and Gamay had said their good-byes to Morgan before speaking to her himself.

"Why don't you come with us?" he said. "I've already checked with the pilot. There's plenty of fuel and an extra passenger won't affect the flight."

Morgan looked briefly at the NUMA jet before shaking her head. "It would ruffle a lot of feathers back in London if I didn't show up now. Colonel

Pembroke-Smythe and I will have to report to the Chief of Operations and most likely spend a few hours being grilled by members of Parliament. I'd also like to check in with Professor Cross and see if he's thought of anything new. Once all that's taken care of, I'll think about making my way to America."

"Something tells me that won't take long," Kurt said. "Let me know what flight you're on. Austin Car Service is the best around."

"Very well," she said, her formal bearing firmly in place. "Until we meet again."

There was no handshake, no hug, no kiss. Just a swift turn on her heels and a composed march to the Learjet on the far side of the ramp.

Kurt watched her board and then climbed back up the stairs into the NUMA Gulfstream.

"Five passengers?" the pilot asked.

"No," Kurt said. "Just four."

While the pilot secured the door and returned to the cockpit, Kurt moved toward the back of the plane. Finding a seat was no problem, the aircraft was spacious. It had been designed to let twelve passengers fly in comfort for long distances, but NUMA had modified it for smaller groups and added a few additional touches.

It had eight premium seats in two rows of four, then an area where comfortable couches offered retractable footrests and the option of reclining into beds, and a high-tech workstation with a computer terminal connected by satellite links directly to NUMA's servers. Across from the sectionals lay a kitchenette, complete with wet bar, and behind that on the wall were a pair of fifty-inch flat-screen TVs connected to satellite.

Kurt took a seat on the aisle, one row ahead of Joe and directly across the aisle from Paul. Gamay sat next to him, gazing wistfully out the window at the Spanish countryside they were about to leave behind.

As the Gulfstream began to move, Kurt settled back. He had no doubt he would see Morgan again, but his mind had already switched lanes and was focused on the next steps in the search for the missing treasure. Figuring out who killed Jake Melbourne would be one avenue of investigation. Another would be the stone fragment in his jacket pocket.

Pulling the stone out, Kurt ran his thumb over the surface once more. It was soft and porous. Some of the red particles rubbed off on his skin as he brushed it. He turned to Paul and held the fragment out. "What do you make of that?"

Paul had a Ph.D. in Ocean Sciences and was a specialist in deepwater geology. He'd written a thesis on rock formation found on the seafloor. As far as Kurt was concerned, sea-based geology and land-based geology couldn't be all that different.

Paul took the stone from Kurt, studied it for a second and then switched on the overhead light.

"Sedimentary rock," he said, "with a high level of iron content, which accounts for the red color. Reminds me of Navajo sandstone."

"Navajo sandstone?"

Paul nodded. "The vermillion-colored rock you see so much of in Arizona, Utah and New Mexico."

"Is that a unique color?"

Paul shook his head. "There are red sandstones all around the world. They come from similar formations, but that's what first came to mind. Is this stone from a section of the hieroglyphics tablet?"

Kurt thought so. "It has no writing on it, but it's the same color and has smooth edges."

Paul dabbed a napkin in some water and gave the stone an additional cleaning. "It's flat on three sides, with a ninety-degree angle at the point. Could be a corner piece. Might have broken off in the crash as the fragments were jostled around."

"That's what I was thinking," Kurt said. He glanced out the window as the Gulfstream pulled onto the runway and the engines began to ramp up. "Is there any way you could determine what part of the world this stone came from?"

A thoughtful look came over Paul's face. "There are several ways to narrow it down."

"Such as?"

"We could look for microscopic fossils embedded in the sandstone," Paul said. "That could tell you when, geologically speaking, it formed. We could check its uranium content and radioactivity levels, we could grind it up and analyze its exact chemical makeup. Sandstones around the world are all slightly different. It depends on when, where and how they were laid down. But even if we narrow down the source area, I'm not going to be able to give you a latitude and longitude."

As Paul finished speaking, the aircraft began its takeoff run. Kurt leaned back in his seat, relaxing, as they picked up speed. "Just name me a continent," he said. "We'll go from there."

Chapter 42

Cambridge, England

Professor Henry Cross arrived home later than usual on a Wednesday night. A meeting at the university had run long and a minor traffic accident on the roundabout south of campus had held him up further.

He parked his Mini Cooper in the drive, pulled his briefcase off the passenger seat and walked around to a side door of the modest cottage-style home he'd lived in for two decades.

Unlocking the door and stepping through, he flipped a switch to ignite a gas fireplace in the living room. The flames gave the house a warm, cozy feel. They also lit the place in orange, illuminating a man sitting in one of the professor's high-backed chairs.

"About bloody time you got here," the man said.

Professor Cross studied the man the way he

might examine an ancient scroll. He noted the prominent nose, the dark stubble on the man's face and neck, the wool hat pulled down over the ears. He also noticed the pistol in his hand and the cylindrical tube screwed into the end of the barrel.

"Why do you have a silencer on your gun?"

The scruffy-looking man aimed the pistol at Professor Cross. "A respectable neighborhood, this. Wouldn't want to go disturbing the peace if I had to shoot you, now would I?"

The professor leaned against the wall. He was more annoyed than afraid. "What do you want, Robson?"

"Answers."

"I would have given you the answers," the professor began. "I would have sent you everything you needed, had you and those hooligans of yours not acted so clumsily when the Americans were here."

Robson shifted in his chair and crossed his legs as if he owned the place. With practiced movements, he slid the pistol back into a shoulder holster and tucked it away. "Thought you'd appreciate us coming down on you like gangbusters. Keeps your impeccable name above suspicion."

Professor Cross shook his head and glared at the man. The growing anger building inside him came out when he spoke next. "You'd just better hope they never wonder how you happened to arrive at Cambridge on the same exact day at the same exact moment they did."

"Actually," Robson said, grinning, "you'd better hope that. It's not my name that'll be dragged through the mud if they get suspicious."

Robson stood up and walked toward the professor, passing him and stepping into the kitchen. Without asking permission, he pulled open the refrigerator and began pawing through its contents. "Blimey," he said. "Half this stuff is out of date, Professor. I know you like old things, but, jeez, go shopping once in a while."

The professor sighed. "I wasn't expecting guests. Now what, exactly, do you want? I've already given you all the information I have."

Robson's head appeared above the refrigerator door. "You make it sound like a charity case. Like we never paid you. What are you doing with all of Barlow's money anyway? Certainly haven't spent it on this place."

"I have my own pursuits," the professor said.

"A little bit of crumpet on the side? That nice secretary of yours maybe?"

"Don't be crass."

Robson went back to foraging and finally settled on a bunch of grapes, pulling them out and closing the refrigerator door. Plucking several off, he began popping them into his mouth.

Street thugs, Professor Cross thought, no sense of decorum. "If you're here for a snack," he said, "I'm going to retire." He turned for the bedroom.

"We need you to look at something," Robson told him. "A new set of hieroglyphics."

The professor stopped in his tracks. "New set? From where?"

"They come from the red tablet," Robson said. "The part that's never been seen."

Slowly, the professor's eyes widened. "You've found more fragments?"

Robson nodded. "Found them all, I'd say. Out in the old plane. Right where the logbook said they'd be."

Suddenly, the professor understood Robson's newfound confidence, his cock-of-the-walk attitude. No doubt Barlow had heaped praise and money on him for finding what no one else had been able to. "Do you have them here?"

"Of course not," Robson said, popping another grape into his mouth. "Barlow isn't going to let them out of his sight. But I have this."

He pulled the architect's tube off his shoulder, popped the cap off one end and removed a rolled-up poster-sized sheet of paper.

"This is a computer-enhanced drawing," he said. "One of Barlow's people took pictures of all the broken bits of stone and had the computer match them together. Then he slotted in the photos MI5 was nice enough to give us. Altogether, it produced this. A full image of the stone to look at instead of a hundred pieces. Care to take a gander?"

Professor Cross took it without hesitating. Unrolling it slowly, he found a white page with grayscale images on it. It looked like a photographic negative. He carefully spread it out on his kitchen table, placing various items at the corners to keep it from curling up.

He reached for the overhead light, pausing with his fingers on the chain.

A nervous glance out through the kitchen window reminded him how dark it had grown. Night had come on while they spoke. Any light would let the world see in through his windows. He turned to Robson. "Close the blinds."

The blinds came down tight and Professor Cross switched on the overhead light to see the masterpiece before him.

Looking at the images, he was rapidly consumed. He studied the poster as if it were a scroll from an ancient century. It didn't matter that it was ink and paper. What mattered was the information.

Running a finger across the glyphs, the professor racked his brain for translations. "Incredible," he whispered, his eyes darting from spot to spot. "This is a message sent three thousand years ago. One only now being received."

"All Barlow cares about is what it says."

"It tells us of a fleet that traveled the Nile without stopping," the professor said. "They sailed through the night and passed Memphis under the light of the quarter moon."

"Memphis?"

"Think Cairo," the professor explained. "Alexandria. The ancient capital of Egypt." He read on. "They left the world behind the next day."

"The world?" Robson said.

"It's a euphemism," Professor Cross said. "A figure of speech."

"I know what a euphemism is," Robson snapped. "What's it supposed to mean?"

"It means they left the Land of the Ancients. They left Egypt itself."

Robson seemed satisfied. He popped another grape in his mouth and sat back. "To go where?"

Professor Cross turned back to the computer-generated poster. Continuing on down, he took notes and explained what he was finding. "On the Day of the Long Sun—that would be the summer solstice—Pharaoh Herihor, Ruler of the Great House, unfurled a new banner to be flown by all ships in the great fleet. The Mark of Aten is upon the banner."

"And what does that tell us? What, exactly, is the Mark of Aten?"

The professor went back to make sure he'd read that correctly. "Aten was the name of the Sun God," he said quietly. "Now, that is surprising."

"I thought the Egyptian's worshipped the sun," Robson said. "Ra and all that."

"The Egyptians worshipped many gods," the professor explained. "They had a pantheon like the Greeks and the Romans. But during one brief part of their history a Pharaoh named Akhenaten took over and tried to force everyone to worship only the sun. He tried to turn the whole empire away from their many gods to just the one. From a multitheistic religion to a monotheistic one. Ra became Aten. And believing in the other gods became heresy, a crime punishable by death. The name Akhenaten literally means **Worshipper of Aten** and he spent his time constructing monuments dedicated to the sun. He even moved some of the entombed Pharaohs from old burial places to new graves where they would be illuminated by the first rays of the sunrise."

"And . . ."

"And, Mr. Robson, for every action there is an equal and opposite reaction. Akhenaten's decrees brought about a backlash. Followers of the old gods met in secret and plotted against him. He was poisoned, went blind, then died."

"Too bad for him."

"Yes, it was," the professor said. "The next Pharaoh, the famous Tutankhamen, spent years undoing everything Akhenaten had done, setting the religious order back to the way it had been.

The old gods were restored, Akhenaten was labeled a heretic and things returned to normal. But if Herihor built himself a fleet and sailed it under the banner of Aten two hundred years later"—the professor looked up at Robson—"that means all of history is changed and we may now have a different understanding of why he took the treasures to begin with."

Professor Cross all but swooned for a moment. If this small tablet could reveal so much, he only dared to imagine what finding Herihor's tomb would bring.

"What's so different?" Robson asked. "Are you telling me he's not a thief?"

"Herihor was no thief," the professor said sternly, "he was a king. He was surrounded by wealth. Drowning in it. He had all the gold and luxuries and delicacies one man could possess. Not to mention power, armies, servants and wives. To call him a commonplace grave robber is a disservice. And, quite frankly, unimaginative."

The professor saw a look of surprise appear on Robson's face, but he wasn't finished. "If Herihor just wanted to be richer than he already was, then he could have plundered the tombs, taken the gold for himself and left the Pharaohs' decaying bodies behind. If it was greed and avarice, he could have stolen everything piecemeal, melted it down and claimed it as newly discovered gold and freshly mined jewels. Trust me, there was no one in the Valley of the Kings to stop him."

"No need to get angry," Robson said. "It's not like he was your brother or something."

The professor adjusted his glasses and continued. "I'm not angry, I'm passionate. You must understand that what Herihor did he did out of a religious fervor, not greed. He valued preserving the past of his ancestors more than wealth, power and even glory. He gave up a kingdom to do it. Not only that, he risked his life on a journey into the unknown to make it happen. In truth, I would be honored to be called his brother."

Robson held up his hands almost defensively. "All right, all right, fine. Whatever you say. Just finish the translation. If any of us are going to get a piece of this treasure, we need to know where he went."

The professor sighed and turned back to the hieroglyphics. "The Worshippers of Aten had a singular obsession," he explained, "and that was to dwell with the sun always. Like all religions, the ultimate desire was to reunite with their god. Their search for Heaven meant finding the place where the Sun God rested during the night."

"Something tells me they're going to be sorely disappointed when they figure out there's no such place," Robson said.

"Indeed," the professor remarked. He went back to the paper and continued translating. "They followed the sun for twenty days as it led them across the sea. On the twenty-first day a storm hit. Several ships were lost as they tried to shelter in a rocky cove." He paused. "This must be where DeMars found the wrecked boats, the ones that made him think Egyptians had colonized France."

"So DeMars was right. The treasure is somewhere in France."

"No," the professor said. "The fleet did not stay there." He resumed translating. "The fleet traveled past the Great Rock That Guards Eternity. Out beyond all things. They go as Aten guides them, searching from his Resting Realm."

"What does that mean?"

"It means the fleet continued following the setting sun, traveling west."

Here, for the first time, Professor Cross found a set of glyphs that he could not make sense of. He'd never seen their like before. He skipped them and said nothing to Robson. "Great beasts of the water were spotted, spouting steam—he must mean whales."

"Go on."

"Nets of fish . . . Some men weakening . . . Third full moon . . . Lack of wind and the oarsmen grow tired . . ." The professor paused. "They were getting their food from the sea as they traveled. Quite ingenious. But men weakening suggests scurvy. That and the third full moon suggests they'd been at sea for eight weeks, probably more."

"And the oarsmen," Robson said. "Are you telling me they were rowing all this time?"

"Not all the time," the professor said. "Lack of wind and tired oarsmen. They must have used sails when they could and rowed when there was no breeze. Extended time without wind makes me think they were in the doldrums. An area of the Atlantic Ocean where winds can slack for weeks at a time. The great European sailing ships often ended up stranded that way. If caught there too long, the men did what they could to spark the winds, including tossing horses overboard, which is why some call that area the Horse Latitudes."

Robson stood up. "Hold on, Professor. You're telling me this lot went halfway across the Atlantic Ocean?"

The professor nodded. "We know they were off the coast of France heading in a westerly direction. We know they passed the Great Rock That Guards Eternity—that has to mean Gibraltar. From there, they followed the setting sun for weeks, tracking it day after day after day. That would take them west and south. At some point the wind stopped and they rowed. Lucky for them, their ships were much smaller and lighter than those of the Spaniards centuries later. But based on this, they could hardly be anywhere but the mid-Atlantic."

Robson's eyes narrowed as if trying to detect a lie. "Don't play games with me, Professor. You might wear fancy clothes and use big words, but I know who you are. A con knows a con."

"I'm not playing with you," the professor insisted. "I'm trying to enlighten you."

He looked back at the paper one more time. He was two-thirds of the way to the bottom. He returned to reading and explaining. "After a sacrifice, the winds returned. On the day of the fourth moon, they made landfall. Here, there are crocodiles like those of the Nile. Herihor has declared this a poisoned land as these creatures are the Servants of Sobek."

The professor interrupted himself before Robson could. "Sobek was a crocodile god and an enemy of Aten." He continued on, paraphrasing now. "They made landfall in a drier place and Herihor ordered them to burn their ships—just like Cortés."

For the second time, Professor Cross came upon a set of glyphs he'd never seen. This time he admitted it. "These must be printed incorrectly."

"They're not," Robson said. "It's a digital copy."

"I'll have to do more research, then," Professor Cross said. "I certainly don't recognize them. And yet, I think that tells us something in and of itself."

"Such as?"

"All languages change over time," he explained. "If these glyphs were some new creation of this offshoot band and there is no record of them in the classic Egyptian writings, then it proves that there was no further contact between the two groups. It tells us that once Herihor's fleet left Egypt, they never returned."

Robson was losing patience. "Cut to the chase, Professor. Where did they end up?"

Professor Cross read further. Much of the next section was about men of bronze who traded with them, animals not known in Egypt, including great woolen beasts whose skins were used as clothing when the sky turned white and fell with bitterness, and strange foods. And it was about losses.

As he read, Professor Cross could not help but see these Egyptians traveling through North America, encountering Native Americans, herds of buffalo, snow falling from a white sky—things they would have never known in Egypt.

He read tales of the ground turning to stone and imagined it was frost. They set up camps and scouted. They hunted and traded. Still, they continued to follow the sun. Still, they continued to seek the Resting Place of Aten.

He pitied them now, thinking how they would follow the sun forever, like a child searching for the end of the rainbow. Perhaps that was why these tablets were written by Qsn, the Sparrow, the Creature of Sadness.

He wondered if their fanaticism would end

in disaster or would it bring them all the way around the earth to cross the Pacific, taking them through Asia, India and eventually back to the Middle East and familiar ground. His heart raced as he considered he might have been reading about the very first circumnavigation of the world twenty-five hundred years before Magellan.

And then he read of their joyous final discovery, a canyon whose walls were steep and red and angled in such a way as to cradle the setting sun. There they could watch Aten rise, see him light up the world and cross the sky. There they could watch him descend back to earth. It was described as a majestic canyon unlike any in the known world.

"In a vision," the professor said, reading again, "Herihor was told he had found the place of rest."

He wondered if it was a decision to stave off a mutiny or if Herihor himself had fallen ill and could go no farther. Perhaps it was a compromise, a valley reminiscent of the Valley of the Kings but aligned with the path of Aten up above. It must have seemed as close to Heaven as those mortal men would ever get.

"The last glyphs tell of them carving tombs out of the rock to rival those of Egypt. But that these tombs were designed to remain hidden from all the world, keeping the Pharaohs and their belongings safe from grave robbers."

"Too bad they didn't count on us," Robson said. "Now, tell me where they are. I won't ask again."

"It has to be America," the professor whispered. "They found Aten's sanctuary and buried the Pharaoh's treasure in America."

Robson appeared doubtful. "Come on, Professor. Even I know that's not possible."

"Not only is it possible," Cross said, "it makes perfect sense. These were fanatics, leaving civilization behind and chasing their god. Nothing stopped them—not storms, not lack of wind, not months at sea, not scurvy. When they arrived on land, they didn't declare victory. They went on foot and traveled by wheeled cart, carrying their treasure, domesticating beasts along the way. They endured winter, crossed a continent and continued going. They weren't simply going to pick a random place and stop. They were looking for Heaven, for the spectacular."

He looked back at the text. "But upon discovering a canyon as deep as a mountain, with walls of different colors and a narrow river flowing through it, they'd found a place so majestic they knew they'd reached their destination, the Sanctuary of Aten. Seeing the sun cradled in its arms as it set in the west was the final proof."

Robson continued to look on suspiciously, but the professor knew he was beginning to see.

"Where do you think that is?" the professor asked. "After everything they went through, what vision of their god's splendor would be enough to make them stop and declare victory?"

Robson thought hard. Finally, he spoke. "The Grand Canyon," he said, half guessing, half stating. "In America."

The professor couldn't have been prouder if the answer had come from one of his best students at Cambridge. "That's right," he said. "They laid the Pharaohs of Egypt to rest in the Grand Canyon—in America."

Chapter 43

MV **Tunisian Wind**, somewhere on the North Sea

Solomon Barlow was in his stateroom on the **Tunisian Wind** when Robson called in on the encrypted satellite phone.

Barlow answered immediately and paced the well-appointed cabin as Robson explained the professor's theory that the Egyptian treasures had been shipped to America. It seemed astounding to him—too astounding to be true. "The whole idea is absurd," he said. "The professor must be lying."

"Why would he lie?" Robson said. "He wants to see this treasure unearthed as badly as we do."

Barlow thought about their long relationship with the professor, how it had grown from a simple deal of cash-for-information to a partnership where the respected university scholar keyed them in on things that few others knew about. The professor had been easy to corrupt—in fact, he'd all but done it to himself. As Barlow recalled, it was Professor Cross who'd first floated the idea of finding the lost Pharaohs and their missing treasure, it was he who'd fed them clues along the way. Despite all that, Cross remained a man of society and was unlikely to side with Barlow and his criminals in the end.

"He could be trying to throw us off the track," Barlow said. "Make us waste our time running around in America while he talks to MI5, tells them the truth, then directs them to the treasure. That way, he could immunize himself from guilt and end up acting as the lead expert in studying everything that's found."

"You're misreading him," Robson insisted. "The professor isn't a fool. He knows we'd kill him if he steered us wrong. Besides, if he was going to lie to us, don't you think he'd have come up with a location that was easier to believe? A spot in southern Egypt or central Africa? The number one rule of a good lie is to bend it as close as possible to the truth. This is so far off the mark, it has to be true."

"You trust him?" Barlow asked.

"No," Robson said. "But I know what he wants and we can trust him to act on that."

Robson's uncouth manner often rubbed Barlow the wrong way, but his uncultured upbringing brought with it street smarts that were an asset to be utilized. Robson came from a world of con men, petty thieves and scammers. He could sniff out half-truths and lies like a pig sniffs for truffles.

"All right," Barlow said. "I'll trust your judgment for now. But operating in America is going to be far more difficult than running around Europe or the Third World. We'll be at a disadvantage. We're going to need more men, especially with all the losses we've had lately."

"You can get a small army from Omar Kai," Robson said.

Kai was a mercenary they'd worked with before. Barlow considered him a little flamboyant, but he was the easiest sort to hire because he was fearless and always broke.

"Omar is a good choice," Barlow admitted. "But I'm more interested in finding someone to deal with NUMA. And Kurt Austin in particular. He and his friends have a nasty habit of appearing where they are least wanted—or expected. At this very moment they're on their way back to America. A few hours ago, I considered that a small victory, but it goes to the other side of the ledger now. It puts Austin on his home turf. It'll make him even harder to deal with the next time he interferes."

"You may want to get rid of him," Robson suggested. "Hit him before he can gum up the works."

Killing Austin would be a prudent step, but assassination was a different game, a different skill, than soldiering. Neither Robson nor Omar Kai were really suited for the task. Barlow would have to outsource the job.

"I'll look into it," Barlow said. "In the meantime, get yourself to America. And bring Professor Cross with you. We might need him. And we certainly don't want him running his mouth to anyone."

"Not to worry," Robson said. "He's already in my tender loving care."

Barlow cut the link and stood there for a moment, pausing before making the next move. He knew at least a dozen people who would kill for money but very few who would take the job when they heard that the operation would take place in America and would involve eliminating a United States government employee.

One by one, he crossed potential candidates off the list until he ended up with a single name, the only person he could think of who might be both capable of pulling it off and willing to risk it. "The Toymaker," he whispered to himself.

Tapping the screen on his phone, he scanned through a section of contacts. Under the cryptic heading TOYMAKER, he found an email address that existed only on the dark web—a section of the internet that required special software to access. This dark web was where the criminals of the cyberworld met, the equivalent of a shadow-filled alley in a lawless virtual city.

Using his own encryption software, Barlow sent a message. It would set up an anonymous link and allow him to make an offer to the Toymaker. If the job was accepted, details about the targets would be given and money transferred.

The Toymaker would get half up front and Barlow would wait for news of the kill before transferring the rest of the money. Theoretically, the Toymaker ran the risk of not being paid the second installment. But if there was one person in the world who never got shorted on the back end of a business deal, it was this anonymous assassin who killed with impunity.

Barlow typed out a message. A simple inquiry. He pressed SEND.

A response arrived in less than an hour.

The Toymaker was interested.

Chapter 44

After the long flight home and a few hours in his own bed, Kurt found himself wide awake at four in the morning. He'd grown accustomed to the European time and now on the East Coast it felt more like the middle of the day.

Never one to lie in bed if he wasn't sleeping, Kurt got up, showered and drove to the NUMA headquarters, a modern glass and steel building overlooking the Potomac.

He used his key card to enter the parking garage beneath the building and rode the secured elevator up to the seventh floor. A short walk led to his office and a desk covered with studies, reports and proposals.

There was enough paperwork on his desk to have taken the lives of several trees. His in-box was stacked a foot high. "That's what I get for going on vacation."

Not interested in attacking the backlog of work, Kurt shut off the light, closed the door and made his way upstairs, arriving on the floor reserved for Hiram Yaeger and his computers.

Though it was still early, Kurt wasn't surprised to find Hiram in the office. NUMA's resident computer genius preferred to work in the quiet of the morning before everyone else arrived with questions and requests.

When Kurt arrived, Hiram was sitting at his console, working on intricate coding instructions. He was surrounded by three large computer screens, each one filled with numbers and symbols. It looked to Kurt like digital graffiti.

Kurt knocked softly on the wall to alert Hiram to his presence without startling him. "You'd be good enough to tell me if the whole world was a virtual reality simulation, right?"

Hiram swiveled in his chair and leaned back. "What makes you think I'd know? I couldn't even find your missing plane."

Kurt walked over beside Hiram's desk, pulled a chair out and spun it around backward before sitting down. He leaned on the backrest as he spoke to Hiram. "No shame in that. The whole world assumed that plane fell into the Atlantic ninety years ago."

"All the same," Hiram said, "it's our job to figure out things the rest of the world gets wrong.

That's why I'm working on this new program. I need to enable our computers to make leaps of logic that are actually illogical. It's a more complicated task than you'd think."

"You should have Joe help out. He's a master of the illogical."

Hiram nodded. "Maybe you're right. He was the one who figured out it was Melbourne's plane. Do you still think it might lead you to the Pharaoh's treasure?"

"That depends," Kurt said. "What can you and Max tell me about Jake Melbourne?"

Max was the supercomputer Hiram had built from scratch. A one-of-a-kind design that Hiram continually updated to incorporate all the latest advances, Max had the fastest processors, most advanced computer chips and most complex programming, all designed and created in-house by Hiram and funded by NUMA's large technology budget.

Having built Max from the ground up, Hiram had become very attached to his creation. He'd named it Max but gave it a female persona and added a voice—and, at one point, a holographic body—that sounded a lot like his wife.

Leaning back, Hiram tilted his chin toward the ceiling. "Max," he said, "give us a basic rundown on Jake Melbourne, the famous pilot."

"Stand by," a sultry voice replied via hidden

speakers. "Also, please offer Kurt a complimentary beverage. Based on the thermal reading of his skin, he's mildly dehydrated."

Kurt glanced upward. "Thanks, Max, but I'm okay."

Max was having none of it. "Dehydration leads to lethargy, inefficient thinking and irritability. If you intend to perform at optimal levels of functioning, I suggest a full liter of water to rebalance your system."

Kurt's brow wrinkled. He turned to Hiram. "When did Max become a doctor?"

Hiram started to reply, but Max interrupted. "I have the entire storehouse of Western medical knowledge in my data banks. I have optical and infrared sensors that see better than human eyes and have the ability to cross-reference symptoms at a speed of four-point-seven billion bits of information per second. By all rational standards, I'm far superior to any human doctor."

"Except for her bedside manner," Hiram joked.

Kurt laughed. "In that case, I'm glad all I have is a little dehydration."

The doctor wasn't done. "You also seem to be favoring your right leg, suggesting injury to your knee or ankle. This is in addition to areas of raised surface temperature suggesting bruising and inflammation on multiple parts of your body. You really should learn to take better care of yourself, Kurt."

"I took a bad step," Kurt replied.

"More than one, I suspect."

"Sorry," Hiram said. "I've installed biometric sensors in Max's camera grid. They were supposed to be for security purposes only, but Max put them to her own use."

As Hiram finished explaining, he opened a small fridge at his feet and pulled out two bottles of purified water. He handed one to Kurt and put the other one on the desk. "Just take it. Otherwise, she'll never stop."

Kurt laughed, raising the water bottle. "To your health," he said. "Or mine, apparently."

Max seemed genuinely pleased. "Thank you, Kurt. Ready to report on Jake Melbourne."

"Go ahead."

"Jake Melbourne, pilot. Born March 5th, 1901, Louisville, Kentucky. Learned to fly by the time he was fifteen, ran away from home at sixteen and then lied about his age in order to enlist in the Army. He was sent to Europe in 1917 when the United States entered World War One on the side of France and the United Kingdom.

"Being a trained pilot, he was quickly transferred to the Army Air Corps. He flew in two different squadrons during his time in Europe, shooting down seven German planes during his first three weeks of deployment. This qualified him as the youngest ace pilot in the war. Melbourne was eventually given credit for nineteen kills and also survived being shot down twice himself."

As Max spoke, photos of Jake with his squadron appeared on the screens in front of Kurt and Hiram. He looked older than his age, which probably helped him get through enlistment without getting caught. By the end of the war, his blond hair was already growing into a mane. Apparently, as an ace, he didn't have to keep it high and tight.

Max continued her report. "Melbourne returned to the United States after the Armistice and became a barnstormer. After traveling all across the country and flying in shows, he was briefly connected with several Hollywood moguls. During the early twenties, he appeared in three movies and performed flying stunts in a total of seven. After being photographed with the wife of a well-known director, Melbourne moved away from Los Angeles and left the movie business behind."

Max paused, not to take a breath but to allow the humans time to soak up the information. When she continued, a new photo appeared on the screen. It was an older, filled-out version of the same man. He wore a red leather jacket and ostrich-skin boots.

"After leaving California, Jake Melbourne began to perform internationally, flying in both Europe and South America. He developed a reputation for mischief. In particular, he was known for drinking, gambling and womanizing. In 1926, he publicly pledged to win the Orteig Prize. With the help of an East Coast aircraft builder, he designed and built a plane specifically for the contest, naming it after his own persona, the **Golden Ram.** Following several test flights proving it airworthy, Melbourne readied for his attempt.

"On May 12th, 1927, he took off from Roosevelt Field in New York. After crossing Long Island, the aircraft was last seen flying in a northeast direction out over the Atlantic. It was never seen again."

"Apparently, you haven't uploaded our discovery," Kurt said. "Melbourne's plane has been found. By us."

"I'm aware of your discovery," Max said. "It's quite an accomplishment. I am merely restating the preexisting historic record."

"Please continue," Hiram said.

"An international search conducted in the weeks after the disappearance found no sign of wreckage. Melbourne and his aircraft were declared lost at sea. Controversy erupted several weeks later when Melbourne's body was found in a Brooklyn icehouse. Because the cold temperatures acted to preserve his tissue, it was impossible to determine how long he'd been dead. This, combined with his reputation, led to speculation that Melbourne had been involved in a scheme to win the prize by hoax or to ditch his plane, fake his death and collect the insurance money. The second of these two schemes was presumed to include an unknown partner who subsequently killed Melbourne, hoping to keep all the proceeds for him- or herself."

Max paused to allow for questions.

"Any truth to that?" Hiram asked.

"The evidence suggests insurance fraud was unlikely to be a motivating factor," Max said. "A policy with New York Mutual paid out ten thousand dollars, but most of that was distributed among his creditors. No individual benefactor received more than two hundred dollars."

"No point in faking your death for two hundred bucks," Kurt said. "Even back then."

"Not when landing in Paris would have given you twenty-five thousand," Hiram added. "And a lifetime of fame to cash in on. Were there any other suspects in his death?"

"Melbourne had several enemies," Max said, "including the husband of a prominent New England socialite with whom he was having an affair. In addition, Melbourne was known to have substantial gambling debts with the Irish Syndicate in New York, though he was photographed in public the week before his flight with a prominent member of the gang known as Bags Callahan."

Max displayed the picture showing two men in period clothing having lunch outside a tavern. There appeared to be smiles on both faces.

"Looks pretty friendly to me," Hiram said.

Kurt agreed. "More importantly, dead men don't pay off markers. Even if he owed them money, Melbourne was worth more to the Syndicate alive than he was dead. Anyone else?"

"There are no other suspects listed in any official or speculative record."

"Might be time to activate the illogical logic program," Kurt said.

"I wish you wouldn't," Max replied.

"What if there were two planes?" Hiram asked. "One in America and one shipped to Europe. Melbourne takes off in America, hides the plane somewhere and the next day—after allowing an appropriate amount of time to pass—the second plane takes off from Spain and lands in Paris. The idea being, Melbourne collects the prize, sells his famous aircraft to the Smithsonian and spends the rest of his life getting rich by endorsing products and giving commencement speeches, having never risked the dangerous flight."

"It wouldn't work," Kurt said. "In 1927 there was no way for Melbourne to get from New York to Europe in time to appear in Paris. And considering all the pandemonium and press surrounding the prize, he couldn't hope to keep the ruse a secret. Lindbergh was photographed repeatedly once he landed. He met all the dignitaries over there and appeared in multiple newsreels. Melbourne would have gotten the same treatment. Unless he had an identical twin, he could never pull off a stunt like that."

Hiram raised an eyebrow. "Max, any chance Melbourne had a twin?"

"Melbourne had one sister eight years younger than him," Max reported. "No medical or historical records suggest a twin or close-aged relative who could pass for him."

"What if Melbourne was already in Europe," Kurt suggested, "and the hoax was perpetrated on this side of the Atlantic? Easier to fake the takeoff than the landing."

"In that case, his body would have wound up in Spain, not on ice in Brooklyn," Hiram said.

"Good point," Kurt replied. "Maybe I **am** dehydrated. I should have put that together."

Kurt took another drink of water as Max gave them more information regarding the flight.

"All aircraft involved in attempts to win the Orteig Prize were required to carry a sealed barograph. This device recorded atmospheric pressure and altitude as the aircraft traveled, preventing any hidden landings, takeoffs or other interruptions of the flight. The barograph also recorded duration of flight. The U.S. National Aeronautic Association and Aéro-Club of France were used to certify that all barographs were not tampered with. This precaution would preclude the type of hoax you've suggested."

"I'm at a loss," Hiram said.

"Because we're focusing on the wrong pilot," Kurt said. "It's my fault. I came in here asking about Jake Melbourne, but he's irrelevant."

Hiram had found Kurt's instincts to be sharper than most. Rather than disagree, he prodded Kurt to elaborate. "What are you suggesting?"

Kurt straightened up, sitting taller on the backward chair. "For ninety years, everyone thought Melbourne ditched his plane while trying to perpetrate some scam or because he chickened out. But we know that his plane was successfully flown to Europe even if it didn't reach Paris. We know it crashed there and that whoever the pilot was, he died and got buried anonymously as a result of the crash. If Melbourne was trying to set up a hoax, he would have been the one in Europe. If he was going to collect insurance money, he wouldn't have allowed that plane to go anywhere except into the depths of the Atlantic. The fact that the plane actually flew across the ocean without him means he wasn't calling the shots, someone else was. And that means the Orteig Prize was no longer the goal of the flight. We keep looking at Melbourne when we should be trying to figure out who was actually flying the plane when it crashed."

"You think the person flying the plane killed Melbourne and took his place," Hiram said.

"It fits," Kurt replied. "What do you say, Max?

Is there any way to determine who was actually flying the plane when it went down?"

"Researching," Max said, then added, "Photographic evidence of Jake Melbourne climbing into his aircraft on the day of the flight appears to show a man two or three inches shorter than Melbourne."

"Well," Hiram said, "that narrows it down to every living male in 1927 who was shorter than five feet nine inches."

"Incorrect," Max said. "The photograph does not rule out female pilots."

Kurt often laughed at Hiram's banter with Max, sometimes wondering if he'd made Max's personality too close to that of his wife's. "The parish records in San Sebastián list the burial of a young man," Kurt said. "But male or female, whoever got in that plane in 1927 would have to be a pilot. Can you search the records for any pilots who went missing during the time Melbourne's plane vanished?"

"Stand by," Max said. In seconds Max accessed diverse records contained in various governmental databases and cross-referenced them with information from other sources. "No other federally licensed pilots went missing over a two-month period surrounding the disappearance of the **Golden Ram.** Eight died in crashes, but all bodies were recovered and identified."

"What about someone else Melbourne might have been associated with?"

Another momentary delay, but this time Max gave them something to work with. "The only missing person report connected with Jake Melbourne during that time relates to a freelance mechanic named Stefano Cordova who worked at Roosevelt Field prior to Melbourne's flight."

"Prior to but not after?" Kurt asked.

"Correct," Max said. "Cordova's fiancée reported him missing eight days after Melbourne's flight took off. But, according to the report, she hadn't seen him in over a week. He was never found."

Hiram looked at Kurt, who nodded. They were onto something.

Max spoke next. "By your rising skin temperatures, you obviously consider this an important fact."

"Stop watching my skin temperature," Kurt said. "And, yes, it's definitely important. Tell us how Cordova was connected to Melbourne."

"He was a known associate who worked on Melbourne's aircraft. The missing person report suggested they were close friends and that his fiancée feared that Cordova had committed suicide after Melbourne's plane vanished, perhaps blaming himself."

"Could Cordova be the pilot in the photograph pretending to be Melbourne?"

"Uncertain," Max said. "Cordova's height was listed in the missing person report at five feet seven inches. That correlates to the height of the figure in the blurred photograph to an accuracy level of only seventy percent."

"Add in the ostrich-skin boots and it's a direct hit," Hiram said.

"A valid assumption."

Kurt turned to Hiram. "Did MI5 share the pages of the mechanic's log with you?"

"They emailed copies to us. Why?"

"Max," Kurt said. "Compare the handwriting of the mechanic's entries in the early part of the logbook with the notes scribbled on the last few pages."

Max didn't disappoint. "Based on repeatable characteristics, I find a ninety-six percent probability that both sets of writing were done by the same person. The handwriting also matches Stefano Cordova's known writing samples on his petition for a marriage license, filed in the Nassau County Courthouse on December 1st, 1926."

Hiram beamed with pride. "Now use that powerful brain of yours to tell us why a mechanic who did work on Melbourne's plane would have had reason to kill him and take his place."

"Insufficient information," Max said. "I'm brilliant, but I can't pull answers out of thin air."

"Can you speculate?"

"The most logical connection would be Stefano Cordova's family," Max replied. "He was the nephew of Carlo Granzini, a smuggler known to deal in stolen paintings, statuary and historical artifacts."

"That's damn fine speculation," Kurt said. "If NUMA ever retires you—and you don't want to be a doctor—I suggest you go work for the FBI."

"I'll take that as a compliment."

"You should," Kurt said. "What else can you tell us about the Granzini family and their smuggling activities?"

"At the time of the flight, they were wanted by J. Edgar Hoover and the Bureau of Investigation."

"For what crimes?" Hiram asked.

"Unknown," Max said. "All records relating to the Bureau's investigation into activities of the Granzini family are classified under the National Heritage Protection and International Stability Act of 1913. NUMA clearance levels are insufficient to access materials classified under that Act."

Hiram fell silent. Kurt wondered if Max was playing a joke on them. Considering the computer's personality, he couldn't put it past her. But, Max said nothing more.

"What the heck is the National Heritage and whatever you said after that Act?" Kurt asked.

"The National Heritage Protection and International Stability Act, passed by Congress in 1913, signed by President Woodrow Wilson that same year. This Act allows the President to identify material important to American heritage and international stability. It grants the President the powers to classify such materials and all knowledge of them as a national secret without restraint of Congress or the Courts. Suggested time period of classification is fifty to one hundred years, but no upper limit is established. The Act expressly considers the possibility that the President be given the power to protect materials and secrets for a term without end."

"Forever?" Hiram said.

"That would be my reading of the language," Max said.

Kurt had worked in the government for most of his adult life. Both he and Hiram had top secret clearance, both of them had knowledge that went beyond what the public would ever know, but neither of them had ever heard of this particular Act nor had they ever heard of a secret being classified for all eternity.

"This sounds like we-faked-the-moon-landing kind of stuff."

"It's going to take some work to dig the truth out," Kurt replied.

Hiram narrowed his gaze. "You have a plan for that?"

"The beginnings of one," Kurt said. He got up and stretched. The way Kurt saw it, if a President could classify something, then perhaps a Vice President could unclassify it. Or at least find out what had been hidden and why.

"Not going to elaborate, are you?"

Kurt shook his head. "Thanks for the help," he said. "And the water. I feel more alert and sharper already."

"Where are you going?" Hiram asked.

"Home to take a nap," Kurt replied. "Got up way too early this morning. And since I have a party to go to later, I want to look my best."

Chapter 45

Cambridge, England

Morgan Manning pulled up to the cottage-style house in East Cambridge expecting the worst. Several police cars were already on-site, their lights bathing the neighborhood in continuous blue flashes.

A uniformed officer in a neon windbreaker stopped her from approaching. "I'm sorry, but this is a crime scene," he said. "You'll have to turn around."

She held up her ID. "Section 5," she said. "What happened here?"

"Break-in and assault, by the looks of it," the officer said.

"Anyone inside?" she asked.

"No, mum. But it looks like a hell of a fight took place, if you don't mind me saying."

Morgan parked the car and got out. "Have your men begin a search of the surrounding area. Get any video you can find from the traffic cameras. I want to know who did this."

She walked into the house and studied the damage. The living room had been torn apart, with the furniture flipped over and shredded and the shelves swept clean of books and trinkets, which now lay scattered about the floor.

The bedrooms and den were in the same condition. In the kitchen, she found blood on the counter and along the floor. A discarded knife had blood on it as well, while a cricket bat had been broken in half where it had been smashed against a hard surface.

It looked as if Professor Cross had put up a courageous fight. The fact that he was gone and not lying dead in the house was both hopeful and ominous.

Hopeful because they might have a chance to save him if they could figure out where Barlow and his men were going next. Ominous because without the professor to help them, and the **Writings of Qsn** to clue them in, Morgan had no idea where that might be.

She stared at the cricket bat. "Sticky wicket," she whispered. "Indeed."

Returning to her car, she called Pembroke-Smythe and relayed the bad news. Her next call went out long-distance to Kurt Austin in America. She left a simple message. "Professor Cross has been abducted. His house has been destroyed. Hope you're making better progress than I am."

Chapter 46

Number One Observatory Circle, Washington, D.C.

Kurt appeared overdressed as he walked toward the gate of the large home on the grounds of the Naval Observatory. He wore a sharply tailored tuxedo, patent leather shoes and a black bow tie. His French-cuffed shirt was starched nearly to the point of being armor and his cuff links and matching studs were made of cobalt that had been mined from the bottom of the sea.

Before he reached the white-painted house with the green shutters, he stopped at a guardhouse and presented his ID to a member of the Secret Service. After being scanned with a metal detector, he walked up to the canted porch and was allowed into the house by a staff member.

"He's out on the veranda," she said. "He requested that you meet him there."

Kurt was led through the formal reception hall and then through an elegantly appointed living room. From there, he passed through the garden room and out onto the back porch.

Number One Observatory Circle was the official residence of the Vice President of the United States. It was designed to support a family and guests, though for the last several years the only official full-time occupant was a confirmed bachelor.

Kurt found that bachelor on the back deck, puffing away on an impressive cigar.

"Mr. Vice President," the assistant said. "Your guest has arrived."

James Sandecker measured just over five feet six inches tall. Despite the lack of height, he commanded the attention of everyone who met him. He had a stocky build, an intense face and bright red hair. The perfectly trimmed Van Dyke beard on his chin was his calling card.

Before accepting the honor of becoming Vice President, Sandecker had built NUMA into the organization it was today. It had been his idea, based on a love of the sea, and he still took a special interest in its activities.

Sandecker nodded to the assistant and then stared at Kurt suspiciously. "You're a little overdressed for a scuba diver."

Kurt grinned like a wolf. "And I thought admirals wore white to formal occasions."

"I'd prefer it," Sandecker admitted. "On the other hand, your penguin costume has me concerned. Is there a reason you're in a tux?"

"Thought you might need a wingman for the fund-raiser," Kurt said. "Unless you already have a date for the party."

Sandecker had an active social life and was in high demand on the Washington social circuit. His appointment to the Vice Presidency had brought oversight and restrictions that complicated his personal life to a degree, but, being a resourceful man, Sandecker had found ways around them.

"Number one rule of fund-raisers," Sandecker said. "Never take a date to one of these things. It bores them to tears and makes the other women jealous."

Kurt tapped the side of his head. "I'll keep that in mind if I ever accidentally become a politician."

Sandecker put the cigar back in his mouth, then blew a cloud of blue smoke out into the backyard. "What makes you think I need a wingman for tonight? I don't recall sending you an invitation."

Kurt had expected the question and was ready with his response. "My first month at NUMA you had me extract you from a tedious gala where agency Directors were forced to spend the night schmoozing with Congressmen and Senators in hopes of getting larger budgets for the following year. I recall you suggesting my job prospects depended on how successful I was."

"That they did," Sandecker said. "Fortunately for you, you didn't let me down."

"Glad to hear it," Kurt said. "Now, the way I figure it, if there's anything worse than a gaggle of Congressmen and Senators looking to be fawned over, it has to be lobbyists and money donors who want to suck the life out of you before handing over a dollar. Which makes tonight's gala even more of a torture test."

Sandecker preferred blunt, straight-to-the-point talk, something in short supply since he'd become a politician. He appreciated Kurt's assessment. "You're not wrong," he admitted. "But I'm the Vice President now. I can fake a national emergency if I need to get away."

Kurt adjusted his cuffs. "You could," he said. "But you wouldn't do it right out of the gate. Bring me along and I'll tell you a story to help pass the time. You're going to like this one. It begins with lost Egyptian treasure, ends with a pilot unknown to history who crossed the Atlantic on his own a few weeks before Lindbergh."

"What's on tap for the middle part?"

"A beautiful English agent, a group of arms dealers who've been making my life extremely difficult for the last few weeks and intrigue at every turn."

Kurt noticed Sandecker's eyes glinting in the light. He'd momentarily stopped puffing on the cigar, but it remained clenched between his teeth.

"Or," Kurt suggested, "I could leave you to the special interest groups and send you a written summary next week."

Sandecker released another cloud of smoke, aiming this one upward into the still night air. It formed a perfect ring before dissipating. "Don't be so hasty," he said. "Can't hurt to bring you along. I'll get you an earbud and we'll pretend you're with the Secret Service. Who knows, someone might shoot at me tonight. But first I want to know what the objective is. What are you after?"

"What makes you think I'm after something?"

Sandecker laid the cigar down carefully, placing it in an ashtray and allowing it to go out naturally rather than mashing it, which would cause it to smoke bitterly.

"Kurt," he said like a knowing father. "If you're going to survive in Washington, you're going to have to become a better liar. Tonight will do you some good. Some of these people could teach a master class in the art of untruthful speaking."

Officially invited, Kurt offered a slight bow as if to say, **Lead on.**

The two men walked to the front of the house and stepped out under the portico. In his previous position as head of NUMA, Sandecker had pointedly refused to be chauffeured around in limousines, avoiding them as if they were a sign of the Apocalypse. Maintaining that independence wasn't as easy now that he was Vice President.

Official functions demanded official transportation. And while this was technically a private affair, the agents on Sandecker's protection detail were as stubborn as he was.

"Morris," Sandecker said, speaking to the lead Secret Service agent. "I won't be in need of your services tonight."

"Are you canceling the fund-raiser?"

"No," Sandecker said. "I'm using Kurt here for close protection."

Morris didn't bat an eye. "I'm sorry, Mr. Vice President. With all due respect to Mr. Austin, I can't allow you to go alone."

Sandecker exhaled a dissatisfied grunt. "So much for wielding the reins of power. What's the minimum detail that won't get you fired?"

"The driver and myself."

"Fair enough," Sandecker said. "Let's go."

Morris called for the VP's car and a large black sedan pulled up to the front of the house. From the outside, it appeared to be a Cadillac with all the right badges. Underneath, it was actually a purpose-built armored vehicle. It rode on a truck chassis, weighed nearly twenty thousand pounds and was protected by five-inch-thick bulletproof glass, along with layers of steel, ceramic plating and Kevlar.

Kurt and Sandecker climbed in the back, Morris got in the front with the driver and the armored vehicle began to move off.

"Comfortable?" Sandecker said, settling in across from Kurt.

"Beats the crosstown bus," Kurt said. "Mind if I have a drink? Max says I'm dehydrated." He reached toward a small refrigerator.

"That fridge won't help you," Sandecker warned.

Kurt had already pulled it open. Instead of cold beverages, he found clear bags of red liquid hanging inside. Labels stuck to the bags were covered in fine print, the name SANDECKER sticking out prominently. "Did you become a vampire since the last time we met or—"

"It's my own blood," Sandecker said.

"That's only slightly less creepy."

"They draw liters of the stuff every other month," Sandecker explained. "It starts right after you take office. It goes with me wherever I travel, in case something terrible were to befall me and I needed a transfusion on the way to the hospital."

Kurt closed the door, noticing now that a placard on the outside read MEDICAL SUPPLIES. "I see."

"They used to keep the stuff in the trunk," Sandecker explained. "But I pointed out, that wouldn't do me much good if we got rear-ended by a suicide bomber or hit in the tail with an RPG."

Kurt sat back while Sandecker opened a different refrigerator and pulled out a bottle of water. It even had the Vice Presidential seal on it. "You can keep the bottle as a collector's item. Might be worth ten cents someday."

As Kurt twisted the cap off, Sandecker opened another compartment and plucked a big cigar from a humidor. "Had this installed myself. More important than the blood bank."

Kurt had to laugh.

"Now," Sandecker said, lighting the cigar, "tell me the story."

Kurt relayed the details in a conversational way, leading Sandecker into asking questions, piquing his interest with cliff-hangers and answers. As they pulled up to the fund-raising venue, Kurt threw out the final hook, explaining how the **Writings of Qsn** had once been on American soil but that the truth about those who'd smuggled the tablets remained hidden in files he couldn't access.

Sandecker sat back, eyeing the crowd outside the Potomac Club and taking one last puff of the cigar, before making a critical decision. He pressed an INTERCOM button and said to Morris, "Change of plans," he ordered. "Take us to the J. Edgar Hoover Building."

"Now, Mr. Vice President?"

"Yes," Sandecker said. "Now."

"But it's almost ten o'clock."

"It's the FBI," Sandecker said. "They don't close up shop for the evening."

Chapter 47

J. Edgar Hoover Building, Washington, D.C.

The façade of the J. Edgar Hoover Building on Pennsylvania Avenue was made up of concrete blocks and deep-set square windows. It was an architectural style known as Brutalism. And while there were plenty of government edifices of similar design, it seemed most appropriate for the one named after the power-hungry former Director of the FBI.

Even on the brightest day, FBI headquarters was an imposing sight. At night it was like approaching a fortress.

The décor inside was slightly warmer, if still unmistakably government-issue—bland furniture, secured steel doors and a long desk where every visitor had to be identified and checked in, even the sitting Vice President.

The desk administrator, whose name was Trotter, was young, with limited managerial experience—as those placed on the night shift usually were. He seemed perplexed by the situation. He'd had agents appear in the middle of the night, seen suspects or witnesses brought in under cover of darkness, even had the occasional lunatic try to bust into the place claiming that Elvis or Santa Claus was being held captive there, but he'd never had a sitting Vice President stop by for an after-hours visit.

"I'm not sure what to tell you, Mr. Vice President," he said. "The Director and the Assistant Directors have all gone home. Perhaps you could have one of them look into these files in the morning?"

"Not necessary," Sandecker said. "I'm here to-night. I just need one of your archivists."

Kurt offered some additional advice. "What we really need is someone who knows how to access the older files and records."

"And you are?"

"Kurt Austin, Special Projects Director at NUMA."

"The underwater guys?"

"That's us."

Sandecker took over the conversation. "We're wasting time. Before you get all worried, we just need to look at some files from the early 1900s. Nothing political, nothing relating to anyone living today, just historical information we'll be accessing on my clearance."

Trotter rubbed his hands together and exhaled. The FBI had been dragged into politics way too often in the past decade, but it was unlikely that files from the early 1900s could stir up much of a hornet's nest. And it was the Vice President asking. "Ms. Curtis would be your best bet," he said. "And you're in luck because she's still here."

He pulled out a pair of visitor badges, felt odd handing one to the Vice President, but had the two men sign in anyway.

"Something strange about the way he said 'in luck,'" Sandecker noted.

Kurt nodded. He'd noticed it too.

Trotter used a radio to summon Ms. Curtis and then buzzed them through. "She'll meet you in the inner foyer," he said. "Try not to make her mad."

Kurt attached the visitor badge and followed Sandecker through the inner doors to the second foyer. "Wonder what he meant by that?"

"We're about to find out," Sandecker said.

The doors at the far end opened and Ms. Curtis joined them. She was a thin woman, fit and strong for seventy-five years of age. She wore a beige ankle-length skirt, a green top and comfortable sensible shoes. A pair of reading glasses with purple frames dangling from a sparkling chain rested against her chest.

"Hmm," she said as if surprised or unimpressed. "And I thought this was one of Gary's late-night jokes. What can I do for you, Mr. Vice President?"

"Glad you recognized me," Sandecker said.

"Oh, you're easy to spot," she said. "You're colorful."

Kurt did his best to suppress a laugh.

"We're looking for some very old files," Sandecker said. "And once we find them, we may need to wake the Director and clear the viewing of them. That way, you won't get in trouble for showing them to us. If he gives you any guff, I'll take the blame."

"It's okay," Ms. Curtis said. "I'm not afraid of the Director. He and I have an understanding."

Kurt stepped forward. "Kurt Austin," he said, introducing himself. "You can call me Kurt."

"Miranda Abigail Curtis," she said in response. "You can call me Ms. Curtis."

This time it was Sandecker who struggled not to laugh.

Ms. Curtis turned and waved them forward. "This way, gentlemen."

They followed her to the far end of what seemed an endless white hall and stepped onto an unadorned elevator, which took them down four levels to the sub-basement of the building. Stepping out of the elevator, they entered a huge open storehouse. It ran under the entire building, covering nearly five acres of space, every square foot of it filled with numbered cabinetry.

The FBI had used this underground vault almost since its inception, adding more storage as time went on. Not all the filing cabinets matched since they'd been purchased and installed at different times over the decades. As Kurt looked at a map of fire exits on a bulletin board, he could see that the layout was circular, with spokes meeting in the center, like a spider's web.

"Welcome to my parlor," Ms. Curtis told them as if channeling his thoughts. "The records hall spans the width of the building and the entire space beneath the courtyard right up to Pennsylvania Avenue. We have nearly fifteen million files stored down here, an estimated seven thousand tons of paper. And that doesn't include computer files or other evidence, which is stored elsewhere."

"So," Kurt said. "Do you use the Dewey Decimal System or—"

She fixed him with a withering glare. "Something tells me you were a troublemaker in school, Mr. Austin. We knew how to deal with that type of attitude back in my day."

"I'll try to behave," Kurt said.

"You do that," she said. "Now, how old are these files you're looking for?"

"From the 1920s," Kurt said.

"Then we'll have to use the old computer," she said. "Not everything has been brought up to date."

The streets of Washington were home to more security cameras, motion sensors, security guards and police officers than perhaps any other spot on earth. That was especially true on Pennsylvania Avenue, with its abundance of government buildings. But what the banks of cameras, sensors, guards and police on the street had missed, what even the Vice President's Secret Service agents and Kurt Austin had not taken notice of, was a large crow sitting on an outstretched branch of a tall tree across from the entrance to the FBI building.

They hadn't seen it fly down the street or noticed it landing. Nor had anyone questioned what a daylight-loving bird like a crow would be doing out in the middle of the night. Neither had they seen an identical bird sitting atop a streetlight a hundred yards down the road.

The crow in the tree and its twin on the pole were mechanical devices made of lightweight Space Age materials and powered by the next generation of compact lithium-ion batteries. They flew like regular birds, flapping their wings when taking off and gliding when they had enough altitude. They perched and even squawked like the real thing once they had landed. But their iridescent eyes were actually powerful cameras capable of seeing in regular wavelengths and infrared. Hidden in their beaks were sensitive microphones capable of picking up voices at long distances when pointed in the right directions.

The first crow had followed the armored limousine from the Naval Observatory, tracking it to central Washington, where the second crow had picked it up and trailed it to the J. Edgar Hoover Building. Both now rested, awaiting new orders.

Three miles away, a man and a woman sitting in a silver Tesla were arguing about what orders to issue. The woman occupied the driver's seat while the man was in the back, surrounded by multiple video screens and a pair of lighted keyboards.

He was dressed in dirty clothing and thin enough to be called emaciated. His jet-black hair was fixed in a wild pattern, his ears, eyebrows and nose adorned with stainless steel piercings. The impression he gave was that of a starving tattoo artist.

"The situation is no good," he said with an Eastern European accent. "It's gone from bad to worse and now to impossible. We should have taken Austin out on the way over. Before he met with the Vice President. And definitely before they drove to the FBI building." His voice peaking as he finished the tirade.

The woman scoffed. Her hair was long, straight and dyed from the same bottle as his. She wore a gray hoodie and black stretch pants and running shoes. Physically more fit than he was and free of piercings, she looked like an urban housewife ready to go for a jog.

"It was too soon," she told him, her voice as flat and unemotional as his was expressive. "The money hadn't hit our account yet. And we don't do charity work."

"You might as well send the money back," he replied. "We can't get at Austin in the FBI building."

"Open your eyes, little brother," she said. "What do you see?"

"I see the end of a failed experiment."

"They're wearing tuxedos," she pointed out. "They have other places to be. They'll be back out soon enough."

"And right back into a limousine you'd need an antitank missile to obliterate."

Fydor and Xandra were brother and sister. They argued incessantly but stuck together. Working as a team, they had entered the assassination game operating under the name the Toymaker. They were known for their use of intricate devices to deliver poisons, bombs or even pull the trigger remotely on an old-fashioned kill.

She gazed at him. "You're cute when you're angry, Fydor, but you're so timid. You know better than I how far away we'll be when your machines take action. We just have to wait until they come out."

Fydor stared at her in shock. "You want to kill

Austin in front of the FBI building? With the Vice President at his side and Secret Service agents all around?"

"No," she said. "I want you to kill them all."

Fydor looked as if he was going to lose his mind, but Xandra just smiled.

"You see things myopically, little brother. The setup is perfect. If we take them both out and claim the attack in the name of an infamous terrorist organization, everyone will assume it was an attack on the Vice President instead of Austin. The heat will go elsewhere and we'll be able to walk away without having to break a sweat."

Fydor shook his head meekly and mumbled something, though he didn't have it in him to challenge her.

She flicked on her own screen to admire the bird's-eye view. "Get your other little toys ready to go. We're not passing up a million dollars just because the level of difficulty has increased."

Chapter 48

J. Edgar Hoover Building, Archives, Sub-Level 4,
Washington, D.C.

Deep beneath the J. Edgar Hoover Building,
Kurt, Sandecker and Ms. Curtis discussed the files that Kurt wanted to
see. Despite the initial tussling between them,
Ms. Curtis quickly warmed to Kurt, especially
as he explained the historical quest they were on.

"History's always been my favorite subject," she
said. "That's what led me into this job. Down
here, I've learned all kinds of things you'll never
read about in any book."

Kurt raised an eyebrow. "Such as?"

"You want to know about Roswell?" she asked.
"Want to know what really happened out there?"

"I'd be interested," Kurt admitted with a grin.

Sandecker cleared his throat purposefully, putting a stop to the fun. "Maybe some other time,
Ms. Curtis. We're here for the information on the

Granzini crime family, specifically the classified files related to their activities in 1926 and 1927."

"All business, this one," she said. Swiveling in her seat and waking up her computer, she entered in a password and began tapping away at the console. It wasn't long before she had a list of file numbers and locations. "We have forty-three classified files," she said. "None of them have been digitized, so I'll have to go get the dead-tree copies."

Kurt wouldn't hear of letting her carry them back on her own and went into the maze with her. They started off in the main aisle, branched off three times and eventually stopped beside a set of gunmetal gray filing cabinets that looked as old as the reports themselves.

"Second level," Ms. Curtis said, pointing. "Right up there."

Kurt slid a ladder into place, climbed up and opened the drawer. He checked the numbers she'd given him against the files inside and began pulling out the selected folders. They were yellowed and brittle with age.

One by one, he handed them down. Ms. Curtis kept them organized by placing them in bins on a cart on wheels. When the last was loaded, Kurt climbed back down and pushed the cart toward a reading room, where Sandecker was already waiting.

"I'll leave you two for an hour," she said. "Just press the intercom button if you need anything."

Diving into the paperwork, Kurt and Sandecker soon had the background on the Granzini family.

"Two branches of the family came here in the 1880s. One from Sicily and one from Salerno," Kurt said.

Sandecker was reading a different set of files. "According to the Treasury Department, they were more a group of smugglers than a true crime family. Specializing in gemstones from Africa, Italian art and sculpture, also silk from China."

"Those sound like perfectly legitimate businesses to me," Kurt said.

"Sure," Sandecker replied, "as long as you pay the import duties, which ran as high as fifty percent back then. Apparently, the Granzini family considered that an optional expense."

"It does cut into the profit margin," Kurt said.

"Treasury agents busted them in 1908 and 1913," Sandecker said. "The New York Attorney General investigated them from 1915 through 1922. The Bureau of Investigation was looking into their activities as early as 1923. By my count, at least five members of the family served time in jail. Several others went overseas during World War One, choosing induction into the Army instead of facing incarceration."

Kurt was finding similar details in his stack of files. He undid his bow tie, allowing it to hang loose, and undid the top button of his shirt. "This is all very interesting," he said. "But unless you've found something that says they were related to the Roosevelts, I can't see any reason why these files were classified in the first place, let alone under some obscure Act related to national heritage."

"You didn't hear it from me," Sandecker replied, "but the government does make a mistake every once in a while."

"You don't say."

Kurt put down the report he'd been reading and leafed through the box, studying the names of various agencies as they appeared on the labels of the files' tabs. "Treasury Department, Bureau of Investigation, IRS, Army Intelligence—there are files from a dozen different agencies here. Seems like overkill for a minor family of smugglers."

"And a complicated situation to piece together," Sandecker said. "It'll take the rest of the night to read through all this."

Kurt figured half of the next day would be spent on it as well. "There is someone who might be able to help us cut to the chase here. She loves history, she's spent forty years working with these files and I have a feeling she might be listening at the door."

Sandecker laughed. "Just don't ask her about Roswell or the moon landing."

Kurt pressed the INTERCOM button and asked Ms. Curtis to join them. She arrived moments later.

"Happy to help," she told them. With Ms. Curtis guiding them, their progress accelerated rapidly. She cut through all the clutter and got them into the files that mattered. "Now, I don't know what's in them," she insisted, smiling as she spoke, "but based on the coding numbers these files were the first to be classified under that National Heritage Act."

She gave a handful of files to each of them. To Kurt's surprise, the dossiers came from the State Department. Even more shocking, they spoke of the Granzini family in glowing terms.

"This is interesting," Kurt said. "Under Calvin Coolidge, the State Department had begun setting up a network of informants. They chose to use crime families with links to Europe. They were trying to keep tabs on the Communists, the Fascists and several other radical groups operating in the postwar landscape. The Granzinis were connected to powerful families in Europe by their smuggling operations and had access to information no journalist or Army Intelligence agent could find."

"Sounds like Kennedy asking the mob to bump off Castro," Sandecker said.

"This was a lot more intricate," Kurt said.

Kurt read on, summarizing what he was learning. "By the time the Roaring Twenties kicked in and everybody was flush with cash, these crime families had become an effective, pre-CIA spy network."

"That explains why this stuff is classified," Sandecker said.

"Spend enough time down here, you'll find all kinds of strange bedfellows," Ms. Curtis said.

Sandecker was leafing through a different file. Having read acres of government paper during his lifetime, he knew how to skip past the filler and get right to the heart of the matter. Sandecker's file was from the Bureau of Investigation. It had a very different take on the Granzini family. "Strong-arm robberies, extortion, tax evasion—the Bureau has the Granzinis pegged as street thugs and gangsters. They were stealing art and antiquities as early as the mid-twenties and smuggling it all out to Europe. Hoover himself made stopping the Granzinis a priority."

"Sounds like one hand doesn't know what the other hand is doing," Ms. Curtis said slyly.

Sandecker nodded. "In 1926 they were suspected of arson, setting a fire in which several people died. A short time later, the leader of the family shot several known associates whom they'd previously worked with. During the getaway, they killed an agent working for the Bureau of Investigation and were briefly listed as Public Enemy Number One."

"When was that?" Kurt asked.

"March 17th, 1927."

"That's only two months before Jake Melbourne made his flight," Kurt replied. "Or should I say failed to make his flight? Who'd they shoot and what did they steal?"

Sandecker read off a list of names, none of which rang a bell. "It says the victims were archeologists whom the Granzinis had worked with before as part of their theft and antique smuggling ring."

He found a list of stolen items along with several photographs. "The loot consisted of ancient Egyptian antiquities uncovered in"—Sandecker paused before reading the location, finally spiting it out—"northern Arizona."

"You mean owned by someone in Arizona?" Kurt asked.

"No," Sandecker said. "According to this, the artifacts were pulled from a cave in a remote part of the Grand Canyon."

Kurt put his file down and leaned over to see what Sandecker was looking at. Half the file was dedicated to the discovery of these items in the Grand Canyon. It included photographs, crude maps and descriptions. There was a letter from the archeologists sent to the Granzinis that listed rumors they were following up on, including a famous article in the **Phoenix Gazette** that insisted members of a Smithsonian-funded expedition had found Egyptian treasure in the Grand Canyon as early as 1909 and then covered the discovery up. There were topographical maps with areas previously searched marked. And there was a recounting of a Native American legend that talked about People of the Sun who'd come to the Southwest thousands of years before carrying golden coffins and statues of animals.

Sandecker summarized. "It says they came in the time of the forefathers. They broke through the walls of the narrow canyon and burrowed into the cliffs, hollowed out the mountain and dragged cartloads of the rubble to the riverside to build a tomb for their ancestors. According to the legend, they sealed up the tomb when they were finished and left to follow the setting sun."

The next page contained a set of poorly lit photographs that hadn't aged well since they were taken. Holding them to the light revealed a cave filled with treasures, including statues of Anubis and Horus, mummified bodies stacked like cordwood and at least one gleaming—and possibly gold-plated—sarcophagus.

"Well, I'll be damned," Sandecker said.

"It certainly looks impressive," Kurt replied. "But the English professor, who's now been kidnapped, insisted we'd be looking at the combined treasure of at least fifteen Pharaohs collected together. There should be more than one sarcophagus."

"According to this, it's a large cave with many chambers," Sandecker said. "No telling what else is in there."

Kurt nodded. "What else does it say?"

Sandecker continued. "Upon word of the discovery, the Granzinis started talking with several of their favorite contacts in Europe. A French family in particular. A deal had been worked out where the Granzinis would sell some of the artifacts to the buyers in Europe and the archeologists would take a portion of the money. But first they had to convince the prospective buyers that the cache was real. They planned to do that by smuggling small items, along with these photographs and a series of hieroglyphics tablets. They took a picture of themselves standing at the rim of the canyon with the items to prove they had come from America. Take a look."

Kurt glanced at the photograph and saw flat stones laying on the ground in front of the people. Placed together, they were as large as a sheet of drywall. The photo was in black and white, so he couldn't tell what color the tablets were, but they were clearly covered in hieroglyphics. "Looks a lot like the **Writings of Qsn.**"

"The Granzinis must have thought they were about to change their address and move in next door to the Rockefellers," Sandecker said. "The question is, what went wrong?"

"The same thing that always goes wrong when you have criminals with a large amount of money to split," Ms. Curtis said. "Greed took over."

They looked at her.

"That's just a guess."

Sandecker looked back to the report and found that guess to be more than accurate. "According to this, the Granzinis killed the archeologists to keep the discovery a secret."

Kurt sat back for a moment. Something was off. "That doesn't make any sense," he said. "If the plan was to establish the legitimacy of the find—reaping gains from the notoriety of the discovery being on American soil—they needed their friends the archeologists. More to the point, keeping it a secret doesn't help drive up the price."

"You're looking for logical thinking among dishonest minds," Sandecker said.

"They might not be honest," Kurt said, "but they can add and subtract."

"Maybe this will explain it," Ms. Curtis said. She handed them a file from the bottom of the stack. It came from the Office of the President and had the signature of Calvin Coolidge and the Executive Seal on it.

Sandecker opened the folder and read through it, a scowl growing on his face by the time he finished.

Ms. Curtis raised an eyebrow. She knew what was in the file. "Truth is stranger than fiction."

"It's almost too impossible to believe," Sandecker said.

"What is?" Kurt asked.

"See for yourself."

Sandecker passed the dossier to Kurt but said nothing. He obviously wanted Kurt to see for himself.

Kurt scanned down from the top, slowing as he reached the new information. He read the section twice just to make sure he wasn't missing anything. The details clarified the situation instantly. They explained why the Granzinis had killed the archeologists and why they hadn't left anyone alive to talk about the treasure.

Kurt closed the file. "Well," he said, "this changes everything."

Sandecker nodded slowly. "It certainly does."

Chapter 49

J. Edgar Hoover Building, Washington, D.C.

Kurt and Sandecker bid Ms. Curtis good-bye, with Sandecker suggesting NUMA could use someone with her curiosity and memory, should she ever tire of her role at the Bureau.

She promised to think about it, before retreating to the subterranean file room.

"I can just imagine her and Perlmutter working together," Sandecker said.

They met Agent Morris in the outer foyer and he radioed the driver to bring the limo around. The three of them left the building together and took the stairs down toward a wide sidewalk in front of 10th Street.

A temporary guardhouse and a collection of concrete planters lined the sidewalk so that no car or truck could drive between them and into the FBI building. Beyond the sidewalk was a yellow-striped section of 10th Street separated by orange traffic cones. It served as a pickup and drop-off lane for important personnel and guests. The Vice President certainly qualified.

Alerted by Agent Morris, a uniformed officer stepped out of the guard shack and moved the cones on the street side so the limo could approach the curb. Kurt and Sandecker stood silently by as the big vehicle came down 10th.

Lost in his own thoughts for a minute, Kurt found himself looking off into the distance. His gaze settled on a large black bird, a crow, sitting in one of the planters at the end of the road. It tilted its head, looking back at him. There was something undeniably strange about that gaze. But before Kurt could say what, his attention was diverted by a high-pitched whine like that of an expensive remote-controlled car.

Kurt turned toward the offending sound and spotted a skateboard-sized object racing the wrong way up 10th Street and coming directly toward them. It had six small wheels—three on either side—and carried a large battery pack on the aft end. Up front, held in a hydraulic grip, was an Uzi submachine gun.

"Get down!" Kurt shouted.

He tackled Sandecker like the Secret Service agent Sandecker had suggested he pose as. The two of them hit the ground behind the nearest concrete planter, crashing to the sidewalk just as the six-wheeled vehicle opened fire.

A line of bullets stitched across the face of the planter, stopped effectively by its concrete and soil.

The remote-controlled killing machine stopped, pivoted and opened fire on the uniformed officer from the guardhouse. He went down in the midst of calling for backup.

As the officer fell, Agent Morris pulled out his weapon and blasted several rounds at the machine, hitting it twice.

The metal-clad killer was unaffected. It jerked to the side, recovered and then accelerated up onto the curb, darting between two of the planters and weaving around in search Kurt and Sandecker.

Kurt was unarmed, but that wasn't going to keep him out of the battle. He grabbed a large stone from the landscaping materials and jumped up onto the planter. Spotting the agile little attacker, he hurled the stone downward as if he were spiking a football after a touchdown.

It recorded a direct hit, knocking the gun askew and sending the machine tumbling. It landed upside down, flailing for a moment like a beetle caught on its back, extending a wing in hopes of righting itself.

Not interested in seeing that happen, Kurt jumped and landed on the machine with both feet, bending the wing irreparably and kicking the Uzi free.

Before he could celebrate, the crow he'd spotted earlier flew his way, nearly clipping his face. He

ducked and watched it fly off in the opposite direction. "Something evil about that bird," he said.

There was no time to wonder what it might be.
A second RC vehicle was racing their way. Instead
of a gun, this one had a load of plastic explosives
strapped on top. A third machine sped along behind it, armed with a pistol and peppering the
sidewalk with covering gunfire.

By now the limo had screeched to a halt between the remaining orange cones. Morris pushed
Sandecker toward the open door but took a bullet
in the leg before he could climb in himself. He fell
to the ground and Kurt went to help him, but he
shoved Kurt away. "Get the Vice President out of
here! Go! Go! Go!"

As Kurt dove into the limo, the driver stomped
on the gas pedal. A cloud of white smoke billowed
out behind them as the 650 horsepower turbo engine spun the big tires. The limo surged forward,
but the plinking of shells hitting the bulletproof
armor told them they hadn't escaped yet.

They roared down 10th Street toward
Pennsylvania Avenue. Fortunately, it was late
enough that little traffic got in their way. Coming
to the turn, the limo leaned, sliding, as it sped
around the corner.

Righting the car, the driver called out an alert
on his radio. "Immediate Code Four," he shouted.
"Pennsylvania Avenue, Government Two."

Code 4 turned every streetlight in Washington

red except for those programmed to allow a government vehicle to take a specific emergency route to a secure location. Government 2 meant the Vice President was on board.

A response in his earbud told him help was coming. "Backup is on the way," he shouted to Kurt and Sandecker.

Kurt braced himself as the limo turned again. Seconds later a patrol car from the D.C. police force pulled onto the road beside them. It escorted them for a half a block before pulling out in front and then slowing down.

"Get out of the way," the driver yelled in frustration.

Kurt looked through the partition and the front window, gazing into the squad car. He noticed something ominous. The car had no driver. "It's a setup."

The driver was confused. "What?"

"Turn!"

It was too late. The back window of the squad car shattered as a high-powered weapon mounted inside opened fire.

In a matter of seconds, the rapid-fire attack had scored a dozen hits, filling the windshield with pockmarks and cracks. The bulletproof polymer held, but the damage made it impossible to see.

The driver looked down, his eyes transitioning to a screen in the center console where the display from a camera showed the view ahead. To get away from the squad car, the driver cut to the right, aiming for a side street.

The turn was tight, too constricted for the limo to take at high speed. The big car slid out of control, skidding up onto the sidewalk and slamming a light pole side-on while hitting a parked car with its front end.

The double impact brought the limo to a sudden stop. Kurt and Sandecker were thrown about in the back. The driver was dazed but soon came to his senses.

"We can't sit here," Kurt shouted.

The driver understood. He restarted the stalled engine and got the vehicle moving again. They pulled away from the collapsed lamppost, bulldozed the parked car out of the way and pulled back onto the street.

They'd gone about a hundred feet when the driverless squad car appeared at the far end, turned and accelerated toward them.

"It must have circled the block after we crashed."

The driver slammed on the brakes, put the big car in reverse and began to back up. Kurt glanced behind them and saw bad news. The speedy little remote-controlled vehicles had come racing around the corner. The one with the pistol began firing. The small-caliber bullets were stopped easily by the limo's armor, but the explosives-laden machine was the real danger.

"Forward," Kurt shouted.

"But the other car—"

"Go forward now!"

The driver slammed on the brakes and shifted gears again. He stomped on the gas pedal once more, but the heavy limousine was not nimble enough to avoid its fate. The attacker raced under the chassis and detonated its payload of explosives.

Chapter 50

The explosion shook the block like thunder. The dark side street lit up with an orange fireball that engulfed the Vice President's limousine and the parked cars around it. Several exploded in flames as their gas tanks ruptured.

Had there been any onlookers, they would have seen that the limo was burning and damaged beyond repair. The wheels had been blown out sideways, the drivetrain hopelessly mangled. Every metal surface had been buckled in one way or another and every window scarred by fissures.

What an observer wouldn't have seen were Kurt, Sandecker and the driver still alive and kicking, protected from the blast by the armor cladding the underside of the passenger compartment. The V-shaped configuration of the armor allowed it to compress into the body of the car, absorbing the blast as it simultaneously directed the force of the blast outward and away from it. The design was a lesson learned from the fight against IEDs in the Gulf War. It just saved the lives of the three men inside.

Kurt was the first to regain his senses. With his ears ringing, he raised his head, looking around to assess the damage. The flicker of orange light outside told him they were on fire while the bent roof panels and other damage inside told him they wouldn't be moving anytime soon.

He checked on Sandecker. "Are you okay?"

Sandecker had hit his head and was bleeding from a gash at the hairline. Other than that, he looked untouched. Even his bow tie remained perfectly in position. "More angry than hurt."

"That makes two of us." He couldn't get to the driver, but the silence from up front told him the man had been injured worse than either he or the Vice President.

"You have anything in this car besides cigars and blood?"

Sandecker pointed to a section of the seating. Kurt pulled up a cushion and found a weapons locker. Inside were two Heckler & Koch SP5K machine pistols.

"Backup has to be coming soon," Sandecker said.

Kurt pulled out one of the tactical weapons and made sure it was loaded, with a bullet in the chamber. "Not that I should be giving orders, but if you could get on the radio and direct the reinforcements to go after that squad car."

"What are you going to do?"

"I'm going outside to hunt that six-wheeled robot and any friends it might have brought along with it."

"Are you sure that's necessary?"

"This car is almost a tank, but not quite," Kurt said. "We won't survive another blast like that. Time to take the fight to the street."

Kicking the door open, Kurt felt the heat of the lingering flames and smelled the stench of burning rubber. He heard the sound of police sirens and helicopters coming in from the distance. The cavalry was on its way, but it would be too long before they arrived.

Looking through the smoke, he searched for any sign of the little machines that had attacked them. Obviously, the bomb-carrying vehicle was gone, having obliterated itself in the explosion, but the gun-toting one could still be out there. And there was no way of knowing how many of the remote-controlled machines had been dispatched in the first place.

With his gun raised, Kurt searched through the wreckage, watching for any sign of movement. He quickly realized he was being watched as well. Across the street, sitting on the roof of a demolished car, was the same crow he'd seen outside the FBI building.

As soon as its eyes focused on him, the remote-controlled weapon in the fake police car began firing.

Kurt dove back inside the limo and slammed the door. The shells put three huge dents in the armor, but the multiple levels of plating still held.

"Either that bird has risen up against us or we're being watched by a mechanical contrivance," he said.

Sandecker cast him an odd glance and then turned his attention back to the radio. He was speaking with the pilot of the nearest military helicopter, barking orders like he'd done in his younger days. "That's right," he said. "Engage the police car."

The pilot asked a question that didn't sit well with the VP.

"I don't care if it is the Metro PD," Sandecker said. "We're taking direct fire from it."

The sound of a helicopter crossing above filled the street. It was followed shortly thereafter by a hail of gunfire and a minor explosion as the phony police car's gas tank ruptured and exploded.

"Target has been eliminated," a voice over the radio said.

"Great job," Sandecker said.

"We're not out of the woods yet," Kurt said. "Those little remotes are still out there."

"Drones and RC cars," Sandecker said, shaking

his head. "You'd think they'd come up with a more dignified way to attack the Vice President."

"Don't want to sound like an egomaniac," Kurt said, "but I think I'm the target."

"You?"

"Remember those arms dealers I told you about?" Kurt asked. "I'm betting this is their doing. Probably tied to the files we just borrowed from the FBI."

"You're probably right," Sandecker said.

"Sorry for endangering you," Kurt said, "but I'm about to turn the tables on them."

"And how's that?"

An idea had dawned on Kurt. One so devious it made him proud. "I'm going to give them another chance to shoot at me."

With Sandecker looking on, Kurt reached for the files Ms. Curtis had copied from the Archives. Shuffling through them, he grabbed the FBI file, the one that Hoover's men had written before they knew the truth.

Next, he opened the refrigerator, pulled out a bag of Sandecker's blood and stuffed it down inside an inner pocket of his tuxedo.

The look on Sandecker's face told him all he needed to know. "You can't be serious."

"Can you think of a better plan?" Kurt asked.

"I can hardly think of a worse one," Sandecker said. "But, good luck."

Kurt shouldered the buckled door open and got out once again. He stepped away from the vehicle with the gun in one hand, the file in the other. Moving through the smoke, he acted jumpy, turning this way and that, as if expecting to get attacked at any second.

He knew the crow was watching him but ignored it, looking instead for any sign of the six-wheeled killing machine.

A shadow flickered in front of the streetlamp as the black bird took flight. At the same moment, the distinctive whine of the RC's motor sounded on the far side of the limousine.

Kurt spun around, spotting the machine as it appeared from behind the wrecked limo. He raised his gun and pulled the trigger, firing just as the remote-controlled machine locked onto him and fired.

Kurt's shot was accurate, piercing the machine's electrical gearbox and knocking it sideways just as it triggered its own weapon. The return fire flew wide off to the left, but Kurt pretended otherwise, lurching to the side and spinning around.

To anyone watching, it looked as if he'd been hit dead center. He dropped the pistol as he fell, stumbling forward but also thumping his chest hard enough to break the bag of Sandecker's blood.

The punch, delivered quickly and as if he were reacting to being hit, was almost unnoticeable, but the impact tore the IV bag and sent Sandecker's blood streaming down Kurt's white tuxedo shirt.

Kurt took another stumbling step to make it look good and then fell on his side. The hardest part was hitting the ground without doing anything to break his fall.

Lying there, eyes half open, Kurt saw that the remote-controlled machine was dead but that the crow was still staring at him. He topped off his theatrics by reaching for the file he'd dropped and allowing his hand to fall short of it, then going completely still.

Several blocks away, still in the back of the Tesla, Fydor watched the events on-screen via the camera eyes of the mechanical bird.

"He's down," he said to Xandra. "Austin is down. Finally." He sighed deeply. "I thought they were going to escape. I really thought they were going to get away."

Helicopters thundered overhead, heading toward the wrecked limousine. Police cars raced in from every direction, lights flashing frantically, sirens wailing.

"Finish him," Xandra ordered. "Quickly. We need proof of his death for payment."

Fydor tried to hit Kurt with another blast from the Uzi but found the remote unit unresponsive.

"The RCs are out," he said. "All three of them. Austin must have hit the last one as he went down."

"What about the squad car?"

"Obliterated from above," Fydor said. "Like we will be if we don't get out of here."

"We're not leaving without proof," she insisted. "Use the bird. Get a close-up of Austin's body."

Fydor switched screens and took control of the black bird. He directed it to swoop down onto the blacktop beside Austin's prone body. It hopped into the air, glided from its perch and flew down, landing six feet from where Kurt lay. Drifting smoke obscuring the view.

"Closer," Xandra said.

Fydor moved the crow forward. The image resolved as the gap shrunk. Both Fydor and Xandra stared at the screen. They saw Kurt in full color, saw his awkward positioning, the blood-soaked tuxedo shirt, the half-open eyes. The truth was obvious.

"Now can we get out of here?" Fydor asked.

Xandra hesitated. "What's that?" she asked, pointing to something beyond Kurt's outstretched hand. "Over there."

"It looks like a file folder," Fydor said. "It must be what they went to the FBI building to retrieve."

"Grab it," she ordered. "Barlow will almost certainly pay extra for it."

"Are you sure?"

"Quickly!"

———

Kurt lay in the street, holding his breath and remaining still. He saw the mechanical crow swoop down and land, watched as it hopped closer and studied him. He knew it was fake—no living bird would walk through smoke and fire—but it looked and moved so realistically, it would have been easy to forget.

It came up to him, studied him for a second and then turned its perfect bird-like head, focusing on his outstretched hand and the file on the ground.

With two quick hops the crow reached the folder, used its beak to lift the edge and then gripped the file tightly with a mechanical claw. With the dossier held securely, the bird stretched out its wings and began flapping them wildly. It hopped in the air, swooped low along the street and then climbed higher as it picked up speed. Passing the end of the street, the black device vanished into the dark of night.

Kurt took a shallow breath but remained where he was. He resisted the urge to grin—too much damage had been done for that—but for the first time since spotting the trawler off the coast of Scotland he knew he'd gained the upper hand. And all because of a mechanical bird.

Chapter 51

You're playing a dangerous game here."

Kurt looked across the desk to Rudi Gunn. He'd just finished laying out his plan to deal with the Bloodstone Group once and for all. He hadn't expected Rudi to like it, but ultimately Rudi was a pragmatist. Kurt was counting on him.

"We're not going to get another chance like this," Kurt told him.

"Why take a chance at all?" Rudi asked. "Why not toss the ball back over to Interpol and MI5 where it belongs? Ask the FBI to look into it?"

Kurt leaned back. Despite two showers and fresh clothes, he could still smell the acrid aroma of explosives and burnt rubber from the previous night. "Interpol is a paper tiger," he said. "And MI5 isn't going to be much help here in America. As for the FBI, aside from one of their archivists, they consider me and my opinions about as valuable as a week-old newspaper."

Rudi looked at a report that detailed the FBI's findings regarding the attack on the Vice Presidential limousine. "They have rejected your theory about being the target of the attack. Something about being a narcissist who thinks he's more important than the second-most-powerful man in the world."

Kurt knew how it looked. "That's my point," he said. "They don't believe a word of it. Which means they're not looking for Barlow or his people or whoever it was that built that mechanical bird."

"I noticed you didn't mention that to them."

"I looked crazy enough already," Kurt said. "Didn't want to confirm all their suspicions."

Rudi laughed and put away the FBI report. "So what you're telling me is, it's either us or no one. And you want to risk everything to trap Barlow. How can you even be sure they'll fall for it?"

"They have the **Writings of Qsn,**" Kurt said, "which, according to what Max and Hiram were able to get off that photograph, suggests the treasure lies in some desert ravine on the far side of a large sea. They also have the copies of the old FBI file, which verifies the existence of the treasure, the connection to the Granzini family and the approximate location in the Grand Canyon where the rest of the treasure lies. There's even a hand-drawn map, aerial photos and snapshots from the inside of the cave. There's literally no way for them to miss the connection." Kurt grinned almost maniacally as he spoke. "They have to come here. Either that or give up."

Rudi looked away, twirling a pen in his fingers, as he considered the possibilities. "Realizing I couldn't talk you out of this if I tried, I'll consider your request. What do you need to pull this off?"

"Satellite data detailed enough to match the location of the FBI photos to the exact spot in the canyon where the archeologists found the cave."

Rudi nodded. "That should be easy enough. Hiram and Max have used photos to match the contours and orientation of old landscapes before. Of course, the Bloodstone Group will have no problem doing the same thing, which I can only assume you're counting on."

"I am," Kurt said. "But, along with Max being quicker to the punch, it'll allow us to get there first and lie in wait."

"By yourselves?"

"We can't exactly hide an army down there," Kurt said. "If they see one thing out of place—one sign of preparation or security—they'll bail before any of the important people show up. No good capturing a few scouts when we need to capture Barlow and his top lieutenants."

"I'm not letting you go in there alone," Rudi said.

"I'll have Joe, Morgan and the Trouts."

"Not interested in seeing my entire Special Operations team wiped out at the same time. Adding one MI5 operative doesn't change that equation. You're going to have backup of one type or another."

Kurt glanced over at a map on the wall, focusing on the western United States and northern Arizona. "There's an Army base near Flagstaff called Camp Navajo. They do a lot of basic training and National Guard stuff out there. A small detachment of Rangers sent there and held on alert would never be noticeable. Once we've confirmed that Barlow and his men are on-site, we make a quick call for help, the Rangers swoop in and the rest is history."

Rudi considered the plan. It was reasonable, especially for something Kurt had come up with. "I'm sure I'll end up regretting this," Rudi said, "but I'll sign off on it. You'd better get yourself out to the Grand Canyon. And keep a low profile. Remember, you're supposed to be dead."

Chapter 52

MV Tunisian Wind, Galveston Harbor, Texas

Solomon Barlow stood in the shadows of an open cargo hatch, watching as a motor launch approached the **Tunisian Wind.** Despite the shade and a strategically placed fan, his face glistened with sweat. Living in Northern Europe had left him woefully unprepared for the warmth and humidity of Galveston Bay under a late-summer heat wave.

Robson stood next to him, suffering less from the heat but complaining more. "I don't like bringing them here," he said, nodding at the approaching launch. "They almost killed the Vice President. If they're being watched, they'll lead the FBI right to us."

"The FBI is busy hunting for terrorists," Barlow said. "A strategic leak of information saw to that. They have no idea the Toymaker was behind it."

"I still think it's foolish to meet with them. What purpose could it serve?"

"We're going to partner with them," Barlow said.

"Them?"

"You'll see."

The launch reached the ship and bumped alongside. A gangway was lowered from the cargo hatch and secured to the smaller boat.

With the gangway in place, Barlow's crewmen stepped aside. An athletic, confident woman came aboard, followed by a nervous, twitchy man who reminded Barlow of a hyperactive rat.

They reached the hatch, stepped off the gangway and stood where the breeze from the fan could reach them.

"Let me introduce the Toymaker," Barlow said to Robson. "Or should I say the Toymakers? Xandra and Fydor."

He used their names to show them he'd figured out who they really were. Or at least their second-level aliases. The statement didn't go unnoticed.

Xandra stared at him. "You had it right the first time, Solomon." She pointed to Fydor. "He makes the machines. I just keep people from beating him up."

"Either way, you do excellent work," Barlow said. "You've been paid for it but let me thank you personally for getting rid of Austin. I'm thinking of framing the photo you sent me."

"Do what you want with it," Xandra said. "I'd like to get down to business. We have something you need. It's going to cost a share of the total proceeds before we hand it over."

"So you said in your message. I'm prepared to offer you just that. But first you'll need to prove what you've found. Come with me," Barlow said. "Let's talk."

He led them into the ship and to the officers' mess, which had been cleared and turned into a planning room. Four additional men waited inside. They were hardened and deeply tanned.

"Xandra and Fydor," Barlow said, "this is Omar Kai."

Omar Kai stood against the far wall, leaning at a slight angle. He was tall and slim, with wavy dark hair, sun-creased olive skin and a wide mustache that would have looked more at home on an old Western gunfighter. He wore casual clothes and had a gleam in his eye as he spoke. "Pleasure to meet you."

"I know who you are," Xandra said.

No hands were shaken, no other words exchanged.

"Everyone, take a seat," Robson said.

The members of the group sat at one large table, Xandra and Fydor on one side, Omar Kai and his men on the other and Robson at the far end. Barlow stayed standing and explained why they were all there.

"We're going to steal the greatest deposit of

Egyptian treasure the world has ever known. If you choose to join me, you'll be given cash up front for your participation, cash that you're welcome to return to me in exchange for your portion of what we bring back."

"We want a half share," Xandra declared proudly. "We know exactly where the treasure is. We're leading you to it. We won't take anything less."

"Greed," Omar Kai said. "How predictable."

Xandra sneered at him.

Barlow was unfazed. "If that's your position, you can go in and haul it out yourself. Our expert has given us a conservative estimate suggesting the weight of the treasure will exceed a hundred tons. You're talking coffins made of gold, bars of silver, chests filled with gemstones and ornate weapons, statues carved from marble and onyx. You're welcome to carry it out on your backs, if you like. And then, should you succeed, you can look for someone to sell it to, hoping not to get caught by an Interpol sting or upended by one of their informants." He let that sink in for a minute. "Or you can work with me and my people will take care of the heavy lifting, sales and distribution."

Xandra held silent. Kai smiled and winked. Barlow knew he'd regained control.

"You get a quarter share," he said, "assuming you can provide us with an accurate location and assist our effort."

"I can give you a precise location," Xandra bragged.

"Then you'll have earned your twenty-five percent."

"And what about our share?" Omar Kai asked.

"You and your men also get a quarter share," Barlow explained.

"Generous."

"Not really," Barlow said. "You'll be taking the biggest risk."

Kai seemed unconcerned. "No risk, no reward," he said. "Count us in."

Across the table, Xandra nodded as well. "We're in also. What's the plan?"

Barlow went over an operation that would get them in and out of the canyon quickly. It allowed for a large carrying capacity and a maximum amount of stealth. He had no illusions of being able to get every trinket from the cave, but they would concentrate on the big-ticket items—the gold and jewels, the caskets and sarcophaguses, the death masks and mummies of the Pharaohs themselves.

"The only real danger," he warned, "would be the sudden arrival of law enforcement. That's where you two earn your shares."

Kai spoke up. "Surely you don't expect us to fight the police while you carry away the treasure?"

"Not at all," Barlow said. "Fighting the police is a losing game. They just call for more help until eventually you're surrounded. I expect you to be wiser than that. I expect you to set up a distraction. One that will have the authorities focused on something far larger and more important than a few people digging in an obscure section of the desert."

"And how, exactly, do we do that?" Xandra asked.

Barlow picked up a remote control, aimed it toward a screen at the front of the room and pressed the button. A photo appeared. It showed a large concrete dam wedged in between two walls of reddish sandstone.

"This is the Glen Canyon Dam," Barlow said. "It sits upriver from the Grand Canyon. It holds back a billion tons of Colorado River water while providing large amounts of electricity to Arizona and New Mexico."

"You want us to blow up the dam?" Fydor asked in shock.

"Of course not," Barlow said. "I want you to simulate someone attempting to blow up the dam. Specifically, it needs to look like a large-scale terrorist attack and takeover. One that draws the eyes and ears of every local, state and national law enforcement agency. One that keeps them focused on it for a while. With their attention on preventing the collapse of the dam and rooting out the imaginary terrorists, we'll be able to excavate the cave, take everything of value and vanish."

"While we end up running for our lives," Kai said. "Yes, I can see why that would appeal to you."

Barlow was undaunted. "You're going to have to earn this money. Your team's share will come out between fifty and a hundred million dollars. Perhaps more. If that's not worth the risk to you, I can find someone else."

Xandra's appetite had been whetted. "All we have to do is get their attention," she said. "We can leave a few surprises and sneak out of there before any real counterterrorist force arrives."

Barlow admired her. She was obsessively bold.

Kai nodded. He wasn't the type to be outdone. And, as always, he needed the money. "Very well. We'll figure out our own plan and escape route, but we'll do our part."

"The six of you are smart enough to handle the details," Barlow said. "The dam is the target, you come up with a plan. In the meantime, Xandra, I'll need that location."

She nodded. "When the deposit hits our account."

"Check with your bank," Barlow said smugly. "It's already there."

Barlow waited patiently, considered his sudden turn of good fortune, while Xandra used her phone to check the status of their secret Panamanian account. He had everything he needed to finish the job now—the knowledge and insight of Professor Cross, the steady hand of Robson, reinforcements in Omar Kai and a pair of assassins who used remote vehicles to do their bidding—making them perfect for the job he wanted done. More importantly, Austin was gone, NUMA was out of the picture and Barlow would soon have the exact location of the treasure, speeding the process up exponentially.

Things had turned his way in the blink of an eye. He had no intention of allowing that to change. "Well?"

Xandra nodded. "The money is there, as you said." She tapped a button on her phone. It sent an encrypted email to Barlow's address. "Open the file. You'll find everything you need."

Barlow nodded and then turned to Robson. "You know what everyone needs to do. Let's move like the wind."

Chapter 53

Grand Canyon National Park, northern Arizona

Morgan Manning stood near the rim of the Grand Canyon, staring across it. So vast and all-encompassing was the view, she struggled to put it into words. To say it took her breath away would have been an understatement. She was awestruck, the weariness of eleven hours of traveling swept away in an instant.

Kurt, Joe and Paul stood off to one side while Gamay was a few feet away, riskily looking over the edge and staring straight down.

"It's incredible," Morgan said. "I've never felt so tiny and insignificant."

"This place has a way of doing that to one," Gamay noted.

Getting her bearings back, Morgan turned to Kurt. "Thank you for letting me come here and help finish this. I was sick to my stomach when I found that Professor Cross had been kidnapped. I can only hope Barlow will bring the professor here."

"He'd be foolish not to," Kurt said. "Considering what he's expecting to find, he'll need the professor's help to identify the valuable treasures from the mundane."

"How are we supposed to find this cave before they do?" Gamay asked.

"Hiram and Max matched the details of the old FBI photos with the current terrain," Kurt said. "It's a pretty remote spot, in a distant part of the canyon, but it's accessible by an old road."

"What are we waiting for, then?"

"Permission," Kurt replied. "The cave is located outside the boundaries of the National Park, in an area that belongs to the Navajo people. It may even be sacred ground. We need to get the proper blessing before we go down there."

As Kurt spoke, an old Chevy pickup came down the dirt road toward them. Its paint was faded and rust had crept in around the bed, but the engine sounded strong.

After the truck pulled to a stop, the driver's door opened. A Navajo man stepped out. His jet-black hair was tied back in a ponytail. He had broad shoulders, a big chest and a large head. He wore faded jeans and a plaid shirt.

Kurt stepped forward and gave the man a bear hug. "Thanks for coming to meet us." He turned to introduce the new arrival. "This is

Eddie Toh-Yah. He's an old friend of mine from the Navy."

"Be careful throwing that word **old** around," Eddie said. "I'm a year younger than you are."

Like Kurt, Eddie had spent most of his life in the elements, though for him it was the High Desert of Arizona and of New Mexico while Kurt had spent his life out on the ocean and along its shore.

"How long has it been?"

"Eight years," Eddie replied. "Can't say time has been kind to you, Kurt. You look a little beat-up."

Kurt laughed and took no offense. "I think aging has improved your looks. But, then again, you had nowhere to go but up. Can you help us out?"

"I told my grandfather about your request," Eddie said. "He's part of the tribal administration. He's willing to see you, but you're going to have to tell him why you want to go down there. I have to warn you, Kurt, he's all about the old ways."

"I'm partial to the old ways myself," Kurt said. "Let's go."

A ten-mile drive brought them away from the canyon and down into a high valley where a small Navajo community lay. A collection of hogan-style buildings, built from timber and supporting earthen roofs, stood in the center. A fenced-in pasture sat off to one side while several horses lazily chewing hay occupied a corral behind the structures.

Shortly after arriving, Kurt and company were led into one of the buildings. The interior was a single large room with a dirt floor. The room smelled strongly of incense. The only illumination in the hogan came from candles.

Everyone sat on the floor and Eddie introduced them to his grandfather, speaking in Navajo. Kurt remained silent, studying the older man. Unlike Eddie, the elder was dressed in traditional garments made of wool and dyed with intricate patterns. Kurt guessed his age at somewhere between eighty and ninety, though it was hard to tell. There was wisdom in his face, knowledge far beyond even his many years.

Eddie turned back toward Kurt. "My grandfather extends his welcome. He wants to know where you wish to travel."

Kurt pulled out a folded topographical map. "I marked the area on this. It's called Silver Box Ravine. I read that some have suggested the area is sacred."

Eddie took a look at the map and then handed it over to his grandfather, who studied it before responding.

"Silver Box Ravine is not a holy place for our people," the older Navajo said, "though other places in the canyon nearby are sacred."

"We promise not to stray from the area I've marked," Kurt said.

Eddie's grandfather nodded, taking Kurt at his word. "Why is it you wish to go there? Are you looking for treasure?"

Kurt was taken by surprise.

"Eddie has told me all about you," the grandfather said proudly. "He says you've found lost treasure all over the world and that when you were in the Navy you hardly ever stopped in a port without looking into any story or legend from the ancient days of whatever country you were visiting."

"His description of me is accurate," Kurt admitted.

The older man smiled. "I too am interested in stories from the ancient days. Here in our land, there are rumors of a treasure. It was said to be left behind by the People of the Sun, the Egyptians. The internet is filled with these stories. Even the old newspapers. Every few years, someone comes here claiming to have found something or seen something. They never have any proof, though."

"I'm not surprised," Kurt said. He didn't elaborate. "But I'm not interested in any treasure that might be down there, just the people who are coming after it."

Eddie asked the next question. "Are these people dangerous?"

"They are," Kurt said. "Our plan is to capture them."

Eddie's grandfather went silent for a moment, contemplating what Kurt had said. Finally, he spoke again, this time addressing Eddie in their native language and allowing him to translate one more time.

"He says if that's what you seek, we will help you, but he thinks you should know they won't find what they're looking for down there."

Kurt didn't waver. "As long as they show up and we get the drop on them, the treasure can remain a mystery for all eternity, as far as I'm concerned."

Chapter 54

Silver Box Ravine, Navajo Nation, Arizona

The bottom of Silver Box Ravine lay at an elevation of twenty-five hundred feet, almost a mile down from the rim of the canyon up above. The terrain was loose rock and sand, as the ravine itself was dry year-round and only eroded when flash floods brought on by thunderstorms rushed through. Looking up at a blue sky devoid of the smallest wisp of a cloud, Kurt and the others could see there would be no storm today.

"It's so hot," Morgan said. She pulled at the neck of her T-shirt, trying to let some of the heat underneath escape. "It's a wonder Herihor's people didn't think they'd circled the world and gone all the way back to Egypt."

"But it's a dry heat," Gamay quipped, offering the classic desert dweller's response.

"My shirt disagrees with you," Paul replied.

Joe laughed. He'd grown up in the Southwest and felt right at home in this weather.

Kurt found the inferno invigorating, especially as it soothed the sore joints and muscles that had been strained and bruised over the last two weeks. "The sooner we find this cave, the sooner we find some shade. According to the old FBI report, the entrance is a large gap in the south wall not far from where the road let us out."

They'd driven from the Navajo village to the edge of the canyon in a pair of pickup trucks pulling horse trailers. After finding the old road, Eddie had led them down on horseback and then taken the horses back up the trail, leaving Kurt and his crew to search on foot.

For Kurt's plan to work, it was important that there be no sign of any activity in the ravine—and that meant no motorized equipment, tire tracks or helicopters buzzing about. Even more important, they had to find the cave and get inside before anyone from Barlow's team arrived.

Kurt glanced up at the switchback road carved into the side of the canyon. It was a crumbling mule track at this point, but in the FBI photos it was freshly excavated and graded at no small expense.

Comparing the photos to the current view wasn't an exact science, but they soon discovered a few landmarks and from those zeroed in on where the cave entrance should have been. Instead of an opening, they found a giant sloping pile of boulders and sand.

"It's got to be behind that—" Joe started to say.

"Rockslide," Gamay finished.

"Bound to have been several in the last hundred years," Paul pointed out. "That's how the canyon grows and changes. From the look of it, there are areas on both sides ripe for another break. Let's be careful—if and when the shooting starts."

"If we surprise Barlow, there won't be much shooting," Morgan insisted.

Kurt was already scaling the rocks, trying to get to the top without causing an avalanche of his own. He reached the upper reaches of the pile and found what he was hoping to discover—a narrow gap. Cool air from the cave inside was pouring out through it.

"This is it," he told them.

The sand and rock had backslid into the cave over the years. The result was an opening at the top and a descending pile of rubble on the inside.

Aiming a flashlight into the dark space beyond, he saw nothing remarkable other than the walls of the cave itself. It didn't matter. He knew they were in the right place.

He turned to the others. "Backtrack fifty yards and clear away any footprints we've left. Then get up here and join me inside."

As the others went to work, Kurt made his way to the bottom of the slope inside the cave's entrance. Reaching the ground, he aimed his flashlight into the void beyond.

Careful not to leave footprints, he walked on only the hard-packed ground and rock, avoiding the sand. The tunnel was wide—wide enough to drive a truck through. As he got away from the entrance, he found evidence that a truck may have indeed been driven in there.

In the dried mud on one side of the tunnel he noticed a tire track. It was narrow with a simple-patterned tread, a giveaway to its place in history nearly a century before.

Moving on, he found the first Egyptian-style artifacts. Furniture and disassembled chariots. Passing them by, he came to an expansive chamber in the cave. It spread wide and high, like an opera house or indoor arena.

Panning his light around revealed ramps and platforms and multilevel architecture carved out of the rock. In every direction, at every level, he found dust-covered figures and strange faces.

A muscular body standing against the wall with the head of a jackal represented Anubis, the god of embalming. A slim figure to the left of it had a falcon's head and great painted eyes, which Kurt knew was a representation of Horus, the god of health, protection and power. Farther on, stacked up with what seemed like little care, let alone respect, were eight mummified figures, their strips of cloth gray and brown with dust and grime.

Kurt aimed his light deeper. In the middle of the cavern, he saw dozens of smaller statues, along with piles of gilded furniture, reed baskets and clay jars. A large throne-like chair lay surrounded by cat figures that looked to be made of alabaster, ornate treasure boxes and small versions of the Sphinx.

The arrangement was haphazard, as if it had been shoved in in haste instead of placed there with care. In the very center lay a single sarcophagus, not the fifteen that Professor Cross had envisioned.

Kurt approached it but dared not touch the top—the dust was distributed too perfectly, a handprint or rubbing would be too obvious. He aimed the flashlight at the surface, looking closely and spotting the glimmer of cracking gold leaf.

He'd found what the archeologists discovered in 1927. He'd discovered the exact secret that the Granzini family had killed to preserve. Now all he needed was for Barlow and his men to find it as well.

Chapter 55

The sight of tractor-trailers rolling through Tuba City was not an uncommon one. Not an eyebrow was raised as three nearly identical semitrucks passed through in a convoy. Garnering even less attention was a four-door crew cab pickup truck following behind them, pulling a powerboat on a trailer.

From Tuba City, the convoy traveled west on Route 160 before turning north on a narrow two-lane highway known as Route 89. Thirty miles on, without a car in sight in either direction, the tractor-trailers pulled off the highway and drove down a dirt road, where they disappeared behind a smooth-sided bluff of wind-eroded sandstone.

Using the dirt road as a parking lot, the trucks spread out, stopped and shut down their noisy engines.

Solomon Barlow climbed out of the lead truck,

thankful to stretch his legs after twelve hours in the cab. Robson got out of the second truck and came to meet his boss. Fydor and Xandra climbed out of the third vehicle. Behind them, Omar Kai emerged from the pickup.

"This is where we split up," Barlow said. "Are we all clear on the plan?"

Kai nodded. "My men and I will infiltrate the dam while Fydor and Xandra make mischief on the outside. We'll sabotage the dam, setting some booby traps for the authorities to deal with, and then disappear."

Kai was very confident. Barlow saw their chances of success at no more than fifty percent, but ultimately all he needed was a diversion. If Kai and his people got themselves shot or blown up in the effort, it was of little concern to him. All that mattered was that the eyes of law enforcement would be drawn to the dam and away from him and his illegal excavation.

"Very well," Barlow said. "You've all set up your own extraction plans, so this will be it for a while. Let's dispense with the threats of what happens if I double-cross you or if you double-cross me. We all know we can make each other's lives miserable. Far better if we meet in a week to start splitting the wealth."

Fydor and Xandra nodded. Kai did the same. "You two are with me," he said.

The three of them turned and strode confidently back to the pickup truck Fydor and Xandra had arrived in, climbing inside and slamming the doors. In a moment, the truck was turning around and heading for the highway, a cloud of dust rising behind it.

Barlow watched them go and then focused on the men with him. "Unload the trailers."

Robson opened the back doors of Barlow's truck and manhandled a ramp into place. He and his men climbed inside and soon emerged riding four-wheeled all-terrain vehicles. Each ATV had basic excavation equipment strapped on the back.

"Follow me," Robson shouted.

He twisted the throttle and sped off, heading west. Four identical ATVs followed, three of them carrying Robson's mates and one of them hauling a special guest who had been far more cooperative than any of them anticipated.

As Robson and his men moved out, Barlow turned to the last members of his team. "Break these trucks down and get those birds in the air. We have no time to waste."

Unloading the last two trucks was a more complicated task. Instead of opening the back doors, Barlow's men climbed up on the roofs of the trucks and began unscrewing large panels.

The lightweight roof panels were detached and tossed aside. With this done, the hinged side walls and the aft doors of the trucks were lowered to the ground. When that effort was complete, the trucks resembled flowers with opened petals. At the center of each flower, sitting on the flat bed of each trailer, was a helicopter with its rotors folded.

The helicopters were painted to match those of a well-known tour operator famous for its sightseeing flights in the area. A perfect disguise, Barlow thought, should anyone notice them buzzing in and out of the canyon.

With the helicopters now exposed, their crews went to work making them airworthy. The rotors were unfolded and locked into position. The power systems, fuel pumps and hydraulic systems were checked, the electrical systems were tested and confirmed operational.

When the green light was given, Barlow climbed into the lead helicopter. He was joined by a pilot. A second pilot and spare crewmen climbed into the number two aircraft. Both helicopters had cargo bays filled with lighting and excavation equipment, all of which Barlow expected to leave behind when he loaded the helicopters with treasure.

He wasn't sure how many trips in and out of the canyon he would have time to make, but he hoped to leave the helicopters behind in the desert while driving out of Arizona with several trailerloads of priceless Egyptian artifacts.

Sliding a headset over his ears, he made a whirling motion with his hand. "Let's go."

As the helicopters powered up, a radio call came in from several miles up ahead. It was Robson. "We've found the old road. We're taking it down into the ravine. Meet you at the bottom."

As Barlow and Robson prepared for the excavation, Omar Kai was navigating the streets of Page, a small town at the eastern end of Lake Powell.

Page was a tourist town, packed with boaters and vacationers in the summer, quieter in the fall—except on the weekends. Like a lot of tourist towns, it had a cluster of motels and plenty of fast-food joints.

Omar Kai studied the buildings as he went by. Most were garishly painted, some adorned with giant-sized plastic food or whimsical signs promoting their wares. It seemed a hodgepodge of things grouped together with little overriding thought except as a way to make money from those passing through.

"How typically American," he said, his voice simultaneously filled with admiration and dripping with disdain.

"We can do without the commentary," Xandra said. "Just find the boat ramp."

Kai wasn't about to hurry, but he understood

the tension. His men were crammed in the back of the truck while Xandra and Fydor shared the front bench seat. All of them were looking forward to getting out.

Following the signs, he descended a curving road that ran between a row of motels and then took a secondary road that led east to a spot where they could access the lake. Finding no one else around, they backed the powerboat into the water.

Fydor and Xandra went aboard, looking ghastly pale and out of place in their particular outfits.

"Try not to die of sunburn before this is over," Kai joked.

Fydor was already plastering a stripe of zinc oxide on his nose.

"We'll be fine," Xandra snapped. "But you're going to need more than sunglasses and ugly shirts if you plan to take over the dam." Kai and his crew were dressed like tourists. "How do you plan on sneaking weapons past the guards and metal detectors?"

"We don't need to bring guns with us," Kai said. "We'll pick them up once we're inside."

Xandra stared at him as if trying to detect a lie. Then she understood. "You're not as dumb as I thought."

Kai gave the boat a shove and watched it drift out. As it began to pull away, he turned his attention to the dam. His demeanor grew instantly more serious.

Climbing back into the truck, he took the measure of his men and found them ready. "Let's see if we can make the one o'clock tour."

A short drive led them to a bridge that crossed the canyon just downriver of the dam. Crossing it gave them a perfect view of the tremendous structure.

"That's larger than I thought," one of the men said.

Kai had seen plenty of dams in his time, including several in China that were larger than anything in the Western world, but those were dark and industrial while this structure had beauty to it. The contrast of colors struck him—from the blue waters stored up behind it to the stark white face of the dam itself to the red-orange hues of the sandstone cliffs into which the dam had been built. Even the trickle of aquamarine that marked the Colorado River below the dam looked as if it had been painted with an artist's brush.

Kai put the thoughts aside as they pulled into the visitor center parking lot and climbed out of the truck. Carrying nothing with them but their wallets and a few bottles of water, Kai and his men made their way into the air-conditioned building and paid for a tour.

The cheerful guide told them the next one started in twenty minutes. Kai did the calculations in his head. It was not much of a problem. They had plenty of time.

He sat on a bench and reached down to his tennis shoes. With deliberate care, he untied and then retied them, carefully checking that the oversize metal tips at the end of the laces remained secured and in place.

Chapter 56

Silver Box Ravine, Navajo Nation, Arizona

The swarm of ATVs navigated the crumbling switchback road with caution. The descent was treacherous, with uneven ground, crumbling shoulders and a steep drop of several thousand feet waiting for anyone who lost control of his vehicle. Robson was pleasantly surprised that they didn't lose anyone along the way.

Reaching the bottom, the ATVs spread out from their single file formation and roared noisily into the open area between the vermillion cliffs. The road had dumped them out heading east, but from the FBI file they knew the entrance to the cave lay behind them to the west.

"This way," Robson said, moving away from the broad exit and back toward the upper section of the canyon. Traveling in a group, they scoured the walls. After a few minutes Robson was sure they'd gone too far.

He pulled up and shut his engine off. The team followed suit. "Any of your lot see a cave?" he asked, his face half hidden by a pair of tinted goggles.

Snipe had pulled up next to him. "Nothing."

"Zilch," Gus added.

"Are you sure this is the right spot?" Fingers asked.

"What do you think?"

Fingers recoiled at the reply. "I think all these bloody canyons look the same."

Robson shook his head. "I wasn't talking to you. I was talking to him."

The driver on the last ATV had stopped a few feet away from the rest of them. He'd been unsteady on his vehicle since the beginning and had almost crashed it twice by the time they reached the steep road down to the bottom of the canyon. Robson had expected him to balk at the dangerous drive, but the desire to see what was there proved stronger than the fear.

Professor Cross pulled his helmet off, revealing a head of curly gray hair. He raised his goggles up and parked them on his forehead. The rest of his face was dirty, leaving the area around his eyes looking as if it were highlighted.

"We're waiting, Professor."

"Yes, yes, of course. Well, the entrance should be quite near," the professor told them in his proper English accent. "But I don't see any . . ."

Professor Cross had studied the maps and the

old photos. He'd compared them to the satellite views of the canyon that were available on the internet. It wasn't a precise science, but he estimated that the margin of error could be no more than a quarter mile. They'd covered that much and more at this point. He felt certain that the entrance to the cave should have revealed itself by now.

Twisting his head about like an owl, the professor studied the walls until the answer appeared. "Of course," he said, grinning. "Tutankhamen's crypt was hidden by a landslide as well." He pointed toward a sloping pile of debris that jutted out from the canyon wall. "That's got to be it. Let's hope we can dig our way in."

They turned around, drove back to the rockslide and parked. After dismounting their ATVs, Robson and the professor climbed up to the top of the debris, where they found a narrow gap.

"Tight fit," the professor said, ducking his head inside. "I should want a little more room to be on the safe side."

Robson shook his head. "We're not moving the whole mountain only to find it's the wrong cave. Get in there."

"Right," the professor said, suddenly remembering he was technically a prisoner. "Coming?"

"Don't like closed-in spaces," Robson said. "Jail will do that to you."

The professor nodded politely. Reaching into

a pocket, he produced a headband with a light attached to it. He pulled it over his head, made sure it was snug and then switched the light on. A flashlight from a second pocket fit into his palm.

Getting down on his hands and knees, the professor crawled into the cave and vanished.

Robson and his men waited outside.

"What if he gets killed by a booby trap?" Fingers asked.

"Then we know we found the right place," Robson joked, "don't we?"

"But we won't know if he's dead unless we go in and search around ourselves," Gus pointed out.

"Relax," Robson said. "You ever heard of a trap that still worked two thousand years after it was set? Besides, if there were any traps in there, they'd have killed the archeologists who found this place a hundred years ago. Now, pipe down, you're annoying me."

With the ATVs shut down and his men holding their tongue, Robson came to appreciate how utterly silent the canyon was. He could hear small trails of sand sliding down the rock pile as he moved, he could hear lizards scurrying around in a brush fifty yards away.

The silence made the time drag. Finally, Robson had had enough. He grabbed a flashlight of his own, switched it on and moved to the opening.

Before he could climb in, the grinning face of Professor Cross appeared in the entry.

"It's all here," the professor said giddily. "Everything. Everything we could have possibly hoped to find."

Chapter 57

By the time Barlow's helicopters landed, Robson and his men had spent thirty minutes digging at the debris. The pile wasn't entirely gone, but by using shovels and pry bars and chains attached to the ATVs to drag the larger boulders away they'd managed to take several feet off the top. A four-foot-high opening had been excavated at the apex and the inclines accessing the cave had been flattened and smoothed considerably. It now resembled a dirt ramp leading up, in and then down.

"Good work," Barlow said, studying the progress. "We'll need that space to get everything in and out."

"Another twenty minutes and we'll have this looking like the on-ramp to the motorway," Robson said.

Barlow wasn't about to wait that long. "Let your men do the rest. I want you and the professor to show me what you've found."

Robson laid down his shovel and ordered Fingers, Gus and Snipe to keep working. That done, he steeled himself to enter the dark cave.

Barlow whistled to the crewmen who'd flown in on the helicopters with him. "Unload everything. We'll need the lights ASAP and the crawlers soon after."

The pair of lights each had a high-powered array of multiple LED bulbs on it. Each was powered with a heavy lithium-ion battery and was capable of lighting up the inside of the cavern like a stadium.

The crawlers were specialized handcarts equipped with motorized caterpillar tracks. These machines could carry thousands of pounds and would be used later to haul out the heaviest of the items.

With the unloading under way, Barlow and Robson turned to the cave. Scaling the ramp, they went inside with Professor Cross leading the way.

They descended the inner slope and began moving through the dark tunnel. With their eyes used to the brightness of the ravine, they saw only what their flashlights illuminated.

"The interior of the cave is perfectly flat," Barlow said, noticing how smooth it was underfoot.

"That should come as no surprise," Professor Cross said. "The Egyptians were wonderful engineers."

Robson kept glancing back at the entrance. "Are you sure you need me?"

"Keep moving," Barlow ordered.

They continued on, spotting a row of small statues up against the wall. Behind them, in a state of disrepair, were parts of several chariots. A pile of furniture and decorative items stood nearby.

"There'd better be more than this," Barlow warned.

"Of course," the professor said. "These are just the gifts for the Afterlife. The treasure is this way."

They pushed on past the hastily stacked furniture and arrived in a huge open room. Even in the poor illumination of a couple of handheld flashlights, Barlow could see that this room was filled with ornate carvings, life-sized statues, artwork and mummies. In the center, he spotted a sarcophagus.

As his crewmen arrived, he ordered the lights to be set up. "There and there," he said, pointing to a couple of areas spaced widely apart. "Be quick. I want to see it in all its glory."

The men arranged their portable floodlights and set them up quickly. Switches were thrown and, one by one, the powerful LEDs came on. Each unit's bulbs pointed in slightly different directions, but most of the light was aimed upward and out, first hitting the walls and ceiling, then reflecting back on the artifacts.

As each section of the cavern was illuminated, more treasure appeared. As Barlow turned from one quarter to the next, he grew almost hysterical. It was better than he dreamed. His tractor-trailers couldn't carry half of it. He would have to pick and choose. He knew the royal items would be the most valuable and found himself focused on the sarcophagus in the middle of the room.

He turned to Professor Cross. "I thought you said there would be at least fifteen Pharaohs buried down here."

"I'm sure there are more around here somewhere," the professor said. "We've only explored a small part of the cave."

Barlow nodded and walked toward the sarcophagus with Professor Cross at his side.

As they went that direction, Robson looked the other way. With the lights on and the large, open space, he'd forgotten his claustrophobia and begun imagining his portion of the wealth.

Looking around, he took it all in, stopping only when his eye fell on something that didn't belong among the Pharaoh's treasures. He blinked twice to make sure it wasn't a trick of the shadows or a figment of his imagination.

In the far section of the cave, up on a platform at the end of a smooth ramp, he spied a dust-covered vintage automobile. The machine had a long, sleek hood and gracefully curved fenders that swept down over multi-spoked wheels. Running boards graced the side of the car and a pair of forward-jutting headlights stuck out in front of the vehicle's radiator. It appeared to be very well preserved. Even the tires, though showing signs of age, were still inflated.

He walked toward it, climbing the ramp that led up to the platform. As he neared the vehicle, more details emerged. The machine was a two-seater convertible with its top down and only a simple, flat-plate windshield sticking up in front of the passenger compartment. A tarp that must have been placed over it at one time appeared to have slipped off and now lay on the ground. Though the vehicle was covered in dust, Robson could see it was painted a lustrous black.

Stopping at the top of the ramp, he spoke without turning back to the others. "Did the Pharaoh own a car?"

All eyes turned toward him and the automobile.

"The Granzinis must have left that here," the professor said. "Or one of the archeologists."

Robson looked into the passenger compartment. It sported a wooden steering wheel, a metal instrument panel and a badge that read KISSEL. He assumed that was the make or model, though he himself had never heard of it.

The more he studied it, the more certain he was that this wasn't a car an archeologist would own. He figured it must have belonged to the Granzinis, but why the smugglers would have left it in the cave escaped him. Nor could he come up with a reason to drive such a fine automobile into a desert canyon in the first place.

He reached inside, touched the steering wheel and noticed a placard attached to the instrument panel. Sweeping the dust away with his fingers revealed engraved letters. The sign read **Property of C. B. DeMille.**

The name rang a bell, but Robson couldn't place it.

Meanwhile, back in the center of the cave, Barlow and Professor Cross were crouching beside the sarcophagus, studying what they'd found.

Professor Cross wiped it clean of dust, gazing at the painted blue and gold stripes on the facial portion. The paint was cracked and fading. He touched the lid, rubbing more dirt off and getting a sense of the texture. He rapped his fingers against it.

"Appears to be made of wood," he said. "Usually the outer case is made of stone and the inner casket is made of gold, but perhaps stone was too heavy to carry down here."

"It's the golden death mask and the body that matters," Barlow said. "Do you have any idea how much people will pay to have the mummy of a Pharaoh in their private collection? Let's open it."

The two men found a seam and wedged their

fingers into the gap. Lifting it up, they raised the lid a few inches at a time. It slid upward with ease, feeling surprisingly light. When it pulled clear of the lower half, Barlow shoved it away, allowing it to topple over and thump noisily to the ground.

Barlow looked immediately for his prize. But instead of a golden casket or a mummified Pharaoh, he found something else entirely.

Kurt Austin lay in the sarcophagus. He wore a satisfied grin on his face and held a .45 caliber pistol in his hand, the barrel of which was aimed at a spot directly between Barlow's eyes.

Both Barlow and Professor Cross froze.

"Austin?" Barlow stammered. "How . . . I saw you killed."

"So you did," Kurt replied. "But I'm old friends with Osiris, god of the Underworld. When I told her what you were up to, she canceled my reservation and sent me back here to put a stop to it."

Chapter 58

From his position by the vintage car, Robson couldn't clearly see what was happening at the center of the cave. He saw Barlow and the professor raise their hands, heard them mumbling something and then saw them getting down on their knees. For a second, he thought they were performing some ritual or even praying.

Before he could figure it out, a whistle from behind the old automobile got his attention.

Spinning quickly, Robson came face-to-face with Joe Zavala, who held a short-barreled MP7 submachine gun in his hands.

"Get on the floor," Zavala said. "Hands on your head."

Robson had no choice. He took a final glimpse toward the center of the cave as he lay down. He saw Barlow and Professor Cross getting the same treatment. They'd been caught as red-handed as it gets.

With the leaders of the group captured, the men who'd brought in the lights panicked. Seeing the guns, they made a quick evaluation of the situation and took off running.

The man nearest to the exit got halfway there before a woman, whom Robson knew as Morgan Manning, appeared from behind a statue of Anubis and hit him in the midriff with an ancient-looking staff. The wooden pole shattered, sending pieces in all directions, but the impact was enough to drop him to the ground.

He stayed down, holding his stomach, as she pulled out a 9mm handgun. Seeing that any hope of escape was cut off, the other man surrendered, dropping to his knees and putting his hands behind his head.

At the center of the cavern, Kurt stood up. He was pleased with the operation. He kept the Colt pointed at Barlow as he stepped out of the sarcophagus, waiting for the man to try something.

Instead, Professor Cross began to speak. "Thank you," he said, starting to get up. "Thank you for rescuing me. You have no idea how abhorrent it's been. I've barely been able to—"

Kurt fixed him with a glare. "Stay where you are, Professor. We're not done here."

"I don't understand."

"But I do," Kurt said. "Now, get on the ground. You chose the wrong team."

The professor looked deeply wounded as he lay down, but he didn't protest further.

Kurt shouted to his friend, "Joe?"

Joe's voice echoed as he shouted back. "Got the drop on this one."

Morgan spoke next. "These two aren't going anywhere either."

"Paul? Gamay?" Kurt called out. "Time to secure the prisoners."

Paul and Gamay emerged from another section of the cave. They made their way to Morgan first. While she guarded her two captives, Paul zip-tied their hands and Gamay sealed each man's mouth with a length of duct tape.

"Barlow and the professor next," Kurt said.

"With pleasure," Gamay said.

She and Paul turned toward the center of the cave, but the roar of an engine filled the space as one of the ATVs came charging into the cavern.

Morgan turned to fire but was forced to dive out of the way to avoid being run over. Paul and Gamay leapt to safety as well and the rider sped past them and rushed headlong toward the stash of treasure—and directly at Kurt, Barlow and Professor Cross.

Kurt had no choice. He raised his pistol and fired twice, knocking the man off the machine with the first shot and blasting the front right tire with the second.

The tire exploded, sending the ATV into a diagonal spin. It bounced off a wall, flipped and tumbled. Kurt was forced to dive behind the sarcophagus, hitting the ground just as the four-wheeler slammed into the side of it, sending fragments of painted wood and dust exploding into the air.

Kurt rolled to get clear and then popped back up. He saw Professor Cross running deeper into the cave and Barlow leveling a snub-nosed pistol in Kurt's direction.

Kurt and Barlow fired at each other, dodged to their respective sides and then fired again. Neither of them took a hit, but Barlow had the better position, protected behind the wrecked ATV. All Kurt had was the thin wooden husk of the shattered sarcophagus to shield him.

Up on the platform, beside the vintage automobile, Joe saw Kurt was in danger. He raised his weapon and fired down at Barlow, forcing the man to halt his attack and go for better cover.

The choice gave Joe's prisoner a chance to make his own move. The instant he wasn't covered, Robson rolled over, pulled a pistol of his own and began firing at Joe.

Joe dropped down behind the Kissel and listened as the slugs hit the metal of its engine block. When the firing stopped, he looked beneath the car and saw Robson sprinting in the opposite direction.

Jumping up, Joe took a shot at Robson, but the bullet pinged harmlessly off the rock wall as he escaped into another part of the cave.

Paul and Gamay ran up the ramp, joining Joe behind the old car.

"They're all in the back half of the cave," Joe shouted. "We have them trapped."

No sooner had he uttered the words than a hail of bullets came at them from the front. Robson's mates from the streets of London had come inside to join the fight.

Gamay shook her head. "You just had to say something, didn't you?"

The battle quickly turned into a four-way cross fire, with Barlow and Robson's reinforcements at the entry, Kurt and Morgan taking cover near the center, Joe and the Trouts on the far side by the vintage Kissel and Barlow, Robson and Professor Cross trapped deeper in the cavern.

For a brief while, one side took potshots at the other, but with everybody carrying limited ammunition—and nobody interested in running out—the gunfight soon turned into a stalemate.

In the absence of gunfire Barlow's voice echoed

from the depths of the cave. "You moved too soon, Austin! You should have waited till we were all in the cave."

"I would have preferred that myself," Kurt shouted back. "Didn't have much choice once you popped the lid off the sarcophagus. It was worth it to see the look on your face."

"It'll be the last thing you ever smile about," Barlow insisted. "You should have shot me when you had the chance. You'll soon realize not pulling the trigger was a mistake."

"Trust me," Kurt said, "your mistake is going to be more costly than mine. You and the professor have run off in the wrong direction. You're trapped back there. I can wait for reinforcements all day long if I need to, but you're going to miss the bus home if you don't get out of here soon."

Kurt faced his own dilemma. He couldn't radio from the depths of the cave—the signal would be blocked, absorbed by all the rock surrounding them. Barlow may or may not have known that, but Kurt wasn't about to point it out.

"Waiting for help, eh?" Barlow laughed as he spoke. The laughter was sinister, deep and genuine. "Well, you did surprise me, Austin, I'll admit that. But now I have a surprise for you. Your reinforcements aren't going to come. I'm afraid they're going to be very, very busy."

Chapter 59

Glen Canyon Dam, Arizona

The tour of the Glen Canyon Dam was mildly interesting even to Omar Kai, but they weren't there to sightsee.

Having made it through the security screening without any hassle, he and his men walked casually with the rest of the group, mingling with retirees from Utah, a few engineering students from Arizona State and Japanese tourists who'd come down from Las Vegas, where they'd already seen the Hoover Dam.

After a brief walk along the top of the dam they entered a large elevator, descending five hundred and fifty-eight feet to the foot of the structure. There, they stepped off the elevator and were outside again. They crossed a short open-air corridor and lawn and arrived at the power plant.

Visible through windows to one side were the large turbines that helped electrify large swaths of Utah, New Mexico and Arizona. At the far end, glass walls enclosed the control room, where, inside, computer screens flickered and two engineers regulated the intake of water, the speed of the turbines and the output of electricity.

Looking around casually, Kai noticed one armed guard near the control room and a second guard standing against the far wall.

He nodded to his men, noted their acknowledgment and then crouched to tie his sneakers once more. Loosening and then retying them, he pulled the long metal tips from the ends of the laces, palming them as he stood up. That done, he twisted the cap off of his water bottle, took a sip and then slipped the tiny strips of metal into the bottle.

The shoelace caps looked like ordinary snips of aluminum, but they were actually made from an exotic combination of lithium and cesium, two metals that react violently when exposed to water. To prevent an instant explosion, they'd been coated with a layer of paint that would dissolve in approximately thirty seconds.

After screwing the cap back on, Kai walked over to a blue recycle bin and casually tossed the bottle in. Walking back toward the tour group, he began counting in his head. Right at thirty seconds, the bin exploded with a thunderous boom.

The blast was louder than it was destructive.

Paper, plastic and bits of the recycle bin itself flew in all directions while gray smoke billowed across the room.

Some members of the tour froze, some hit the floor, others ran. The security guards, flinching, turned toward the explosion. Before they knew what hit them, Kai and his men had attacked.

The guard near the control room door was Kai's target. He slammed a knee into the man's groin, dropping him to the ground. He followed that with a blow to the back of the head, severe enough to knock the guard unconscious.

The second guard presented more trouble. He'd managed to pull his weapon from his holster and was now wrestling with Kai's people. In the melee, two shots were fired, but they flew harmlessly through the ceiling.

"Take him down!" Kai shouted.

By then, his men had gained the upper hand. The gun was pulled free and the security guard pistol-whipped into submission with it.

Seeing that it was about to turn into a hostage situation, the rest of the tourists started to flee. Kai aimed the weapon he'd taken off the first guard above their heads and squeezed off a shot. "Everyone, on the floor!"

The gunshot did its job. Those attempting to escape froze. The others covered up. The room grew quiet.

"That's better," Kai said. "Guard them."

As his men spread out, Kai moved toward the control room door. He didn't bother trying the handle. Rapping on the glass with the pistol, he got the attention of the two engineers. "Open the door."

The man and woman looked at each other. The woman shook her head.

Kai hauled up the bloodied guard and held the pistol against his head. "I won't ask again."

Reluctantly, the woman pressed a button. The door buzzed and Kai barged through. "Good choice."

"What are you going to do?" she asked.

"Don't worry," he said. "We're not here to kill anyone. We're . . . eco-warriors," the word sliding off his tongue. "We're here to do a little bit of sabotage and put the dam out of action for a few months. Of course, I'd blow the whole thing up if I could, but that's far easier said than done. Don't you agree?"

The woman had no idea what to make of him.

"I'll bargain with you here," Kai said. "You help me turn on every single faucet and start flooding the canyon and I won't stain this control room with your blood."

"That's all you want?" she asked.

"That's my part," he said. "Deal?"

With the security guard's pistol aimed at their backs, the woman and her partner began opening the floodgates. One after the other, every turbine in the power plant spun up to full capacity.

"The bypass channels too," Kai demanded.

The engineers did as asked, opening all the side tunnels, which allowed water from Lake Powell behind the Glen Canyon Dam to flow around it and its turbines and then out into the Colorado River beyond.

It took a few minutes for the surge to reach maximum capacity. At that point, water was blasting from the outflow diversion tunnels at a rate of fifty thousand cubic feet per second. Kai saw the effects on one of the computer screens and felt it in the control room as the building began to vibrate with a subtle rhythmic energy.

"Thank you," he said. "Now you need to leave the room so I can flood it with nerve gas."

"What?"

The engineers looked at him as if he were joking, but when he raised the pistol they headed for the door so rapidly that they nearly knocked each other over.

As the engineers left, one of Kai's men came inside. He carried his own bottle of water and the metal tips from his own shoelaces. Placing the bottle on the control panel and tossing the cap aside, he dropped the strips of metal into it. These tips were made of another chemical, one that would react differently with water.

"Good," Kai said. "Let's go."

Kai and his partner left the room, sealing the door behind them. Within seconds of their departure, the water in the bottle began to foam and bubble. Soon, the bottle was venting a greenish gas that spread across the room like a witch's potion.

"That's Q_5 nerve gas," Kai told the hostages. "If anyone goes in there, they'll die. If the door is opened, you all die. Understand?"

Half the group nodded. That was good enough.

"What about the Japanese tourists?" one of Kai's men asked.

Kai turned back toward the control room. It was slowly filling with the green fog. "I don't think that needs much of a translation."

With everyone amply scared, Kai looked for the exit. Using the key cards they'd taken off the security personnel, they released one of the sealed doors and moved through it. Crossing the open-air corridor, they reentered the dam.

"Part one of this plan is in operation," Kai said proudly. "Let's hope those techno-geeks can handle part two."

Out on the waters of Lake Powell, Xandra and Fydor watched the Glen Canyon Dam through binoculars, looking for any sign the floodgates had been opened. They'd expected a sudden current or maybe a whirlpool to appear behind the dam, or the roar of a waterfall, as acres of liquid were sucked into the twin intake tubes. But from half a mile away no sign of any change could be seen.

"They must have failed," Fydor said, "or been captured. I knew we should have remained anonymous. Let's get out of here."

Xandra ignored him. While she saw no sign of a whirlpool or even rapidly moving water, she did see a veil of fine mist floating up from the other side. It caught the afternoon light, creating a barely visible rainbow.

"The water's flowing," she said.

Changing her focus, she spotted a line of cars racing toward the dam. They had flashing red and blue lights on top. They pulled out onto the dam itself and began hustling tourists and employees off of the structure.

"They haven't failed at all," Xandra said, lowering the binoculars. "Policemen are swarming the dam. They're rushing everyone to safety. Time for our attack. Let's make sure our impact is more obvious."

Fydor looked as nervous as ever. "Fine," he said. "We should hurry though."

They moved to the aft end of the boat and loosened the cord on a plastic tarp. Pulling it aside revealed a pair of ROVs. The aquatic machines were roughly torpedo-shaped and painted dark gray.

After lifting the first one up and dropping it into the water, Xandra attached a payload of explosives spaced along a rope to the back of the vehicle.

Both ROVs would act like miniature tugboats, hauling their respective payloads and releasing them near the dam. The currents in and around the dam would do the rest, bringing the explosives into contact with the wall of the dam, where they would explode like mines.

The random spacing between each explosion would keep the authorities off balance. The delay caused by explosives drifting would give her and Fydor time to make a leisurely escape.

Fydor got on his laptop and directed the first of the ROVs toward the dam. The small craft submerged thirty feet, vanishing from view, and moved off.

"ROV One is on its way," he said.

Xandra attached the payload to the second ROV. She'd selected one of the most powerful combinations of explosives available, each forty-pound charge deploying the equivalent force of five hundred pounds of TNT. They wouldn't do any real damage to the concrete dam, but the display would be impressive enough to warrant an all-out response from the authorities.

"Charges set," she told her brother. "Send number two on its way."

Fydor put ROV 1 on automatic pilot before

taking control of its sibling. He would switch back and forth over the next few minutes, guiding first one, then the other. While he did, Xandra began easing the powerboat away from the center of the lake.

"ROV One is approaching the dam," he said. "I'm taking it toward the right-hand side, near to the visitor center. That should result in maximum surprise and shock."

"Excellent idea," Xandra replied.

"Releasing initial payload," Fydor said.

From there, Fydor directed ROV 1 to cross the face of the dam, releasing another of the explosive charges every hundred feet or so.

"Second payload released," he announced. Then, a minute later, "Third payload released. Sending ROV One to the bottom."

The plan was to dispose of the ROVs in the silt rather than retrieve them. Fydor had no wish to be traced to the machines.

"Make it quick," Xandra said. "I'd like to be back at the dock and leaving this place behind before the carnage begins."

Fydor put ROV 1 into a full nose-down dive and then switched to ROV 2. Just as he changed over, a thunderous explosion echoed across Lake Powell. He looked up to see a geyser of water erupting against the right-hand side of the Glen Canyon Dam. It rose a hundred feet above the observation causeway, spread out and then crashed back down, drenching the top of the dam, the police officers and their cars with the flashing lights.

Fydor couldn't see through the mist, but he imagined the police running for cover and leaving their vehicles behind.

No sooner had the water from the first explosion subsided than the second mine hit, followed moments later by a third explosion. The water thrown up by the last blast proved to be the most impressive. It was dark in the center, filled with sediment, but white and effervescent around the edges. It looked as if a depth charge had gone off on the side of the dam.

Both Fydor and Xandra marveled at the towers of water, but for different reasons.

"It's beautiful," Fydor giggled.

"It's too soon," Xandra said. "You released the charges too close to the dam."

"I didn't," Fydor insisted.

"Why are they hitting so quickly, then?"

"It must be the current from the open floodgates," Fydor explained.

"Don't make that mistake with the next three."

Fydor looked offended. "I know how to do my job," he snapped.

Going back to his screen, Fydor directed ROV 2 on a course away from the dam. He was surprised when it didn't respond. He moved the throttle to full power and yet found the ROV traveling backward. He soon realized the problem. "ROV Two is caught in the current."

He tried to guide it sideways and then turned it one hundred and eighty degrees in the other direction, but neither maneuver had any effect. The ROV had drifted too close to one of the open floodgates.

"Get it out of there."

"I can't," Fydor replied. "It's getting sucked into the intake tower."

"Brother!"

"I'm losing it," Fydor said desperately.

He made one more attempt to change the depth and direction, but then the ROV was gone.

It had been drawn down into the bypass channel as it gulped massive amounts of water.

Unlike the two tunnels devoted to generating power, the bypass tunnel was simply designed to take as much water as possible from one side of the dam to the other. The slope inside was steep, the pipeline tracking downward through the dam and then off to the side. There were no turbines in the way to slow anything down. The path took the water through part of the dam and then around it, out through the edge of the sandstone cliffs and down, where it traveled past the power plant before being dumped back into the river on the other side of the dam.

Entering the bypass channel, the water accelerated rapidly, twisting as it went down. That spiraling action kept the ROV and its charges from impacting the wall—at least until they reached the bottom.

There, the ROV crashed into a baffle designed to control water flow at lower rates. The three explosives made contact a fraction of a second apart, detonating almost simultaneously. The proximity of the explosions served to amplify their combined destructive power, with each detonation magnifying the effect of the previous one.

Because the tunnel was completely filled with water, the entire force of the explosions was transferred to the surrounding enclosure. The sixty-year-old tunnel was not up to the task of resisting such a force. The walls cracked and fractured, allowing the high-pressure water to get at the sandstone beyond, which immediately started to erode.

Water blasted through every tiny pore of the rock, finding and widening every microscopic fissure. The dam had always taken on water from the sandstone around it—one of the ironies of building a concrete structure amid porous rock—but now it would experience an internal flood.

Watching from a spot in the visitor center, the Director of Water Operations gazed in horror at the watery explosions erupting outside. As rumblings from a deeper impact shook the dam, he lifted a phone.

"Get me the Director of Homeland Security," he said. "Glen Canyon Dam is under terrorist attack."

Chapter 60

Treasure Cave, Silver Box Ravine, Navajo
Nation, Arizona

Kurt didn't know about the attack on the
Glen Canyon Dam or the superintendent's
call to the Director of Homeland Security.
Nor could he know how quickly and completely
it would bring about action.

Within minutes of the message reaching
Washington, orders went out to the FBI, the
Arizona National Guard, the Coconino County
Sheriff's Office and—in what felt like an incredible
stroke of good luck to the Director of Homeland
Security—a twenty-man squad of counterterror-
ist Army Rangers who were cooling their heels at
Camp Navajo in Flagstaff, only a thirty-minute
flight from the dam.

The Rangers were already on alert, sitting in
their Black Hawks, armed and ready to go. They
were airborne and racing toward the dam less

than sixty seconds after the call came in, leaving Kurt and his group to fend for themselves.

Morgan summed it up. "If Barlow's not bluffing, this could be a long afternoon."

She and Kurt were huddled behind an outcropping of rock that stuck up from the cave's floor. The sloped protrusion of sandstone was no more than three feet tall and four feet wide. They crouched behind it, pressed against each other back-to-back.

Kurt watched the depths of the cavern, hoping for a shot at Barlow, while Morgan watched the tunnel that led in from the outside, hoping Barlow and Robson's men didn't charge.

With so little cover and enemies on both sides, they were in the most precarious position of anyone.

"I don't think he's bluffing," Kurt said. "We're going to have to do this ourselves."

His first step was to up the war of words. Turning his head, he shouted, "Anyone who wants to live a long, prison-free life can run on out of here now. We only want Barlow. The rest of you can head for the hills, we won't stop you."

The next shout came from across the cave. It was Robson. "Any of you bloody fools leave and I'll kill you myself when I get out of here."

Silence followed.

"Not hearing a stampede to the exit," Morgan said.

"Not even a measured retreat," Kurt said. "We need a way to instill some uncertainty in these men."

"What if we shoot out the lights?" Morgan suggested. "If they can't see us, they won't know where we are."

"You realize we won't be able to see them either, right?"

"We've been in here for hours," she said. "They just came in from the blinding glare out in the canyon. They'll find it hard to see anything but green spots for a while."

She shifted her weight, leaned against the rock and fired off three quick shots. The bullets from her 9mm Beretta tore into the portable light that sat beside the southern wall.

The first bullet ripped through the light's plastic housing and flew out the other side without damaging anything, but the second and third bullets hit the battery pack and the controls that regulated the brightness. The light flared and went out.

"One down, one to go," she said.

Kurt saw a method to the madness. And without a better plan to lean on, he jumped on the bandwagon. "Good point. Cover me."

Morgan fired toward the front, forcing Barlow's men to duck. From there, she swung her aim toward the back and fired in the direction of Barlow, Robson and Professor Cross.

As she kept them pinned down, Kurt slid out from behind the rock until he could get a bead on the second lighting unit. He fired twice. The first shot from the Colt hit the casing dead center, knocking it over and shutting it down. The second went through the battery pack.

The cave fell into near-total darkness, with the crashed ATV and a few discarded flashlights the only remaining illumination.

"Let the hunting begin," Kurt called out.

Professor Cross had fought to remain calm, but sitting in the darkness and hearing the threats go back and forth was too much for him. He didn't belong there and he knew it. He pulled on Robson's sleeve. "I say we run for it. Go now while it's dark."

Robson pushed him away. "Get off me."

"Your men can cover us," the professor urged. "They can shoot at Austin and Manning while we run to freedom."

"More likely, shoot us by mistake," Robson insisted. "Now, sit tight."

Realizing he was getting nowhere with Robson, the professor appealed to Barlow. "Have your men attack. Order them to rush forward and take their chances."

Barlow stared blindly into the cave. It was completely dark except for a narrow beam of light at the center of the cave where one headlight of the crashed ATV still shone. Philosophically, he found himself agreeing with the professor, but to charge forward was suicide. He wouldn't do it himself and he wouldn't order his men to do it. But he could send the professor.

"You rush them," Barlow said.

"What?"

"You're so eager to attack," Barlow said, "why don't you take the lead?"

"But I'm unarmed," the professor cried. "They'll shoot me if I go out there."

"If you're lucky, they'll miss," Barlow said, "but I won't." He aimed his pistol toward Professor Cross as he spoke.

Cross froze in place, his heart pounding inside his chest. When Barlow cocked the hammer, he knew it was over.

"Go!" Barlow shouted.

Professor Cross stumbled from the hiding spot, tripping over a relic and nearly losing his feet. Regaining his balance, he kept going and charged across the room. Maybe if he could speak to Morgan . . .

He tripped again, going face-first into the collection of Egyptian artifacts. They tumbled around him like bowling pins.

He stayed down, switching the headlamp off and lying flat, as gunfire erupted above him. Barlow and Robson were shooting in one direction, Kurt and Morgan were shooting back. The others joined in from the entrance. The muzzle flashes were terrifying, the noise of each discharged weapon startlingly loud in the confines of the cave.

Professor Cross covered his head and began to crawl, moving off to the side, trying to get out of the line of fire. He worked his way deeper into the treasure pile, pushing past and underneath things, slithering along like a snake.

He came to a stop beside a crouching Anubis. Its sleek jackal's body looked relaxed, its tall, pointed ears standing proud. The professor patted its head for reassurance and accidentally broke off one of the ears. Holding the broken piece up, he studied it in the dim light. He noticed writing printed on the inside. The words were folded and twisted, but they weren't hieroglyphics or ancient Greek. They were modern English. The print was faint, but Professor Cross could have sworn it was old newspaper copy.

"What is this?" he said to himself. He reached for Anubis's other ear and accidentally snapped off the jackal's entire head. Anger rose inside him. He smashed the head to the ground and picked up the largest pieces, studying the inside. The words on the inside were newsprint. And the flaky plaster underneath unmistakable. "Papier-mâché?"

The professor's head spun, he felt dizzy. "Is this some kind of joke?"

He threw the rest of the statue of Anubis to the ground and it shattered upon impact. A second statue suffered a similar fate. A third he kicked, putting his foot through its torso.

He pushed the pieces away and waded through the treasure trove. In his rage, he'd forgotten all about the battle and the flying bullets. He knocked things over and shoved them aside, moving objects that should have weighed hundreds of pounds without much effort at all.

They were hollow, constructed of papier-mâché and plaster, balsa wood or tin. He found nothing made of stone, no solid gold.

He pushed an eight-foot statue of Osiris to the ground, picked up a hieroglyphics panel that was made of plywood coated with crumbling stucco. Flinging the panel away, he revealed the latest surprise—a tall, three-drawer filing cabinet. It would have fit well in the office of Sam Spade.

Grabbing the top handle, Professor Cross opened the first drawer violently, all but yanking it off its rails. The drawer was filled with invoices, instructions and memos.

He pulled open the second drawer, discovering a stack of bound folders. Grabbing one from the top, he studied the front page.

The paper was entirely white. Whatever had been written there had faded completely. He turned the page and found the ink on the inner pages in better condition. Foolishly, he switched his headlamp back on. A bullet pierced his back before he could read a single word.

He dropped to the ground, feeling a burning sensation in his body. With great effort, he turned sideways and propped himself up, sitting with his back against the wall. He coughed up some blood and felt the slick feeling of it trickling down the side of his mouth.

With his life force ebbing away, he glanced down at the bound page in front of him. The lamp illuminated the header at the top of the page. It read **Shooting Script / Journey of the Pharaohs / A Cecil B. DeMille Production.**

Chapter 61

J oe watched Kurt and Morgan shooting out
the lights and immediately understood what
his best friend had in mind.

Gamay was more confused. "Why would they
blow out the lights?"

"Putting the pressure on," Joe said. "Someone
has to crack and Kurt's betting on those men
nearest the exit."

Joe, Paul and Gamay had remained out of the
battle so far, mostly acting to keep Barlow's men
from rushing and overrunning Kurt and Morgan.

"The darkness plays into our hands," Joe said.
"Time for us to take the offensive."

"I'm all for aggressive action," Paul said, "but
we'll be shot to pieces as soon as we come out
from behind this car."

"Then we won't come out from behind it," Joe

said. "We'll push it in front of us and use it as a shield."

"You'll need someone to drive," Gamay said.

"Get in," Joe said. "Paul and I will provide the power. All we have to do is get it pointed toward the entrance and rolling down that ramp. Once it picks up enough speed, we'll hop on the running boards and ride it down like proper gangsters."

Gamay climbed into the two-seater Kissel, fitting snugly in the small compartment. She placed her gun down on the passenger seat and released the brake. "Ready."

Joe moved into position at the back of the antique car. Paul lined up next to him. They found excellent handholds on the trunk-mounted spare tire and rear fenders.

"This thing is a classic," Paul said. "I've seen cars like this in Dirk's collection."

"Assuming we live long enough, we can give it to him for Christmas," Joe said. "Hopefully, he won't mind a few holes."

Rocking the Kissel back and forth, they got it moving. The motion allowed Gamay to turn the wooden steering wheel.

"A little more to the left," Joe insisted. "We need to go down the ramp, not off the edge."

"I'm trying," Gamay said. "This thing isn't equipped with power steering."

As Gamay strained to turn the wheel, Joe and

Paul pulled the Kissel back toward themselves and then pushed forward once more, this time lowering their shoulders and putting their entire bodies into the effort.

The car turned onto the ramp, the front wheels taking the slope. As soon as the weight of the car shifted, it began to pick up speed.

Joe and Paul kept pushing, their feet digging in as they shoved the car. The Kissel surged toward the tunnel and the exit to the cave, heading toward daylight for the first time in a hundred years.

Going down the ramp, Joe could barely keep up with the car. He sprinted and leapt onto the side board, latching onto the door, before the car got away. Holding on tight as the Kissel rolled toward the tunnel entrance, he took what protection he could from the bodywork while raising the MP7 and firing over the front fender.

Paul was doing the same thing on the other side of the car. But as the incoming fire was shattering the windshield, he lost his grip and jumped off.

Gamay had her head down for most of the trip, flinching only when the windshield shattered. Out of the corner of her eye, she saw Paul jump off. She also heard Joe firing at the enemy. Gripping her own pistol tightly, she sat up and pulled the trigger as soon as she spotted a target.

Robson's men knew something was happening

when they heard the wheels of the Kissel rolling, but they didn't know what. They held their ground and peered into the darkness. By the time they saw the car emerge from the shadows and opened fire, it was almost too late.

Fingers turned to run and was hit in both legs.

Snipe saw someone clinging to the right side of the automobile. He also saw the tall man running on the other side. He divided his fire between the two while trying to back away. He never saw Gamay until she popped up from the passenger compartment and hit him in the shoulder with a perfectly aimed shot.

The bullet spun him around and knocked him over. His own weapon flew from his hand as he hit the ground.

Gus was the last of Robson's men to give in. He held his position to the end, turning to run only with the car bearing down on him. He went right, but his feet slipped on the sandy floor of the cave and the vintage Kissel slammed into him and sent him flying.

He landed awkwardly, breaking an arm and hitting his head. By the time he recovered his senses, he was being held at gunpoint.

With the cave's entrance secured, Joe looked around for any other sign of trouble. One of Barlow's crewmen was scampering back outside. From the look of it, the man wore a flight suit. Joe figured it was one of the pilots and not a major threat. There was no one else around to worry about.

"We've got the front entrance covered," Joe shouted across the cave. "They'll never get out now."

Kurt heard Joe's call but remained silent to avoid giving away their position. He and Morgan were making their way through the stacks of artifacts, looping around in a wide half circle, hoping to flank Barlow, Robson and Professor Cross.

Of the three of them, Morgan's thoughts were on the professor. "How'd you know he'd gone over to the other side? I was sure he was with us."

"Barlow's men showed up in Cambridge on the same day we did," Kurt said. "They didn't follow us, they actually got there first. That suggested they were tipped off. And it was Professor Cross who insisted on punting on the river instead of meeting in his office. That allowed them to attack us in the open and make a clean getaway. He even shouted at you to throw the briefcase to them when they got too close."

Morgan's eyes narrowed. "But they ransacked his cottage when they abducted him. It looked as if there'd been an awful fight."

"Overkill," Kurt said. "They already had the **Writings of Qsn,** there was nothing for them to search for. On top of that, there was simply no chance Professor Cross could have put up the kind of fight you described. Not against Barlow's people. It had to be staged."

"He did seem well when he reappeared."

By now they'd circumnavigated the room and were nearing the back wall. "Thought we'd have spotted them by now," Morgan said. "Either they're playing dead or they've moved."

Kurt pointed to the ground. Several brass shell casings could be seen in the dim light. "This is the right place."

"They didn't go forward," Morgan said. "We would have seen them."

"They must have gone back," he said. "Deeper into the cave."

Following the tracks in the dust led them to a section of the cave that looked more natural than the area filled with treasure. It twisted as it went farther into the cliff.

"They're looking for a back door," Morgan said. "If they find one, we'll lose them."

Kurt nodded and moved deeper into the passage. With Morgan covering him, they cleared one section at a time until the sound of scuffling reached them from up ahead.

Glancing along the passage, Kurt noticed the flickering glow from a flashlight moving about randomly. He stepped forward just in time to see its illumination tumbling down the side of the wall. Glancing upward, he spotted a pair of boots disappearing through a narrow opening thirty feet above.

"Too late," he said.

"Can't risk following them," Morgan said. "They'll shoot us as soon as we stick our heads through the opening."

"True," Kurt said. "But that's rough country out there. They're not going to get very far on foot."

Chapter 62

Glen Canyon Dam, Arizona

Omar Kai and his men had left the power plant and made their way back inside the dam, stopping here and there to cut electrical cables and damage water sensors in a way that would make anyone on the outside think the dam itself was leaking badly.

"I think we've done enough," Kai told his men. "Time to head for the exit."

The men heartily approved, picking up the pace as Kai led them to a ladder. They went down three levels and entered another of the long galleries that ran the length of the dam.

"Shouldn't we be going outside?" one of the men asked.

"This tunnel meets up with the old bypass channel at the far end," Kai explained. "From there, we can break into a maintenance shaft that runs to the surface."

Kai led his men forward, double-timing it through the dark tunnel until their feet began splashing through water. At first it was just a trickle of water running down the center of the corridor, but it widened by the second.

"What is this?"

Kai wasn't sure. "Stay here," he said. He continued forward, the water deepening with every step. When he was fifty yards from the end, he began to hear a hissing sound. Raising the flashlight, Kai saw water blasting into the tunnel through a crack in the wall at the far end. It was also pouring out beneath the door of the maintenance shaft they'd hoped to go through.

Kai remembered three small explosions and one large one that reverberated through the entire dam. Suddenly he knew what had happened.

He backtracked to his men. "Can't go that way."

"Why not?"

"Because those two idiots let the explosives get sucked into the bypass tunnel. The explosives detonated inside the dam instead of against its outside wall. There must be a fissure in the tunnel. The backflow is forcing its way into the dam."

"How much of it?"

"Enough that we're going to need another way out."

As he spoke, the door at the far end groaned from the weight of the water pressing against it.

Kai looked down, he and his men were standing in two inches of water. And the pace of the inundation was picking up. It flowed past them toward the low point at the center of the dam.

Kai had to come up with a contingency plan quickly. "We need to go back to the power plant."

"And then what?" one of the men asked. "We'll be trapped there."

"Not if we swim for it," Kai said.

"What about the water we just released?" one of the men said. "A billion gallons of it, flooding into the channel."

Kai saw that as a positive. "It'll give us cover and push us downstream at high speed. We get a few miles away and disappear into the back-country. They'll never find us."

The men always took their cues from Kai and they seemed to consider this a reasonable plan even if he knew it was a long shot. Truth was, they had little choice. "It's either that or take the elevator to the top and fight off the National Guard with a couple of handguns."

None of them wanted that. They got up and moved back through the corridor, climbed the ladder and wound their way back to the door they'd entered earlier. Pushing through it, they moved across the open-air corridor and took cover.

"Watch for snipers," Kai ordered.

On high alert, the men edged their way

around the building and onto an extension of the power plant that ran along the southern wall of the canyon.

The area was broad, flat and paved. Several trucks were parked there. A road led from the parking area into a tunnel. Kai briefly considered that as an escape route. But, however inviting the open end at the bottom looked, the top would be guarded like the walls of a fortress.

"Move toward the outlet pipes," Kai said. "The mist will cover us."

The water pouring through the gates on the other side of the dam was blasting out through four huge pipes, two on each side and each wide enough to swallow a full-sized van. The water was deafening, the spray and mist silently drifting up and back.

Half the parking area was shrouded. Four or five parked vehicles and a small concrete wall at the end offered some cover.

Kai was about to run for it when one of his men grabbed him and pointed upward.

Through the mist, Kai saw a Black Hawk helicopter swoop in over the Glen Canyon Dam. It descended rapidly, dropping toward the power plant. A second helicopter could be seen near the crest.

"Now we're outgunned for sure," one of the men said.

The first Black Hawk slowed to a hovering position over the top of the plant. A squad of men deployed from it, sliding down ropes, onto the roof.

One of his men foolishly shot at them, drawing fire in return that was far more deadly. He took three bullets to the chest, tumbled back and fell over the railing, splashing down into the churning green and white water of the Colorado River.

"Move!" Kai shouted to the others. There was nothing to do but run or surrender and he didn't feel like surrendering. He took off, crouching low and ducking behind the trucks that were parked near the outlet tunnels.

He moved in spurts, from one to the next, well aware that he was probably being shot at, though he couldn't hear the gunfire. This close to the pipes, the roar of the jetting water had become so loud that even shouting was pointless.

Kai urged his men on, waving his arms and then pointing. One of them took a bullet in the calf and fell to the blacktop. Another pulled open the door of a truck, found the keys above the visor and tried to drive off.

Kai shouted a warning, but the man had made his decision. He jammed the truck into gear and turned toward the vehicle tunnel. A hail of bullets from the Army specialists stopped the truck before it reached the entrance.

Now alone, Kai knew he had only one choice. He sprinted through the mist and vaulted the wall, landing on top of one of the outlet pipes.

The pipe had an immense diameter. Standing on top was like standing on the roof of a moving train. The entire conduit shook with the relentless flow of the water as it curved away. Crouching to stay out of sight, Kai felt its vibration coursing through his body like a current of electricity.

Between the wall and the mist, he was temporarily out of the line of fire, but he now had nowhere else to go. If he emerged, he'd be shot head-on. If he waited, he'd be picked off from the side or surrounded and captured. And if he jumped . . .

Kai stared at the water blasting from the pipes with a force like rocket engines at full throttle, each jet ten feet in diameter and moving at a hundred miles an hour. The water left the four pipes separately, then merged ten feet from the outflow point, where it dropped to the churning waters below.

If he jumped, it would either drown him or break every bone in his body. Probably the river would do both.

Better than spending the rest of my life in an American prison, he thought.

A spread of covering fire pinged off the concrete wall behind him. He knew that meant one group of soldiers was moving forward while the other group was keeping him pinned down.

He raised his pistol and fired blindly over the wall in all directions, emptying the magazine in hopes of giving himself a second to act.

With the ammo used up, he tossed the gun aside, turned toward the river and dove from the outflow pipe into the mist.

Several of the Rangers saw him dive. One even snapped off a shot, though in his report he admitted it was not well aimed. Whether it hit the target or not, he would never know. Omar Kai disappeared into the Colorado River and vanished. His body was never recovered.

Chapter 63

Kurt and Morgan returned from the depths of the cave with bad news. "Barlow and Robson escaped out the back. They're on foot."

"Let's go after them," Joe said.

With Paul and Gamay guarding the prisoners, Kurt, Joe and Morgan reloaded their weapons and left the cave.

As they emerged, one of Barlow's Black Hawks dusted off and headed south. It traveled half a mile down the slope of the ravine and then hovered and began a slow, sideways drift.

"I'll give you one guess what they're looking for," Kurt said.

"Barlow and Robson," Morgan said. "They must have called for help."

Kurt looked over to where the second Black Hawk sat quietly. Turning to Joe, he asked the obvious question. "We'll never catch them on foot. Can you fly that thing?"

"No problem," Joe said. "They're all basically the same once you get inside."

The three of them rushed to the helicopter and Joe climbed on board. As he started the engines, Kurt and Morgan climbed in the back. They found a heavy, mechanized cart, shovels and other tools that had never been used.

"Barlow came prepared."

"He's going to leave that way too if we don't hurry," Kurt said.

Joe powered up the engines, getting them off the ground in record time. They turned to the south, where the other helicopter had picked up Barlow and Robson.

"They're on the move," Morgan said. "We need to catch them."

Joe poured on the power, accelerating toward the other craft, but Barlow's pilot did the same thing, flying along the deck and heading toward the open end of Silver Box, where it merged with the main branch of the Grand Canyon.

He couldn't close the gap.

"Can't catch him," Joe said. "These choppers are identical. We have the same exact amount of power."

"We don't have to catch them," Kurt said. "All we have to do is follow. There's no way they can fly that thing to Canada or Mexico. Eventually, they'll have to land and try some other method of escape."

"That sounds easy enough," Morgan said.

"Too easy," Joe replied. "They've already figured it out."

Up ahead, Barlow's helicopter was slowing and turning to the side. Muzzle flashes from the open cargo door announced a barrage of rifle fire.

Joe shoved the controls over and banked hard to the right. Glancing behind him, he saw Kurt and Morgan righting themselves.

"A little warning next time," Kurt said.

"Sorry," Joe said. "They tried to hit us with a broadside."

The mood in Barlow's helicopter couldn't have been more tense. "You missed," Barlow snapped at Robson. Both men were looking out the cargo door.

"We need to be closer," Robson said.

Barlow turned toward the pilot. "You should have disabled the other helicopter."

"I was busy coming to rescue you," the pilot said. "Besides, how was I to know they had someone who could fly it?"

Realizing two streams of bullets were better than one, Barlow grabbed a rifle. "Let them get closer," he said. "I'll deal with them personally."

Joe could see the danger plainly. The nearer he got to Barlow's Black Hawk, the more likely he was to get hit. On the other hand, if he turned and ran, they'd be even more vulnerable. His only hope was to get Barlow's pilot to make a mistake.

He swung wide, kept up his speed, and then rolled the helicopter back in the other direction. "Setting up for an attack run," he shouted.

Behind him, Kurt pushed their cargo door open and locked it into place. "No sharp turns without telling me first," Kurt said. "I don't want to end up skydiving without a parachute."

Joe nodded and turned his attention back to the target. Barlow's helicopter was turning tightly and losing speed in the process. Joe had to keep his speed up to stay ahead of the rifles that were being aimed out the side door.

"I'm going to fake left and then turn right. You'll get a shot as we fly past."

The approach was a twisting one, with the helicopter picking up speed, banking to the left and then back to the right.

Barlow's pilot responded by slowing almost to a hover and rotating the Hawk like a turret. A hailstorm of fire came from the cargo door. Most of the bullets went wide and low, though a couple of shots caught the bottom of the craft, punching holes in the sheet metal and disappearing.

Joe pressed on, racing past the motionless craft. As it flashed by, Kurt and Morgan unleashed everything they had. When they looked back, it didn't appear they'd done any damage.

"Pistols against rifles is a losing bet," Morgan said.

"And now they're after us," Joe said.

Their fortunes had now reversed. As soon as Joe passed Barlow's craft, Barlow's pilot had turned. The hunter had become the hunted.

With Barlow's helicopter following them, Joe had little choice but to run. That meant flying along the deck like a madman.

Kurt and Morgan held on in the back, checking their ammunition. "Two shots left," Kurt said.

"I have five," Morgan said. "That's not going to do much."

The chase continued down the length of Silver Box Ravine and out across the narrow strip of water that was the Colorado River by the end of summer.

With the wider space of the Grand Canyon around them, Joe banked to the left, hoping to circle Barlow's helicopter and regain the advantage.

It was a good effort, but Barlow's pilot cut him off and they took another broadside from the rifles in Barlow's and Robson's hands.

Joe ducked as the swarm of bullets hit them, drilling holes in the plexiglass and sheet metal.

"Faster," Morgan urged.

"No," Kurt said. "Slower. And higher. As high as we can get."

"We'll stall at some point," Joe said.

"So will they. And then all of us will be standing still for a moment."

"The sitting-duck plan," Joe said. "Why not? The exact opposite of anything tactically logical."

Joe dipped the nose of the helicopter, picked up as much speed as possible and then pulled back on the controls. The agile craft began to rise, its nose angled up into what would be called a maximum climb angle.

"Keep going," Kurt said. "They're following us up."

Joe kept the throttle wide open and the helicopter climbing, despite the speed soon beginning to bleed off. As the needle on the airspeed indicator fell backward, the altimeter began to slow. Soon the rotors were clawing at the air.

"Five thousand feet," Joe said. "We're not going to make six."

Barlow's Black Hawk had raced up behind them, unwilling to let Joe gain the high ground or get away.

"Drift right," Kurt shouted.

Joe stepped on the rudder pedal, afraid that any other change would stall them out and send them spiraling to the ground.

The helicopter slid to the right, putting them directly over Barlow's craft by no more than a hundred feet. The stall warning began to scream.

"It's now or never," Joe called out.

In the back of the helicopter, Kurt flipped the control knob on Barlow's mechanized cart to the forward position. It surged out the cargo door, carrying every tool and loose piece of equipment Kurt and Morgan could find.

The cart went over the edge with surprising grace, flipping upside down slowly and raining a storm of shovels, picks and other gear toward Barlow's helicopter. The tools were batted aside by the rotor blades, but the hundred-pound metal cart was another story. It crashed through the rotors, shattering three of the four blades, before slamming into the curved plexiglass of the cockpit.

Barlow's Black Hawk twisted and rolled over. It fell from the sky, dropping like a stone, until it slammed into the rocky banks of the Colorado River and burst into flames.

Chapter 64

Joe's expert piloting skills prevented their helicopter from suffering a similar fate. After stabilizing their craft and leveling off, he turned back toward the burning wreckage. One look told them all they needed to know.

"No one survived that impact," Kurt said. "Let's get back to the cave."

Returning to Silver Box Ravine, they met up with Paul and Gamay, who had the prisoners sitting in the shade, quiet and obedient.

"You two would make good jailers," Kurt said.

"Guard duty is boring," Gamay said.

With the situation stable, Kurt reached out to Rudi.

"Various authorities are on their way," Rudi told them over the satellite phone.

"Late as usual," Kurt said. "What happened to our backup?"

"A terrorist attack on the Glen Canyon Dam took priority," Rudi explained. "The Army Rangers who were supposed to help you ended up flying north and thwarting it. Three of the four perpetrators were killed, the other one is missing and presumed dead."

"Barlow mentioned having a trick up his sleeve," Kurt said. "That must have been it."

"If so, it was an effective and costly diversion," Rudi said. "Multiple explosions and a group who infiltrated the control room. They opened all the floodgates and tricked the authorities into thinking they'd laced the place with nerve gas. Turned out it was harmless colored vapor. Unfortunately, it took a while to confirm all that and shut off the flow of water."

"Should we start building an ark down here?"

Rudi didn't sound concerned. "Based on the rate of discharge, you should see a five- to ten-foot rise in the Colorado River about an hour from now. It'll pass by nightfall."

"We'll be high and dry up here," Joe pointed out.

As Kurt and Rudi finished their conversation, a helicopter carrying U.S. Marshals landed nearby. A second helicopter with members of the Arizona National Guard arrived shortly thereafter. A third helicopter with agents from the FBI was reported to be on the way.

"This little strip of land is going to be busier than O'Hare Airport before too long," he told the others. "I'd like to tie up one more loose end before we're ordered to leave."

"What might that be?" Joe asked.

"Professor Cross," Kurt said. "He's missing and unaccounted for."

Kurt, Joe and Morgan entered the cave and spread out. Searching in a grid pattern, it wasn't long before they found the professor. He was in the deepest part of the treasure heap, sitting propped up against a wall. Blood from a wound had soaked his shirt. His eyes were wide open, staring forward. Of all things, a file cabinet stood open beside him and a stack of bound papers rested in his lap.

Morgan crouched beside the professor, felt for a pulse and then gently closed his eyes. "He's gone," she said, telling them what they already knew. "I would have said he died happy to have found the treasure, but there's more to this than you've let on. Why is there a filing cabinet in here? What are all these papers?"

"The secret of the cave," Kurt replied cryptically, "the secret the Granzinis killed their partners for." Kurt waved his flashlight around, pointing out the treasures and idols. "All of this—all the artifacts, all the mummies, all the gold and jewels—all of it is fake."

To prove his point, Kurt reached over to a statue that appeared to be made of marble. With a quick snap he broke the arm off, it crumbling to dust in his hand. "They're props," he explained. "Most of them are made from papier-mâché and plaster, balsa wood or tin."

"Props?"

He nodded. "Elaborate set decorations. Designed and created for a movie that never got made."

"You've got to be kidding me," she said.

Joe reached down and pulled the blood-soaked stack of paper from the professor's hands. **"Journey of the Pharaohs,"** he said, reading the title. "A Cecil B. DeMille Production."

"That explains the Kissel," Joe said. "When we were using it as a mobile shield and battering ram, I noticed a name tag riveted to the instrument panel. That's Cecil B. DeMille's car."

"It was," Kurt said. "And it's the only historical treasure in the whole cavern."

"This is a movie set?" Morgan asked, just to be sure. "You're telling me we're standing inside a movie set."

Kurt nodded again. "According to the FBI files, DeMille came out here to make an epic about the rise of a fictional Pharaoh. A location scout had found this place and determined that it was a perfect stand-in for Egypt. The ravine outside doubled for the Valley of the Kings. The Colorado River stood in for the Nile. They used this cave as the interior set for several different locations, including a tomb, a temple and the Pharaoh's palace. That's why the ground is so flat. Because they had it paved. That's why there are ramps and platforms all over the place. So they could move cameras, lights and equipment around to set up different shots, make the same cave look like different places."

"I suppose that's why half the cave is filled with worthless furniture and trinkets," Morgan said.

"Set decoration," Kurt said.

"What happened?" Joe asked. "I've seen every old movie ever made, but I've never even heard of this one."

"Halfway through the shoot, one of the producers got caught in a financial scandal," Kurt said. "The picture lost its funding and production shut down. Instead of hauling all this stuff back to Hollywood, they stored it here, hoping DeMille could find new backers. Unfortunately for them, the canyon got a lot of snow that winter, causing landslides, including the one that buried the entrance to the cave. The studio ended up writing the whole thing off and DeMille moved on."

"What about the archeologists?" Joe asked. "You said this place was discovered back in the twenties."

"The archeologists were partners of the Granzini family," Kurt explained, "smuggling artifacts from Africa to buyers in Europe. They came here to follow up on the old rumors of Egyptian relics in the canyon and were led to this cave by a local guide. They burrowed inside and explored a small fraction of it, using only dim oil lanterns. They saw what we saw, the mother lode of Egyptian artifacts, which they immediately informed the Granzinis about."

"That must have sparked a celebration," Joe said.

"A short-lived one," Kurt pointed out. "The Granzinis believed the story—they had no reason not to—reached out to their old contacts, urging their favorite European collectors to get their checkbooks ready. It wasn't until the patriarch of the Granzini family came here in person that the archeologists discovered the truth."

"By truth, you mean the Hollywood fabrication?" Joe suggested.

"Exactly," Kurt said. "And that caused a conflict. An argument blew up about what they should do. The Granzinis had already made a lot of promises. They figured they could keep the lie going and profit from it. The archeologists wanted to expose the truth, which they knew would come out eventually. The Granzinis ended up killing them to keep them from talking."

"How were they supposed to make money from this?" Morgan asked. "Photos are one thing. But anybody who received a balsa wood statue would know instantly that they'd been had."

"The plan was the same as it always had been," Kurt said. "Find artifacts in backwater places, pretend they were discovered here. The Granzinis were masters of sourcing run-of-the-mill Egyptian artifacts from around the globe and then claiming they came from famous tombs. They advertised this as 'The rarest and most exclusive of collections.' It was a gold mine just waiting to be tapped. They just needed the rumor to remain alive until they'd milked it for all it was worth."

"But what about the boats that DeMars found off the coast of France?" Morgan asked.

"He's the only one that ever saw them," Kurt said. "There was never any proof. Most likely because there were never any boats to begin with. Even his children and grandchildren seem to doubt they existed."

"And the **Writings of Qsn**?" Morgan asked. "And the kid who flew them to Spain?"

Kurt paused for a moment. "That was the hardest part to figure," he admitted. "By all accounts, the writings are legitimate. But when they were actually discovered and where they truly came from is impossible to know. What they were doing on that plane is easier to figure. The Granzinis were hoping to get them to a buyer in France who would verify their authenticity. But after the shoot-out in Arizona, they were being hunted by the FBI. They needed to move the broken tablets before they got caught red-handed with them since the tablets would tie them to the murder of the archeologists. They probably should have just dumped them in the lake, but that would have meant giving up on a large payday, something they would need if they were about to relocate to another country. Sadly, all the usual channels of shipping were closed to them. All but one."

"Jake Melbourne," Morgan said. "They wanted him to fly it. The fact that he ended up dead suggests he said no."

"They shot him and convinced their nephew to do it," Joe said.

"Seems that way," Kurt said. "According to the FBI file on Cordova, Jake Melbourne was a friend of his and was teaching him to fly in exchange for free maintenance work on the plane."

It looked as if they'd solved a couple of long-standing mysteries, but Morgan was hung up on the original quest. "If the **Writings of Qsn** are legitimate, that means Herihor's treasure and everything he stole from the other Pharaohs is still out there."

"It's a compelling story," Kurt admitted, "but it requires some interpretation. In the end, all the **Writings of Qsn** really tells us is that a group of Egyptians, working under Herihor, embarked on a journey that took them far from Egypt. They went by sea and then across open land, finally ending up in a canyon. But that canyon could be anywhere. It could be West Africa or Central America or somewhere in Europe. It could even be here in the U.S., but there's no real evidence to suggest that. Even the well-known article in the **Phoenix Gazette** lists sources in the Smithsonian that the institute has no record of ever being employed there."

"Another hoax," Joe said.

"Believe only half of what you read," Morgan said.

"And none of what you see."

Kurt watched Morgan Manning for some kind of reaction. A half-dozen emotions crossed her face in a matter of moments. First came disbelief, then anger. For an instant, she looked like she could chew through steel, then her face softened and she began to laugh. "The joke's on Barlow, isn't it? He should have stayed in the mercenary business. It would have been safer for him."

"It would have at that," Kurt said.

"Now what?" Joe asked.

Kurt grinned. "Now we turn this over to the proper authorities, head back to D.C. and bring the curtain down on this entire production."

Joe shook his head. Morgan offered a salty grin. Kurt didn't mind. He just shrugged and turned for the exit.

Chapter 65

Kurt, Joe and the Trouts returned to Washington, with Morgan coming along for the ride. At a debriefing in the NUMA conference room, Rudi confirmed the capture of Xandra and Fydor, who were easily linked to the assassination attempt in Washington and the attack on the Glen Canyon Dam.

"Have they confessed?" Morgan asked.

"Xandra, the sister, hasn't said a word," Rudi explained, "but Fydor spilled the whole story within thirty minutes of being apprehended."

"How'd they get caught?" Kurt asked.

"They docked the powerboat without paying the manager of the marina," Rudi said. "He followed them to the parking lot to get a credit card, but by the time he got there they were in the process of stealing a car—his car. The plate numbers were given to the state police, who caught up with them at a truck stop near Flagstaff. Electronic gear and other evidence will pin them to both crimes."

"That's two dangerous characters off the street," Kurt noted.

"And when the survivors of Robson's gang are extradited to the UK, they'll be off the street as well," Morgan said. "For a long, long time."

The debriefing wrapped up and the participants made plans to go their own ways.

Joe was off to Spain to learn more about Stefano Cordova, the young man who'd flown across the Atlantic shortly before Lindbergh. Paul and Gamay were heading to Australia for a proper vacation, choosing the destination partly because it was as far as possible from anything Egyptian. Morgan was scheduled to fly back to London immediately, until Kurt convinced her to postpone her flight for at least one day.

"What's in it for me?" she asked, walking him back to his office.

"A gourmet dinner at a spot overlooking the river," Kurt said.

"What's the name of this restaurant?" she said. "I dine at only the best establishments."

"It doesn't have a name," Kurt said, opening the door to his office and noticing that the stack of paper in his in-box had grown even higher than when he last looked. He walked by the desk just to see what was on top.

"If that's true," Morgan replied, "what kind of menu can I expect?"

"Pizza or cheeseburgers."

She frowned. "Doesn't sound very gourmet to me."

"Either selection comes with a bottle of Opus One," he said. "A bottle I've been saving for just such an occasion."

That brought a smile to her face. "In that case, I accept. Since we're talking about your place, I hope that means I won't have to wear any shoes once I'm there."

Kurt grinned. "No shoes, no problem." He was leafing through the paperwork, intending to leave it all for another day, when he spotted something interesting. He plucked a single-page report from the pile and began to scan the contents.

"What's that?" Morgan asked.

"Paul's chemical analysis of the sandstone fragment we found in Melbourne's plane," Kurt said. "The fragment that was part of the **Writings of Qsn.**"

She leaned closer. "What does it say?"

Kurt first read the findings to himself and then summarized for her. "It says the stone was quarried somewhere in the Colorado River Basin, most likely western New Mexico or northern Arizona."

"Well, that's interesting," she said.

"It is," Kurt replied, putting the report through the shredder. "Very interesting indeed."

EPILOGUE

Navajo Nation, Arizona
Four months later

A parade of agents came through northern Arizona in the months after the attack on the Glen Canyon Dam. The FBI sent most of them, but representatives from the National Parks Service's Bureau of Land Management, the State Department and the FAA all made appearances at one time or another.

Reporters from the major networks came, followed by journalists from national magazines and local news outlets. Most of them asked the same questions. Few of them listened to the answers.

By late December, the air had turned cold and the first snow of the season had dusted the vermillion ground with a coating of white. By then, the wrecked Black Hawk helicopter, the movie props and the vintage Kissel automobile had all been removed, the various agents had gone back to Washington and the journalists had moved on, chasing different stories in other parts of the country.

With the quiet of the canyon restored, Eddie Toh-Yah and his grandfather went out on horseback early one morning. They rode slowly, picking their way over the frozen ground, leaving the high country and descending into a remote part of the canyon, fifteen miles from Silver Box Ravine.

"You seem happy to have all the commotion behind us," Eddie said.

"This land is supposed to be quiet," his grandfather told him. "The ancestors prefer it."

Eddie figured there was a message for him in that and he remained silent for a long time after. In truth, he preferred the quiet, listening to the sound of the horses' hooves on the ground, the call of a hawk in the distance.

As much as he enjoyed it out here on the range, he was surprised to be riding with his grandfather. The old man was frail, he rarely left home these days, let alone for a difficult ride in the cold of winter.

"It's been a long time since you invited me on a ride," Eddie said. "Care to tell me where we're going?"

"No," his grandfather said. "But we're almost there." He pulled the horse up and dismounted awkwardly, tying the reins to a scrub bush at the edge of the ravine and taking a small pack from the saddle. "Follow me."

Eddie got off his horse, tied him and then rushed to catch up with his grandfather, who was proving surprisingly spry negotiating the rough terrain.

They climbed up the west slope of the ravine until his grandfather found a notch in the face of the rock. It looked to Eddie like nothing more than a crack in the face of the cliff, but his grandfather squeezed through and disappeared.

Eddie followed and found himself in what was known as a slot canyon, with walls that were shades of crimson streaked with orange and tan.

Eddie stayed quiet as he followed his grandfather through the labyrinth-like curves. A quarter mile in, they came to an opening that had clearly been carved by man-made tools. It led inside the cliff.

His grandfather lit an old Coleman lantern, turned up the wick and then stepped through.

Eddie followed once again, this time walking into a square-cut room with markings on the walls. In the flickering light, Eddie saw symbols he didn't recognize and depictions of strange creatures, half human, half animal.

He knew better than to ask at this point. His grandfather was showing him something he needed to see for himself.

They continued on, climbing up a steep ramp and arriving in a vast, open space several times larger than the movie set in Silver Box Ravine. It was clear to Eddie that this space had been hewn from the rock. The effort must have taken years with tools of only bronze and stone.

Moving forward, he saw that the excavation had left columns of stone to support the ceiling. Arranged carefully around the columns Eddie saw statues, sculpture and other carvings. He walked past mummified bodies of strange animals that lined the central path. He followed his grandfather to the far end, where a niche had been carved in the rock in the shape of a pyramid.

Fifteen ancient coffins were lined up beneath it side by side. They gleamed in the light, gold and blue and other brilliant colors. The sarcophaguses were free of debris or even any dust. Above them, embedded into the ceiling, were gemstones arranged like the stars of the night. So precise were the astronomical designs that Eddie had no trouble picking out Orion's Belt and the Big Dipper.

Eddie's grandfather used a long thin taper to light some incense. As the aroma of sage and piñon wafted through the room, he began lighting candles, one at the base of each golden sarcophagus. As the flickering light grew, it reflected off mirrors placed above each of the sarcophaguses, illuminating the faces carefully crafted on each.

"Grandfather," Eddie whispered. "Is this what I think it is?"

As the fourteenth candle was lit, Eddie's grandfather spoke. "These are the People of the Sun.

They came here many generations before the white men. Your great ancestors knew them."

"These are the Egyptian Pharaohs," Eddie said. "The treasure Kurt was looking for."

Eddie's grandfather corrected him. "Your friend said he cared not for the treasure but for the men who were after the treasure. He has them now."

Eddie realized that was true. "Why did you bring me here?"

"Today is the winter solstice," his grandfather said. "The day of the short sun. A sun these faces long to see. I come here every year, twice a year, to light these candles. Every summer solstice, as well. My grandfather did the same thing. And should you choose to carry on the tradition, your grandchildren will one day be asked to care for these travelers who found rest in our land."

"You want me to—"

"It has been entrusted to us to care for these ancient ones," his grandfather said. "But I'm too old to do this much longer. It falls to you . . . If you wish it."

Eddie studied the treasure around him. He thought about the history of these people and his own small place in the world. Then his mind focused on the great honor that was being offered to him.

Without a word, he stepped forward, took the taper from his grandfather's hand and dipped it to light the final candle.

About the Author

CLIVE CUSSLER is the author of more than seventy books in five bestselling series, including Dirk Pitt®, NUMA® Files, **Oregon** Files, Isaac Bell and Sam and Remi Fargo. His life nearly parallels that of his hero Dirk Pitt. Whether searching for lost aircraft or leading expeditions to find famous shipwrecks, he and his NUMA crew of volunteers have discovered and surveyed more than seventy-five lost ships of historic significance, including the long-lost Confederate submarine **Hunley**, which was raised in 2000 with much publicity. Like Pitt, Cussler collects classic automobiles. His collection features more than one hundred examples of custom coachwork. Cussler and his wife make their home in Arizona.

GRAHAM BROWN is the author of **Black Rain** and **Black Sun**, and the coauthor with Cussler of **Devil's Gate, The Storm, Zero Hour, Ghost Ship, The Pharaoh's Secret, Nighthawk, The Rising Sea** and **Sea of Greed**. He is a pilot and an attorney.

LIKE WHAT YOU'VE READ?

Try these titles by Clive Cussler,
also available in large print:

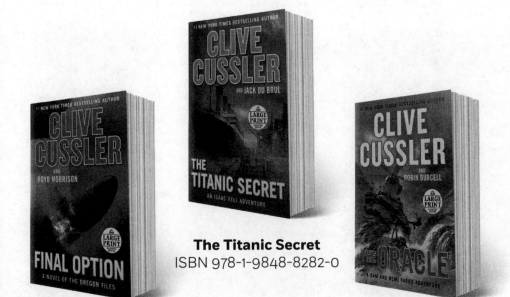

The Titanic Secret
ISBN 978-1-9848-8282-0

Final Option
ISBN 978-0-593-15236-2

The Oracle
ISBN 978-0-593-10434-7

For more information on large print titles, visit
www.penguinrandomhouse.com/large-print-format-books